1

'Thank you for asking me to tea,' Sadie said and offered Sally Harper a half-smile. 'To be honest, I am worried to death about Marco. I haven't heard from him since he left last December.'

It was now the end of January 1918 and the New Year had not started well. London and the south-east of England had recently endured a night of heavy bombing. To Sally, it seemed that all the optimism they'd felt before Christmas that the war would soon be over, was misplaced. What with the terrible pit disaster in North Staffordshire and the confusion at May Island, as a big Royal Navy fleet had sailed down the Firth of Forth, bound for exercises in the North Sea, and several accidents had occurred, sinking various vessels and causing the deaths of over a hundred men, January had been a sad and terrible month.

'It is early days yet,' Sally did her best to reassure the young woman about her husband, despite her own anxiety for her friend and former employee. 'I expect he has been busy training and getting ready to go wherever they decide to send him...' Yet in her heart, she knew that Marco would write if he could, because he was a caring person and understood that Sadie worried for him.

'Marco did his military training some time back,' Sadie told her. 'He said that he thought he would be sent overseas almost immediately.'

'Yes, I can understand why you're worried.' Sally agreed that it was likely Marco would have been sent to join a fighting unit immediately. He'd been returned to frontline duties by his commander, who had been furious about his refusal to be sent to Russia as a spy. Marco had known he could not be of use there and stuck to his guns, but the officer who had sent him to spy in France had been resentful of his decision. Sally's husband, Ben, had hinted at the reasons for him being sent to the Front and Sally had guessed the rest. Besides, the Allies needed manpower and although the Americans were now putting their might behind the war effort that didn't mean Britain could let up, so every able-bodied man was being thrown into the mix. This war with Germany was relentless and without constant effort it could easily be lost despite the gains made recently. 'But letters take longer from overseas and I'm certain that Marco will write as soon as he can.'

'Yes, I know...' Sadie sighed. 'It's just that I feel a bit lost now that Marco isn't around.'

'I'm sure Pierre keeps you busy.' Sally glanced at Sadie's son, who was happily playing with a pile of bricks. Jenny, her nearly five-year-old daughter, had graciously allowed him to share her toys and seemed intent on her dolls. One of them being a new toy that Ben had bought her for Christmas.

'Yes, to a certain extent,' Sadie replied. 'I just need more to do.'

'I thought Marco said you might like to return to nursing?'

'Yes, I would have...' Sadie's face showed her disappointment. 'I went to the hospital and asked to help. I didn't mind what I did, but they said as I hadn't finished my training, I wasn't suitable.'

'Oh, that is a shame – and it is so stupid,' Sally exclaimed. 'The hospitals are short-staffed, because so many nurses have gone over-

VICTORY BELLS FOR THE HARPERS GIRLS

HARPERS EMPORIUM BOOK 6

ROSIE CLARKE

First publish[...]

Copyright © Rosie Clarke, 2022

Cover Design by Colin Thomas

Cover Photography: Colin Thomas

The moral right of Rosie Clarke to be identified as the author of this work has been asserted in accordance with the Copyright, Designs and Patents Act 1988.

A CIP catalogue record for this book is available from the British Library.

Paperback ISBN 978-1-80162-253-0

Large Print ISBN 978-1-80162-254-7

Hardback ISBN 978-1-80162-252-3

Ebook ISBN 978-1-80162-256-1

Kindle ISBN 978-1-80162-255-4

Audio CD ISBN 978-1-80162-247-9

MP3 CD ISBN 978-1-80162-248-6

Digital audio download ISBN 978-1-80162-250-9

Boldwood Books Ltd
23 Bowerdean Street
London SW6 3TN
www.boldwoodbooks.com

seas to nurse the wounded. Why on earth are they so stuffy about these things?'

Sadie shook her head, her fair hair moving negatively about her face. 'I suppose I let the side down. I wasn't supposed to get married and have a child...'

Sally considered for a moment. 'I suppose you can only do part-time anyway?'

'Yes,' Sadie agreed. 'My mother is happy to have Pierre for a few hours a day, but she couldn't manage the whole day.'

'Let me think about it and see what I can do,' Sally suggested. She didn't say anything, however, she had an alternative in mind for Sadie but would explore all avenues before offering her hope. 'In the meantime, enjoy your cake. Mrs Hills made it especially for us.'

'I am enjoying it,' Sadie assured her and laughed. 'I know I'm impatient, Sally, but I just wish I could hear from Marco. I have a horrid feeling something may have happened to him.'

'Oh, that is awful for you,' Sally sympathised, 'but try not to worry. I'm sure you will get a letter soon. Marco knows more about fighting than either of us realises and he will be fine.'

'He's strong and brave,' Sadie said, 'but out there in the trenches, it isn't how brave or clever you are – if the mortar lands near you or a bullet has your name on it—' She shuddered. 'I lost one man I loved to this war. I couldn't bear to lose Marco too.'

'You do love him very much, don't you?'

Sadie looked at her for a moment, then, 'Yes, I do. It didn't start out that way... Marco married me so that I could come back to England with my son. He is the child of a Frenchman who died resisting the Germans, but Marco loves Pierre like his own son.'

'Yes, I guessed as much,' Sally said softly. 'I think all that is in the past and you will both be very happy together.'

'*If* he comes home,' Sadie said, a choke in her voice

Sally touched her hand. 'Please, have faith, Sadie. Ben and I both love Marco and want him home again, and I am certain that he will come. I just feel it inside.' Sally's eyes filled with tears. 'We know that we've lost some of our young men who went to fight... one of them was only seventeen. Ernie lied about his age to get in and died within days of reaching the Front.'

'I am so sorry. How did you know?'

'His mother had a telegram and she came to see me. He was a cheeky, lively lad and it hurts to think we shan't see him again. Fred Burrows – he's the stores' manager – was very distressed, because they had been working together and he liked the lad.'

'How sad,' Sadie sighed. 'I know I must have faith – but it is so hard...'

Sally realised that her visitor was in need of something and decided to speak sooner than she'd planned. 'I will see if I can find you an opening at the hospital I visit, but if that is impossible – would you consider working for me?'

Sadie stared. 'As a sales assistant?' she asked dubiously.

'No – as a nurse and a childminder at the store,' Sally said. 'I can see that in the future some of my staff may need to bring a child or a baby to work with them. Your nursing experience would make you ideal for the position, Sadie. Besides, sometimes, members of staff feel unwell. You could administer a powder for headaches and take temperatures. You would know whether they just need to rest, go home, or be sent to hospital... and you could bandage a cut hand. Young Nicky – one of our recent recruits to the stores – cut his hand on broken glass yesterday and had to go to the hospital.'

Sadie was smiling now. 'I could probably have saved him a trip. If you provide the materials, I can stitch a small wound. I can even give injections if I have what is needed. I think it is a wonderful idea. I'd love to take the job. May I bring Pierre with me for part of the time? My mother will have him in the afternoons, but she needs the mornings to do her chores.'

'Yes, of course. I didn't think you would say yes immediately, because it isn't true nursing, but it is very worthwhile.'

'I think it is so clever of you to think of it,' Sadie said. 'Women who work all have the same problem of what to do with their children. You must be either the first or one of the first to think of this...'

'I don't know about that, but I know I would have found it difficult at times if I couldn't take Jenny with me to the office – and that made me realise how impossible it must be for others.' It was an idea she'd had for a while, but Sadie's restlessness had forced it to the front of her mind and made her act on what had only been a thought.

'Where will the nursing department be?' Sadie asked.

'I thought we would put it next to the toy department,' Sally said and smiled. 'Children's toys are so difficult to find at the moment and I don't need half the space we have dedicated. After the war, well, we'll have to see how things work out then.'

'I hope you will keep it going, not just for my sake, but for all the women it will help.'

'We need to think of our female workers,' Sally replied seriously. 'I know that when the war is over many of them will no longer wish to work – they came to Harpers because their men were away, but some will continue especially if—' The unspoken words lingered and Sally cursed herself as she saw the fear in Sadie's eyes. 'Some women will not want to give up their independence even when the men return.'

'What will happen then?' Sadie asked. 'Surely the men will want their jobs back and the women will be dismissed?'

'In some cases – jobs more usually held by men – will be given back to them. You won't see women driving trams or buses as they do now, but at Harpers we have always employed quite a few women and I don't intend to change that.'

'I'm glad,' Sadie replied, then, 'Have you heard from Maggie recently, Sally?'

'Yes, I had a letter this morning, she is well and happy, I believe.'

Sadie smiled. 'I am glad. I wrote to her two weeks ago, but she hasn't answered yet. I expect she is busy.'

Sally looked at her. 'I hope you will make friends with Becky and some of the other girls at the store?'

'Mrs Burrows has been to see me and Mrs Bailey is friendly if I visit her department – but Becky Stockbridge seems distant. She made an excuse when I invited her to tea. Perhaps I've upset her in some way?'

'I am sure you haven't. Becky is being a silly girl at the moment – it isn't anything you've done, so don't blame yourself. Once you are working at Harpers you are bound to make more friends. Ben and I have some very good friends we met through the store.'

'Thank you, Sally. How is your husband?'

'Ben's shoulder is much better,' Sally said and sighed. 'He had hoped to give up his work for the war effort, but they still need him, it seems. He isn't travelling as much, which is better for us both – but he still has several meetings and masses of paperwork, for a while anyway.'

'Don't you find running Harpers alone is a lot of work for you?' Sadie asked.

'I don't run it alone,' Sally said and laughed. 'Ben might not have much time to spare and his sister, Jenni, isn't around these days since she moved to the north, but I have lots of young women to help me and a few of the senior men who were too old to fight. Mr Stockbridge, Harpers' manager, Mr Brown, who looks after the men's department and advises on the buying, and Fred Burrows in the stores department. I do not know what I would do without any of them. And, of course, Rachel and my other ladies keep Harpers running...'

'But you oversee it all.' Sadie looked at her curiously. 'You must be very close to your time, Sally. When will you take time off to have your second baby?'

Sally placed her hands on her belly, which was the evidence of the soon-to-be-birth and laughed. 'If Ben had his way, tomorrow. I expect it will be any day now. My husband has put his foot down and forbidden me to go into the office for the time being, but I'll continue at home while I can. Jenni will come down next week and she'll stay until after the birth, which they tell me should be in another month or so – but knowing what happened last time, it could happen any day if I'm lucky.' She smiled at Sadie, who had cheered up a little. 'Leave this job idea with me, Sadie, and I'll have a word with Ben and then get your department up and running as soon as we can.'

2

Becky Stockbridge emerged from the staff restroom, feeling drained. She'd had to excuse herself yet again to be sick and the corset she'd laced so tightly was killing her. She was terrified that someone would guess her secret and she'd seen her father looking at her once or twice. Had he noticed that she was putting on weight? What would he say when he learned that she was carrying the child of a man she barely knew?

Shame washed over her. When she looked back now, she could scarcely believe it had happened to her. Minnie – her stepmother – had persuaded her father that she was old enough to be taken to the theatre by a gentleman they'd trusted. Becky had trusted him, too, and it had been last November that she'd known she truly loved him, when he came back on leave and explained why he hadn't been able to visit for some months. He'd been busy working overseas and it had been too difficult.

'I thought about you, Becky,' he'd said and his voice was as soft as a caress. 'You were in my mind all the time – and I came as soon as I could manage it.'

Becky believed him absolutely. He was an officer in the Army and a doctor and she'd fallen for him the very first time she saw him at the first-aid classes. How she wished she'd never gone with Maggie Gibbs and Marion Jackson to those wretched classes. If her purse hadn't been stolen, Captain David Morgan would never have taken her home and she wouldn't have fallen in love with him. He hadn't visited her often at the start, though he'd had tea with her and Minnie once or twice, and the uncertainty about his feelings for her had made her edgy and a little jealous of friends like Maggie, who was married to Colin Morgan – the man she loved.

It was strange that her lover had the same surname as Maggie's husband and so, she'd asked David if there were related one afternoon when they were walking in the park, and he'd told her that he was the son of Colin Morgan's grandfather's brother's son.

'Some sort of distant cousin, I suppose,' he'd told her. 'His side of the family inherited the land and money. My father died young and Mother and I had a difficult time until I was able to work and earn enough to pay off outstanding debts. My mother died two years ago so my distant cousins are my only family.'

'I wasn't prying,' Becky had said, looking at him shyly. 'It just struck me as odd that you were both Army officers and both had the same surname.'

'Ask what you like, sweet little Becky,' he'd said and tipped her chin up so that she looked at him. 'You do know that I adore you and want to marry you when all this is over. You're a little young yet—'

'I'm nearly eighteen,' Becky had said and David had laughed and reached for her, kissing her on the mouth. Somehow it had gone from a gentle, teasing kiss to something more passionate. He was older, perhaps by ten years or so, and sophisticated, with a charming smile.

* * *

Nothing had happened then, but the next time they'd met, by arrangement on this occasion, David had taken her to his apartment overlooking the park. It was a special place, filled with exquisite furniture and lovely things in mellow old cabinets that gave the place a comfortable, homely but luxurious feel and she was a little overwhelmed.

'I wanted you to see your home if we marry,' David had told her with a look in his eyes that took her breath. Becky was young and innocent but not too innocent to know what that look signified. 'It is possible that I won't come back and I wanted you to know how much I love you – and to give you something to remember me by...' He'd taken a velvet box from his jacket pocket. When she opened it, Becky had gasped in shock because it was a parure of choker necklace, bracelet, drop earrings and a ring and they were all beautiful sapphire and diamond pieces. 'This set was my mother's when she married and she would never sell it, despite being hard up. She left it to me for my wife when I found the right girl... That girl is you, Becky. I'd like you to accept it now. I want you to be my wife, but it is too much to ask you to wait, because I have to go back to the Front, where I'm needed – so I want you to have this just in case.'

Becky had flung herself into his arms, crying and begging him not to say such things, telling him that she loved him and would be his wife now if he wished it.

'I leave almost at once,' David had told her. 'I wish I'd told you how I felt sooner, but I thought it was too early, because we hardly knew each other – and that you were too young—'

'I'm not a child! I'm a woman,' Becky had cried and pressed herself against him. Perhaps to him she seemed young, because he was nearly thirty, and yet he seemed the perfect age to her. So strong, confident and his smile made her heart ache with love for him. 'I love you so much,' she'd whispered and then, suddenly, she was in his arms and he was carrying her through to the bedroom.

They settled on the bed together, just kissing and touching, whispering silly little things at first. Then David had made love to her so sweetly and she'd given herself without reserve – just that once.

How could life be so unfair that she'd fallen for a child when other people were married for ages and could never have a baby? Becky's feelings alternated between shame and happiness at the memory of that afternoon. She still had the beautiful jewels David had given her and she knew his family had come from decent folk – surely, he would marry her when he came home... *if* he came home? After they'd made love, he'd told her that as far as he was concerned, they were engaged and that was nearly the same as being married, wasn't it?

'We'll be married as soon as I get back,' he'd told her as he kissed her lingeringly. 'Never doubt that I love you, Becky, and I will marry you, I promise. I want you as my wife.'

'Will you write to me?' she'd asked.

'All the time,' he'd promised. 'Don't worry, nothing will happen. You won't fall for a baby the first time – though I want at least two children when we are married. A boy and a girl.'

He'd seemed so sincere and she'd been so young and so besotted – and now she was carrying his baby and she was terrified. Who could she talk to – who could she ask for help? It would shame her too much to confess it to her father... He knew that she'd been out with David a few times, but he wasn't aware of her passionate love for the man *he'd* only met twice – and he didn't know that they had met several times just by chance. When Becky had been leaving work and on Sundays when she'd gone out for a walk or to meet friends – but had those meeting really been chance? In her heart, Becky knew that David had come looking for her whenever he had time – so he *must* love her. Surely, he did?

'Becky...' the voice calling to her was Mrs Harper's and Becky halted, looking at her in trepidation. Had Mrs Harper noticed something? Surely it didn't show yet?

'Ah, Becky,' Mrs Harper said and smiled at her. 'I wanted to have a little talk to you but...' She placed her hands on her stomach. 'I've been a bit preoccupied, but when my baby is born, I want you to visit me at home so we can have a talk privately. Is that all right?'

'Yes, Mrs Harper.' Becky looked at her intently. She seemed so kind and friendly – would she help Becky if she confided in her? She certainly needed help and would be forced to go to someone eventually. 'If you wish.'

'I do,' Mrs Harper replied. 'I care about all my girls, Becky – and that includes you, don't forget.'

'Thank you, I'll remember.'

As Becky returned to the office, she felt a flicker of hope. Perhaps Mrs Harper could help her keep her secret from her father and Minnie, because she couldn't bear them to know what a wicked girl she was.

* * *

'I reckon we'd best have a carpenter in, Mrs Harper,' Fred Burrows advised when Sally told him her plans later that morning. 'We'll erect a partition wall that can come down when we need it to.'

Sally looked at him doubtfully. 'I want it to look professional and be safe, Fred...'

'Yes, of course you do,' he agreed. 'Now, why don't you get off home and leave it all to me? I know what you're after and I'll sort it for you. We need a small room with a bed that can be used if a member of staff is unwell – and another bigger one for the children to play in. I'll see to it.'

'What about the toys?' Sally looked about her. 'It won't leave much room for them up here?'

'Why don't we do what Mr Harper suggested and put the toys downstairs for now?' Fred asked. 'We could divide the confectionary department in two – I think there is far too much empty space there at the moment.'

'Yes, perhaps you are right...' Sally sighed, because although the space gave it a luxurious feel, it could be put to better use, especially with things the way they were at the moment. She felt a little tired and too big and ungainly to cope. Ben would be cross with her for coming into the store when she should have been resting. 'You know, Mr Burrows, I think I do need to go home and leave this to you.'

'Good.' He smiled at her. 'I'll ask Beth to come and visit you this evening and make sure you're all right.'

'Thank you. Ben has had to go away for a couple of days. He said it would be the last trip before the birth, because he wants to be around when I need him.' She smiled. 'I've got more than a month to go yet.'

'That's as maybe,' Fred told her. 'You should be at home resting, Mrs Harper. You were very ill last year, remember, and none of us want to lose you. I don't know what our Beth would do if anything happened to you. Thinks the world of you, she does.'

'I do of her,' Sally said, smiling at the thought of one of her very best friends. They had started working at Harpers together at the very beginning and their friendship had continued ever since, getting stronger all the time. Sally, Beth, Rachel and Maggie were four of the original Harpers girls, when Ben had first opened the store in 1912. Maggie was now married and living in Devon, Beth had two sons and Rachel still ran the department closest to Sally's heart – the bags, jewellery, hats and glove department – but she now had a little girl named Lizzie that she was hoping to adopt when her husband returned from the isolation hospital. 'I'll be in touch, Mr Burrows...' Sally said and left him to get on with reorganising the departments. She was suddenly feeling very weary and her back had started to ache. She asked Ruth to call her a taxi as soon as she reached her office. It really was time she stayed home to prepare for the birth of her second child or she would end up having it in the store!

* * *

'I came straight round as soon as Dad told me he was concerned about you,' Beth Burrows said that evening. Married to Fred's eldest son and the mother of two small boys herself, she'd been immediately anxious. 'How are you, Sally love? You look a bit uncomfortable?'

'I am,' Sally agreed with a little moan. 'My back started to ache this morning and it hasn't stopped...'

'You don't think you've started your labour?' Beth asked. 'I mean, I know you think it isn't due for another four weeks or so but—'

'I was nearly a month early last time,' Sally agreed and sighed. 'I don't think it is coming yet, Beth. Ben has me booked into Doctor Symonds' clinic for the birth and I suppose that is the right thing, especially after I was so ill at the start of my pregnancy.'

'It is much the best,' Beth told her firmly. 'Having it at home would upset Jenny. She wouldn't understand why you were in pain and all the stuff that goes with it. If you feel anything is happening, get a taxi at once.'

'Yes, all right, I will,' Sally replied with a tight smile. 'Mrs Hills asked me if I wanted her to stay tonight, but I sent her home. I'm sure I'll be fine, Beth. Anyway, how are you – and the children?'

'Jackie and Tim are fine,' Beth said. '*I'm* getting too fat.'

'Of course you're not,' Sally assured her. Beth might be a size thirty-eight hips since the birth of her children, but she carried the extra weight well and looked as lovely as always, her long hair swept up at the back of her head. Sally's own reddish-brown hair was always cut short because she preferred it, but sometimes she envied Beth's glossy blonde locks. 'You've put on a few pounds; that is only natural after having two children. Besides, it suits you...'

'I don't like it. None of my clothes fit,' Beth complained. 'I'm going to diet, but the doctor won't let me until I stop breastfeeding Tim.'

'Won't he take the bottle yet?' Sally asked.

'Sometimes,' Beth replied. 'Fred's friend, Vera, doesn't approve of bottle feeding – but Jenny was fine on it, wasn't she?'

'Absolutely,' Sally said. 'It isn't easy to make the decision, Beth, but you should begin to wean him now anyway.'

'You're not going to give up your job then?' Beth laughed at the look in Sally's eyes. 'As if! So you think I should ignore Vera's advice and bottle feed then?'

'I would – but it is your choice—' Sally gasped out loud. 'Ouch! I'm not sure, but I think Baby has decided that he wants to be born—'

'You've decided it's a boy this time then?' Beth asked. 'Should I ring for a taxi, love?'

'I don't—' Sally was about to say she didn't know for sure when the doorbell rang. 'Will you answer that please?' She gasped and slumped in her chair as she felt the pain in her back intensify. In the hall, she could hear Sadie's voice and she called out that she should come in.

'I brought that list round...' Sadie began and then all three women gasped as Sally's dress became wet. 'Your waters have broken... you can't get to the clinic now, Sally. We'd better get you in bed and then ring for the doctor...'

'Oh no, not again,' Sally moaned. 'I thought this time it would all go smoothly... Ben wanted to be here.'

'Well, your baby is in a hurry to be born,' Sadie said. 'Don't worry, Sally. I did this during my nursing course. Even if the doctor doesn't get here, I am certain we can manage.'

* * *

Two hours later, Sally looked up at her friends as she held the newly born child in her arms, a beautiful boy this time, and smiled at them.

'Oh, he is so lovely,' she said, tears in her eyes. 'Thank you both so much for helping me. It was all so quick...'

'No, it wasn't,' Beth contradicted. 'You'd been in pain all day, but, as usual, you ignored it. It's a miracle Sadie was here – because I couldn't have done what she did and that doctor still hasn't turned up.'

'He was attending another patient,' Sadie said practically. 'Besides, we didn't need him. Sally did it all by herself. You were very brave and good, Sally. Your little Jenny slept through the whole thing.'

'What about Pierre though? You only came to deliver a list...' Sally said sleepily.

'My mother is with him.' Sadie looked at her. 'You just relax. You have a gorgeous little boy, Sally.'

They all heard the bell ring and Beth went to answer it. The doctor had arrived together with the midwife. They were both astonished when they heard the baby cry.

'We shall take a look at you just the same,' Doctor Symonds said. 'If I am satisfied that you can remain at home, Nurse Martin will stay with you this evening – but you should not be alone. Why didn't you call me earlier?'

'I thought it was just backache,' Sally sighed. She was very tired now. 'It is all right – Sadie is a nurse, but she has to go home to her family now.'

'I'll come and see you tomorrow,' Sadie promised.

'You go too, Beth,' Sally said. 'I'll be fine – and thank you, both...'

'I was happy to do what I could,' Sadie smiled and left.

'I'll just make sure you're both all right – shall I make another pot of tea before I go, Nurse Martin?' Beth asked.

'Yes please, I should like some tea,' the efficient nurse said, nodding at them. 'We just need to look at mother and that fine little chap while you make it...'

Sally submitted to the examination but was told everything was just as it should be.

'Your friends made a good job of things – you say one of them has nursing experience?' Doctor Symonds enquired.

'Sadie was a nurse in the war. She left because she got married and had a child.'

'Ah yes,' Doctor Symonds said. 'Well, if she ever wants a part-time job she may apply to my clinic. I am always looking for good midwives.'

'I will tell her,' Sally promised. She drifted into sleep as Nurse Martin removed her son from her arms and she vaguely heard Beth say goodnight.

* * *

When Sally woke, it was to see Ben sitting beside the bed with a huge bunch of pale pink roses in his hands and it was morning. He smiled at her and reached for her, kissing her softly on the lips. 'How do you feel, my darling? I got home late last night to find that I had a wonderful little son. Please forgive me for not being here, Sally. I am so sorry I wasn't around when you needed me.'

'You couldn't know...' She smiled as he placed the flowers beside her. 'They are lovely – but have you seen our son?'

'Nurse let me hold him,' Ben said and looked elated. 'He is a fine big boy, Sally – and I'm told you had no one but Beth and Sadie to help you – the doctor arrived too late.'

'I was fine,' Sally said. 'The doctor said so...'

'I know. The nurse told me – but she has to go now if you feel well?'

'Yes, I'm fine. You can look after me,' she said, smiling.

'Mrs Hills is here. I rang her and she came in early.'

'Good...' Sally yawned sleepily. 'What are we going to call our beautiful little boy?'

'What about Peter?' Ben asked. 'It is a nice name – and we can add family names as well, but I like Peter...'

'Whatever you like,' Sally agreed. 'Peter Ben Harper... Yes, I like it. Oh, I've got something to tell you.'

'Is it about Harpers?' he asked and she nodded. Ben squeezed her hand. 'It will do later, my darling. You are going to have a nice breakfast and then a little wash and tidy-up – and then we'll talk all you like.' He sighed. 'I could do with a shave and something to eat too... I've been travelling for hours to get home. I had a feeling you might give birth sooner than we thought and I was worried.'

'You didn't need to worry,' Sally replied. 'I was fine and Sadie was wonderful.'

'I must thank her,' Ben said and bent to kiss her. 'Now, here comes Mrs Hills with your breakfast. Make sure you eat it...'

3

'It is wonderful news that Mrs Harper has had her baby – a boy this time. I'll bet Mr Harper is pleased?' Marion Jackson said when Rachel Bailey called to see her that evening after first visiting Sally at her home. 'Thank you for coming to tell me.'

'Yes, Mr Harper is very pleased,' Rachel said and smiled at Marion. She often visited the young woman, whose husband was serving in the Army, just to keep in touch. Marion had worked in her department until Christmas, when she'd needed to take time off to have her baby. 'Mr Harper went round every department telling the staff and everyone is getting an extra half-crown in their wages.'

'Gosh!' Marion gasped. There were a lot of staff at Harpers and it would be expensive – but it was a gesture the staff would appreciate. 'That was nice of him.'

'Yes, everyone was pleased. He said it was so we could toast the new baby, but for the younger staff it is a lot of money. One of Fred's young assistants, Sam, only earns five shillings a week so it was a fortune to him and he's already said he's giving his mum a surprise gift with his bonus.'

'Ma doesn't get much,' he'd told Fred, who had then told Rachel. 'She had six of us to bring up and with Dad in the Army, half his wage doesn't leave a lot for her.'

When young Sam had made an appearance in her department later that day, Rachel had found him a pretty scarf left over from a previous sale. There was no actual fault it in, just that it was a bright yellow colour and no one had wanted it, but Sam said it was his mum's favourite colour so she'd wrapped it in tissue and given him a smart bag for his gift, which he'd carried off as if it were the Crown Jewels.

'I came round to bring you your bonus and ask how you were,' Rachel concluded, looking at Marion who had another few weeks to go before she gave birth to her first child. 'Are you keeping well?'

'Yes, I am,' Marion smiled. 'I'm glad I'm not standing behind a counter, though. Sarah won't let me do much. She fusses over me like a mother hen and my mother-in-law is always bringing me something nice to eat.'

'Well, that is nice,' Rachel glanced approvingly at Marion's sister-in-law, Sarah. 'Have you heard from Maggie recently?'

'She wrote to me at Christmas and sent a gift for the baby,' Marion replied, 'but I haven't heard anything since.'

It was February now and the papers were filled with hints that women were at last to receive the vote, though it was thought it would only be those over thirty. However, many restrictive laws concerning property were going to be scrapped and all male resident householders would now have the vote. It was a step in the right direction and the prominent members of the Women's Movement were pleased but intended to press for more when things settled down after the war – which everyone hoped could not last much longer.

'And when is your husband coming home?' Marion asked now. 'I know you've been expecting him since Christmas.'

'He had a chill so they kept him a little longer, but he should be home this weekend,' Rachel replied. She hesitated, then, 'I wrote and told him about Lizzie. I want to adopt her as our own – but I need William's permission for that...'

'He will surely give it.' Marion looked surprised. 'He must know how much it will mean to you – you love her so much.'

'Yes, I do,' Rachel agreed. 'However, I am not sure that William will approve. He may not want the bother of a young child – and Lizzie's father is a wanted criminal...' Rachel had rescued Lizzie from a careless grandmother and when Lizzie's father returned from the war, he'd quarrelled violently with his mother over her treatment of his child and struck her. She'd died and, now wanted by the police, he'd given Lizzie into Rachel's care.

'She can't help that and she didn't do anything wrong,' Marion objected and Rachel silently agreed but sighed.

'I just hope that William feels the same,' she said. 'Anyway, as well as your bonus from Mr Harper, I've brought you some gifts. Several of the staff wanted to put together and they've chosen some lovely things for you. Marco's wife contributed – and Sally says she is coming to work at Harpers. There is to be a crèche for our children if required and also a restroom where Sadie will dispense headache pills and care for us if we injure ourselves.'

'Oh, isn't that just like Sally Harper!' Marion exclaimed. 'I do admire her – having children and yet continuing to run Harpers. I don't know how she does it, but she always manages to get what we need and at good prices.' Harpers had continued to be reasonably well stocked throughout the war, which was more than some stores that had been forced to shut their doors for the duration.

'Sally Harper is a marvel,' Rachel agreed. 'She is a good friend and I am very fond of her and Mr Harper too. He is a generous man and much more approachable since he married Sally. When he first opened the store, he seemed a little distant, but that all changed when he married and became a father.'

The two women nodded in agreement. Ben Harper and his sister, Jenni, owned the store, although they both believed it was Sally who had made it what it was – a store that was still busy and popular even in the dire circumstances of the war.

'Has anyone heard from Mr Marco?' Marion asked with a worried frown. Their window dresser was very popular and so good at his job and he was sorely missed now that he was away serving in the Army. 'We were all so pleased to have him back last year after he was sent home injured for a rest – but then they sent him back out there...' A little shudder went through her. 'In Reggie's last letter, he said things had been rough but he was all right. I wish it was all over – don't you?'

'I think the arrival of the Americans is gradually turning the tide,' Rachel said. 'Besides, the Germans can't go on fighting forever. They must be running out of everything, just as we are. The war will have to finish because it will grind to a halt in the end for lack of men and willpower, let alone money. I dread to think what this terrible war has cost us all.'

'The Government will put up the price of everything, I suppose,' Marion said with a grimace.

'Are you finding it difficult to manage now that you're not working?'

Marion hesitated and then shook her head. 'We can manage because Sarah earns some money with her sewing. Reggie sends most of his pay and my brother, Dan, sends money to Sarah, so we're all right. My sister, Kathy, wants to leave school this summer and start work. She's been helping in the kitchens at school as part of her lessons – since she wants to be a cook – but she doesn't earn anything yet. She is learning a lot, but she thought they would pay her something and I think she is disappointed.'

'Perhaps she should leave and get a job somewhere else?' Rachel suggested, but Marion shook her head.

'The wages she would get while she's learning would be so small that it isn't worth it – they expect young girls to work such long hours in these restaurant kitchens, even worse if she goes into service. It's almost as bad as being in a sweat shop. Kathy made inquiries at a hotel who wanted kitchen staff and was told she would need to start by doing the washing-up and it would be years before she could call herself a cook. If she stays at school, she will have quite a lot of experience when she leaves.'

'If she is getting the training she needs, she is better off there,' Rachel agreed.

'She will get a diploma to say she can cook,' Marion said and smiled. 'But she is growing up now and she wants to earn money so that she can buy new clothes instead of having to ask me all the time.' With her elder brothers absent in the army, Marion had been the main breadwinner for her family. Her youngest brother worked on the docks but her youngest sister, Milly, was still a child and Kathy had been at school until now.

'If you needed help, I could lend you a little,' Rachel offered, but Marion shook her head.

'No, thank you. I can manage and once the baby is born, I shall return to Harpers and earn a little extra.'

'Yes, I know Sally really wants you back.' It was probably partly for Marion's sake that their employer had set up the crèche for the children. Other women would need it, too, but Marion's flair for design was important to Harpers, more than ever if Mr Marco were not to return – God forbid!

* * *

Sadie checked her letters that morning – just a bill for the coal she'd ordered but nothing else. Ice trickled down her back as she thought about the reasons why her husband had not written. Marco would know she would be anxious. He would have written to her if he could.

'Mumma...' Pierre's plaintive cry brought her back to reality. She still had the son she adored and she must make sure he was all right rather than sit in a corner and worry over the man she'd fallen in love with.

When they married, Sadie had liked Marco a lot. She'd thought him brave, kind and courteous, but soon she had come to realise he was so much more. He made her laugh a lot and he was good company, intelligent, clever at what he did and a wonderful husband and father. Their marriage was different to most, because she knew that Marco's first love had been a young man – he had never forgotten Julien, but he'd told her he didn't want that kind of relationship again.

'I could never replace him in my heart,' he'd told her, 'and casual relationships are shallow and not for me.' The look in his eyes had told her that something in his past grated, but she hadn't asked. Marco was a private man and entitled to his secrets. Their marriage was not the passionate one she might have shared with Pierre's father, but it was good enough and she wanted him back so badly.

'Please come back to me, Marco...' she whispered as she picked up her son, washed and changed him, pressing her nose into his softness and enjoying the freshness of soap and powder. Babies smelled so gorgeous when they'd been washed and dressed in clean linen. She knew she was fortunate to have him – to have them both. If only Marco returned to her...

'We're lucky that Mummy has a new job starting soon,' she told her son as she tickled him and smiled as he giggled and wriggled in her arms. 'Daddy left us money to take care of us – but it is best if Mummy works. Mrs Harper has made it possible for us to be together a lot of the time.'

Sadie knew her mother would be happy to have Pierre for part of the day, but it was good that she didn't have to ask too much. Her mother had a sharp tongue and if she'd guessed that Pierre was not her husband's child, she would have been scalding in her condemnation. She thought that her daughter had done well, getting a husband like Marco with a good job and education.

'Your dad and me, we left school at fifteen,' Sadie's mother had told her. 'That was a year later than a lot of our friends, so we were lucky. I was taken on as a seamstress in a lady's household and I rose to be her personal dresser. Your father became supervisor at the nuts-and-bolts factory and we were able to give you a better start in life – and now you've repaid us by marrying well and giving us a lovely grandson.'

Both Sadie's mother and father were proud of her and that made her feel guilty. Her mother had asked why she didn't return to nursing, but now she was as pleased as punch that Sadie had a job in the prestigious store.

'I've never heard of such a thing – a department for looking after children, well I never! Most women have to ask relatives, except for rich women,' she'd said, shaking her head in wonder. 'This Mrs Harper must be a very generous woman.'

'She is a good businesswoman, Mum,' Sadie had told her. 'That shop is always busy despite the difficulty of getting the right stock – but, more than that, it has a nice, warm feeling of welcome. You don't always get that, do you?'

'No, that you don't,' her mother had said with a little sniff. 'Some of them posh places up West don't even want to serve the likes of me. The girls look down their noses at me, as if I smell...'

'Mum, I'm sure they don't,' Sadie had laughed. She'd known

what her mother meant though. Some of the stores were run with regimental precision and the girls were frightened of putting a foot wrong, which made them appear stand-offish.

'Well, it makes me uncomfortable,' her mother had retorted. 'But I like Harpers. Everyone smiles and speaks to you – and that manager told me to go up to the canteen and have a cup of tea once when I was feeling a bit faint.'

'You were feeling faint – when was this?' Sadie had asked.

'Oh, last summer, when it was so hot,' her mother had replied. 'It's nothing to worry about, Sadie. The doctor told me my heart sometimes has a bit of an erratic beat, but I'm as fit as a fiddle.'

'Are you sure?'

'Of course I am,' her mother's voice had been sharp. 'Don't you start fussing over me, girl!'

Sadie knew that the last thing her mother would want was a lot of fuss, even if she was ill, but it had given her a little jolt. She'd always taken her parents for granted and if anything happened to her mother... but it wouldn't. Sadie was letting her imagination run away from her. It was the anxiety over her husband. Marco would write when he could – and he would come home after the war. Pray God it wouldn't last for much longer! Surely it couldn't?

Shaking her head, she decided that she would write to her friend, Maggie, that afternoon and tell her about her new job at Harpers. They'd met when they were both training to be nursing assistants before the war started. Sadie had done several jobs until she joined the VADs, a volunteer group of women who had done vital work throughout the conflict. Maggie had worked in Harpers as a counter assistant. Sadie knew that she'd loved it once – but she was married now to a badly injured soldier she'd met in hospital, while recovering from a fever herself, and she'd assured Sadie that she was perfectly happy. Sadie smiled at the thought. Perhaps she too could find happiness working at Harpers? At the moment, all she could do was to pray for Marco's safe return from wherever he was...

4

Maggie was in her favourite sitting room when Colin came in that cold morning February, wheeling his chair and looking windblown, his cheeks red from the fresh air. He had been out on the estate from early morning and the air and exercise were making him stronger. He looked healthy, though it was still difficult for him to transfer from his bathchair to a normal armchair. However, he could now manage it alone and Maggie made no move to help her husband as he did so. One thing he couldn't abide was fuss and once he could do something without help, woe betide anyone that offered. Although loving to her, his temper was not always even and if anyone thought they could take advantage, they were soon cut down to size by his manner of speaking.

'That damned fool of a stockman bought a bull that is no good for anything but eating hay,' he complained. 'Twice we've put him in with the heifers and so far, there's nothing to show for it.'

'Perhaps he's just lazy,' Maggie suggested with a smile, but Colin shook his head.

'No, he performed all right, but he's a dud – a bit like me,' he said with a twist of bitterness that cut her to the heart. She'd hoped that the resentment he felt in being confined to a wheelchair after sustaining terrible injuries in the war was over. They were happy in the marriage, which was as normal as they could make it, though not quite as he might have wished.

Maggie flinched. 'Don't say that, Colin,' she protested. 'I am perfectly happy as we are, you know that – don't you?' Their marriage had proved happier than she could ever have expected, but now and then Colin would let his hurt and anger show. Maggie loved him and did her best to ease his mental hurts, as well as the physical ones, but it was not always enough.

He smiled at her wryly and shook his head. 'Sorry, Maggie. I had high hopes for that bull... Dad had similar hopes for me. He wanted a grandson, but I told him it is unlikely it will happen.'

'Perhaps one day,' she said and offered her hand. 'You can sell the bull – and we're in no hurry, are we?'

'I fear that Frederick is probably for the knacker's yard,' he said and kissed her hand. 'A bull that doesn't breed is no use to us.'

'Poor Frederick – can't you just keep him for a while, retire him like you do the horses...?'

Colin gave a snort of laughter. 'What would I do without you, Maggie? I could never have talked about these things to most women. It just wouldn't do for a lady's drawing room. Anyway, I might as well tell you why I'm in a foul mood... it isn't the bull.'

'No, I thought not,' Maggie agreed with a laugh. 'What has your father done now?'

He smiled at her. 'You know us so well, Maggie. I told him I was thinking that we might adopt a child – an orphan...'

'Yes, we've discussed it as a possibility,' Maggie agreed. 'Is your father against the idea?'

'He says we could bring bad blood into the family... and he doesn't like it,' Colin said, his eyes stormy. 'He threatened to disinherit me if we went ahead and adopted a boy. He said a girl would be all right, because the land would then go to a distant cousin, I've never heard of... one David Morgan... Apparently he is also serving in the Army as a captain.'

Maggie saw the anger and frustration in his eyes and knew how cruelly his father's words had struck him. How could he even suggest that if Colin had no blood heirs, he would leave the estate to a distant cousin? It was an outrageous thing to say and she wasn't surprised it had angered Colin.

'That was very unfair of him,' Maggie said. 'He begged you to come home and look after the estate and now...' She shook her head. They had found a way of making each other happy in bed, but it was still unlikely that they would be able to have children – their own children. Maggie had settled in her mind that they could adopt a child that needed a family, but she could not ask or want something that might rend the family apart for good. 'A little girl would be nice, Colin....'

'I don't mind whether we have our own children, or whether we adopt a girl or a boy – but for him to make that threat... Damn him, Maggie. I've a good mind to go back to London to live. I don't need his money. I only came here because he told me he was ill and, despite his behaviour, I care for him and the estate.'

'I know.' She empathised with him. Maggie's own father had been wonderful to her, but she'd had an uneasy relationship with her mother. Colin cared about his father but he didn't make it easy to live with him.

'How do you feel about living in London?' Colin asked her suddenly, his eyes narrowed. 'You have friends there?'

'Yes, I do,' Maggie said, 'but I'm happy here with you. It's up to you, Colin. What do you want to do with your life? I don't mind what you decide.'

'I'm damned if I'll build this place up for Cousin David... whoever he is.' Colin's eyes sparked with anger. 'I could paint,

Maggie. I could actually spend my life doing what I love instead of worrying about bulls that don't give us calves.'

Maggie suddenly saw the funny side of it and laughed. 'Poor old Frederick,' she said. 'Maybe he just needs a bit more time – and perhaps your father does, too, love. He still isn't used to the fact that I came from the East End of London and not one of your county families.'

'Rubbish! He does like you, Maggie. You know he does, even if he doesn't show it often.'

'Yes, he has been kind to me,' she agreed and touched the pearl brooch her father-in-law had given her for Christmas. He knew that Colin would never have come home if she had not agreed to marry him and be with him. 'But he isn't always kind to you, and I know it is because you are both alike and both have quick tempers – so if you want to move, I'm happy to do so, Colin.'

'I'll give it some thought,' Colin said darkly. 'I do care about this place, Maggie – but if he is going to hand it over to a distant cousin just because we don't have an heir...' He shook his head. 'You really wouldn't mind leaving here if I decided I'd had enough of him and his bullying?'

'I shall be happy wherever I am,' Maggie said and smiled at him, then bent to kiss him softly on the lips. 'I love you, Colin. That's all I need.'

'How did I get so lucky?' he asked and his expression softened with love. 'Would you like to visit London soon – stay at a decent small hotel and visit your friends? You can buy yourself a few pretty things in Harpers...'

'That would be lovely – but what will you do?'

'Oh, I have things to do,' Colin said vaguely. 'I think we'll go up next weekend...'

* * *

The headlines on the newsboy's stand were proclaiming a victory for the Australian cavalry against the Turks; they had taken Jericho, to protect Palestine from one of Germany's allies. On another board, it said that President Wilson had declared there could be no peace with Germany and Austria because of Prussian autocracy, which was at odds with a free society in the modern world.

Colin wheeled himself over and bought a paper, tucking it beside him in the wheelchair. 'This friend of yours,' he said to Maggie. 'Ben Harper – he said he would arrange transport to the hotel?'

'Here he comes now,' Maggie told him as she saw her former employer weaving his way through the crowd on the station. Men in uniform made up most of the crowd, but there were wives and sweethearts, children too. Colin had not yet met Ben Harper, because he had not been able to come for their wedding as he was working for the war effort. However, he was mostly based in London now and had taken the time to come and meet them himself. 'Mr Harper...' She smiled as he approached. 'I wasn't sure if you would know me.'

'Of course I remember one of Sally's best friends,' Ben replied warmly as he shook hands with them. 'Welcome to London, Captain Morgan – and Maggie. I've booked you into the Clarendon, a nice little suite. I have to warn you that two days a week the hotels and restaurants have no meat on the menus now. It is to help with a shortage of food at the moment.'

'We've brought some food with us,' Maggie said. 'We do have a surplus of game on the estate and our own bacon. It is in a box in the porter's van.'

'I'll see to it,' Ben told her with a smile. He turned and summoned a porter and had a word with him. 'He will bring everything to the car, which is waiting outside. My driver is a rough-and-ready sort – but he can offer assistance if you need it, Captain Morgan?'

'I may need a bit of help transferring – and someone will need to see to the chair,' Colin replied. 'Thank you for coming yourself, Harper. You must be a busy man?'

'At times,' Ben admitted. 'I have cut back as much as I can, but we're still in the thick of it, as I'm sure you know – and they need me, so...' he smothered a sigh. 'Anyway, Sally says you're to dine with us this evening. I'll take you to your hotel and you can settle in first.'

'We don't want to impose on you – it was good of you to do this,' Colin said.

'Sally cares about her friends,' Ben replied. 'She quite rightly wouldn't have spoken to me for a week if I'd let you fend for yourselves.' He glanced around at the busy station. Men in every kind of uniform were everywhere. 'We've had a lot going on lately. I think they're getting ready for a big push – but that's not official.'

'Well, the enemy can't stand against the Americans for long,' Colin said as he wheeled himself outside the station to the waiting car. 'They have a lot of men and a lot of money and that's what we lacked.'

Maggie listened as the two men talked about the war, clearly enjoying each other's conversation. It was clear that they'd hit it off immediately and she smiled. It would do Colin good to get away from the estate and his father for a while.

She breathed in the air of London, the underlying odour of the station that smelled of oil and other less pleasant things. In the street, the rush and noise of the traffic and raised voices assailed her ears after the peace of the country. Costers were calling their wares from their barrows, a lorry had spilled its load not far away and there was a lot of shouting and raised fists. Maggie smiled. This was home to her and always would be – but she'd told Colin the truth. She would be happy anywhere with him.

Yet as they drove through the streets to the hotel, she felt herself relaxing. Here she was – the Maggie she had always been – and she didn't have to be careful of what she said to Colin's father. It would be a lovely holiday and she was looking forward to meeting her friends.

* * *

'Beth is so excited,' Sally told her that evening when the car Ben had sent delivered them at her apartment. It smelled of a mixture of perfume and baby powder. 'She is really looking forward to seeing you, Maggie dearest.'

'I'm looking forward to being with all of you,' Maggie said as they hugged. 'I'm coming to Harpers tomorrow and I want to see everything and everyone.'

'We're much the same as always,' Sally told her. 'Struggling to keep the shelves stocked. It isn't just food we're short of now. I've had to pull everything out of the stockroom to keep us looking decent. Sometimes I wonder if we'll get through this war without having to close some of the departments.'

'Oh no, Sally. Surely it isn't that bad?'

'Not yet, but if it gets any worse...' Sally shook her head. 'I'm not going to talk about that this evening, Maggie. You look so healthy, dearest.' Maggie's hair shone with health and her eyes were clear and bright, her figure back to what it had been before she'd lost so much weight during her illness, after she'd caught a fever while nursing wounded soldiers in France.

'I think it's the country air – and I must admit we live quite well. We have a fair amount of game on the table these days.'

'I saw what you sent us,' Sally said and shook her head. 'You shouldn't have done it, Maggie, but it is so welcome. Ben enjoys meat for his evening meal and we don't get much now – only twenty ounces a week for every adult.'

'Yes, it isn't ideal,' Maggie agreed, 'but some people can't afford to buy meat even when it is available.'

'Rachel reminded me of that when I was moaning that I couldn't buy steak for Ben...' She laughed. 'I must sound spoiled, but, as you know, when I was young, I didn't have any of these things.' She gestured to her home and smart furnishings. 'You don't know this, but when Mum was forced to leave me in that home, she meant to come back for me – but, when she did, the nuns wouldn't tell her where I was because they didn't consider her fit to be a mother.'

'That was cruel,' Maggie replied sadly. 'I am so glad you've found her now, Sally.'

'She actually found me,' Sally said. 'Although she wasn't brave enough to tell me for a long time.'

'And then you were ill.' Maggie looked at her intently. 'Are you better now? Are you over the birth of your new son?' She produced a small gift wrapped in tissue from her bag. 'I made this for him. I hope you like it.'

Sally opened the parcel, smiling as she saw the soft white wool of the baby coat. 'It's lovely,' she said and touched her friend's hand. 'I'm fine, Maggie, but they won't let me do much. Mrs Hills prepared the meal this evening and Pearl looks after the children a lot of the time – all I do is look at catalogues and try to persuade firms to give me more than they want to on the telephone.'

'You're not going into Harpers yet?' Maggie inquired.

'Ben won't hear of it,' Sally said with a sigh. 'He says I must wait until next month before I set a foot in there.'

'He loves you.' Maggie glanced at Colin. He was talking earnestly with Ben. 'Our husbands are getting on well, Sally...'

'Yes. Ben has great respect for Captain Morgan. He says he was a hero and deserves to be treated as one.'

A shadow passed across Maggie's face. 'I know nothing about his war service. He won't speak of it.'

'Well, I was told in confidence, so I can't say much – but his actions saved lives and he has been awarded a medal.'

Maggie looked at Colin. 'Does he know about the medal? He hasn't told us...'

'He may not know yet,' Sally said. 'Ben gets to hear of a lot of things.' She paused, then, 'He was making enquiries about Marco when he saw this memo about Captain Morgan.'

'Is Mr Marco missing?' Maggie asked in concern.

'I think he may be,' Sally said. 'Please do not mention this to Sadie when you see her – he was involved in an action that several men were killed in last month. I don't think she has heard yet and I'm not sure of anything. Ben is making further inquiries. Quite a few men were listed as dead, but Marco's name wasn't on the list... However, it is believed that the Germans took prisoners. Marco may be amongst them... or he could be dead or injured but unlisted.'

Maggie stared at her in dismay. 'Poor Sadie. I think they had settled well together and her last letter told me that she loved him...'

'I am sure she does,' Sally said. 'And that is why I asked Ben to make enquiries as to his whereabouts. It just isn't like him not to write to any of us. If he could, I am certain he would.'

* * *

'How are you, love?' Beth asked when she and Maggie met and embraced the next morning at Beth's home. 'This is a wonderful surprise. I couldn't believe it when you said you were coming for a visit.'

'Colin just decided it suddenly or it seemed that way to me,' Maggie said. 'I'm not sure yet, but there is a possibility that we might spend more time up here.'

'That would be lovely,' Beth said, her eyes searching Maggie's face. 'You look well – are you happy?'

'Yes, I am,' Maggie replied. 'Happier than I imagined. I do love Colin, Beth.'

'You didn't at the hospital, though.'

Maggie laughed. Their first meeting at the military hospital had been stormy, but she'd soon understood why Colin was so angry at being confined to a wheelchair and she had come to like him and then to love him.

'At the start, I admired him for his courage and he made me laugh, but we were lucky, Beth. We found love and we're both happy – at least, Colin is happy with me, but his father makes him angry. They don't always get on, I'm afraid. It's one of the reasons we came away, to give them both time to calm down.'

'That's a pity,' Beth said. 'Jack and Fred get on so well – and I love my father-in-law. He's such a dear man and so good with the children.' She smiled. 'He has them whenever I want to go out in the evenings – and his friend, Vera, looks after them during the day if I need to go somewhere, though that isn't often.'

'They are beautiful boys. You must be proud of them?'

'I love them both, but they can be naughty.' Beth gave an indulgent laugh. 'Jack says I spoil them...'

'How is Jack?' Maggie asked. 'Have you heard from him recently?'

'Yes.' Beth smiled happily. Her husband was serving in the Merchant Navy. 'His ship is due home next month. He was in Gibraltar recently and I got a letter. He doesn't often send anything, but he said a friend was returning on another ship and would post it here – so I got it just yesterday. Jack expects to have a few weeks' leave this time, so that will be lovely for the children. Tim has hardly seen him and Jackie misses him when he's away.'

'It must be so hard when he's away for months on end,' Maggie said sympathetically.

'He used to be away all the time when we first started courting,' Beth reminisced. 'But then he gave up the sea to run that hotel but went back to help the war effort – I'm not sure what he'll do when it ends.' Beth looked sad for a moment. 'This war has changed our men, Maggie. I suspect that some of them will never be the same. They've seen too much.'

'Yes, that's true,' Maggie agreed. 'What they've been through is terrible, Beth. Here, at home, we know it's bad, but it's only when you see them brought into the hospitals... and even those who can still walk... the tiredness and the grief in their faces. I am certain that a lot of wives will not recognise their husbands as the same men. It will make life difficult in a lot of homes – how can we know what they're seeing in their minds? The pain, fear and sheer despair they've had to face in awful conditions.'

'You witnessed it at first hand,' Beth said. 'I don't know how you managed to do all that nursing, Maggie. You were so brave. No wonder you got ill.'

Maggie shook her head. 'The men were the ones suffering. We just wanted to do whatever we could for them...' She sighed. 'It has been a long war, Beth. I think in the end, it was just the fatigue and the strain that got to them – and us. A lot of the girls had to come home after their first six months because they were so weary.'

'You were out there for two years...' Beth shook her head over it. 'But you're home and safe now and I'm glad you're happy, Maggie. At times, I thought your marriage was just a reaction to losing Tim...'

'I did love Tim.' Maggie sighed. 'It all seems so long ago. We were very young then and I thought life would be so easy...' She closed her eyes for a moment. 'I'm glad I did what I did, Beth. I wish Tim hadn't died. I think Fred feels it deeply.' Tim was Jack's brother and Fred's youngest son; he was a brave pilot who had died in the early days of the war.

'Yes, he does. He loves Jack and the children, but I know by the look in his eyes sometimes that he's thinking of Tim...'

'Yes.' Maggie lifted her head, determination in her eyes. 'Life goes on, Beth. Fred has you and the children and Jack too – and Harpers. I think he loves his job there and they rely on him so much.'

'He has two assistants now,' Beth told her and laughed. 'They're both school leavers and Fred says it takes half his time keeping them in order – but, actually, I think he feels proud that his department is so important. Sally told him that she needs to know exactly what they have in the store, so he makes a report for her every two weeks.'

'He hasn't asked Vera to marry him yet then?' They'd speculated on the possibility of Fred getting married to his friend, but although Vera was often in the house these days and came for meals most weeks, there was still no sign that they were thinking of getting married.

'No. I think Vera would like it,' Beth said, 'but Fred isn't in any hurry. He has me and the children to keep him company – but if we moved out it might be a different matter.'

'Will you move?' Maggie asked.

'We're thinking of it,' Beth said. 'Not out of London, but to a house of our own somewhere. The trouble is that we need a nice big garden and Fred's house suits us.'

'Sally says Ben talks of a big house and garden in Hampstead, but she isn't sure she wants to move. Their apartment is close to Harpers and Mrs Hills is only a short bus ride away – but if they move out to Hampstead, she would have a longer journey to work and Sally thinks Mrs Hills might leave her.'

'When did she tell you that?' Beth asked, surprised that Sally hadn't said anything to her.

'She didn't – Ben told Colin that he'd suggested the move and Sally wasn't keen. He's seen a big house he likes, but she won't go and look at it apparently.'

'Oh, there are some lovely houses there,' Beth said. 'I expect she'll give in in the end. She could get another housekeeper, I suppose... perhaps a live-in one...'

'That's what we have at the estate,' Maggie told her. 'She is like one of the family and loves Colin.' She smiled. 'I never thought I would settle when I first went there, Beth, but I have – if we come to London, I shall miss it.'

'You should tell Colin how you feel.'

Maggie shook her head. 'I can live wherever he wants,' she assured her friend. 'And it means I'll see my friends at Harpers more often – but it is such a beautiful, peaceful spot...'

'It sounds lovely,' Beth said and hugged her. 'I can hear Jackie upstairs... they've woken after their nap. I'd better fetch them down to meet their Aunty Maggie.'

5

Maggie saw Becky as she was on her way to the department run by Rachel Bailey. She loved visiting the department she'd worked in and smiled. It was such a treat to be in the exclusive store again; the smell of perfume and the warmth of everyone's faces as they saw her gave her a feeling of coming home.

'Becky!' she said, sure that her friend had seen her. 'Wait a moment...'

Becky turned to look at her and she was shocked at the change in her; her face was puffy and her eyes had red rims, as if she'd been crying. For a moment, Becky seemed as if she would hurry away, but then she nodded and forced a smile. 'How are you, Maggie?' she asked. 'Up on a visit are you from your big house in the country?'

There was a distinct note of bitterness in her voice and Maggie flinched. They'd been such good friends once and she hadn't expected such a reaction.

'It isn't my house,' Maggie told her. 'It belongs to my father-in-law, not me. I just live and work there.'

'What work do you do?' Becky asked almost rudely. 'I bet you've got servants that wait on you hand and foot...'

'We do have some,' Maggie admitted, 'but I do a lot of things, in the house and in the village.' She hesitated, then, 'Something is wrong. This isn't you, Becky. Can I do anything to help? You're my friend and if you're in any trouble.' Maggie's eyes narrowed as she saw Becky flinch. She moved forward, taking hold of her arm. 'You are, aren't you?'

Becky hesitated and then inclined her head. 'I do need help badly – will you help me, Maggie? I'm sorry I was nasty just now—'

'It doesn't matter and, of course, I'll help.' She looked at her intently. 'What time is your lunch break?'

'In half an hour.' Becky bit her lip. 'I don't know what to do...'

'I'll meet you downstairs in half an hour,' Maggie offered. 'We'll go somewhere to have a cup of tea and something to eat.'

'Yes, all right – I'd better get back to the office.'

Maggie watched her go. Becky had put on weight. There was no other outward sign other than the puffiness in her face, but Maggie's instincts told her that Becky was with child. Becky's father and Minnie would be so upset. No wonder Becky was snapping at everyone!

Shaking her head over it, Maggie walked into the bags, jewellery, hats and glove department. Despite the war, Sally had kept this department much as it had been before the conflict. Some of the best silk scarves were unavailable, but hats had not been affected and nor had the jewellery and leather bags by the look of things – just the skin bags and imported silver jewellery was missing.

Rachel smiled at her. She was serving a customer, but as soon as she'd finished, she came to meet her. 'How lovely to see you, Maggie. I was hoping you would come in today. Will you come and visit me at home – either this evening or at the weekend? I'd love you to meet my Lizzie.'

'That's the little girl you've adopted. You said her grandmother neglected her and then died just after you took the child,' Maggie said, immediately interested and aware of a new animation about Rachel. 'I'd love to meet Lizzie. What does your husband think to her?'

'As yet, he hasn't said anything,' Rachel replied. 'William got home at the weekend from the isolation hospital and seems much better in himself but a bit quiet.' Rachel's husband had served in the Army for a time but had been invalided out. He'd then developed TB and spent time away from her in isolation recovering from the debilitating disease.

'Do you think he is angry because of Lizzie?' Maggie asked her, picking up her fears, and Rachel frowned.

'He hasn't said a word against her, but he hasn't said he will adopt her. I tried to do it legally, but it seems I can't without his permission. It would break my heart to part with her.' Rachel's eyes darkened. 'No one disputes my right to have her – but to make it legal William must sign the papers...'

'Well at least, *you've* got the vote now,' Maggie said. 'We campaigned for it, Rachel, and some of us have it at last... but women still have to ask their husband's permission for so many things.'

'It still doesn't make us equal,' Rachel said and sighed. 'We are still frowned on if we walk into a bar or a restaurant without a male escort – but I suppose it is a start.'

'Yes, it is a start,' Maggie agreed. 'I don't think the Government had much choice after what women have done in this war – but they're all men and didn't give more than they were forced.'

'I suppose they think it is enough, but we shan't stop

campaigning until we all have the vote and equal rights, if I have my way...'

'I think you and the Movement will have a long campaign to get equal rights,' Maggie said, laughing. 'I wish you good luck though and with Lizzie.' She glanced over her shoulder to see who was nearby. 'I thought one or two of the windows looked a bit tired. You're really missing Mr Marco's flair...'

'Yes – we're missing Marion and Sally's input too,' Rachel said. 'With all three of them away, the windows have been adequate but lacking in that special magic they had before the war.'

Maggie looked around the department. 'This floor still looks good, though.'

'Yes, I'm pleased with the girls I have at the moment. Shirley is coming on nicely and Sarah Jenkins is new but a good salesgirl – but I oversee the displays myself now that Marion has left us. I think Shirley may take her place in time, but Marion had a really good eye for it.'

'Yes, she did,' Maggie agreed. 'I'd like to visit you on Sunday if that is all right? Colin has an appointment for the afternoon – so I could stay for a couple of hours or so.'

'I shall look forward to it. Come to tea,' Rachel invited as a customer walked purposefully towards her.

Maggie nodded and moved away. She spoke briefly to the girls in the department. The new sales assistant seemed pleasant and efficient, though a little shy. After a few moments, she left them to their work and then went down to the ground floor in the lift. She just had time to look round before meeting Becky.

* * *

'You won't tell anyone else if I tell you?' Becky asked and Maggie promised that she wouldn't. 'You remember Captain Morgan – the one we met at the first-aid group?'

'Yes. I met him again when I was training for my nursing.' Maggie smiled. 'He has the same surname as my husband.' Maggie had forgotten the Army doctor until Becky mentioned him again. Since she'd heard nothing of him for a long time, she had assumed that her friend had forgotten him, too, but now saw that was far from the case.

'His Christian name is David and he is a distant cousin of your husband's,' Becky said and Maggie gasped with shock. 'Didn't it occur to you that he might be?'

'No. I didn't even know that Colin had a distant cousin until recently,' Maggie confessed. 'I knew you were sweet on him once, but you haven't written to me for months and you stopped speaking of him ages ago... I do just remember him, but he's very different to my husband. They don't look alike, so I didn't think there was a connection.' Maggie hadn't given him a second thought after she was shipped to France to take up her nursing. The years of caring for wounded soldiers and the horrors and pain she'd endured had pushed any memory of David Morgan to a far corner of her mind.

'David told me about that branch of the family. Their grandfathers were brothers and David's grandfather was the younger son so didn't inherit much but...' Becky breathed deeply. 'David asked me to marry him and he gave me something very valuable that belonged to his mother just in case...' Tears began to shed from her eyes. 'I was in love with him, Maggie. Do you think me very wicked to... you know... go with him?'

'No, not wicked at all.' Maggie looked at her seriously. 'After Tim died, I wished I'd made love with him. I wished I was having his child – and I would have done.' She hesitated, then, because Sadie's secret wasn't hers. 'A friend of mine in France had a love affair. She fell for a baby and her lover died before she could tell him – but she was lucky enough to marry someone else, a friend.'

'I don't know what has happened to David,' Becky told her. 'He promised to write and said we would marry when he got home – but I haven't had one letter.'

Maggie shook her head. 'Something is wrong, Becky. The man we met at those classes – I am sure he would never do that to you...' David Morgan had been a gentleman and surely not the kind to deliberately deceive a young woman?

'I think he must have been badly injured or killed,' Becky said and caught back a sob. 'I love him, Maggie – I don't believe he meant to hurt me, but what am I going to do? I can't have this baby... my father would disown me. Even if he didn't, I couldn't bear to see the shame and disappointment in his eyes – and I can't bring a child up alone.'

'You don't think your father would forgive you?'

Becky shook her head in horror at the thought of telling him, and Maggie hesitated, not quite sure what she could do.

'Let me think about this, love. If you really want to keep this a secret, we have to get you away for a while – when is it due?'

'In August,' Becky whispered. 'I've laced myself in so tightly that it hurts. I don't show much yet, but if anyone comes into my bedroom at night and sees me without my corset, they might guess. My father will be so angry and ashamed...' Tears squeezed from the corner of her eye. 'I have to get away.'

'That could probably be arranged,' Maggie said thoughtfully. 'I would have to talk to Colin though...'

'You promised you wouldn't...' Becky cried and made to get up, but Maggie held her arm and she sat back down. 'Why do you need to tell him?'

'Because I would go away with you while you give birth and then... I'd tell everyone I'd adopted the baby from an orphanage.

Colin would have to know and approve...' She squeezed Becky's arm. 'If you can keep your secret a little longer, I'll ask my husband if he is willing – if you agree, of course – and in confidence.'

'Perhaps...' Becky looked doubtful. 'Why would you want to adopt my baby?'

'Because I may not be able to have one of my own,' Maggie said truthfully. 'We are considering adoption – and this baby is distantly related by blood so...'

Becky stared at her oddly. 'I'm not sure...'

'I'm sorry,' Maggie apologised. 'If you don't like the idea of us adopting the child, I could still help you – but what will you do with the child? Will you leave it at an orphanage?'

'I hadn't thought...' Becky bit her lip as the reality struck her. She'd obviously been trying to block it from her mind but was now thinking about the future. 'I'm sorry, Maggie. It's a lovely idea of yours – my baby would be safe with you...'

'Yes, he or she would be loved.' Maggie smiled and nodded. 'If you're happy for me to do so, I'll talk to Colin and let you know what he thinks – but if he says no, I'll still help you somehow.'

'Thank you,' Becky said and wiped her cheeks with a lace handkerchief. 'I'd better get back to work – but when will you know?'

'I'll talk to you on Saturday,' Maggie promised. 'Don't cry any more, Becky. We'll think of something, I promise.'

* * *

Maggie chose her moment carefully. Colin had told her he had appointments all day and he was back at their hotel in time for tea. After they'd eaten delicious hot crumpets with butter and strawberry jam in the hotel lounge, they went up to their room.

'Did you meet all your friends?' Colin asked, sighing as he relaxed in a comfortable chair. 'You weren't bored on your own?'

'I wasn't on my own much,' Maggie answered with a smile. 'I went from one department to the other and I saw Rachel and Beth – and Becky too—' She took a deep breath. 'Becky is in trouble, Colin. I have her permission to speak to you about something...' Pausing for a moment, she said, 'Becky is unmarried and carrying a child and her father would be terribly shocked if he knew the truth. So... she wants to keep it secret and have it adopted. We want to adopt – how would you feel about taking on her child...?'

'Your friend is unmarried and with child?' Colin whistled in surprise. 'That does take the breath away – poor girl. Who is the father?'

'That is the difficult bit as far as you are concerned...' Maggie hesitated, then, 'His name is David Morgan and I think he may be the distant cousin your father spoke of the other day.'

'Good grief!' Colin's eyes flashed with anger. 'What a bastard – leaving a decent girl to fend for herself. He should be made to marry her!'

'I met him a couple of times. He is – or was – an Army doctor and seemed decent enough,' Maggie said carefully. 'He promised to marry her when he returned, but he hasn't written – it is possible he may have been killed overseas. He is with the Army, so...'

Colin's gaze narrowed. 'You met my father's cousin? Why didn't you tell me?'

'I had no idea he was related to you. Besides, it was at least two years before *we* met and I'd forgotten about him. He was never of interest to me, Colin. He was kind to Becky, giving us a lift home when her purse was stolen – oh, and he gave a lecture to the VADs once. I didn't know how far their relationship had progressed; she kept that very quiet, and, as I said, I went to France and forgot him. I didn't connect you to him when we met. How could I guess that a man I'd met briefly was related to you?'

Colin looked doubtful. 'What kind of a girl is she – to lie with a man she hardly knows?'

Maggie was silent for a moment, then, 'I have always thought her a pleasant girl and I would never have expected her to do something so reckless and hurtful to her family. Her father and stepmother will be so distressed if she is forced to tell them...'

'Surely she has no choice?' Colin asked, brows raised. 'Do you think he took advantage of her innocence?'

'Becky says she was swept away by love and I can understand why it might have happened – he was leaving for France and they both knew he might not return, but she is younger than me... so yes, I feel that he acted badly. He was her first and only boyfriend and she probably didn't truly know what she was doing.' Maggie looked at him. 'It hurts to part from someone you love and it is hard to resist the urge to make love when you may never see them again.'

'Was it hard for you when you parted from Tim?'

'Yes. He didn't ask me to give myself to him – had he done so I might have.'

Colin nodded. 'I know that you didn't, Maggie – but she did. My father's cousin was severely at fault to have taken advantage of her; even if his love overwhelmed him, he should have considered her and what might happen. In such a situation, a man is the one who should take responsibility and control his urges for the sake of the girl he loves.'

'Apparently, it was only once...' Maggie sighed. 'She is my friend, Colin. I must help her.'

Colin looked at her. 'Perhaps it doesn't matter who the father is – it would be our child, just as any other we adopted.' He hesitated, then, 'But how will you arrange it so that her family do not know anything?'

'I thought if I invited her to stay with me,' Maggie said. 'I shall say that she is visiting the estate, but in actual fact, we'll go somewhere we aren't known until the child is born and then we'll take the baby home and tell your father... If it is a boy, we could tell him of the connection.'

'Yes...' Colin nodded. 'That could work... but supposing my father's cousin isn't dead? What happens if he returns, offers to marry her and wants his child?' His eyes met hers. 'It might be best if I try to find out what happened to him. Ben Harper could do it discreetly.'

'That would be wonderful – you need not tell him why.'

'No, of course not – David Morgan is a distant cousin, reason enough.' He looked thoughtful. 'If Becky changes her mind about the adoption or her lover returns, how would you feel about giving up the child?'

'I dare say I should feel disappointed, but then we should adopt an orphan as we'd planned,' Maggie said and smiled at him. 'I think we need more than one child to make your great big house a home that rings with laughter, Colin. A little girl or boy. I do not mind which...'

'Half a dozen of them if it pleases you,' Colin said and gave her a loving glance. 'It was my father I was angry with, Maggie, and not this cousin – it will not matter to me or stop me loving the child, because he is the father.'

'We should only do it if you are sure?'

'Yes, I am,' he replied. 'I was shocked at first – but it makes a kind of sense, doesn't it?'

'In a way.' Maggie touched his hand and looked at him enquiringly. 'Where did you go today – may I know?'

Colin's smile faded. 'I had hoped to give you better news, Maggie. I saw a consultant – a top man – and I asked him if he thought I would be able to father a child one day. He said he thought it unlikely as my lower body has been damaged too much. So your friend's baby will be ideal...'

'I'm sorry you were disappointed,' Maggie told him and bent to kiss him softly on the lips. 'I don't mind, Colin. Truly, I don't – Becky's baby will be ours and any other child we choose to adopt.'

'If you are there at the birth it will help to bind you to the babe,' Colin said thoughtfully. His smile returned. 'The slightly better news is that I managed two steps unaided for the consultant and he thinks I may regain some more mobility if I keep doing those exercises. Oh, I'll never be able to run a road race, but I may be able to manage many things I can't yet...'

Maggie smiled lovingly. 'That is far more important,' she told him. 'So I can arrange Becky's visit then?'

'Yes, ask her if she is happy with the arrangement and I'll get my lawyers to draw up the proper papers...' He paused, then nodded to himself. 'I'll speak to Ben Harper. He knows a lot of people at the War Office. Perhaps he can discover something about Captain David Morgan...'

'Yes, please do,' Maggie agreed. 'He is already making enquiries about Mr Marco – the man I told you about, Colin. He was the window dresser at Harpers, but in France he was a very brave spy. I promised I would never tell anyone else, but there is no harm in telling you.'

'I'm hardly likely to speak of it,' Colin replied. 'He must be very brave, for I would not like to be in his shoes if he has been captured.'

Maggie felt a chill at her nape. 'If Mr Marco was captured by the enemy and his time as a spy was discovered, he would be shot and quite probably tortured. Poor Sadie must be so worried not knowing where her husband is...'

6

Sadie lay wakeful, her mind going over and over the few short months that she had been Marco's wife. He was a wonderful father to Pierre, who adored him and missed him and was constantly asking where Papa had gone. He didn't understand about wars or anything that might happen, he just knew he missed the man who nursed him when he was teething, threw him into the air and always caught him safely and made him giggle. He was missing him dreadfully and so was Sadie.

She turned over in bed, aware that she had a sore throat and a bit of a headache. She must have a cold or something. She was starting to ache all over. If Marco was here, he would get up and make her a drink of hot cocoa and make a fuss of her. It was horrid feeling unwell when you were alone – of course, she had her darling son, so she wasn't alone, but he wasn't big enough to know that Mummy felt a little under the weather...

At least Sadie had her new job to go to at Harpers. Sally Harper was a good friend to her and she was beginning to get to know other people. Sighing as her thoughts went back to Marco, she felt the tears wet on her cheeks. She missed him so much and wondered if he would ever return. Was he alive and suffering or was he already dead?

* * *

He woke to a blinding headache, groaning as the light hurt his eyes when the cell door was opened and the guard entered. 'You, out!' the guttural voice ordered and the rifle was jerked at him impatiently.

Marco stood a little unsteadily and lurched at his tormentor. He knew what was coming and he didn't fancy yet another beating at the hands of the sadistic soldier who was leering at him with malicious satisfaction. After his capture on that hectic day, when they'd been ordered over the top of the trench, Marco had, at first, been treated with rough respect by the German officer who had been in charge. His slight head wound had been tended by a doctor and he'd been kept with other prisoners in a hut at the rear of the enemy lines, but then things had changed on the third day when a new officer arrived – a certain Captain Wenger.

Marco knew the instant he saw him that he was in danger. Captain Wenger had known him as the nightclub entertainer who had gathered secrets for the British and was wanted as a spy. Marco had tried to avoid looking at him, hoping not to be noticed, but on the second day of Wenger's posting to the prisoner of war camp, Marco had been taken out, beaten and then brought to this small hut where he'd remained alone ever since. Twice, he'd been beaten but no questions asked, but this morning it was different. He was taken to a large old barn that the officers used and which he'd seen only briefly before.

Captain Wenger was seated at a desk, his uniform as pristine as ever, his expression a satisfied smile that sent a cold shiver down

Marco's spine. 'So, we meet again, Marco. How are you, my friend? I trust we have been treating you well?'

'Do you?' Marco said through gritted teeth. Wenger certainly knew that he'd been beaten. He must have given the order. 'What have I been brought here for?'

'I was hoping you might clear up a little mystery for me,' Wenger said in a deceptively pleasant tone. 'You are a spy are you not, Marco? The charade of the nightclub entertainer was just an act – was it not?'

'I don't know what you're talking about,' Marco replied. 'I am a British soldier captured in battle and according to the rules of warfare, I should be treated as a prisoner of war and kept with my comrades.'

'Yes, you were certainly captured in battle,' Wenger agreed, his eyes like shards of ice, glittering with malice. 'Which I find most amusing. What happened that they sent you to the Front, my friend? Did you disobey an order? I find myself here because of you.' His gaze narrowed, intensified. 'I was due for promotion, but I failed to pick you up when I was ordered to arrest you – for that I was sent to the front line, but I didn't die. I saved my men from being routed and so they decided to give me this job to get me out of the way... I was a hero, but they continued to punish me because I let the spy slip away...'

'Unfortunate for you,' Marco spoke carefully, 'but nothing to do with me.'

'I am not a fool and to treat me as such is stupid.' Wenger's menace became almost palpable as he leaned closer to Marco. I know you are the spy – but the network you set up seems impossible to penetrate. They continue to cause trouble. If I could break it, I might be given the promotion I deserve – so why don't you just tell me?'

'I am Captain—'

'I know who you are,' Captain Wenger didn't let him continue. 'You are of mixed blood, but your father was British. He worked in the diplomatic service and you worked for Harpers Emporium in London.'

Marco was silent. Wenger had discovered a lot about him; how or why he'd taken such an interest he had no idea.

The officer smiled and nodded. 'Yes, I made it my business to find out about you. You underestimated Shultz, Marco. He was a traitor but not a fool. He picked up all the information he could about you, little things you probably didn't know you'd told him – and I went to a lot of trouble to piece them together.'

Marco's guilt almost swamped him. The young German soldier he'd befriended during his time undercover had known he was a spy and had deliberately given him information, in return for a promise that Marco would help him to live in London after the war – and because of that he'd been tortured to death. Something that would remain on Marco's conscience for a long time.

'Shultz wouldn't have told you anything,' Marco retorted and realised almost instantly he'd made a mistake as Wenger's eyes flashed with triumph. He crossed his arms, taking a firmer stance. What was the point in trying to lie? Wenger knew him from his time as a spy, when Marco had masqueraded as a nightclub entertainer, and he would use any means necessary to get whatever information he wanted. Yet Marco knew very little. Marie and her mother, who had given him a home on his second visit to France, were safely out of Wenger's reach and the other members of the partisan group would have changed their set-up by now. He decided to be bold, to attack rather than defend. 'You should know that I can't tell you anything relevant.'

'No?' Wenger smiled. 'A few names perhaps? Safe houses – the route you took when you escaped? Small things that mean nothing to you but might mean promotion for me.'

'None of that is relevant,' Marco told him. 'It will all have been changed – so what do you really want?'

'Ah, clever,' Wenger said and nodded. 'What did you offer Shultz? He was a promising young soldier and loyal until you corrupted him...'

'It was Hoffmeister who did that,' Marco replied. 'Shultz hated him. He wanted a life in England after the war – I said I'd do what I could...' Kurt Shultz had been bullied and abused by his superior officer and, while Marco was posing as a decadent nightclub entertainer during his first mission as a spy, he'd helped Shultz escape the officer's unwanted attentions. Shultz had craved a life in London after the war – the kind of life he believed Marco lived as a nightclub entertainer – and he'd given him valuable information as proof of his loyalty. However, he'd taken too many risks and been arrested and tortured to death by the man he'd hated.

Wenger was glaring at him. 'Germany will win the war. You British will not be in a position to do anything.'

'If you really believed that you would have had me shot instead of beaten,' Marco replied. He saw the startled look in Wenger's eyes and knew he'd guessed right. 'So what do you think I can do for you?' The German officer must want something he thought Marco had access to and was prepared to go to any lengths to get it.

'I want money,' Wenger said and smiled coldly. 'I know the group you set up gets money from the British. I want enough money to live in the country of my choice when the war is over.'

Marco laughed, because he knew that was never going to happen. 'I'm sorry, Wenger. I don't have any money – and if I radioed Britain and asked for money for you, all I would get is a bullet in the head from one of the partisans. I should be shot as a deserter and a traitor.'

'I know the partisans have gold and a lot of it,' Wenger said and his eyes gleamed with avarice. 'With the money and ammunition they got from the British, they attacked and robbed a supply train. On that train were boxes of gold bars belonging to the German people. I want that gold back...'

'For yourself or your country?' Marco asked and saw the answer in the other man's face. He considered he'd been slighted and he wanted payment. To recover stolen gold and keep it would give him great satisfaction. 'So how do you think I can help you get it?'

'I can arrange for your escape. The partisans trust you, Marco. You will discover the whereabouts of the stolen gold and inform me of it.'

'How do you know I won't just re-join my unit and go on fighting?'

'Because I have something you value,' Wenger said and rang a small bell. A door opened and a soldier entered dragging a woman. He shoved her forward and she fell to her knees in front of Marco.

He gave a cry of startled recognition and bent to pick her up. Marie saw him and burst into tears. 'Marie, I'm so sorry,' Marco said. 'I put you all in danger...'

'It wasn't you.' She looked at Wenger and stopped. 'Ignore him, whatever he says, Marcel. Do not trust him...' Marie used the name he'd been given while he stayed with her, but it was clear that Wenger knew all about the deception.

'Have you been ill-treated?' Marco asked and the look he threw at Wenger spoke volumes. If she'd been hurt, he would find a way of taking revenge if it cost his life.

'Not since I was brought here,' Marie said, clinging to him so that he could feel her silent sobs. 'He will use me to make you betray your friends and your country...'

'I know.' Marco looked at Wenger. 'Let her go and I'll do what you want.'

'I told you not to think me a fool...'

'I am not a fool either and if you release Marie, I'll keep my word to you – but if you harm her, I'll kill you. Unless you free her, you can do your worst to me and I won't help you – let her go with me and I will do what you want.'

Wenger met his gaze for a long moment, then inclined his head. 'If I do, remember I found her and took her once before. Betray me and I'll make her wish she'd never known you before she dies.'

'No!' Marie begged. 'Don't do it, Marcel. Let them kill me if they wish...'

Marco held her tighter for a moment, whispering in her ear. She nodded and he let her go. 'Do not be foolish, Marie,' he said aloud. 'We can all be better off – Captain Wenger won't mind us sharing a little of his wealth, will you, Captain? We only need a small amount of this gold...'

'The gold is mine, whatever else the partisans have stashed away is yours,' Wenger said grudgingly. 'The woman goes free – she can vouch for you to your friends. And you will discover where they have hidden their gold and tell me.'

'Yes,' Marco said and met his eyes steadily. 'You have my word as a gentleman on that – but how do I find you?'

'I shall find you,' Wenger said and his gaze narrowed in suspicion. 'How can I be certain you won't betray me?'

'You can't,' Marco said, 'but you have no choice. Unless you free Marie with me, I won't do what you want – I'd rather you went on beating me or just got on with it and shot me. I have nothing to lose, but you do – a fortune in stolen gold...'

'Yes, you are clever,' Wenger said between gritted teeth, 'but don't underestimate me, my friend. Try to betray me and I'll destroy you and everything you love – including the woman and child in England. Oh yes, I know about them, and don't think I can't reach them, because I can – even if I'm dead. There will be a letter to a relentless assassin with instructions to kill them if I die...'

Marco swallowed hard. He hadn't thought Wenger could touch

Sadie, but there was no mercy in those cold eyes. Yet there was nothing he could do but agree. If he refused, Marie would be tortured and murdered, and if he agreed – then he became a traitor to all that he honoured and loved.

'Agreed,' he said without hesitation. 'I'll get you the gold, Wenger. You leave me no choice...' Already the beginning of a plan was forming in his head...

7

Sally could see that Ben was excited the moment he came in that early-spring evening. The nights were just beginning to pull out and the weather wasn't quite as cold as it had been throughout January and February. Ben's face was alive with hope, his eyes glowing with an inner satisfaction. He walked towards her and gave her a hug, before kissing her.

'Something has pleased you – what is it?' she asked him, her heart racing.

'Marco is alive,' he told her. 'He was wounded slightly and taken prisoner but a few days ago made a daring escape and has contacted the group he was working with in France,' Ben told her without hesitation, knowing that she'd long ago guessed Marco had been a spy for the British.

'That is wonderful news,' Sally said. 'Oh, thank goodness! Am I allowed to tell Sadie?'

'Not about the group in France,' Ben said. 'You can just say that he is believed to have escaped and be somewhere in France and should be coming home soon...'

'Won't he be forced to return to his unit?'

'London has sent instructions that he is now high priority and they want him back.' Ben hesitated and his expression warned her not to ask for more details. He'd told her what he could, and though she didn't doubt there was much more, she knew he wouldn't say. Then, he surprised her by saying something she hadn't expected, 'They are sending me out there to liaise with him and bring him back safely.'

'Ben! Why? I don't understand – why do you need to go out?' Sally was shocked and frightened.

'There's something going on,' Ben said. 'I'm sorry, I can't tell you, Sally, but because I know Marco so well, they just need me to be the one to make contact and I said I would. He is in difficulty and needs help, Sally, and he is my friend.'

'Yes, I know...' A shiver went down her spine. She swallowed back the protests and the tears. 'It's just that it was so good having you back in London with me.'

'I know – I want to be here, too, but Marco is special to us both, isn't he?' She nodded, holding back the urge to cry. 'So I'll pop over, help him out and we'll both be home before you know it – and he won't be going back until the war is over and nor shall I.' He was deliberately making it sound easy, like a little day trip to the sea, but Sally knew that was far from the truth.

'Promise?'

'On my word as a gentleman,' Ben said solemnly and kissed her. 'I love you and I love my children, Sally.' He smiled at her. 'While I'm away, won't you take a look at that house, I told you about?'

'Yes, I will,' she agreed. 'I suppose if we had a house with a garden, we could have a puppy? Jenny does so want a little dog of her own.'

'See if you like it and we'll talk about it when I get home,' Ben said. 'And now I'd better pack my stuff.'

'Oh, Ben,' she said and sighed. 'Leave it to me – I know what you need. You keep it all in the special drawer and I'm much better at packing than you are.'

'The most important thing is that nothing tells the enemy who I am should anything go wrong – but of course it won't,' he hurried to add. 'I promise I'm not going near the front line.'

* * *

Sally passed on what she could of the good news to Sadie. Marco's wife had tears in her eyes as she thanked her.

'Please thank Mr Harper for discovering the truth,' she said and squeezed Sally's hands. 'It was so good of him to go to so much trouble...'

'He was only too pleased,' Sally said and hesitated, then, 'Ben has had to go away for a while, but as soon as he's back and there is more news, I shall let you know – but at least we know that Marco wasn't killed in that action.'

'Perhaps they will send him home soon – or at least he may be able to write to me now...' Sadie smiled wanly at her. 'I don't know how to thank you...'

'Seeing you smile is thanks enough,' Sally assured her. 'Fred Burrows told me that the restroom and nursery are almost ready, Sadie. I'm sorry it has all taken longer than I'd hoped, but you should be able to start work soon now.'

'That's wonderful,' Sadie said. 'I'm so looking forward to it – and I can't thank you enough.'

'You may not when you have a dozen small children screaming and pulling at your skirts,' Sally teased, 'but the news about Marco is wonderful...'

She crossed her fingers behind her back, because Ben still had to bring Marco safely back from France and she had a feeling that it wasn't all as straightforward as her husband had told her...

8

'That is beautiful, Sarah,' Marion paused to admire her sister-in-law's exquisite needlework. It was so fine and delicate and would fetch a fortune in the West End shops. 'I could never embroider like that...'

She wasn't bad at plain sewing, but the delicate lingerie Sarah was making for a young woman's wedding was beyond her. The silk was so thin and soft and the pattern of fronds and flowers worked into scrolls was lovely.

'I like doing it,' Sarah said as she folded it and put it away carefully, 'but it isn't something you can do too much of at one time. I think I earn more from the plain sewing you help me with, Marion.'

'That is easier and no one wants to pay what such intricate work is really worth these days.' Sarah had offered her work to a shop she'd thought might appreciate it, but they hadn't wanted to pay her what it was worth so she only worked on private commissions.

'I get more from the alteration work I do for Harpers' dress department than I could selling garments to other stores,' Sarah said and smiled at her. 'It is much easier and I enjoy going in to fit the ladies when it is finished. It always smells lovely...'

'That's those perfumes Mrs Harper bought in before the war. It was a good thing she bought such a good stock. I think they bring in a lot of customers just for the pleasure of smelling them.' She hesitated, then, 'You really should show Mrs Harper this lingerie, Sarah. I don't think she knows how beautiful it is, because I am sure she would order some for herself, even if she didn't sell it in Harpers.'

'Perhaps I will,' Sarah said and sighed. 'I could do with a cup of tea – what about you?'

'Yes, I'm more than ready.' Marion had been working on clothes for her expected baby. She shook her head as Sarah made to get up. 'Let me do it – I've just been watching you for the past hour or so...'

Sarah sat back and allowed her to get on with it. With both their husbands away, they shared the housework, though Sarah did more than her share of the cleaning at the moment, because she said Marion should rest when she could. Marion had got so big these past weeks that it was difficult to do some of the jobs that she had always done so easily. However, she could dust, polish, make cups of tea and help with the cooking as well as her sewing and nothing would dissuade her from doing her share.

As she brought the tray of tea to the kitchen table, where they had been working, they heard the letterbox go. It sounded like the second post of the day and Sarah went eagerly to pick up the envelopes. She came back smiling and showed Marion what she'd found.

'There's one for me from Dan and you've got two from Reggie.'

'Really?' Marion felt a surge of delight as she took them. For a few minutes, they sat in silence as they read their letters. Sarah let out a sigh as she put hers away.

'Dan sent this from Gibraltar, but he doesn't expect to come home for a while. He says he won't be able to write again soon, but I'm not to worry and he hopes to get leave in the summer.'

'Oh, I am sorry, Sarah,' Marion said sympathetically. Letters were all they had to bring their husbands closer and months without a letter were hard to bear. Sarah had only seen her husband a handful of times since their wedding. She'd come to Marion when she was heavily pregnant and her father had thrown her out, not because she was unmarried, but because she'd married a man he disapproved of and he was a selfish, horrid father. Marion had gone round to his house for a second time and managed to get a few more things that belonged to Sarah, but he had never forgiven his daughter or asked about his grandson. She resumed reading her letters and gave a little cry. 'Reggie says he thinks he may be sent home to England soon. He has been wounded again... in his leg this time, as well as a few other small cuts, and it means he can't fight. He is in hospital but says he's fine and will be able to walk when it's healed...'

'Poor Reggie,' Sarah said. 'That's the second time he's been wounded in action.'

'Yes... Oh, that's good...' Marion opened the second letter. 'He's getting on well and he's been told that he will be put on non-active duties for the next few months. That means he will be in this country for some time.'

'I thought they were only allowed to say certain things,' Sarah queried. 'It is a wonder that letter hasn't been censored...'

Marion read on and then smiled and nodded. 'That's because he wrote this in a military hospital in this country; his first letter was delayed. He's home, Sarah, but he doesn't say where and I can't visit until he's better.' She looked down at herself ruefully. 'Not that there's much chance of me going far at the moment...'

'He hasn't told you where to write?' Sarah questioned, puzzled.

'No.' Marion shook her head. She looked at the postmarks on the two letters. One was sent through the usual channels from abroad and the other one was impossible to read. 'I can't make out the postmark either.' She shrugged. 'I expect he forgot to tell me where he is. As long as he is home and out of danger, I don't really mind.'

'Well, I'd better get started on the dinner,' Sarah said, finishing her tea. 'Dickon will be home soon – he said he might be earlier this evening.'

Marion's youngest brother had been working all hours on the docks for months. At one time, he'd hoped to follow his elder brothers into the Army or the Merchant Navy, but his job was important and he'd been refused permission to join up. With the war raging on for so long, most of Dickon's friends had joined one of the armed forces and his family knew he felt resentful at being told he must remain in his job.

'I'm one of the few skilled men they have left,' he'd told his sister and Sarah. 'I know they can't operate the shipyards without us – but I get a lot of nasty comments from folk who don't understand why I'm not in the Army.'

'Mr Harper kept getting white feathers at the start of the war,' Marion had contributed by way of comfort. 'Mrs Harper told me how upset and angry he was – but it's different for you. The Government has made a lot of people do jobs they don't want to do rather than join up.' And she, for one, was glad that Dickon didn't have to fight.

Some younger lads had been sent to work in the mines rather than being allowed to join the Army. The essential jobs had to be protected or the country would grind to a halt, but some of the men resented it, because the Army had more appeal than hard, dirty work that broke men's spirit and sometimes their backs in the dark and dangerous conditions of the coal mines. Dickon knew it was his duty to stay home and help his sister and Sarah and continue the necessary repair to ships damaged by warfare, but he envied his brothers what he saw as their adventures, visiting places like

Gibraltar, Malta and America. He'd told his sister that once the war was over, he was going to change his life.

'I'm going to America or Canada,' he'd said to Marion and his eyes had lit up. 'I'm a skilled man and I reckon I'll find work there...'

'Yes, you should if it's what you want,' she'd told him. 'I'd tell you to go now, Dickon, but I think if you left your job they might put you in the mines – or worse still, prison...'

'Yes, I've been told that I would be in trouble if I left,' Dickon had said, looking angry at the idea of forced labour. 'It isn't right, Marion. They treat us as if we were criminals if we mention being allowed to leave and do something else.'

'I think it's hard on you and other young men who want to do something different with their lives,' Marion had replied, 'but the country is at war, Dickon. I know in Ireland they've had difficulty with the general conscription they're bringing in and there are conscientious objectors amongst our Englishmen who won't fight...'

'Why don't they send them down the mines or make them do the job I do?' Dickon had said petulantly, showing his youth. He'd left school at fourteen and did a man's work, but three years on, he still sounded like a boy at times and Marion was glad the authorities considered his job to be protected, even though she knew how much he resented it at times.

'Could they do your job?' she'd asked, because she knew that he was skilled at carpentry, welding and various other jobs that were much needed in shipbuilding. 'You are a shipwright and most of the men they're recruiting are labourers. They couldn't do what you do.'

He'd nodded reluctantly, fed up with the long hours he'd had to work for months on end, because of the shortage of skilled men available. Too many had flocked to join the forces at the start of the war and so the authorities had had to put a stop to it.

Their meal of a delicious chicken casserole was simmering

nicely in the range oven when Dickon entered the house and threw his rucksack onto the old settee. He hung his work jacket up and then looked at his sister.

'What is for tea? I hope it's ready because I'm going down the pub...'

'It is almost ready to come out of the oven,' Sarah answered just as there was a rap at the door.

Marion went to open it and gave a little cry of shock as she saw the telegraph boy.

'Telegram, missus,' the boy said and thrust it at her. 'It's one of them...'

He got on his bike and pedalled away furiously, as if he couldn't bear to hear the distress he had caused. Marion took it into the kitchen and looked at it. Her hands trembled as she opened it because these telegrams were never good news.

'Oh no!' she cried. 'It's Robbie...' She went cold all over. 'He has been killed – it says lost in action, believed dead...' Her second eldest brother – the one who was always smiling and helping them all – the one who had gone so happily to fight the enemy – the one who was now dead.

Dickon stared at her and then sat down, his face drained of colour. 'He can't be...' he muttered in a choked voice. 'Not our Robbie. He sent me a letter telling me he'd met a girl he liked... he was going to get married after the war...'

Marion stared at him, hardly registering what he'd just said, tears trickling down her cheeks. Robbie was her sweet brother, darling of the family, and the pain of his death was nearly unbearable. She was still stunned when Kathy walked in, looking tired and fed up.

'What's wrong?' Kathy asked, looking round for her youngest sister. 'Where's Milly?'

'She's next door with Mrs Jackson,' Sarah told her. Marion was too upset to speak and the silent tears kept running down her cheeks.

'It's Robbie...' she said at last and handed the telegram to Kathy.

'No! It can't be true...' Kathy cried and burst into noisy tears. 'I can't bear it. I can't lose him too...'

She rushed out of the room and up the stairs. They heard the slam of her bedroom door and then deep sobbing.

'She has never got over Mum's death,' Marion said to no one in particular. She felt numb, unable to take it in – her middle brother dead. It was impossible, too dreadful to accept. Robbie was younger than Marion but older than Dickon, Kathy and Milly. Dan was the eldest and had spent much of his adult life at sea – but Robbie was still so young and would have been at the beginning of his adult life if it had not been for the war. He'd become a man overnight when he'd joined up – and now he was dead. The thought was devastating and Marion's heart felt as if it had been stabbed.

Sarah was looking at her sympathetically but saying nothing.

'I'd better go up to her...' Marion said at last, but Sarah took her arm.

'Let her cry it out,' she advised. 'Kathy was already upset when she came in. I saw it in her face. It's best if she calms down and then she'll talk to us...'

'Yes, I suppose.' Marion accepted that Sarah was right. Kathy was suffering, but so were they all. Dickon had picked up his work jacket. 'Are you going out? You haven't had your tea—'

'I'm going to the pub and I'm going to get drunk,' Dickon said defiantly. 'I'm sick of this rotten war and everything else...' He went out and slammed the door behind him.

'Dickon!' Marion said, but she felt unable to go after him or try to reason with him. The wonder of it was that he'd put up with his life all this time and normally never came home drunk. Yet she feared for what might happen if the drink should take control of him as it had their father. He'd ended up a murderer and a wife batterer all because he couldn't handle his need for strong drink and when under its influence, he lost all control. Marion couldn't bear to see that happen to Dickon – and yet what else did he have? He was tied to a job he didn't much like and there was no prospect of him being able to change things until the war ended. And now the brother he'd adored and looked up to was dead.

* * *

Kathy came down an hour later, looking red-eyed and sullen. Sarah's casserole was still in the oven, because no one had felt like eating and Milly was staying with Mrs Jackson, next door. She spent more and more time with her 'granny' these days and Marion was glad. It would be just too hard to tell her little sister about Robbie. She wouldn't fully understand, though she'd be upset and cry a lot, and Marion felt close to collapse herself. One day she would explain to Milly, but not just yet.

'I've given notice and left my job at the school,' Kathy announced as she sat down at the kitchen table. 'I'm just a drudge there, Marion, and I won't put up with it...'

'I thought it was what you wanted?' Marion said. 'If it's money, I can give you an extra shilling or two for yourself...'

'No, it isn't,' Kathy said. 'All they let me do is prepare vegetables and wash up. That isn't what I was promised and I don't want to stay there.'

'I can ask about a job at Harpers – if that would suit you?' Marion suggested.

Kathy thought for a moment and then inclined her head. 'Yes, please, Marion. I'll work in the canteen or as a sales assistant – but when I've saved some money, I'll take cookery lessons. It's still what I want to do – but not where I am...' She sighed and then decided to confide in her sister. 'It's the kitchen manager. She picks on me the whole time and never gives me a chance to show what I can do – and don't say you'll talk to her because she says our whole family is rubbish, because of what Dad did...'

'She sounds like a nasty woman,' Marion said. 'How long has this been going on?'

'Since Mrs Milligan retired last January. She was the one who offered me the job. I was supposed to get five shillings a week and be taught cooking – well, this one told the headmaster that I wasn't worth paying and she hasn't taught me a thing. I can cook better than her, too.'

'You should have told me before that you were unhappy,' Marion said. 'I'll go in to Harpers on Monday and speak to Rachel Bailey. She will see what roles are available there and then you'll have an interview – is that all right?'

'Yes, thank you,' Kathy replied and lifted her head. 'You've had enough to worry about, Marion. I didn't want to bother you – but I walked out this afternoon and spent hours mooching about before I could get up the courage to tell you and then...' A flicker of pain went across her face. 'Is it certain about Robbie?'

'We can't be sure he is dead, but the tone of the telegram isn't hopeful.'

'No...' Kathy swallowed hard. 'I hate this war and I hate cruel people. Why do they want to start wars and cause so much pain?'

'I don't know, love,' Marion said. 'I will make inquiries at Harpers and, with any luck, they will have a junior position for you.'

Marion saw her sister smile faintly and nodded. She would go to the headmaster at Kathy's school and tell him what her sister had told her – it was wrong that a young girl had been treated so shamefully and Marion wasn't going to let them get away with it!

* * *

'I have every confidence in our kitchen manager,' the headmaster of Kathy's old school said confidently. 'She has excellent references.'

'Perhaps you should check them again,' Marion suggested in a firm but polite manner. 'She treated my sister shamefully and deprived her of the small wage and the experience she'd been promised.'

'I was told she was lazy and insolent,' he protested as he recognised Marion's underlying steel.

'That is something my sister has never been,' Marion replied coldly. 'Please check your records in future, sir. I would advise you to contact Mrs Milligan or the teachers who knew Kathy best. She is a polite, industrious girl, but if you treat someone badly it will make anyone turn against you.'

'I am sorry you feel that way...'

'I do,' Marion replied. 'I cannot force you to do anything, sir – but my sister is owed several weeks in wages and unless she receives either a written apology or her back wages, I shall be writing to the Board of Governors.' Marion pulled on her gloves. 'You may think me a woman of no importance and no influence – but I have friends at Harpers – friends in a position to help me and also in the Women's Movement. If I were to tell them...' She smiled now. 'I do not imagine you would care for a protest outside your gates...'

And with that she left him, still sitting behind his big desk with his mouth half-open and a look of shock in his eyes. In reality, there was probably little she could do to touch him or the woman who had treated Kathy badly, but at least she'd made him think!

9

Becky burst into tears when Maggie told her that Colin had agreed to her suggestion that they would take the baby and no one need ever know the truth. 'It is lucky we're still here. We only came for a few days but have stayed longer than expected – now I'm glad we did, because I can help you.' Maggie told her.

'I don't know how to thank you,' she said, dabbing her eyes with her handkerchief. 'But what shall we tell my father and Minnie?'

'I've been thinking about that,' Maggie replied. 'I believe our best approach would be for me to tell them that I've been a little unwell and feel in need of a friend. It would be a lie, but unless you want to confide in Minnie...?' Becky shook her head. 'She might understand if you gave her the chance...' The suggestion just made Becky look upset.

'I should be so ashamed,' Becky told her. 'I love Minnie and I don't want her to be disappointed. She might tell my father...'

'I am certain she would not,' Maggie said but realised that it would not change her friend's mind.

Although it felt uncomfortable to do it, Maggie went straight from their meeting to the home Becky shared with her father and his wife and told Becky's stepmother the story she'd prepared.

Minnie was so pleased to see her, greeting her with hugs and kisses and spoiling her with cakes and pots of tea, that it made Maggie feel wicked to lie to her – but perhaps Becky was right and it would be too hurtful for her stepmother and father to know the truth.

'You want to take Becky to live with you for a little while?' Minnie looked startled and then thoughtful, surprising Maggie when she nodded. 'Yes, perhaps that would be the best thing, dearest. I know she has been unhappy lately...' She looked into Maggie's eyes. 'I know you will look after her and bring her back safely when... you can...' The pause was significant and Maggie felt a little shock of recognition. Minnie knew the truth. She was almost certain she did, but she wasn't saying. As Maggie met her gaze, she saw no anger or recrimination, only love tinged with sorrow.

'I promise I will,' Maggie said at last. 'You know how fond I am of you and Becky?'

'Yes, dear Maggie, I do,' her friend said gently. 'I haven't had much chance to tell you how proud I was of all you did out there – and I'm proud of Becky too. I want you both to be happy.'

'Oh, Minnie, I do love you,' Maggie said and hugged her. 'Will you speak to Becky's father – make him understand it is for my sake?'

'Yes, I will. He has noticed she is unhappy – and she does not need to work for a while. We are perfectly able to support her and I know she will be fine with you.'

'Yes, she will, I promise you,' Maggie said. 'I'll take care of her and bring her back when we're ready.'

'Good, that is much the best for both of you,' Minnie said. 'So when will you leave?'

'Colin has some appointments this week, so we'll go next,'

Maggie told her. 'Becky says they have plenty of staff in the office and she won't be missed. I don't think she ever settled there. I know she trained for the work, but she liked it better in the department, but then...' Maggie looked at her steadily. 'She believes the man she loves to have been killed in action.'

'Yes, I thought that was it,' Minnie agreed, her face pale with sorrow. 'I know you lost someone too, my dear, and I understand how that can hurt, because I was forced to part from my dear Mr Stockbridge for so many years – but you have found happiness and perhaps she will too.'

'I am sure she will one day,' Maggie assured her. 'Together, we can find a way, Minnie.'

'Yes, I trust you to take care of her for us,' Minnie said and smiled. 'Are you settled in your new home, dear Maggie?'

'It is a lovely place,' Maggie replied, 'but I should be happy anywhere with Colin. I love him very much.'

'Then that is all you need,' Minnie told her. 'I wasn't able to marry Mr Stockbridge when we were young and I never loved anyone else – but I am content now. Love is more important than anything, as I am certain you know.'

'Yes, I do,' Maggie kissed her on the cheek. 'Becky is very lucky to have you for her stepmother.'

'I think I'm the lucky one. I just hope she knows that I love her – and whatever she does, I always shall.'

Minnie knew. Maggie's eyes brimmed with tears that she didn't let fall. 'I am sure that she does,' she said. 'I'll write to you and let you know how we are, Minnie.'

'Thank you, my dear. That would be kind – but then, you always have been kind. Take care of yourself too.'

* * *

Maggie's heart felt full as she walked back to her hotel after leaving Minnie. Minnie's story had been so sad. Obliged by duty to stay with her sister after their father's death, she'd turned down the man she loved and had to endure years of loneliness and regret, until they met again when she started work at Harpers after her elder sister's death – but now she was happy. Maggie had no doubt that Becky's stepmother had guessed the truth but she'd accepted that what they were planning to do was the best outcome for Becky. If Minnie told her husband that his daughter needed to stay with her friend for an extended holiday, he would accept it. Becky could have her baby somewhere she wasn't known and then give it to Maggie and return to her old life – or start a new one if she knew what she wanted to do...

Colin and Maggie would have the first of the children they intended to adopt and things would work out all round. Maggie smiled, pleased with her life. She had accepted at the start that she could not expect to have her own children – but there were so many orphans needing homes that she knew they could fill their house with the sound of children laughing. Becky's child would be theirs just as much as if they had given it life themselves.

* * *

Colin was waiting for her in their hotel room and he smiled as he saw her face. 'It went all right then?' he said and held out his hand to her. 'I'm glad, my darling – and now I have news for you?'

'Something nice?' she asked as she saw the look of satisfaction in his eyes.

'I have bought a pretty little house for us in Hampstead, not far from the Heath,' he said, a note of excitement in his voice. 'It has five bedrooms, three reception rooms and a large kitchen and bathroom. We shall not have live-in staff as we do at the estate, but a

housekeeper will come in each day to look after us. It will be somewhere for us to escape to when my father becomes unbearable...'

'Oh, he doesn't upset me,' Maggie said, 'but it sounds wonderful. When may I see it, please?'

Colin laughed in delight. 'This afternoon if you wish. It means
that I shall remain in London for a while after you and your
friend leave – but don't worry about me, I shall be staying in a
clinic where they will look after me. I want to see about some
work that needs doing at the house and have some treatment on
my legs and spine while I'm here... but when I can, I shall visit
you.'

'Oh, Colin, that is wonderful news,' Maggie said and bent to kiss
him. 'I love you so much. I shall miss you...'

'I shall miss you too,' Colin replied and touched her cheek. 'But
this is what we need to do for the future – for both of us...'

Maggie nodded. 'What will you tell your father?'

'It isn't necessary for me to be there the whole time. Once I've
finished my business here, I'll go and make sure things are as they
should be. If the staff know I'm keeping an eye on them, I think it
will be fine. Most of them are good honest folk, as you know.'

'Your father needs *you*, Colin. You must visit regularly. Even if
he is grumpy and stubborn at times...'

'Just as I am,' he agreed and laughed. 'I know – we are too much
alike, but lucky we have you to keep the peace.'

'I think I'm the lucky one.'

'That is what makes it so perfect,' Colin agreed and then his
expression became serious. 'You can manage everything alone? I'll
see you have money and I'll come to you as soon as I can, my love.'

'I shall be looking forward to that day,' Maggie promised, 'but I
can manage. After what we endured in France, I think I could cope
with most things...'

'Yes, you had a bad time out there – we all did...' He smiled at her. 'Did Sally Harper tell you that I am getting some sort of medal?'

'Yes, she did. Ben discovered it when he was making enquiries about a friend.'

Colin nodded. 'It is a pity he had to leave so soon. I liked talking to him.'

'I am sure we shall see a lot more of them when we have our house here. We shall be able to ask them to dinner.'

'Yes, God willing,' Colin replied, a shadow passing over his face. For a moment he looked sombre, but then he was smiling again.

'Is anything wrong?' Maggie asked, but he shook his head.

'Just memories, my darling. Things in the war – things I would prefer to forget...'

Maggie nodded. She had a lot of those memories, too, and like her husband she would prefer to forget them.

'We shall leave next Monday,' she said. 'I shall telephone that number I found in the *The Lady* magazine and make arrangements to rent the cottage they have advertised for three months. It sounds perfect for what we need – a quiet village near the sea. There is a small cottage hospital for Becky to have the child and shops where I can purchase the things we shall want. The advertisement said there was someone who would clean and cook if required.'

'You should accept those terms, Maggie. I'll feel better if I know you have someone looking after you.'

'Yes, I shall, too,' she agreed. 'It will be a little holiday... but you still haven't said what you will tell your father about the adoption?'

'Oh, I'll simply tell him that it was our choice to adopt. If he refuses to accept the child, we'll come and live in London and let him do whatever he chooses.'

10

Sally turned over in bed. She felt cold, restless and anxious. Where was Ben? What was he doing? He'd been gone for weeks now. She knew that he was somewhere in France and that he would be trying to help his best friend, Marco, to escape from whatever trouble he was in, but she didn't believe it would be as simple as he'd made out.

'Ben, be careful,' she whispered in the silence of the night. Fear made her shiver. She didn't know what she would do if her husband never returned... but she wouldn't let herself think that way! No, she had to stay strong for the children and Harpers.

Feeling restless, she got out of bed and went into the kitchen to make herself a hot drink. Sometimes it was easier to get up and do things rather than lie in bed and think. She wanted Ben home with her and the children and felt a little cross with him for risking his life, even though she understood that Marco meant a lot to Ben. Their friendship went back many years, long before the store was opened in London.

Sipping her tea and munching one of her favourite Bourbon biscuits, Sally curled up on the sofa and began to read through her department accounts. There were so many people relying on Harpers and it would help take her mind off Ben. Though as she tried to concentrate on the stock figures, her mind kept returning to Ben – where was he and had he found Marco yet? What was he really up to? Far more than he'd told her, she was certain...

* * *

'I've had the devil of a job finding you,' Ben said as he saw Marco enter the meeting place. 'Where have you been hiding?'

'So London believed me then?' Marco said as he gripped Ben's hand firmly. 'I thought they might doubt it was me and I would find myself being shot as a German spy or a deserter. Andre knew where to find me but I've been lying low, because there are those that would betray me...'

'Your friends were reluctant to help me at first,' Ben said wryly. 'I think they thought I might be a spy or something.'

'They have learned to be cautious,' Marco told him with a smile. 'I had no idea the man who was looking for me was you – or I'd have shown myself sooner.'

'London asked me what I thought – if you were to be trusted – and I said that if it was definitely you, they could believe every word you said. That was when they asked me to come out and verify your identity.'

'It's a bit of a coil,' Marco said. 'The lives of at least two women could depend on what I do next, Ben. If I just go back home, Wenger will take it out on Marie and her family and also Sadie – and yet, how can I betray my own country? To find that gold for Wenger is a betrayal of the men who risked so much to get me home – of Pierre who gave his life for mine...'

'Then don't.' Ben looked at him earnestly. 'We made a plan to protect Sadie. She will be watched from a distance and whisked off to safety if anything goes wrong here. As for Marie, it was suggested that she and her family are taken to London until we can sort Wenger out.'

'He says there is a letter to someone to make sure his vengeance is carried out if I kill him.'

'He may be bluffing, but forewarned is forearmed,' Ben said. 'Besides, you are not going to kill him. I am—'

'—you! But that is madness and too risky,' Marco said, looking at him in alarm. 'You have no experience of armed conflict...'

'No – but I learned to shoot as a young man,' Ben said. 'Now, listen, before you pour cold water on it – this is what we plan to do. You are going to hand over the gold to Wenger and walk away. After that, you just leave things to me and a few friends...'

'So you won't be taking him on alone?' Marco smiled in relief. 'I thought for a moment—'

'I'll be there directing it and, if forced, I'll do it myself, but I doubt it will be necessary. Captain Wenger is simply going to disappear – there will be no corpse, nothing to show that anything untoward has happened. Your wife should be in the clear. No one is going to spend time looking for her when they believe Wenger has disappeared with his gold...'

Marco nodded. 'If we had the gold, it could work... unless he has an accomplice watching...'

'That part isn't for you to worry about,' Ben told him firmly. 'You will hand over the gold and then leave. You will make your way to the rendezvous and we'll leave for England together.'

'Simple,' Marco replied with wry humour. 'Now all I have to do is find the stolen gold, explain why I want it and somehow appease the anger of the men who risked their lives to take it... and then avoid being shot as a traitor.'

Ben laughed. 'I think you can leave most of that to me. When

London confirms the plan, we shouldn't have any trouble convincing the partisans to lend us the gold for a short time...'

'Lend.' Marco nodded appreciatively. 'Ah, I see – now I think I understand. Yes, that could work, as long as Wenger doesn't suspect anything or trick us...'

'Always possible,' Ben agreed, 'but the partisans can't lose either way. London has promised to replace it if everything goes wrong.'

'They've promised a fortune just to get me back...?' Marco looked at him oddly. 'How did you manage that? I'm not that important.'

'To me you are,' Ben said. 'It was just a bit of arm-twisting for favours done.' He smiled teasingly. 'The windows at Harpers are not inspiring at the moment, old chap. The plain truth is we need you back.'

'Well, I don't know how you persuaded them,' Marco replied doubtfully. 'I found it difficult to get money out of them – but I'm glad you did. I can't wait to get it over with and be on my way home.'

'You'd better take me to meet these partisans,' Ben said. 'We have a lot of talking and explaining to do and I want to get on with it. Harpers and our wives need us back home in one piece.'

11

'Will you go back to the counters yourself when you return to work at Harpers?' Sarah asked Marion, placing her needlework basket on the kitchen table. 'Or will you just concentrate on the window displays?'

'It all depends if Mr Marco comes back from the war,' Marion said and poured boiling water into the large brown teapot. 'I should like to just do windows for a few hours a day – but if they have him back, I might not be needed.'

'Mrs Harper told you they wanted you back too...'

'I do like working with Mr Marco. He says I have a definite flair and under his guidance, I could become a window dresser rather than a shop girl.'

Sarah nodded. 'Let's hope he comes home safely and is of the same mind,' she said.

Marion nodded and bent to pick a pin from the floor. 'Ouch!' she said as she straightened up. She put a hand to her back and grimaced. 'That one was really sharp...'

Her sister-in-law looked up from the book by Marie Stopes she had just picked up, having borrowed it from the library. It was an interesting, perhaps startling view of married love, which urged women to seek contraception rather than continue having children. 'Is it the baby, Marion?' she asked, because they knew the baby could come any day now.

'I think it might be,' Marion said and forced a smile. 'I couldn't sleep much last night, because of my back aching. I wasn't sure; I thought it might be another week or two yet...'

'I was early too, remember?' Sarah said, looking at her anxiously. 'Would you like me to help you upstairs?'

'I want a cup of tea first,' Marion said and bit her lip as she felt a sharp pain. However, dogged determination wouldn't let her give in and she drank the tea she'd poured, gritting her teeth when the pain came again as she finished it.

'That was quick,' Sarah remarked. 'I think I'd better get you up to your room and then fetch Mrs Jackson.'

Marion nodded and it was at the top of the stairs that she felt the water soaking through her dress. 'You'd better let my mother-in-law know her grandchild is on its way,' she said and clenched her teeth. 'I hope she hasn't gone out because I think we're going to need her fairly soon...'

* * *

It was, however, some hours after Mrs Jackson arrived that Marion's baby showed any sign of being born, during which time her screams could be clearly heard by everyone downstairs in the kitchen. Dickon was home from work and sat at the scrubbed pine table drinking a cup of tea, his knuckles white and strained on the handle. Kathy sat on the settee with Milly, her arm about her protectively as she tried not to cry.

'Will Marion die?' she asked, sounding terrified.

'No, of course she won't,' Kathy said but looked anxiously at

Sarah as she entered the kitchen to fetch more hot water. 'How is she?'

'Marion is doing well,' Sarah said and smiled at them. 'Mrs Jackson thinks it can't be long now – but she wants you to go for the doctor just in case, Dickon.'

He nodded, jumped up and grabbed his jacket, clearly relieved to be sent on an errand.

'You didn't need the doctor...' Kathy said and Sarah smiled.

'He came afterwards and took a look at me to make sure all was well, but we thought Dickon needed something to do...' A shout from upstairs warned her that she was needed and she picked up the kettle and went back up to the bedroom swiftly.

Milly pressed against Kathy and they held each other as the screaming began again. Then, mercifully, it stopped and they heard another cry – the cry of a newborn baby. The two sisters looked at each other in delight, because neither of them could imagine a life without Marion.

Upstairs, in the bedroom, Marion was looking anxiously at her mother-in-law as she wrapped the child in a big clean towel. 'A little boy?' she whispered, tears brimming with emotion. Her heart was filled with love for her little son. 'Oh, Mum... Reggie will be so pleased...'

'Like a dog with two tails.' Mrs Jackson laughed and placed the baby in her arms so that she could hold him and see his face. 'He's beautiful, Marion, and looks perfectly healthy to me – and you know Reggie would be happy with a girl if that's what you'd had...'

Marion nodded and smiled tiredly. She knew she'd been luckier than most because her labour hadn't been as long as it might have been, but she still felt exhausted and fell back against the pillows as her mother-in-law took the child and then gave him to Sarah to bathe while she made Marion more comfortable.

'Thank you – you were very kind to me,' she said as her eyelids closed

'You're a lovely, hard-working girl. You've given me a gorgeous grandchild and my Reggie is lucky to have you.' Mrs Jackson smiled at her as she settled the covers back around her. 'With any luck, he'll be home soon – and I reckon he's done his bit and more...'

Marion nodded sleepily. She just wanted to drift off and not think about anything for the moment, but she did hope that her mother-in-law was right. If Reggie came home and was perhaps given a new posting to a training camp to help with the new recruits, she would see more of him and he would be able to see his son growing up.

* * *

Dickon came up to visit his nephew and talk to Marion late that evening. He brought the cup of tea and ham sandwich that she'd requested when she woke from her exhausted sleep to find Kathy taking her turn by her bedside. Kathy had gone down to make the tea but Dickon had wanted to bring it up.

'He's a lovely little chap,' he told her now as he looked at the baby. 'I'm glad you're both all right, Marion – and I'm sorry for the way I behaved the night we got the telegram...'

'I understood,' she said softly as she saw the remorse in his eyes. 'We were all of us upset that night.'

He sat down in the chair by the bed and looked at her. 'It's rotten luck for Robbie – and for you. You've had to bear all of it, Marion. Mum's illness, her dying and all that business with Dad – and now Robbie. Your husband has been wounded twice and then I slammed out as if it was your fault. I'm sorry I'm not more help to you.'

'Dickon, you're my brother and I'm glad you're here. Your wages have helped to keep food on the table – especially since I had to stop work.'

'I don't give you as much as you need for all of us...'

'No, but I have Reggie's money, too, and when I'm ready, I'll do part-time work... if I can.'

'You mean if Reggie will let you,' Dickon said and frowned. 'I think it's daft the way a lot of men say their wives can't work – if you can manage it and you enjoy it, you should.' He smiled at her. 'Women like you deserve equal rights and if I had my way, you'd get them.'

'Bless you, love,' Marion said. 'I don't mind about the vote, but I would like to continue at Harpers.'

'I should think so too. All women should do what makes them happy – as long as it is decent.' He rolled his eyes and Marion laughed at his joke. She knew that most women would prefer to live decent lives and most that went off the rails did so because of poverty and necessity.

'Well, I can only think about going back, because I have Mrs Jackson next door and Sarah. If it were not for them, I'd have to pay someone to take care of my son and then it wouldn't be worth it.' Marion sighed. 'I wouldn't have gone back to standing behind a counter at Harpers, even though I loved it and miss all the beautiful things there. That would be too much with a baby to care for – but I do enjoy the window dressing, and it isn't every day.'

'No, once a window is done it stays the same for a few weeks, doesn't it?'

'We rotate them,' Marion said. 'We have four big windows to dress and we do one a week, occasionally we change two if it is for a special event. It means that each week people come to see what is different and that brings trade to the shop.'

'I like to window shop,' Dickon replied thoughtfully. 'Some of the shops leave their displays longer than Harpers does these days.'

'We had some wonderful displays before the war, especially for the Women's Movement, but it isn't as easy now, because we don't have as much stock or as much variety.' Marion sighed. 'Mr Marco used to have some unusual props, but it is hard to find anything now.'

'It's the same story wherever you go,' Dickon told her. 'All the shops have a limited stock and if you ask for something you bought before the war, they just shake their head at you and remind you how long it has been going on.'

'I know – too long,' Marion agreed. 'Sometimes it has felt that it will never end.'

'I was talking to someone at work,' Dickon said. 'He remembers his father talking about the Crimea War – says it didn't affect the population like this one.'

'Well, it wouldn't have,' Marion replied. 'No one dropped bombs on us before this, did they?'

'Well, they didn't have the LZ 36 Zeppelins or Gothas bombers during the Crimea War,' Dickon quipped, grinning at her.

'It's terrifying when they raid us,' Marion said, shuddering as she remembered the first year of the war when the raids had been at their heaviest and had terrified the population. 'I always think of you exposed on the docks.'

'We've had a few near misses,' Dickon admitted, 'but so far we've been lucky where we are.' The enemy planes had dropped incendiary bombs not far from where he'd been working once, but they'd landed on a patch of waste ground and some went into the river. Other yards and some warehouses had been bombed and gone up in flames. Despite several raids in the district, many of the bombs dropped went astray and although people had been killed and fires started in London and elsewhere, the devastation was perhaps not as bad as it might have been. He gave her a half-hearted grin. 'I know I moan a lot, but I felt tied to my work – but now, well, Robbie's death has brought home to me how much worse things could be.'

'I know how much you loved him. I did too and I miss him.' Marion reached for his hand and held it. 'We'd been lucky as a family until then, but so many of our friends have lost brothers, sons or cousins...'

Dickon nodded. 'War is awful, Marion. A part of me wants to strike back for Robbie but...' He shook his head as she gripped his hand. 'No, I shan't do anything daft – but it feels weird knowing our Robbie won't come back.'

'Yes, I still can't quite believe it,' Marion agreed and felt a sharp pain in the region of her heart. 'I keep thinking it was a bad dream or they made a mistake. Death is so final and I wasn't ready to say goodbye.'

'I certainly wasn't. I thought he would come home when it was all over and everything would be the same.' Dickon stood up. 'I'd better leave you to sleep, Marion. You must be worn out?'

'Not too bad now,' she said and turned her head as her son's cry reached her. 'I think he's probably in need of a feed. Could you get him for me, Dickon?'

Her brother went to the cot in the corner and gently picked up his nephew. He smiled down at the baby before putting him into his mother's arms.

'He is so beautiful. What are you going to call him?'

'I thought Bobby if you don't mind?'

'After our Robbie,' Dickon looked thoughtful. 'Yes, Robbie would like that. Do you think Reggie will mind?'

'Why should he? We can give him Reggie's name as a second name if he likes, but he hates his own name anyway...'

'Reggie doesn't disagree with you much,' Dickon said. 'I'd better get some sleep or I'll never get up in time for work.' He paused at the door and glanced back as she held the baby to her breast. 'He'll keep you busy. I'm not sure you'll have the energy for work if he keeps you awake half the night.'

Marion rested her head against the pillows as she settled her baby at her breast, where he seemed to know exactly what do to with the minimum of prompting. She smiled and allowed her thoughts to drift. For the moment, she was content to lie here in peace and let the future take its course. Her thoughts went to Harpers and the job she hoped to restart when she could. They needed Mr Marco's skills. She often thought about him and wondered where he was and if he was all right...

12

'Why should we let you take our gold and give it to that bastard?' Andre demanded. 'Men have given their lives for it – or at least the power it gives us. We need that gold, not just now – but after the war, to rebuild lives. Look at the wanton damage they did to homes in the village in reprisal after you escaped. Marie's farmhouse was destroyed by fire.' He looked at the group of stony-faced men. 'We've all lost too much.' His gaze was fierce as he looked at Marco. 'Have you forgotten that Pierre gave his life for you?'

'No.' A nerve flicked in Marco's cheek. 'That is something I shall never forget.'

'It will save the life of an innocent woman,' Ben Harper said into the silence. 'Besides, we don't intend that Wenger will live to enjoy it. You'll get your gold back – or be compensated for its loss by the British Government.'

'How can we be certain?' Andre looked suspicious. He and his men had worked with Marco, destroying enemy trains and causing as much trouble as they could. When Marco life was in danger, they'd got him away to the coast and back to England.

'Because you have my word,' Ben replied meeting his fierce gaze steadily. 'We just need to borrow it – and you can help make sure it doesn't go astray.'

'How? Wenger will be expecting a trap. He'll make sure the handover is on open ground so that he's certain he won't be caught by a surprise attack.'

'But he won't expect it here,' Ben showed him the spot on the map he and Marco had selected for the ambush. 'If you are waiting for him out of sight...'

'Supposing he brings a patrol with him?' Andre said. 'Why should we have to fight for it again after we already have it safe?'

'He might not take that route back,' Jacques, another member of the group, pointed out. 'He could go that way...' he gestured to the map.

'He could if British planes were not attacking the only bridge over the river at this very moment,' Ben replied. 'Once that is down, Wenger will have no choice but to return by this road and you can attack and kill him – and any men he has with him here.'

Andre looked at the map and nodded slowly. 'Yes, it could work. I would like to see that sadistic bastard dead. He deserves it.' He looked round at the assembled group. 'Shall we do it, my friends?'

'If you think it can work,' one of the younger men said. 'I don't care who they are – if they're the enemy, I'll kill them.' He stroked his rifle lovingly.

'I still don't see why we have to get involved,' Jacques objected. 'The gold is ours – why should we risk our lives for an Englishman?'

'Because he did as much for us,' Andre nodded at Marco. 'He didn't have to come here and help us – and he has been honest with us over this. It wouldn't have taken him much thought to work out where we hid the gold and steal it from us.'

'In the passage leading from the church vault?' Marco nodded as he saw his answer. 'We have to move it from there, Andre. If Wenger knew about that, you'd have nowhere to hide or escape from. We'll put it on a truck and I'll drive it to the meeting place and hand it over.'

'And I'll be with you,' Ben said, but Marco shook his head.

'No, you won't, Ben. I don't trust that snake. He may well shoot me once he has the gold. I am prepared for that if it happens – but you're needed back in England. Sally would never forgive me if anything happened to you.'

'I came out here to fetch you,' Ben began to protest.

'You've done your part,' Marco said firmly. 'You will keep out of it, Ben – or the whole thing is off.'

Ben nodded, though there was a look in his eyes that Sally would have understood. 'Have it your way,' he said and turned to Andre. 'So we're in agreement then? I can tell London you will go along with it?'

'Yes – and if the gold is lost, they will replace it?'

'Yes, I guarantee it.' Ben offered his hand and they shook on the promise. Everyone looked at Marco.

'It's up to you to contact Wenger then.'

'I have already left a message where he told me,' Marco said. 'It is on for tonight and the pick-up is here, just as Ben told you.'

They all nodded in approval because they knew the area well. There was an open stretch of land by the river and Wenger would not suspect a trap there. When Marco turned up driving a truck with the gold on board, Wenger could just take it and go – but he was unlikely to simply leave without exacting some revenge because once he had the gold, Marco would be of no further use to him...

'It's a good place,' Andre nodded to Ben. 'Do it your way, Marco. We'll be there at the ambush point waiting. Wenger and whoever he brings with him won't be going far with our gold...'

* * *

The night air was rent with gunfire. It was a fierce fight to the death and both sides were driven by hatred. The partisans had more to lose and their desire for revenge was strong. It had happened exactly as they'd expected – in betrayal and vengeance.

'Is he dead?' Jacques asked as the shooting died down and they knelt by Marco's still body on the long grass that was wet with his blood. 'I knew that devil wouldn't just take the gold and go away. It's just as well that Marco didn't know the real plan.'

'He is still alive, thank God! We must get him back to the safe house.' Ben felt for a pulse, his expression grim as he found the wound. 'Give me your scarf to staunch the bleeding.' Ben pressed down hard and bound the wound as best he could. 'The plan I gave Marco was the back-up plan,' he told Jacques as he continued to help his friend. 'We always intended to take Wenger and his men out here. If we'd let him drive away, there's no telling which way he would have gone.'

'That story about the bridge being blown up by the British was false then,' Jacques nodded his satisfaction as Ben completed the make-shift bandage. 'I didn't see why they would go to that trouble just for some gold they weren't going to get.'

'They wouldn't have done it for him either,' Ben said flatly. 'I had to twist a few arms to get them to let me come out here and bring him back. His wife has received protection back home, even though she probably doesn't know it or need it, because ten to one Wenger was bluffing about being able to get to her – but the British Government would not have lifted a finger to save Marco.'

'You did though,' Andre said, looking at him with satisfaction. 'I never believed that story for a moment. I knew they wouldn't compensate us – but I saw what Marco meant to you.'

'Thank you, but I would have done what I could to keep my word to you, even if it took me years.' Ben lifted Marco in his arms. 'We'd best get him back to the doctor you have standing by.'

He carried Marco to the lorry that contained the gold. Wenger and the three heavily armed men he'd brought with him hadn't had time to drive it away as they'd planned to do after shooting Marco. As Wenger had drawn his pistol, pointing it at Marco, a lone shot had rung out and taken him perfectly in the head, because he'd never noticed the man with the rifle hidden in the tree beside the river.

As Wenger fell to the ground, the men with him started shooting and yelling. Almost at once, Andre's men arrived, driving up fast in another truck. The crack shot in the tree killed one of them and the other two were killed by a hail of fire from the new arrivals, who had appeared from where they'd been hidden a way back behind an old barn, but before they could get there, Marco had been shot in the leg and the chest. It was a miracle that he hadn't died instantly.

'Clear this lot up and get rid of their vehicle,' Andre barked at his men. He helped Ben lift the unconscious Marco into the back of the truck.

Ben knelt beside him, pressing his jacket against the wound to Marco's chest, which was bleeding profusely. 'Come on, damn you,' he muttered. 'Come on, Marco. I can't lose you now...'

For a moment, he thought that Marco's eyelids fluttered as if he knew and was trying to come back. Ben smiled grimly in the darkness. His daring and slightly crazy plan had worked far better than he'd hoped, despite Marco's wound. At first, when he'd put his idea to Andre, he'd thought he would refuse, but the man had proved to be both honest and stalwart. He'd told him that some of his men might not want to go along with it, but in the end he'd carried them with him.

Ben had realised that he would need to deceive Marco, too; if he'd known the whole plan, he would never have gone along with it. Marco had known the risk to himself but he'd insisted on going through with it, because of Wenger's threats against Sadie and Marie, but Ben would never forgive himself if he died of his wounds.

'You're my friend,' he muttered as they reached the farmhouse where a doctor was waiting, prepared to treat any injuries. 'Sally would never forgive me if I let you die now...'

* * *

Sadie woke from a bad dream and shivered in the darkness. She couldn't recall exactly what she'd been dreaming but knew instinctively that it concerned Marco. Something bad was happening to him, she felt it inside and the pain was sharp, as if her flesh had been pierced with something hard.

Shaking her head, she jumped out of bed and pulled on a dressing gown, unable to sleep. She was shivering as she went to her son's room and peeped in at him, but he was sleeping peacefully. Continuing through to the kitchen, Sadie filled a kettle and put it on the gas cooker, striking a match to light the ring beneath it. As it flared to life, Sadie became aware that her cheeks were wet with tears and knew that whatever she had seen in her dream it had affected her deeply.

If she lost Marco... No, it was just too painful to consider. Sadie realised just how important he had become to her and prayed that he wasn't dead. Her head had begun to ache again and she felt awful, but she supposed it was this English weather, warmish one day and cold again the next. For four years, she'd been used to the warmer climate of France and preferred it. Perhaps one day she and Marco would go back and visit Marie, who had been so kind to them both.

'Please come home to me,' she said aloud. 'Please don't be dead, Marco. I do love you so very much...'

13

'How does Jenny feel about the new arrival?' Jenni Harper asked and Sally raised her brows, because her daughter tended to demand attention when the baby was being nursed. It was late spring now and Jenni had come down to London to visit, bringing a silver rattle for the baby. 'I wanted to get you something different – and I'm sure you have all the baby clothes you need?'

'Jenny isn't quite sure yet but I'm trying to let her see that she is still loved just as much.' Sally smiled up at her sister-in-law from the settee. 'I am lucky as far as baby clothes go. Our suppliers sent me quite a few things as gifts.' She laughed. 'I suppose it is as good a way of ensuring I see their stock as any.'

'They all know the war can't go on forever,' Jenni quipped. 'Your orders will be worth having once the war is over and the restrictions end.'

'I shall be so glad when that happens.' Sally sighed. 'It has been hard this last year, Jenni. I can't even buy the knitwear seconds now because everyone is doing the same thing. We're just having to apologise to the customers when the stocks are low.'

'I know how bad things are. Andrew says it's much the same as far as medicines are concerned.' She paused, then, 'I hardly like to tell you my good news when you have so much to worry you...'

'Good news?' Sally sat forward. 'Now that is something I could do with – please tell me.'

'I have two interesting things...' Jenni paused, then, 'My husband in America has agreed to divorce me. He wishes to marry again and started the proceedings – and I've just discovered I am expecting a baby. It should be born in time for Christmas...'

'Oh, Jenni! That is wonderful,' Sally jumped up from the settee to hug her. 'I am so delighted for you, dearest. It is exactly what you wanted – a divorce from Henry and now a baby... You are pleased, aren't you?'

'Yes, of course,' Jenni said. 'Andrew says we'll get married as soon as the divorce comes through. He wants his son to have his name.'

'Or daughter?' Sally said, laughing. 'I am so happy it has all worked out.' She looked Jenni in the eyes. 'You are happy this time, aren't you?'

'Yes, I am, very,' Jenni replied. 'I wanted to ask – you will come, you and Ben, to the wedding?'

'Yes, of course – at least, I shall, but Ben isn't here at the moment.' Sally bit her lip. Ben had been gone for three weeks and she was beginning to worry. 'He had to go away again—'

'I thought he'd finished his work for the British Government?'

'He intends to – but something came up.' Sally shook her head. 'It's no use looking at me like that, Jenni. I don't know either.'

'You're worried, I can see that,' Jenni said. 'I shan't plague you – but I shall have something to say to that brother of mine when I see him.'

'He'll be back soon,' Sally said. 'Shall we go to Harpers now? Come and see my new nursery department.'

'Nursery?' Jenni's brows shot up. 'That sounds intriguing?'

'It was an idea I had because of the children,' Sally told her. 'I was lucky because I had Pearl and Mrs Hills – but there must be a lot of married women who have to stop work because they have a child, so I have employed Marco's wife to look after them. We actually have four children in there at the moment, but I am sure we shall get more as time goes on. Sadie is a trained nurse and she looks after any of the staff that become unwell at work – and the children.'

'What a wonderful idea!' Jenni's face lit up. 'I think that is great, Sally. Most women have to give up work as soon as they have a family – but that means many more of them will be able to return as soon as they are over the birth.' She looked thoughtful. 'It's an idea I might steal from you.'

Sally looked at her in surprise. 'What do you mean?'

'I'm thinking of opening a store in Newcastle,' she explained. 'Once the war is over.' Jenni smiled. 'Henry was so anxious to marry his new love that he offered me fifty thousand dollars to give him an amicable divorce. I accepted of course.' She shrugged. 'I could have asked for more – his family have millions.'

'So you're thinking of opening your own store.' Sally stared at her in surprise. 'What will you sell?'

'I'm going to start quite small,' Jenni replied. 'I thought I would stick to clothes – men, women and children's. I've sourced some good woollens for Harpers in the past and I know all your suppliers.' She laughed excitedly. 'It will be fun and I've missed it, even though I keep in touch with Harpers.'

'Harpers is half yours too...'

'Yes, and I shan't be changing that in the near future. One day, Ben can buy me out if he likes, but until then, I'll keep my money invested.'

'Good.' Sally's relief showed. 'We couldn't afford to buy you out yet, Jenni. I haven't had to touch the loan you made us, thank goodness – but it has been nice to know it was there if needed.'

'Well, I don't need it for what I want to do – not yet.' Jenni smiled. 'I wouldn't do that to you and Ben at a time like this.'

'No, but if you needed it…'

'Well, I don't, so no need to worry.'

'Thank you,' Sally said. 'What will you call the new store – Harpers of Newcastle?'

'No.' Jenni shook her head. 'My business won't be big enough to be a Harpers store – not yet. I shall call it Jenni Alexander. Andrew agrees and is prepared to help me if I need it.'

Sally nodded. It was Jenni's decision, of course, but she was glad she didn't intend to call her shop Harpers. Ben's store was exclusive and it was possible that one day he would want to expand to other towns himself. It would be confusing if Jenni chose to call her new business Harpers, because although for the start it would only be small, with Jenni's flair and drive it would surely grow.

* * *

'Mrs Harper,' Sadie greeted her and Jenni with a big smile as they entered the department. 'How lovely to see you.'

'Sadie – I don't think you have met my sister-in-law, Jenni, have you?'

'No, I haven't. How do you do?' Sadie said a little shyly.

'I'm fine,' Jenni said. 'Don't stand on ceremony with me, Sadie. I'm curious about your role here. I think Sally has come up with the most marvellous idea and I want to hear all about it from your side.'

Sally smiled as they began to talk. 'I'm going to pay a visit to the hat department,' she said to Jenni, who just nodded and continued to speak with Sadie.

* * *

Rachel noticed her as her customer left and she finished tidying up. 'Mrs Harper,' she said, using the formal manner she adopted at work. 'How good it is to see you in the store. You look very well.' It was the first time Sally had visited since the birth. 'How is that lovely baby boy?'

'Gorgeous. You must come and see him again soon.'

'I will,' Rachel promised. 'But should you be here? Are you well enough?'

'Yes, I am, and it is lovely to be here,' Sally said. Her eyes moved over the stock. 'Those bangles seem to be selling well – but then the jewellery usually does.'

'People need something to cheer them up,' Rachel replied and nodded. 'A piece of silver jewellery or indeed something like those new photograph frames on the ground floor make lovely gifts. I bought one of those for Hazel for her last birthday and placed a picture of Lizzie in it. She was delighted.'

Hazel was the mother of Rachel's first husband and loved Lizzie, the little girl she was hoping to adopt, and was like a granny to her.

'What does William think of Lizzie?' Sally asked her. William had spent much of the past year in an isolation hospital with TB. Home at last, Rachel had told her he was still not back to his old self. 'And how does he seem, now? I know you said he was a bit quiet when he first got back.'

'He is still looking a bit pale and tired.' Rachel said sighed. 'However, he says he feels much better than he did...' She hesitated. 'Lizzie is still staying with Hazel. William has met her on several occasions and says she is a sweet little thing but...' She shook her head. 'Perhaps he just isn't ready for a child in the home.'

'It may take time for him to adapt to the idea,' Sally said. 'Do you miss her very much, Rachel?'

'Yes, I do. I see her every day, but I can't spend as much time with her as I'd like to.' Sally saw the sadness in her eyes. It was hard for her friend having to leave the child at her old mother-in-law's home. 'However, she loves Hazel and is very happy there. Hazel says she will miss her when I take her home.'

'Of course, but she will see her regularly,' Sally said and Rachel nodded.

* * *

After a few words with the girls on the shop floor, Sally went in search of her sister-in-law and found Jenni playing with a little boy on the floor of the nursery.

She looked up at Sally and smiled. 'He reminds me of Henry's son.'

Jenni had been fond of her husband's son – and he of her – but Henry had refused to let the boy write to her after they'd parted. However, unknown to his father, he had set up a way of getting letters to and from England without his father knowing and had told Jenni that when he was older, he would visit her in England.

Sally recalled Jenni's distress when she'd realised the mistake she'd made in marrying a cold man and had been forced to make the huge decision to leave him. However, she had now found happiness with a brilliant doctor, whom she'd met when he visited Sally. Sally had earlier persuaded him into giving them some of his precious time in London and after meeting Jenni, Andrew had made the journey more often. In the end, he'd asked Jenni to live with him, which she had eventually agreed to.

Jenni was smiling as she got to her feet, brushing at her smart dress. 'This was certainly one of your best ever ideas,' she told Sally.

'It seems popular,' Sally said. 'I am hoping it will entice Marion Jackson back to work a bit sooner. Mr Marco thought she had potential talent as a window dresser and we've certainly noticed the difference since she left just before Christmas... Marco was sent abroad then too.' Sally felt an icy trickle down her back. Where were Ben and Marco? She'd heard nothing for weeks and she was certain something had gone wrong, because Ben had thought he would be back by now. However, she was determined not to let Jenni realise she was worried about him. There was no point in upsetting her too.

'Has Marion had her child yet?' Jenni asked as they continued up to the office.

'Yes, she has a little boy. I haven't seen him yet, but Rachel has and she says he's lovely.' Sally smiled. 'Peter will be awake soon and you can hold him when we get home.'

'I am looking forward to that.' Jenni looked pleased, then frowned, 'I suppose you've heard nothing of your Mr Marco yet?'

'No, unfortunately not,' Sally said, trying to keep her voice light. 'Ben heard that he'd survived the action he was in but nothing more.'

'So when is my brother coming home?' Jenni looked a bit annoyed. 'When he rang me last month, he said he was based here – and I wanted to ask him to be my witness. It will be a small private ceremony, of course.' She placed a hand on her stomach. 'We don't want to make a big thing of it, but I did want Ben here.'

'When is the wedding?' Sally asked and Jenni looked surprised.

'Didn't I say?' She wrinkled her brow. 'Probably next month and we'll marry here in London... that's why I came down, to make the arrangements.'

Next month could mean a week or two or three, Sally just hoped that Ben would be home in time and she would never have to tell Jenni that her brother had gone off on another risky adventure.

14

'This is lovely,' Becky said, looking around her with pleasure at the picturesque cottage. They were in Devon and about fifty miles distant from Colin's father's estate. 'How did you know about it?'

'When Colin knew what I wanted to do, he thought of this – it belonged to his grandmother, of whom he was fond. She lived here after her husband died and Sir Edmund took over the estate. It was left to Colin and he keeps it for sentimental reasons. Sometimes he rents it out, but it has been empty for a few months,' Maggie explained.

The sitting room was furnished with old things that had acquired a comfortable mellow look, though the chair coverings and curtains all looked bright and fresh, a pretty chintz that gave it a cosy feel. Knick-knacks were on the dresser and the mantle, as well as on the little tables dotted here and there about the room.

'She clearly loved her things,' Becky said and went round the room touching the little pieces of glass and porcelain. 'Some of these have been broken and glued together.'

'Have they?' Maggie smiled at the thought of the old lady patiently sticking her things back together. 'You'll be all right here?'

'Yes, of course. It is lovely,' Becky said. 'Dad's house is fine, but it's on a busy street and he only has a small garden at the back – he would love this.' She looked out at the big front garden and Maggie joined her.

The spring flowers were just coming into bloom and it was a riot of colour, a little untidy but beautiful as the bulbs burst into life and the first blossom flowered on the almond tree.

'Colin had the place cleaned and aired,' Maggie said, 'but they haven't done much to the gardens, I'm afraid.'

'It was short notice,' Becky replied. 'Perhaps we could do it together?' She looked at Maggie shyly. 'I don't know how to thank you for what you've done for me...'

'I told you – this is as much for us as you.' Maggie touched her hand in sympathy. Becky's face had clouded, because she was at heart a good honest girl and this deception felt wrong to her. She would have to keep the secret for the rest of her life and that was a heavy punishment for a young girl. 'Don't feel guilty or too sad, Becky. What you're doing is to protect your father – his feelings and his reputation. I know you feel he would be shamed by what you've done, but it isn't so very wicked.'

'Isn't it?' Becky looked doubtful. 'He sacked a girl from Harpers only three weeks ago, because she'd become pregnant and was unmarried. He told Minnie that she'd brought shame on her family.' Tears welled in Becky's eyes and her hand trembled. 'I feel so wicked...'

'You're not! It was a natural thing to do and David should have protected you – there are ways, I believe,' Maggie said as Becky shook her head. 'He loved you and he ought to have taken more care of you.'

'Do you think he did love me?' Becky asked tearfully. 'I believed he did, Maggie. I truly did and I loved him... I just didn't think about what might happen to me if...' She swallowed a sob. 'If it were not for you—'

'Don't cry, love,' Maggie comforted. 'You can see the baby whenever you wish, I promise.'

'No...' Becky shook her head. 'I don't want to – it's best to make a clean break.'

Maggie remained silent. Becky's emotions were all over the place. She felt now that she didn't want to see her baby in the future, but as time passed, she would surely think of it and regret her decision?

'Well, it is your choice,' Maggie told her. 'Come on, let's go and see the bedrooms.'

'Mrs Morgan,' the friendly woman, who would clean daily during their stay, entered the sitting room at that moment. 'I'm off now – unless there is anything you need?'

'No thank you, Mrs Neal,' Maggie said. 'You will be back later?'

'I'll come in at four every afternoon to cook a meal for you,' Mrs Neal said, 'and my daughter Evangeline will be in to see Mrs Becky Morgan tomorrow to examine her. She is a good girl my Evangeline and will look after you when the baby comes, Mrs Morgan.'

Becky blushed to hear herself called by the name they'd decided on. It was her lover's name and seemed appropriate as she was wearing a wedding ring, which Maggie had loaned her.

'Thank you,' she said faintly. 'That is very kind of her.'

'Evangeline is a good nurse and midwife, though I do say it myself,' Mrs Neal said. 'Nursing was all she ever wanted to do and she qualified in a hospital. Before she took up the position here, there wasn't a proper midwife for miles around and quite a few young women died in childbed.' As Becky gave a gasp of alarm, Mrs Neal laughed. 'It won't happen to a healthy young lady like you, not with my Evangeline to look after you.'

'I am glad to hear it,' Maggie said, feeling cross that the woman had put such an idea into Becky's head. It was quite true that women were often subjected to inadequate treatment during birth and that the name of 'midwife' was often given to women who had no professional training. At least Becky would have the benefit of a trained midwife, which was fortunate. 'Thank you, Mrs Neal. We shall look forward to meeting her.'

After the woman had gone, Becky looked at Maggie. 'Do you think she heard us talking? Will she gossip about me?'

'I don't think she could have heard anything important,' Maggie said, though it was possible. 'I am sure she won't gossip – Colin said she was very reliable.'

'Thank you,' Becky looked on the verge of tears again. 'Can we go upstairs please? I should like to rest for a while.'

Maggie nodded. Her friend looked close to collapse. No wonder Becky had been snapping at everyone at Harpers. She'd worried so much and slept so little that she'd become tired and listless. The good fresh air and a little exercise in the garden would help her to recover before the birth. Childbed was dangerous for a woman at times and Maggie couldn't bear the thought that she might lose her friend...

Had she been right to suggest this plan to Becky? Would she regret giving up her child one day? Perhaps it might have been better if Becky had faced up to the truth and told her father and stepmother – and yet she had not been able to bear the idea of her father's shame.

Maggie pushed the doubts to one side. Whatever happened, she would do all she could to help Becky through this time of worry and uncertainty.

* * *

Alone in her room, Becky fought back her tears. She was so grateful to Maggie for helping her, because she could not have borne the shame of having to tell her father about her child – but it was hard to give up the child.

Maggie was looking forward to caring for it and had told her that Colin was preparing a nursery at their home and also at the house in London, for they intended to spend some time there in the future. How lucky Maggie was to have so much. Becky felt envious but knew she ought not – Maggie's life wasn't perfect. Her husband was in a basket chair and they might never have their own children.

Sniffing, Becky wiped her tears away. She should be thanking Maggie for all she was doing and she had – but it seemed so unfair and she couldn't help feeling sorry for herself.

Oh, why had she allowed herself to be carried away? Why hadn't David written to her as he'd promised? Where was he and would she ever see him again?

Sometimes, it was more than she could bear and she wished she could just lie down and die so she need not think about it ever again...

15

'Do you feel ready to go home?' Ben asked as Marco opened his eyes and looked at him. Outside, the sun was shining and the birds were calling, but inside the small room it was hot and airless, stuffy with the smell of sickness. 'Andre wants to move us if he can. They haven't had a German patrol through here for many months but...' He left the sentence unfinished. They both knew that it wouldn't go well for the partisans if an enemy patrol decided to come this way.

At the start of the hostilities, the German soldiers had come into the small border town often, sneaking in from behind their lines, because of the nightclub and the girls there, but the war had been going their way then. Now, it was finely balanced and seemed to be turning in favour of the Allies, but it could still happen that a patrol might be sent to investigate the disappearance of Captain Wenger. It was unlikely any trace of him would be found or his friends and their vehicle. It had been removed far enough from the scene to ensure that could not happen and they hoped it would look as if the missing men had deserted. It was not uncommon for men to desert when things were not going well and, with any luck, after a rudimentary search it would be assumed the men had disappeared of their own accord.

'They want to get rid of me,' Marco said and smiled weakly up from the bed. 'I'm lucky to be alive, Ben...'

'If it hadn't been for the cigarette case in your pocket, you probably would be dead,' Ben replied. 'How did you come to have it?'

'It was a gift from...' Marco moved his head negatively. 'When I acted as a spy, I left it at home, but I took it into the trenches with me. The guard who searched me at the prison camp never found it. I hid it in my boot and for some reason he didn't look there.'

'Well, it saved your life,' Ben said. 'The bullet should have entered your chest just above your heart, but, although it went through the silver, it was deflected and came out through your shoulder.'

'Luck of the devil,' Marco quipped and then winced as he moved to the side of the bed. 'Hurts like hell, but I dare say I can walk.'

'They are going to try to take us to the coast in a truck,' Ben told his friend. 'You couldn't make it on your feet. Andre has a cousin who will take us back to England in his fishing boat.'

'I'm so much trouble,' Marco muttered. 'I don't want anyone else to be killed for me.'

'They have their gold and the satisfaction of knowing a man they hated is dead,' Ben said. 'We searched his body, but there was no sign of the letter he threatened to send to an assassin and I would doubt he ever wrote it. That was just bluff, Marco. Wenger couldn't have got to Sadie in England – or he would have had her kidnapped the way he did Marie.'

'Marie is all right?' Marco questioned anxiously.

'Yes, fine. Before she was taken to a place of safety, she thanked you for helping her and said to give her love to Sadie. She will probably be in England now, where she'll stay with distant relatives until the war is over. Andre is going to use some of the stolen gold to rebuild her home when this is all over.'

'If it ever is.' Marco sat up, his face contorting with pain. 'Have you got a cigarette?'

'Yes.' Ben took one out of the packet of French cigarettes in his pocket and lit it before giving it to Marco. 'Don't make yourself cough; it will hurt.'

'Damned right,' Marco said. 'So when are we leaving?'

'Tonight, as soon as it is dark. Andre has arranged it and if we miss the deadline, it could be weeks before they can do it again – otherwise I wouldn't ask you to make the effort.'

'I know,' Marco nodded his acceptance. 'I owe you my life, Ben. If you hadn't been such a damned fool as to risk yours, I'd be dead.'

'I didn't do much – the shooting was all down to Andre's men,' Ben replied. 'I just organised it.'

'You're good at that.' Marco stood up and nearly fell but caught hold of the chest of drawers next to the bed and sat down again. He grimaced. 'They may have to carry me down the stairs.'

'Yes, we're prepared for that – but it has to be done, Marco. I'm sorry. I would have preferred that you rested for another week or two.'

'We've been here long enough as it is,' Marco said, wincing. 'Don't worry – I'll go if it is the last thing I do.' His grimace might have been a smile but was too much effort and he fell back against the pillows. 'We've risked their lives too much already.'

'And you didn't risk yours for them?' Ben smiled oddly. 'You made good friends here, Marco. I'm going to bring Sally over after the war. She would love it here.'

Ben left him to rest and went downstairs to the small parlour where Andre was sitting drinking red wine with another member of the group.

'Will he manage?' Andre asked. 'We're planning something – and it's best he's gone. There may be reprisals.'

Ben nodded, meeting the other man's gaze. 'Obviously it is important or you wouldn't do it right now – so good luck whatever it is.'

'The order came from London,' Andre said. 'They didn't mention you or him.'

'No, they wouldn't,' Ben replied. 'It was made pretty clear to me that I was on my own – and I was told bluntly not to mess things up. I hope I haven't done that?'

'Wenger's body hasn't been found,' Andre said. 'With any luck, it won't be – but not everyone in the area likes the British, my friend. Some think it would be better if the Germans won the war – so the sooner you've gone, the better.'

Ben nodded. He'd become increasingly aware that they'd worn their welcome out as Marco lay tossing in a fever and it was touch and go whether he would survive. Thankfully, two days earlier, he'd opened his eyes and known Ben as he bent over him.

'You're not as pretty as Sadie,' he'd muttered. 'She nursed me last time – and she was a lot better at it...'

'Thanks,' Ben had replied and laughed, because it told him that his friend hadn't lost his sense of humour and was back with them. He'd improved since then but was certainly not well enough to make a long journey. For Marco, the truck drive and then the journey by sea was going to be a nightmare filled with pain, but it had to be made. They needed to remove themselves from danger and their wives would be worrying.

* * *

Sally sat with her pen poised over the illustrated list of men's clothing. She couldn't make up her mind whether to buy the new tweed jackets and fawn slacks that were being offered. If Ben had been here, she would have asked his advice. He had a good eye for clothing and before the war had taken an interest in the stock they sold. A sigh broke from her. When would all this uncertainty be over? It seemed to have been going on so long and she was worried about Ben.

He'd promised he wouldn't be gone long and it was well over a month since he'd left to bring Marco back. What was going on? Something had delayed their return and she couldn't help being anxious – although something inside told her than he was still alive. She would have known if he was dead. Ben had told her he would not be in any danger, but the mission could not be without hazards. She'd known that when he first told her he was going – but she couldn't have stopped him. Once Ben made up his mind, he wouldn't easily change it – but he'd seemed confident and promised her he would be back soon. So where was he?'

Hearing her son start to cry, Sally put down her lists and went to fetch him from his cot before he woke Jenny. No doubt he needed a feed and perhaps his napkin needed to be changed. She picked up Peter and looked into his eyes as the crying miraculously stopped. His eyes reminded her of Ben and she felt a shaft of love mixed with pain.

'It's all right, darling, Mummy is here,' she told her son and bent her head to kiss him. Yes, he definitely needed changing before his feed.

Carrying him through to the sitting room, Sally felt better as she went through her routine. Nothing had happened to Ben. He would come home as soon as he could and he would bring Marco with him. She just had to be patient and carry on looking after the store and her children until he did. Sally was no worse off than thousands of other wives. Rachel's husband had only recently returned from the isolation hospital. She'd had hardly any time with him since their marriage. War had broken out almost immediately and then, when he returned home, it was discovered that he had consumption. Fortunately, he'd recovered and was back with her again.

Sally nodded to herself. Ben would come home and it would all be fine...

16

Rachel looked at her husband as she walked into their sitting room that spring evening. William was sitting in his favourite armchair by the fireplace, reading his paper, only he'd fallen asleep by the look of it and the paper had dropped from his hand to his knee. For a moment, her heart caught, because he looked so still that she feared the worst, but then he opened his eyes and looked at her, smiling.

'Are you all right, dearest?' she asked and dropped to her knees by his side. 'I shouldn't have left you alone so long... I'll tell them at Harpers that I need time off to be with you.'

'I haven't been alone,' William corrected. 'Hazel brought little Lizzie round to see me and we had a lovely time. She had ham sandwiches for her lunch that Mrs James prepared for me, as you asked her – and plum crumble and cream for afters.'

'Lizzie was here?' Rachel asked. 'Is that why you were so tired you fell asleep?'

'Oh, I sleep a lot in the afternoons,' he replied. 'They let me come home, Rachel, but I shall be a while before I'm back to what I was – if ever. I fear I am a sad disappointment to you—'

'No, how could you be?' Rachel cried. 'I love you.'

'Do you, my dear?' William looked sad. 'I expected to be a proper husband to you – hoped we would have many good years, but that wretched disease has taken the stuffing out of me, Rachel. I'm not sure how long it will be before I can take you out anywhere nice again.'

'I'm happy as I am,' she told him and meant it. She hesitated then, 'Would you be content for us to go ahead with the adoption legally and have Lizzie to live with us?'

'Yes, if it is your wish,' he said and sighed. 'I had news today, Rachel – news that has made me a little sad but may change the way we live in future...'

Rachel looked at him uncertainly. 'What news, William?'

'My mother has passed on – it seems she had what they thought was a chill but it turned to a fever and she died in the night. My sister has informed me that she intends to marry now and that means my country house in Hampstead will be empty for the first time.' He looked at her oddly. 'I could never take you there to live while it was my mother's home, because you would not have been happy. She was a difficult woman – and I would not subject you to her criticism. I fear she never approved of me marrying you, Rachel, and might have made you suffer – but now the house is ours, as it should always have been.'

'I would never have expected that,' Rachel exclaimed.

'Nor wanted it either, I dare say,' William replied. 'When it has been cleaned and my mother's things have gone with my sister – I'll take you down and see how you feel about living there. It is a lovely house and the garden is perfect for a growing child.'

Rachel nodded but was unable to answer at once. She knew his ancestral home meant something to her husband, though because of his family's attitude he hadn't wanted to live there while they were in residence. If he wished to make his home there now, it would mean that Rachel would have to resign from Harpers – and that would cause her some heartache. To leave London and all her friends would be a wrench, but she loved William very much and Lizzie would thrive in the countryside. She always enjoyed their outings to the park and there she could have the pets she'd hinted at wanting recently. Lizzie seldom asked for anything, but in the park, she'd seen a little dog, which she had fallen in love with. It was a small, brown dog with curly fur and big brown eyes that seemed always to be sad and melted your heart. Rachel saw how much Lizzie wanted it, but they couldn't really have it here in their London home, because it wasn't suitable.

'May I wait to tell you my thoughts until we've visited, William?' she asked.

'Of course, my dearest. I hope you know that I would not force you to live there, Rachel? If you prefer to continue your life here and go on with your work, I shall understand. I think that a quieter life in the country will suit me – but I shall come up to town and, of course, you could bring Lizzie to visit.'

Rachel looked at him, feeling as if the air had suddenly left her body. Was her husband suggesting they might live separate lives? She knew that it was not unknown in the circles in which William had been raised. His parents had lived apart for most of their lives; his mother preferring her country home and his father enjoying the faster pace of town life until his untimely death. William was considerate to offer her the choice. However, she knew her duty was to go wherever her husband wished to live – the more so because of his uncertain health. They had been forced to live apart while he was in the isolation hospital but now... Rachel smothered the sigh that rose to her lips. If he wanted to live in the country, then so would she.

'It's time I got our supper, William,' Rachel told him. 'I thought something light this evening – would you be happy with an omelette and salad?'

'That sounds delightful,' he said and smiled at her. 'You're not too tired to prepare it?'

'No, of course not.' Rachel bent to kiss the top of his head. 'When shall we visit your home, dearest?'

'Oh, sometime next month,' he replied. 'There is no rush. I intend to go down for the funeral tomorrow and I'll stay a few days – make arrangements for the place to be looked after once my sister has gone, but you need not bother your head over it, Rachel.' He pressed her hand. 'I want you to enter the house as its mistress and not be made to feel as if you're an intruder – so I'll wait to take you down after my sister has left.'

Rachel nodded and went into the kitchen to begin preparing their supper. She was glad of a few weeks to gather her thoughts. Harpers had been her life for some years now and she knew that if she decided to accompany William to the country she would miss it – and yet if she stayed on in town their marriage would not be what she thought of as marriage at all.

* * *

Perhaps it was because her thoughts were not entirely on her work the next day that the theft of a silver and moonstone bracelet happened right under Rachel's nose. She was turning away to replace a leather bag in the cabinet behind her and when she turned back, the bracelet had gone from the counter. Rachel frowned, refusing to believe her own eyes at first as she saw the back of the man as he left the department. He'd seemed genuine and she'd believed he would buy the bracelet for his wife and so she'd looked away for a moment.

'Stop, sir!' she cried, but of course he kept going. She saw that

Shirley was not busy and summoned her to the counter with instructions to put everything away while she went in pursuit. 'A bracelet has been stolen...'

Rachel saw the shock in the young girl's face even as she hurried after her quarry, but by the time she reached the stairs, there was no sign of the thief and she realised that he must have gone down in the lift. She ran down the stairs in the hope of finding him before he left the shop but he'd gone and she felt distressed that her carelessness had led to the theft.

There was no point in putting it off. Rachel knew that Sally Harper was not in the store. She was recovering from the birth of her baby and did not yet come in often. So she must report the theft to Mr Stockbridge and alert the manager. The staff must be warned that a thief had successfully taken an expensive bracelet so that they were on the lookout for him.

Mr Stockbridge was in his office and looked at her sorrowfully as she reported the loss. 'I am surprised that he managed to steal something from your counter, Mrs Bailey. A woman of your experience is not normally careless about these things.'

'It was entirely my fault,' Rachel admitted. 'I am prepared to pay for the loss, Mr Stockbridge.'

'Well, that isn't for me to say,' he told her, looking grave. 'I shall speak to Mrs Harper and see what she feels about it – and it will be her decision, as I know she takes a personal interest in your department. However, I must tell you that I do not think it sets a good example to your staff. Can you reasonably expect the girls who work under you to take the care they must if you do not?'

'I am aware that I have let the girls and Harpers down,' Rachel said, feeling wretched. 'My mind was on personal matters. Would you like me to resign, sir?'

'Oh no,' he said and looked shocked. 'I am sure that will not be necessary. I shall speak to Mrs Harper – and we will let her have the final say. I must admit I am a little disappointed that you allowed your personal problems to intrude into your working day.'

Feeling chastened, Rachel returned to the department. Shirley had tidied the counter and was checking the stock register.

'I checked, Mrs Bailey. As far as I can see, it was just the one bracelet...'

'I had only one on the counter,' Rachel replied. 'I should have picked it up when I turned to replace the bag. Let my mistake be a lesson to us all.'

'It is upsetting for you,' Shirley said, looking sympathetic. 'I know that Selfridges have lost several items in recent weeks. The thieves distract the salesgirl and then snatch something and walk off with it, but they work in groups and pass the items on, so if they're caught, they don't have the stolen goods on them.'

'How do you know that?' Rachel asked.

'I have a friend who works on their jewellery counter. She says they always have two of them now, because there were several thefts in a week. You need to keep one of us with you, Mrs Bailey. Next time, it might not just be one bracelet...'

'That is very worrying,' Rachel said. 'I shall have to think about it. We are a little short-staffed at the moment.' Besides Shirley, there was one other salesgirl present on the floor and Rachel herself. Normally, they had a junior, but the last girl had been lazy and they'd had to dismiss her. 'I shall have to ask if we can have a new assistant.'

Shirley saw a lady approach the scarf and glove counter and went off to serve her. Rachel took out her stock book and wrote 'stolen' beside the bracelet, frowning at her own lack of care. It ought never to have happened.

When she glanced up, she saw Marion Jackson enter the department and walk straight towards her. She smiled as she saw the girl looked well and relaxed.

'How nice to see you – have you left the baby with your sister-in-law?'

'Yes, Sarah has my little Robbie with her,' Marion replied. 'I've come to ask a favour, Mrs Bailey. I ought to ask Mr Stockbridge but I thought you might do it for me...'

'Are you returning to work?' Rachel asked hopefully.

'No – although I hope to come in a couple of mornings a week soon.' Marion hesitated. 'I wanted to ask if there was any chance my sister could get a job in the canteen here? She wants to be a cook... and she is a good plain cook already. She is going to night school to learn special types of cooking but needs a job.

'I thought she worked at her old school?'

'She did, but she isn't happy there,' Marion bit her lip. 'She is a good girl, Mrs Bailey.'

'I am sure she is.' Rachel smiled at her. 'I will speak to Mr Stockbridge. I need a new junior here, too, because... well, the last one wasn't very good.'

'Kathy really wants to work in the canteen, but I suppose she might be happy to work here...' Marion said doubtfully.

'Oh no, I didn't mean that,' Rachel replied, 'though if there isn't any work in Harpers' canteen, she might consider it.'

'Yes, perhaps,' Marion agreed.

They talked for a little longer and then Rachel turned her attention to a customer and Marion spoke to Shirley for a moment before leaving. Rachel paid particular attention to her work, but after her customer had bought two pieces of silver jewellery and left, she thought about what Marion had said concerning her sister.

Rachel seldom used the canteen so had no idea if there was a job vacant, but she would ask and then let Marion know, as she'd promised.

* * *

Sally popped round to see Rachel that evening. She kissed her on the cheek and told her not to worry about the theft. 'I know it must have upset you, but these things happen,' she said. 'I've heard that Selfridges have had a problem too. Their staff are doubling up where there are valuable items on sale – and I've told Mr Stockbridge to get you a new assistant. It is better to have more staff than lose stock.'

'Thank you – but I know it was my fault.' Rachel bit her lip. 'I was thinking about William rather than my work,' she admitted and then it all came out. 'I don't know what to do, Sally. If I go with my husband to the country, it will be goodbye to my job – and I should miss that a lot.' She sighed. 'Yet he's my husband and I love him.'

'Oh, Rachel love, I'm so sorry,' Sally said and gave her a quick hug. 'But you know my answer to that?' Rachel shook her head. 'William comes first, Rachel. You love him and you'll be happy with him and Lizzie in the country – and I'll still be here. You can come up and visit when you wish.'

'Oh, Sally…' Tears stung Rachel's eyes. 'You make it all sound so simple.'

'Well, it is,' Sally told her. 'It was lonely and miserable when he was in isolation – now isn't that true? You missed him and hardly knew what to do with yourself until you had Lizzie.'

Rachel thought about it and knew she was right. Sally had spoken from the heart, even though she would be losing her friend and a loyal member of staff. 'Yes, I know – and William is happy for us to adopt her, which is wonderful,' she admitted. 'Still, I don't like letting you down.'

'We'll find someone else,' Sally told her. 'I'll miss you, Rachel, but you can visit now and then – can't you?'

'Of course I can,' Rachel said and smiled. 'I'll tell William I'm ready to go when you've found my replacement.'

'I'll speak to Mr Stockbridge,' Sally promised. 'We may promote someone from the shop floor and take on more new assistants. I think that loyalty deserves reward – so if there is anyone you think would do well as supervisor, tell me.'

Rachel nodded. 'I'll think about it,' she agreed and looked regretful. 'Beth has two children and no time to work – Maggie has her own life and now I'll be leaving you, Sally. That makes me feel a little sad for you...'

'Yes.' Sally sighed deeply. 'I shall miss you when you go, just as I missed Maggie, but life moves on, Rachel. I still see both Maggie and Beth sometimes – and I don't go into the store as much as I did, though I hope to be able to do more in future.'

'Is there any word from Ben?' Rachel asked. 'He's been away for several weeks now, hasn't he?'

'Yes.' Sally bit her lip. 'I haven't heard, but I'm hoping he will be back soon.'

'Marion is hoping for the same thing,' Rachel said. 'Which reminds me – her sister wants to work in your canteen at Harpers – and I can tell you she is a jolly good cook.'

'If you think she's a good cook, I'll write to her myself,' Sally said. 'We can always do with good staff at Harpers.'

17

Marion finished nursing her baby and burped him, patting his back gently to bring up the wind. She heard the post come and looked at Kathy as she went to fetch whatever had arrived that morning.

'Is there anything for me?' she asked hopefully. Kathy smiled and nodded as she brought the letters back.

'There is one for you, one for Sarah – and one for me. I think it is from Harpers – at last.'

Kathy placed Sarah's letter on the table, handed Marion hers and ripped open her own. She gave a squeal of excitement as she read it.

'I've been given a job in Harpers' canteen,' she reported eagerly. 'They have a cook leaving to have a baby and they've offered me the job as a junior cook. Do you think that was Mrs Bailey's influence?'

Marion looked up from her own letter, which she'd opened almost as soon as Kathy gave it to her. 'Yes, I shouldn't be surprised. Mrs Bailey has always been lovely to work with – I'm sorry she is leaving to live in the country.'

'It's because her husband was so ill, isn't it?' Kathy asked and Marion nodded.

'Yes. He needs the quiet of the countryside; that's what she told me when she visited. I shall miss her visits – and when I go into Harpers again. I shan't be working in the department, of course, just helping with the windows.' Marion sighed.

'Well, you like that,' Kathy replied, looking happy. 'It's wonderful about my job – the letter says they are paying me thirty shillings a week to start, but once I'm trained, I'll get nearly three pounds.'

'That's more than I got in the hat department,' Marion replied, looking surprised.

'It's two pounds, seventeen shillings and sixpence – and that sounds like a fortune to me.'

'I didn't realise cooks got that much,' Marion said, pleased for her sister. 'I suppose a good one is hard to find.' She'd always thought Kathy's determination to be a cook was just her sister's way of doing what she liked but now realised that it could be a good life for her – everyone needed cooks. Fewer girls were going into domestic service now and wealthy people would pay highly for a good cook. Once Kathy had her qualifications, she would have many opportunities.

'I knew it could be good,' Kathy crowed, over the moon with her news. 'It was just that I didn't know how to get started – but I must thank Mrs Bailey for putting in a good word for my cooking.'

'She went to the top,' Marion said. 'Mrs Sally Harper runs things at Harpers and Rachel Bailey is her friend; they started working there together – Sally was just a salesgirl then, but she became the buyer and then married Ben Harper.'

'Maybe I'll get to be head cook one day,' Kathy dreamed mistily. 'I shan't marry Ben Harper or anyone else – but I might still get a top job, mightn't I?'

'Don't see why not!' Marion said and smiled at her. 'I'm glad you've had good news, Kathy, because I have too. Reggie says he feels better and is coming home on leave next month.'

Kathy ran to her and gave her a quick hug. 'I know you've been expecting him for ages – and this will be the first time he's seen his son.'

'Yes, the first time he's seen Bobby,' Marion agreed and laughed with excitement. 'He thought they might send him home weeks ago but they didn't – but he says it is certain now.' She turned the page but there was not very much more. 'He says he can't wait to get home.'

'Is he really better now?' Kathy asked. 'He'd been wounded again last time he wrote...'

'He doesn't say much about that,' Marion said and reread the brief letter. 'Just that he hopes we're all well; he's all right and looking forward to coming home when he can.'

'Well, perhaps he was in a hurry,' Kathy said. 'I'm sure he must be all right or he would have said something. He always tells you everything, doesn't he?'

'Yes.' Marion let a small sigh escape. 'It seems such a long time since he was home and I wanted to visit the hospital in Portsmouth, but he said it was too far for me to go while I was pregnant and he didn't want me to come, but surely I could now—' The door opened and Sarah entered with the pushchair, in which she'd taken her son for a walk. She had called in at the pie shop and the smell of hot food assailed their noses. 'What have you brought us, Sarah?' she asked, smiling. 'It smells good...'

'I bought a chicken pie and chips each for our lunch, Marion. I know it is extravagant, but I got a big order for my sewing this morning and I thought we all deserved a treat.'

'You spoil us,' Marion said and smiled at her. 'Kathy is making a beef stew for us, but that is for this evening. I was just planning on some toast for lunch.'

'I know, but this order is so big that I decided to splash out.' Sarah saw the envelope on the table and swooped on it with delight. 'A letter from Dan...'

Kathy took the little boy from his pushchair and held him up, making Sarah's son chuckle with joy as she teased and kissed him. 'I got good news too,' she said as she saw Sarah scan the letter swiftly, smile and tuck it in her pocket to read again later. 'Everything all right?'

'Yes, Dan is fine. He says not to expect a letter for a while but not to worry.' Sarah smiled as Marion set out plates that were warm from the rack over the kitchen range. 'What was your news then, Kathy?'

Kathy told her in detail while Marion was setting the table and then they all sat down to eat, looking at each other in companionable pleasure. For the moment, everything was right with their world and they all had something to look forward to. Sarah's reputation as a fine seamstress was growing and both Kathy and Marion would soon be working at Harpers. Reggie should be coming home soon and Dan was fine when he'd sent his letter. Life was good for their family just now and Sarah's idea to bring them a treat only made it even better.

* * *

Kathy looked around her in wonder at the canteen kitchen at Harpers. It was all so much more than she'd been expecting. The ovens and hobs were all gas, which she'd learned to use at the school kitchens, though she preferred using an old-fashioned range. However, she would enjoy working here. There were lots of work surfaces, freshly painted cabinets and two large pantries with wide shelves filled with produce, as well as a big dresser that stored all the plates and dishes. Everything was spotless, due to the hard work of two young women whose job it was to prepare vegetables but also to clean.

'This is very nice, Mrs Harper,' she said, looking at her new employer with respect. 'I shall enjoy cooking here.'

'You come highly recommended,' Mrs Harper said. 'Rachel said your cooking is excellent. For the moment, you will be working with Mrs Hilda Higgs. She is our main cook, but I'm sure you'll get on. She has been with us from the start.'

Kathy looked nervously at the big woman who was preparing a large cottage pie, but her anxiety vanished as she got a huge smile and a cheerful voice told her to come and have a look.

'That's right, lovey,' Hilda Higgs said as Kathy approached. 'Let me take a look at you...' She nodded her approval. 'You look just what we want, Kathy – and you can call me Hilda. I don't have none of this formal nonsense in my kitchen. If you've done looking round, you can start preparing the rice pudding. You don't need me to show you?'

'No, thank you, I can make rice pudding,' Kathy said and laughed. 'But I am hoping to learn from you...'

'I'll share my secrets, don't you worry,' Hilda told her. 'I've been a cook all my life. Started off as a kitchen maid when I was twelve, I did – but by the time I was sixteen, I was cooking for the family. It was long hours in service and I got fed up with being told when I could have a night off – here I'm finished by half-past six in the evening and I can please myself what I do.' She beamed at Mrs Harper, who was having a word with the girls chopping carrots. 'She's one in a million that Sally Harper. I've been offered more money to return to service – but you won't catch me falling into that trap. You take my word for it, young Kathy – this is a better life.'

'Everything all right, Hilda? You have all you need?' Sally Harper asked as she approached.

'Yes, thank you, Mrs Harper,' Hilda said and beamed at her. 'I made some nice oat biscuits first thing – would you like them with your coffee this morning?'

'Yes, please. You spoil me,' Sally Harper said and looked at Kathy. 'Do you think you will be happy here?'

'Oh yes,' Kathy said. 'Thank you so much for giving me this job.'

'You're welcome.'

Kathy looked around her with satisfaction as Mrs Harper left the kitchens. She was thrilled with the prospect of working at Harpers and knew that like Hilda she was far better off than in many jobs she might have been offered. If the rumours were true and Harpers was going to open a new restaurant, she might soon have a chance to do the kind of cooking she'd begun to learn about in night school.

She was thoughtful as she checked with Hilda what quantity of pudding was needed and began to fetch out the simple ingredients she would need: rice, milk and a little nutmeg. Sarah and Marion seemed to live for the times their husbands came home, but Kathy had decided long ago that she would never marry. She would never be at the mercy of any man's whim, however nice he might be. She'd seen what her father had done to her mother – witnessed the pain of her mother's fear of yet another beating from her husband – and she'd known *that* life wasn't for her.

Kathy was going to be a successful cook and she was in the right place to start.

18

Ben looked down at the sweat-ridden face that was contorted with agony and cursed. Marco had survived the truck journey to the coast and they were safely on board the ship taking them back to England, which was both a miracle and a blessing, but it had taken a fearful toll, and Ben wasn't sure his friend would survive the voyage. His fever had descended again and Marco was calling out names in his agony of mind and body, begging for forgiveness.

The poor devil was haunted by past tragedies and seemed to have become lost in a nightmare of pain and grief. Ben dipped his cloth into cool water and bathed Marco's face again. There was little he could do until he got him back to England, because there was no doctor on board this fishing vessel and he himself suffered as it pitched and dived buffeted by the sudden squall that had struck soon after they put to sea.

Below decks in the stuffy cabin that smelled of vomit, Ben gritted his teeth as the ship plunged and bucked as it rode out the strong winds, the small ship shuddering from bow to stern. It wasn't a winter storm, but at sea, even a squall made for a rough passage.

Marco called out in his agony, some of his words clearly a name from his past, others undecipherable. He was burning up, the wound he'd received had been treated in the French house they'd stayed at for a short while and the fever had abated, but the rough journey had brought it on again. Peeling back the bandages, Ben saw that the stitching had torn open and Marco's injury seemed to be weeping yellow puss.

'Got to do something about this, old chap,' Ben muttered. But what? he wondered. Glancing about the tiny cabin, which had been kindly given up to them by the ship's captain, he saw a bottle of brandy on a shelf. It was secured with rope to save it from falling during the storm and Ben had to wrestle with it for several minutes to free it.

He looked again at Marco's puckered flesh and decided that it had to be cleansed, even though he knew little about such things and feared he might make the situation worse. There was a storm lamp on the desk, which had a stubby candle inside, used when all else failed, Ben supposed. He used Marco's own cigarette lighter to light the flame and then held the blade of his penknife in the flame. When he thought it was probably hot enough to kill any germs lingering on it, he used it to cut open the clumsy stitches the doctor had sewn. Puss and blood seeped out and Ben wiped it away with his cloth and then, after using a torch to look closely, to make sure all the nasty stuff had gone, he rinsed the cut with brandy.

It must have stung terribly because Marco bucked and cursed and opened his eyes. 'What the hell?' he questioned as his fevered gaze fell on Ben. 'It hurts, damn you...'

'Sorry, but it had to be done,' Ben told him.

As Marco fell back with his eyes closed, Ben prayed he'd done the right thing. He'd read about such procedures being used when the situation was dire but had no idea whether he'd done it as it should be done. All he could hope was that he hadn't made the infection worse.

Marco groaned a few times as he bound him with a clean bandage.

'Sorry, old chap, I've done messing you around now.'

Marco settled back and lay quietly for such a long time that Ben thought he might have killed him. Who was he to play doctor when he'd no idea what he was doing? He felt for a pulse and discovered it was still there – and, miracle of miracles, Marco was cooler to the touch. Maybe, just maybe, the fever had broken.

Ben dashed away the tears that trickled down his cheeks. Good thing no one was here to see him – it was probably the rum he'd just drunk, but he felt like sobbing with relief. His clumsy ministrations hadn't killed Marco; they might just have helped to ease him because he did seem to be resting more peacefully now...

* * *

It was sunny and warm when Sally and Pearl took the children to the park that morning in May. Sally had bought a newspaper and they looked at the headlines anxiously. There was rarely much good news and the paper was reporting the Royal Navy's attempt to seal off the U-boat base at Zeebrugge in a raid. They had manged to sink two ships to try to block the enemy boats escaping, but the action had only had partial success, because the position had not been quite right and within a few days the German U-boats were able to get through again.

'Do you think this war will ever end?' Pearl asked.

'Ben thinks it is going our way, but I can't see any sight of the end yet,' she said and then called to Jenny, who was playing ball with a friendly little dog they'd met that morning. 'Come along, darling. That's enough. We have to go home.'

'She does so want a dog of her own,' Pearl said. 'If you move into that big house in Hampstead you looked at the other week, she could have one.' Sally had taken Pearl and her daughter with her to view the property Ben liked, leaving Peter with Mrs Hills, who loved him and was like a grandmother to both the children.

'Yes, I suppose she could,' Sally agreed. 'We'll have to see what Ben thinks when he gets back.'

'He's been gone a long time, hasn't he?' Pearl said and then bit her lip. 'Sorry, Mrs Harper. I know I shouldn't have asked.'

'Oh, he'll be back when he's ready,' Sally said, pretending a casualness she didn't feel. Ben had been gone weeks longer than she'd expected and she was very anxious but trying not to show it. Where was he? It was all supposed to be straightforward – had something gone wrong? 'Let's go,' she said. 'I've got a meeting with a new supplier this afternoon and I need to go into Harpers.'

* * *

The young woman who presented herself that afternoon was a milliner. She had started to make hats because her husband had been killed in the trenches early in the war and she needed a job to support herself.

'I've made my own hats for years, Mrs Harper,' she said. 'My husband never wanted me to work, but I like to be busy – I thought about what I should do when I got the telegram and it seemed like a good idea, to set up for myself rather than working long hours for an employer. Only...' She bit her lip. 'Not everyone I've written to has given me an interview.'

'How many orders have you taken so far?'

'Just three from friends of mine...' she faltered.

'Well, Mary, I'm pleased about that, because I want you to design and make hats exclusively for Harpers,' Sally said and picked up the beautiful creation the young woman had brought to show her. 'I want lots more like these – how many can you make for me in a month?'

'About twenty to thirty,' Mary Sawston replied confidently. 'I made this one yesterday. It was created for you – because I am an admirer of what you've done here, Mrs Harper.'

'Thank you.' Sally smiled at her. 'Do you have any trouble getting hold of materials? I might be able to put you in touch with suppliers.'

'I haven't so far, but I would appreciate any addresses or phone numbers just in case.'

'When can I expect my first delivery?' Sally asked.

'Next week. I have twenty ready to show – but could only bring these four with me today.'

'How will you deliver them? I can give you the number of a man who might help. He has a small van and makes deliveries locally – and you live in Southwark so that shouldn't be a problem.'

'Thank you – that was a consideration. Someone else asked how I would deliver and I said I would bring them in a few at a time but that wasn't considered satisfactory.'

'These hats are too beautiful to refuse,' Sally said. 'I would still buy them if you could only supply a few at a time, but twenty-five a month will be perfect for a start – and then, if we need more, perhaps you could take on a girl to help you?'

'Oh, do you really think you might need more?' Mary Sawston looked surprised but pleased. 'That would be wonderful – I do know someone who would like to help. Her work at the moment is very hard and I'm sure she could do this sort of thing, under my supervision, of course.'

'If she does them as well as you, then engage her,' Sally advised. 'If you are to make your business a success, you will need to grow it and delegate and I am sure you can.'

'Thank you so much for believing in me,' Mary said. 'It is so kind of you – when Selfridges turned me down because I had no means of transport, I thought I stood no chance.' She gulped back a sob of relief.

'If Harry Selfridge turned you down, he's not the man I thought him,' Sally replied, 'but I'm glad he did, because now you will be exclusive to Harpers.'

'Oh, I didn't see *him*... it was one of his buyers.'

Sally smiled. 'I wouldn't like to be in that man's shoes when he finds out.'

'Oh, I don't suppose he'll care; he must have lots of suppliers.'

Sally didn't comment. She knew a bestselling line when she saw it and these hats were just what women needed to cheer them up, so beautiful and frivolous that there might never have been a war – and she fully intended to purchase this one for herself...

* * *

It had been a pleasant afternoon, Sally thought as she approached the building where she lived. She felt that she had not only discovered a major talent in Mary Sawston but a potential new friend. After they'd finished their business, they'd sat and chatted for a while and Sally's heart was touched as she learned that the young woman had a two-year-old daughter she was bringing up with the help of her mother – who was also a widow and had moved in with her – so that she could care for the child while Mary worked.

'We hoped for more children,' Mary had told Sally, 'but then the war came and I know that I am lucky to have one. Alfred was home for a visit after a wound and I fell for my little girl then.'

War was a terrible thing, Sally reflected as she entered her building. The porter was busy with some new tenants and she reached the lift before he was aware of her.

'Mrs Harper—' He called something as she closed the door but she wasn't sure what. If he had a package for her or a letter, he would bring it up to her later. She was thoughtful as the lift whirred to a halt and she walked out. If she lived in Hampstead the postman would come to her door...

Sally's heart caught as she opened the door of her apartment and saw a man standing looking out of the window down into the busy street. 'Ben... Oh, Ben, you're home at last,' she cried rushing towards him. 'Where have you been and why didn't you let me know?' He turned and she saw the grief in his face. 'What is it? Marco – is he dead?'

'Marco is in hospital and very ill,' he told her gravely. 'No, it isn't him, Sally – it's his wife... I went to his home to let her know he was back in England and her mother was there, taking care of the lad. Sadie had been rushed into the isolation infirmary two nights ago. She had a fever... her mother wasn't sure what it was, but... she's dead, Sally. Her mother said she got the doctor to her as soon as the neighbour told her Sadie was ill but she died in the night... Apparently, there have been a few cases of this fever and they can be fatal.'

'But she was at work two days ago...' Sally said, bewildered. 'I knew she hadn't come in today, because Mr Stockbridge told me he'd sent one of the girls to take her place, but he'd sent her home early the day before with a nasty cold – she thought that was all it was...' Sally was shocked and stunned by the news. 'You got Marco back and he's ill and now this...' She sat down heavily as her legs went weak, and all the breath seemed to have drained out of her. 'Sadie dead – I can't believe it. It is too awful!'

'How am I going to tell him?' Ben asked, looking suddenly tired and drained. 'I know he cares for her – he was willing to do... anything for her.'

'Yes, I believe he loves Sadie,' she agreed. 'It might be different from the way you love me, Ben, but he does love her and the boy.'

'Her mother has taken the boy home,' Ben said. 'I know Marco loves him like a son – but I'm not sure whether he could claim him if Sadie's mother wants the boy.'

'Oh, Ben – he suffered enough when Julien killed himself,' Sally said tearfully. 'I am so sorry.' The years had passed since Marco's young lover had taken his own life because his father had disowned him, but it had seared itself into Marco's mind and he would never forget. Now he was in danger of losing his adopted son as well as his wife.

'I was so relieved to think I'd got him back alive...' Ben shook his head. 'Don't ask, Sally. It's a sordid story of betrayal and revenge and one it's best I don't reveal to anyone. If Marco wants to talk about it, that's up to him, but I don't. I just feel wretched that when he recovers – if he does – I have to tell him that he's lost his wife and perhaps his son, too.'

'I could tell him perhaps,' Sally suggested, but Ben shook his head.

'He's my friend, Sally. Thanks for the offer but I'll tell him when I think he's ready.'

'Yes, I suppose you have to,' she admitted and went to him, putting her arms around him, feeling his deep shudder. 'You look so tired, exhausted.'

'When I think of what we did,' Ben said, a note of despair and regret in his voice. 'All that planning and scheming to protect her... and then she dies of a cold...' He shook his head over it.

Sally didn't understand what he meant by his remarks, but Ben wouldn't or couldn't tell her and so she just nestled her head into his chest and let the tears run silently as they grieved for their friends together while thanking God that they still had each other.

19

Alone in the sitting room of the cottage in Devonshire, Maggie opened her letter from Sally Harper and smiled as she read the good news. Mr Marco was alive and Ben had managed to get him home to England. That was lovely she thought, but the next moment her smile disappeared as she read of Sadie's sudden death.

I am so sorry to give you this news, but I know you were close to her. As yet, Marco hasn't been told because he is still too ill – but I thought I should let you know. I am so sorry...

Sally had written.

Maggie closed her eyes as the tears stung. It was good that Mr Marco was back but so sad that Sadie had died. Sally had gone on to say it was a chill or a fever, but Maggie couldn't bring herself to read the rest of the letter just yet.

She looked up as Becky entered the room, dashing the tears from her cheeks.

'Becky – are you all right?'

'Yes, just a bit tired,' Becky replied. 'But you've been crying – why? It isn't your husband?'

'No – Colin sent me some letters that he'd received for me at home. One was from Sally Harper – and she told me that my friend, Sadie, has died of some kind of a fever—'

'Oh, I'm sorry,' Becky said. 'I don't think I knew her?'

'She was Mr Marco's wife.'

'Oh yes, I did see her in the store once or twice,' Becky murmured. 'Is there anything I can do, Maggie?'

'No, I'll be fine in a moment. I just need to be quiet for a while.'

'I just came down for a drink,' Becky replied. 'I'll take a cup of tea to my room and leave you for a while. I am sorry, Maggie.'

'It isn't your fault,' Maggie said. 'But we went through a lot together out there.'

Becky nodded and left the room.

Maggie sat down as the tears trickled down her cheeks.

* * *

Lying on the bed upstairs some two hours after her conversation with Maggie, Becky watched as the midwife stowed her bits and pieces in the battered leather bag she carried and then placed a light shawl about her shoulders. She turned to say goodbye as she prepared to leave.

'Why don't you get up and come downstairs, Mrs Morgan?' the midwife asked. 'The sun is shining and your friend is sitting in the garden. It would be best if you did too – or even better, go for a nice walk together.'

'Thank you, Evangeline,' Becky replied languidly. 'You are very kind, but I feel too tired. I would rather stay in bed for a while longer.'

'Lying around doing nothing will not make you feel better.'

Evangeline frowned at her. 'I really must urge you to get up, Mrs Morgan. It isn't healthy to sit around too much at this stage of your confinement – I mean, there is no need to stay indoors on a lovely day.'

Becky sighed. Evangeline was a good-natured woman in her early thirties and kind, as well as reassuring, but she did tend to try to push her into doing things when all Becky wanted was to lie here. No one – not even Maggie – seemed to understand the depth of her despair. She'd thought herself loved and wanted, but David had deserted her and she would never get over the shame of giving birth to an illegitimate child in secret.

Maggie had promised her to keep the secret always, and she would take her baby and care for it as her own – but that still left Becky to cope with the birth and then her guilt. She wasn't sure she could just go home and take up her old life as if nothing had happened when it was all over. How could she look her father in the eye? It meant that she must go on lying to him for the rest of her life – and she could never marry, because of what she'd done. She was a wicked girl. Only a wicked girl would sneak off like she had and lie to those she loved...

'You're not listening to a word I've said,' Evangeline exclaimed. 'I am sorry, Mrs Morgan, but this is for the sake of the child you carry. Unless you eat and take more care of yourself, you and the baby may die.'

'Perhaps that would be best.' Becky couldn't look into her reproachful eyes as she lied once again. 'I told you, my husband is dead – how will I live alone?' So many lies but what else could she do?

'That is a very selfish attitude,' Evangeline retorted. 'Your child deserves the chance to live even if you don't wish to. I lost my husband a while ago, but I didn't just give up. I decided to devote my life to helping other women as a midwife. Give yourself a chance and you will learn to live with your grief.'

Becky shook her head. If Evangeline knew the truth, she would probably refuse to look after her. She didn't understand that Becky wasn't just mourning a husband, and lover, she was dying of shame, because of what she'd done.

After Evangeline had gone, Becky turned her face to the pillow and let her tears fall. Why had this happened to her? Why had all her friends married and found happiness – why did she have to be the one to fall for a man who had let her down?

* * *

Maggie was just entering the parlour as Evangeline came down the stairs. She smiled and asked her if she would like a cup of tea and Evangeline agreed, following her into the cosy parlour to sit down.

'I'm worried about your cousin-in-law's life,' she said and Maggie nodded. She'd told Evangeline and her mother they were related by marriage, as they might have been if David Morgan had kept his word to wed Becky. 'Becky seems to have lost interest in everything. She ought to be up, walking in this lovely sunshine, not lying in her bed all the time.'

'She does get up for a while sometimes,' Maggie said. 'But she is very lethargic recently – grieving, I think...'

'For her husband,' Evangeline nodded. 'It is only to be expected, Mrs Morgan. Losing one's husband is bad enough but she is so young – and with the child coming—'

'Yes, she has become very melancholic,' Maggie said. 'I am not sure what I can do to help her – and I'm worried for her survival and the child's.'

'I completely understand that, but there is nothing physically wrong with her,' Evangeline told her. 'It is her mental state. I could ask the doctor to call if you wish?'

Maggie shook her head. 'I don't think he could do much at the moment. I wondered if you had seen melancholy in other young mothers – is it common?'

'It can be. Some women are anxious until the birth is over and then overjoyed, but some behave in the opposite manner; although they want their baby, once it is born, they become unhappy and at times even reject the child.' Evangeline looked thoughtful. 'I believe in your cousin's wife's case it may just be grief.'

'Yes, well, I dare say that is right,' Maggie replied sadly.

'I believe whatever is upsetting her is just in her mind. Her body is carrying well and she is young enough to recover... if she wants to.' Evangeline looked grave. 'I have known young women to go into a decline after the birth and die...' She paused, remembering. 'But I am sure it will not happen in Mrs Morgan's case. We must just be patient with her.'

Maggie poured her tea and handed the cup to her.

Evangeline sipped the hot sweet tea. 'You know you may call on me at any time and I will move in for the last two weeks of her confinement. Because it is quite possible that she may give birth early. Now I really must go.'

Maggie went to the door with her. The sun was shining and she followed her out into the garden, watching as she pedalled away on her bicycle. Evangeline had been married young but her husband had died after just a year of marriage from a fever and she'd never had a child of her own or married again.

'I could never have loved again after Robert died,' she'd told Maggie during one of their chats. 'It was one of the reasons I took up nursing.'

Evangeline had found comfort in looking after the sick, just as Maggie had in France after Tim had died and that gave them a lot in common. Once or twice, Maggie had felt as if she would like to confide in Evangeline, but it wasn't her secret, it was Becky's, who'd become a little hysterical when Maggie had asked if she wanted Evangeline to know.

'You promised you would never tell anyone...' she'd cried resentfully.

'And I shan't – without your permission,' Maggie had replied. 'I just thought it might help to talk about it.'

'What difference could it make?' Becky had asked. 'It won't bring him back if he's dead and if he isn't—' She shook her head, looking so tragic and heartbroken that Maggie had felt actual pain in her chest in sympathy for her. 'Then he doesn't care...'

'I am sure that David would come to you if he could,' she'd said, using his Christian name because to call him Captain Morgan was confusing.

'You didn't know him... not really,' Becky had said and looked at her resentfully. 'How can you say what he might do?'

At first, Becky had been so grateful for what Maggie had done, always thanking her, but recently she'd become resentful and withdrawn, as if blaming Maggie for being happy while she was so wretched. Her attitude had changed after Colin came to visit for a couple of days and she'd witnessed them laughing together. Maggie had tried to cheer her and to comfort her, but she seemed to have made up her mind to be miserable.

* * *

Returning to the house, Maggie went upstairs to Becky's room and knocked.

'Come in,' Becky invited. She was lying against a pile of pillows and had some copies of *The Lady* magazine next to her. 'What's wrong?' she asked.

'Evangeline said you were a little down,' Maggie replied. 'Is there anything I can get that will help, Becky dearest?'

Becky's eyes filled with tears. 'Why are you always so kind to me? I'm not very nice to you. I want to be and I am grateful but...' She gave a little sob. 'I am so ashamed of myself, Maggie.'

'You should not be ashamed,' Maggie said instantly. 'What happened – you were not the first nor yet the last to make a mistake. You were young and you loved him.' Maggie sat on the edge of the bed and took her hand. 'Believe me, dearest. I am sure that David meant to marry you one day. For some reason, he hasn't been able to come to you or let you know.'

'I would almost rather he was dead,' Becky said. 'At least I wouldn't feel used and stupid then.'

'Stop saying such things!' Maggie said sharply. 'I am certain Captain Morgan would not have used any young woman in that way. He was a gentleman – and what you did may have been thoughtless in a moment of passion, but you are not stupid.'

Becky leaned forward and squeezed her hand. 'Thank you – and I know you care for—' She stopped as they heard the back door open and then a man's voice called to them.

'That is Colin,' Maggie said. 'I wonder why he is here. He didn't say he was coming... Excuse me, Becky. I'll come back when I've greeted him.'

'I'm going to get up and come down.'

Maggie smiled and nodded at her, but felt anxious as she went quickly down the stairs. Colin hadn't planned on coming back just yet.

Colin was sitting in his chair in the hall. A young man was standing just behind him. 'This is my new driver, Maggie. He was one of my men and has been invalided out. Ken asked for a job and so I gave him one.'

'Oh, pleased to meet you, sir,' Maggie said with a smile.

'Private Ken Higgins, ma'am,' the young man replied and smiled. 'I was right pleased to see the captain – we all thought he wouldn't make it when they shipped him home.'

'Thank you,' Maggie said. Her gaze turned anxiously to her husband. 'I'm so glad you've come, Colin. I've had some upsetting news.'

'Yes, I've just heard the news about your friend, Maggie, and I came straight down. I am so sorry, my dearest. I know how fond you were of Sadie. I sent Sally's letter on with some others when it arrived for you – but I didn't realise what was in it. I only heard when I spoke to Ben Harper.'

'Yes, I had the letter and it made me cry.' Maggie dabbed at her eyes. 'Poor Sadie – and poor Mr Marco and her son. What will happen to Pierre now?'

'I believe her mother has claimed him for the moment, but when her husband returns, no doubt he will live with him.'

Tears were running down Maggie's cheeks. She went into the sitting room and sat down. Colin sat beside her and held her hand, giving her a handkerchief to dry her tears.

'She was so happy when Ben discovered that Mr Marco was alive and there was hope of getting him home.' Maggie mused aloud. 'How could it happen that she died with a chill?'

'There have been a few cases of it, apparently,' Colin said. 'Some new sickness, it seems. Not that it helps to tell you, my love. I am so sorry to have brought you such terrible news.'

'I was so fond of her,' Maggie said and looked up at him, brushing away her tears. 'We trained together as VADs and then worked together in France. Sadie was like a sister to me, Colin. I can't believe that she has died just like that...'

'Are you speaking of Sadie?' Becky asked, coming into the room, and nodded as Maggie confirmed it. 'It is very distressing, but you already had the news...?'

'Yes. Colin came because he knew I would be upset.' Maggie smiled gratefully at her husband.

'There is other news...' Colin said and she saw it was not good. 'Ben Harper told me that Mr Marco is back in England – however, he is very ill in hospital. He was dreading having to tell him that his wife was dead.'

'Sally told us!' Maggie said. 'We were both upset, because Mr Marco is popular with all the staff at Harpers, kind and funny. It is so sad—'

'Yes, it is,' Becky looked shame-faced. 'It makes my problems seem insignificant by comparison.'

'Becky,' Colin turned to her, his expression grave. 'I have something to tell you, too. I am not certain yet, but I have information that leads me to believe my cousin David may be alive, though very ill...'

'Alive?' Becky stared at him, clearly shocked. Her face paled and she sat down, her hands trembling.

'Yes, my dear,' Colin said carefully. 'I have been told of a man lying in a hospital bed – unfortunately, he doesn't know who he is and no one else is sure, because his head and face were badly burned. He was in a military hospital compound in Belgium when it was attacked by the enemy, about seven months ago, and he was dragged from the carnage barely alive. At first, he couldn't walk or talk, even though they patched him up – but now he can do both. He can't recall anything, except that he was a military doctor and he has not long recalled that... but it is a good sign.' The incident must have happened soon after David had left England to join the war and might explain why Becky had heard nothing from him.

Becky swallowed hard. 'Why do you think he is your cousin?'

'Because a rather distinctive gold watch was recovered when he was rescued. It was put away in a safe when he was taken to the hospital and has only just been discovered and given to him... It was seeing the watch that made him remember that he was a doctor in the army. Inside, it has the inscription: *"To David on his becoming a doctor, from his loving mother, Maud Morgan."* As my cousin's mother was named Maud, I think perhaps there is a good chance that it is him.'

Becky's eyes closed and tears trickled from beneath her lashes. 'Is he dreadfully disfigured?'

'I believe some skilled work has been done to help – but he will hardly be recognisable. His former commanding officer has been to see him but wasn't certain it was him, though he claims to have seen the watch before and thinks it must be him – that is why my father was informed. He asked me to investigate, but I would not know David if I saw him – we never met.' Colin looked at Becky. 'I wondered if you might visit... but if it would be too much for you it does not matter—'

'Of course I shall!' Becky cried and looked from him to Maggie in agitation. 'Where is he?'

'He is in a hospital not too far from here,' Colin told her. 'I have arranged for a visit tomorrow. If I can help him I shall.'

'Please – may we not go now, this afternoon?' Becky cried.

'Tomorrow,' Colin said and smiled at her. 'He has been told to expect visitors then – and will need time to come to terms with the idea. The poor man has been through months of pain and uncertainty,' Colin told her gently. 'You must not expect too much, Becky. He may not remember even when he sees you – and he is never going to be the man he was, though he is much better, I am informed. He can walk and he can see – but he is disfigured and his mind may not be recoverable.'

'What does that mean?' Becky faltered, looking uncertain.

'At the moment, he has terrible nightmares and calls out – for someone or something – and the doctors do not know what to do for him. He has had various treatments, like cold baths and some sort of electrical shocks to his body, but none of them help much.'

'How cruel,' Maggie said. 'I would have thought it best to just let him recover in his own time or simply allow him to forget.'

'Apparently, he volunteered to try because he so desperately wants to remember.'

Becky lifted her head and looked at them. 'I shall visit and tell him who he is and what happened between us,' she said proudly. 'If he accepts me then, perhaps, I can help him to recover... as Maggie helped you, Colin...'

Colin met her look and then nodded, before turning to Maggie with a smile. 'I did not want to live until she came into my life,' he admitted. 'Love gave me the will to live – so maybe it will help David, if it is him—'

'It is,' Becky said confidently. 'I think you were meant to tell me, Colin, and now you have given me something to live for too.'

20

The sister in charge of the ward looked at them doubtfully. 'I'm not sure you can see him yet,' she said. 'He had treatment this morning and is still feeling its effects.'

'He is expecting us. I spoke to his doctor yesterday and was asked to come today,' Colin informed her.

'Please, may I just see him for a moment?' Becky took a deep breath. 'I think he may be my husband...'

She looked at Maggie, her eyes full of a silent appeal not to tell the stern nurse the truth, and Maggie gave a slight nod. 'We'll wait outside,' she offered. 'You speak to him first and tell us what you think.'

'Well, I suppose – just for a moment...' the senior nurse relented.

'If he is Captain David Morgan, he is my cousin,' Colin said. 'We are all concerned for him.'

'Only his wife may visit.' The stern look faded as Sister saw Becky's condition. 'It must be just a quick visit, Mrs Morgan, but in view of your situation – just a few minutes.'

'Thank you so much!' Becky's eyes welled with tears. She sent a watery smile at Colin and Maggie, leaving them standing outside in the sunshine as she went through the open French doors into the ward.

The ward was just a small one, sunny and pleasant on this warm day with all the windows open. Just four beds, two each side, and in three of them the men lay with their eyes closed, pale faces, various parts of their body bandaged and clearly very ill. Becky didn't know any of them, but when she reached the fourth bed, she saw a man sitting on the edge with his back towards them. Something about the way he was sitting and the back of his head made her catch her breath. She was sure it was the man she loved and tears rose to her eyes. She couldn't see much wrong with him until he turned and the shock of his injures made her gasp sharply. One side of his face was still red where a large scar was healing, but the other side had patches of tight, shiny white skin that didn't look natural. Perhaps those patches were where he'd had treatment to help him heal, and his injuries had altered his appearance completely. Yet Becky was certain it was him – David Morgan, the man she'd given herself to so lovingly.

'Captain Morgan – this is your wife,' the nursing sister said. 'I have permitted her to visit for a few minutes... if it is your wish?'

For what seemed an age, the man stared at her and then he nodded, 'Let her stay.' His eyes narrowed as the nurse departed. 'Am I your husband?'

Becky hesitated, then inclined her head. 'Yes, David,' she whispered, convincing herself that it was him. 'I'm sure you are... and I love you. I thought you were dead and I'm so glad you're alive.

'Even though I look like this?' he persisted. 'Even though I'm a monster?'

'You're not,' Becky whispered, her throat closing with emotion as the tears welled over and streamed silently down her face. 'You're hurt badly and I'm sad that you've been through so much – but I'll always love you.'

'Will you?' he asked, a touch of bitterness in his voice. 'How can you be sure – no one else knows me. I don't even know myself...'

'I know it is you – the shape of your head hasn't changed and the way you sit so straight – and your voice is the same.' The more she looked at him, the more certain she became, the more she wanted to believe. 'I know you don't remember me, but I'll never forget you...'

'How can you be so sure?' he demanded harshly and then his gaze narrowed. 'You're carrying a child – is it mine?'

'Yes, certainly...' Becky faltered. 'There was only ever you.'

He stared at her for a moment or two longer, then inclined his head. 'They told me I had no one – but I knew there was someone... When did we marry?'

Becky glanced over her shoulder and then at him. 'We were going to marry when you came home – you promised me that afternoon... I didn't want that nurse to know the truth, because she wouldn't have let me see you.'

'I made love to you and you fell for my child out of wedlock?' He frowned at her. 'How can I believe you? You could be lying – that could be anyone's child...'

'Why would I be here if it wasn't yours?' Becky asked. 'Why would I lie so that I could visit you – if you weren't the man I fell in love with? You swore you loved me and promised to marry me or I wouldn't—' She hung her head, a flush in her cheeks. 'I'm not a bad girl. I don't do things like that.' Tears were still trickling down her cheeks. 'Don't tell Sister or she won't let me visit again.'

He looked at her for a moment more and then glanced in the direction of the sister and nodded. 'She's going to make you leave in a minute – you'll come again, please? I need to think about what you've told me, to try to make sense of it.'

Becky swallowed hard. 'Yes, I'll come as much as I can.' She placed a hand on her swollen belly. 'I'm due in a few weeks so I'm not sure how long I can visit...'

'I don't even know your name.' He clutched her hand, suddenly urgent. 'Please tell me...'

'Becky Stockbridge.' She glanced at the nursing sister who was beckoning to her. 'But I'm using the name of Mrs Morgan... I'm staying with your cousin's wife.'

'I have a cousin too?' He tried to hold her as the sister approached. 'Please, I need to know...'

'Captain Colin Morgan and his father are your family,' she said. 'I'll visit soon and tell you as much as I can.'

'Promise?'

'I promise,' Becky told him. 'If I can, I'll come tomorrow and every day until the baby comes.'

'Come along, Mrs Morgan,' the sister said firmly behind her. 'You may visit again if you wish – but this is enough for the first time.'

Becky turned and smiled at David. 'I'll come tomorrow – is there anything you want? Some toffees perhaps?'

'Why would I want them?' he frowned.

'Because you like them.' Becky smiled. 'I'll bring your favourite if I can get them –treacle toffee.'

He frowned and didn't answer, but sister was clearly annoyed and so Becky had no choice but to follow her from the ward. At the entrance, she looked back and saw that he was still watching her from his bed, looking puzzled.

* * *

'How can you be certain it is him?' Colin asked as his driver took them home. 'If his face is so changed – can you be sure?'

Becky stared at him, feeling less certain now. 'I think it is,' she said slowly. 'The back of his head and the way he sits – and there's something left in his face that makes me think it is him. I can't know one hundred per cent...' She felt a niggle of doubt. David had told her he loved treacle toffee, but when she'd offered to take him some, he'd seemed to doubt that it was his favourite. Had she been too swift to acknowledge him because she so much wanted it to be David? 'There was the watch – you said it was from his mother and must be a treasured possession...'

'He might have come by that in several ways – picked it up from the ground, been given it to bring home by a dying man – or simply stolen it.'

Becky bit her lip, staring at Colin through eyes misted with tears, but then she shook her head. 'He wouldn't have stolen it,' she said. 'I know he wouldn't – but I can't be sure of his identity, naturally, and yet my instinct says it is him.'

'Perhaps the treatment will bring his memory back,' Maggie suggested.

'I'm going to visit him again tomorrow.'

'Is that wise?' Maggie asked. 'Supposing you get involved with him and then it turns out it is someone else? You may not even like him.'

'I have to visit, I promised,' Becky said and felt her confidence return. 'I am sure inside it is David.'

'Instinct is often the best guide,' Maggie agreed. 'Let's hope he does remember of his own accord – but what happens then?'

'He will marry me,' Becky declared more confidently than she felt inside. 'He will marry me as soon as he can...'

'And what of the baby?' Colin asked her.

Becky faltered, looking guilty as her eyes met his. 'I'll keep my baby,' she said with a touch of defiance.

'Of course she will,' Maggie chimed in before Colin could

become angry on her behalf. 'It is the natural and right thing, if she is happily married, Colin.'

'What about her promise to you?' he demanded.

'We'll find another baby that needs a loving home,' Maggie told him softly. 'If a miracle has happened and David is alive in that hospital, he will want his child and so will Becky.'

For a moment, Colin seemed as if he would fight the decision, but then he shrugged. 'If you're happy, Maggie...'

Maggie smiled at him. 'I did this mostly to help Becky and I would have loved the child – but I'm not desperate for a baby, Colin. When the time is right, we'll adopt a child, perhaps more than one – but Becky is my friend and she must do as she wishes.'

'Thank you.' Becky stared at her for a moment longer, then burst into tears and when the car stopped outside the cottage, she immediately ran from it.

'Had you better go after her?' Colin asked, but Maggie shook her head.

'She will go to her room to be alone for a while. Let her cry,' she said. 'She has been through such a lot and this is all too much for her. It must be unbearable to see his poor face like that and not to know for sure.'

'At least she didn't scream and run away when she saw him,' Colin remarked. 'That is the worst thing you can do to someone who has suffered so much, poor devil.'

'Will you tell your father about him and Becky?' Maggie asked. 'Or does he already know?'

'I told him there was a possibility that David might have a wife...' Colin sounded uncertain. 'Father wants us to go home, Maggie. He apologised for his behaviour and said in the matter of adopting a child you must do as you wish.'

'He has missed us,' Maggie said and smiled. 'I don't mind, Colin – but how do you feel?'

'I need to finish some treatment I'm having and then I'll decide.'
He looked thoughtful, then raised his eyes to hers. 'Now that we're
alone, how do you truly feel about her change of heart?'

'Disappointed, of course,' Maggie said, 'but any child is better
with its mother – providing she is kind and decent, which Becky is,
of course. She had been a little out of sorts these past few months,
but considering her situation, I think she has coped well.'

'You went through as much and worse.' Colin's eyes never left
her face as she paused for a moment.

'Yes, I went through a harsh experience – but I didn't have a
father who would have been ashamed of me. My father would be
proud of what I did out there, but I know that if I'd been in Becky's
position, he would have stood by me.'

'Everyone who knows and cares for you is proud of you,' Colin
assured her. 'You've been so patient with Becky. I do not think I
could have put up with her sulks and her tantrums.'

'No, perhaps not,' Maggie agreed with a smile. 'She is my friend,
Colin, and she is under a terrible strain. When this is all over, you'll
see another side to her. She can be funny and kind, generous too.'

'Well, as long as you're happy to continue in the circumstances?'

'Yes.' Maggie walked to him and bent to kiss him in his wheelchair. 'I'll see it through, dearest. I don't know about you, but I
could do with a cup of tea after all that.'

'Make mine a sherry,' he said. 'I think I need something
stronger.'

21

Maggie was relieved to get home. It was a warm day and they had been to the hospital yet again. When he'd visited, Colin had brought several more letters for her that had been sent to his home in the country and she had replied, but there had been no time recently to write further. Becky insisted on going every day to sit with David Morgan for a while and they'd been for eight days in a row now. Colin had returned to London to continue his treatment and Maggie did not feel she could let Becky travel to the hospital alone, even though there was a local bus and it was only a short journey. Becky was so close to her time that she ought not to go, but she would not consider herself, even when Maggie asked her to think of the child.

'I must visit David so that he remembers me,' she had said, looking so anxious that Maggie could not find the heart to refuse her. 'Besides, Evangeline said it was good for me to go out and do things.'

'I thought she said it was good for you to walk in the sunshine,' Maggie had reminded her, but Becky would not listen and so they went every day, even though it caused Becky such pain to see him suffering from the treatment he was having, and his emotional distress at being unable to remember who he really was.

As she went to put the kettle on, Maggie heard the cry from upstairs. She abandoned her task and went swiftly to find Becky doubled over with pain. 'What is it?' Maggie asked, looking at her in concern. 'The baby isn't due for another week or so...'

'I've had a backache all day,' Becky said, gasping as she felt the contraction. 'I'm sure it is coming, Maggie. Yes—' She sat down on the edge of the bed. 'Don't leave me. Please, stay with me—'

'I am going to pop next door and ask the neighbour's son to fetch Evangeline. We are going to need her soon, Becky.'

Becky nodded, forcing a smile. 'Please, ask him to fetch her – but don't leave me for long.'

'I won't,' Maggie promised and went downstairs. Their nearest neighbour was a few yards down the leafy lane and it took several moments to explain what she wanted. When she returned, she heard Becky crying and calling out for her and ran back upstairs. 'I am sorry, dearest,' she said. 'Is the pain very bad?'

Becky nodded, gritting her teeth. 'If she doesn't come soon, it will be too late,' she muttered. 'It's awful, Maggie. I'm not sure I can bear it!'

'Your baby is coming whether you like it or not,' Maggie told her firmly. 'Just settle down on the bed and breathe deeply. If your baby comes, I shall deliver it – but I don't think it will be that quick. Babies often take much longer.' She reached for Becky's hand and held it.

'Oh, let it be quick,' Becky said through gritted teeth. 'It hurts so much.' She looked at Maggie in fear. 'Am I going to die? Am I being punished because I did something bad?'

'No, of course not – no more silly talk,' Maggie said as Becky gripped her hand tightly. 'You will be fine, Becky. The pain will go when it is over.'

Just then, they heard a voice from downstairs and then footsteps coming up. Evangeline appeared in the doorway. She looked at Becky's strained face and smiled. 'It seems I've arrived just in time, Mrs Morgan. Maggie, could you go down and boil some water for me please? And you might make us a cup of tea and bring Mrs Morgan something to eat. We could have a long night.'

'Yes, of course.' She smiled at Becky as she clutched her hand. 'I shan't be long, dearest, and Evangeline is right – we may have some time to go yet.'

* * *

Becky's baby was born in the early hours of the next morning. She had screamed and struggled throughout the long night, but just as it seemed her strength was ebbing, her child was born. She lay back against the pillows, cheeks wet with tears as she asked, 'What is it – is it all right?'

'Yes,' Evangeline assured her. 'You have a beautiful little girl, Mrs Morgan. She is healthy and quite big – so that's why she caused you some pain.'

'Can I hold her?' Becky asked and struggled to sit up against the pillows as she strained to see the baby. Maggie had been bathing her and brought her back, the smears of blood washed from her face, and cosily wrapped in a large towel. 'She is beautiful, isn't she?' Becky looked at Maggie tearfully. 'My baby...'

'Yes, Becky,' Maggie said and smiled. 'She is gorgeous. You're very lucky to have her.'

'Yes, I am – and you as my friend.' Becky reached a hand out and Maggie squeezed it.

'Well, I should go,' Evangeline said after she'd finished tending to Becky. 'You will be fine now, Mrs Morgan – and Maggie is perfectly able to care for you both, I think. I need some rest, but I will pop in later to see how you're both doing.' She shook her head as Maggie walked to the bedroom door with her. 'I can see myself out – you know what to do now?'

'Yes,' Maggie assured her. 'Thank you for coming. You were wonderful.'

'I just did my job as it should be done,' Evangeline said with a slight smile. 'It was a long night and I should sleep – but if you need me, just send word.'

'Yes, of course,' Maggie nodded. 'I don't think we shall – mother and baby seem fine, very healthy.'

'Yes, she has improved a great deal of late,' Evangeline said. 'I suppose it is because she now believes her husband is alive.' Becky had told Evangeline that her husband was in hospital, explaining that he'd lost his memory. Maggie wondered at the wisdom of it, because nothing was certain yet, but Becky had made up her mind that she had found the man she loved and was just as sure he would marry her when he was better and had recovered his memory.

'Yes, I am sure that made a big difference,' Maggie agreed.

'Has her husband made any improvement – his memory returned at all?'

'No, I fear not – but he is getting better. The nurses told us that he now looks forward to Becky's visits and his health is gradually improving, so we have hope.'

'Hope is everything,' Evangeline said. 'I will see you later.'

* * *

Maggie returned to Becky's bed and watched as she nursed her baby. 'Give her to me now, dearest,' she said when she'd finished. 'I'll put her here in the cot for you – and you must rest. You are exhausted.'

'Yes, I am,' Becky admitted and her cheeks were wet with tears. 'I'm so lucky, Maggie. You've been so good to me – thank you.'

Maggie nodded. She heard their housekeeper arrive for the day and went downstairs, giving her the good news. Mrs Neal smiled at her as she took off her hat and coat.

'You get some rest now, Mrs Morgan,' she said. 'I'll go up to Mrs Becky in a moment. I've had three myself so I can manage them for a while. It's wonderful news. She must be so happy?'

'Yes, she is,' Maggie agreed, but as she went to lie down on her bed for a while, she wondered about the future. Becky still had several problems to sort out. Firstly, she had to wait for the man she visited in hospital to recover his health, and then, if he did not recover his memory, even if he believed her and wanted to marry her, she still had the hurdle of telling her father about the child.

The whole point in bringing her away to have the baby and agreeing the plan for Maggie to adopt the child had been to protect Mr Stockbridge. How was Becky going to solve that problem? Even if she married, she couldn't hide the fact that she'd born a child out of wedlock.

Maggie wasn't sure that her friend had thought things through. They couldn't stay here forever. Once Colin decided where he wanted to live in future, he would take her home, and whilst Becky was welcome to stay for a while, she might not want to go far from the hospital where David was recuperating.

Was she capable of managing alone? And what reason would she give her father for not returning to London? Had she given her baby to Maggie as agreed at the start she might have managed to keep her secret but now it was bound to come out.

22

'I am so glad that Marco is getting better,' Sally said and hugged Ben when he returned from visiting his friend in hospital that Sunday morning. 'Like you, I feared he might die...' She hesitated, sensing something, then, 'Did you tell him about Sadie?'

'I had to,' Ben said and looked upset. 'He asked about her, why she hadn't visited, so I had to tell him how she'd died.'

'How did he take it?' Sally asked. 'Was he very cut up over it?'

'He closed his eyes and I saw a tear slide down his cheek, but then he just nodded and looked at me, asking after Pierre.' Ben sighed. 'He asked me if I could visit him and discover if he was happy with his grandmother. He said that if I thought the child was happy and thriving to say nothing, but that if I had any doubts, I was to tell her that he wants his son back and then help him engage a children's nurse.'

'Oh, Ben, that is difficult for you – what did you say?'

'I promised I would – I already have, Sally. I went to the house immediately after leaving the hospital. I am relieved to say that Sadie's mother is willing to give the child up. It seems that she has found having a small child around all the time is more than she can happily cope with and her husband isn't keen on having the boy around too much – so now all I have to do is find a nurse for him.'

'Pearl could look after him with our two for a while,' Sally suggested, 'but long term he is going to need a live-in nurse.'

'Yes, and that is easier said than done these days,' Ben said. 'So many young women went off to nurse the wounded.'

'I know,' Sally said ruefully. 'I lost Maggie for a long time, because of the war – and there was another young woman, Joan Galloway, who worked in the dress department for a while, before taking up nursing. I think her parents might have come from Ireland but she was born here.' She looked at Ben. 'I suppose some of them may have returned home after their posting. We could put an advert in the paper. I am going to need a nurse for Harpers.'

'You intend to continue the department then?' Ben frowned. 'I thought perhaps you'd set it up for Sadie's sake?'

'I did to a certain extent – but I still think it is a marvellous idea. It means all our ladies can return to work after the birth of their children should they so wish.'

Ben nodded. 'Oh, I see the point of it, Sally, but I am not sure a lot of men will agree with it. Once they begin to return from the war, they will want their wives at home – and it surely can't go on much longer? The Germans are running out of resources and will be forced to give up soon enough – we'd be in the same boat if it were not for the Americans. Thank God they came in when they did.'

'You're an American,' Sally said with a smile. 'Had you forgotten?'

'No – but I feel British now.' Ben's eyes twinkled. 'This is my home and it's where I live and work, Sally. I've done all I can to help the British during this war – even though some of them are ungrateful so-and-sos – but most are decent enough and I've got you, my love, and two beautiful children, so I have a lot to be thankful for.'

She moved towards him and they kissed. 'Me too. I love you, Ben. You are a wonderful husband, but I'm grateful to your country for all the help they're giving us. I just want this war to be over so everyone can come home and get on with their lives.'

'The men that return will be asking for their jobs back and expecting to get them, as they were promised. A lot of women will lose their jobs and have to return to being housewives.'

'I suppose so,' Sally agreed. 'I'm going to keep all those I can, Ben – but some of them will have to take a step back. The men were managing their departments before they went to war and will expect to again.'

'They won't work for a woman head of department in the men's section,' Ben agreed. 'It won't make too much difference at Harpers, but it will be a different story when in the factories and some offices.'

'Yes, I know you are right, but I think some women will not go quietly,' Sally replied. 'The militants in the Women's Movement will be on the march again, demanding rights for all women and not just the over thirties.'

'Do you feel in need of more rights, Sally?' Ben asked her with an odd smile.

'No, because I'm married to you and I've already got what they are fighting for. I might not be able to vote, but I have a loving, liberal husband and a family I adore and a job I love – what more do I need?'

Ben's smile widened, becoming satisfied. 'Good, I am glad you feel that way, Sally. However, once we get things going properly again and I can get round to it, I am going to sign half of my shares in Harpers over to you. You should have the right to vote when decisions are taken and to feel that you're working for something.'

'I already do feel that way,' she said and smiled. 'And I'd never use my vote against you, Ben.'

'Never is a long time,' he replied. 'I want Harpers to be yours if something should happen to me – oh, it isn't likely to yet, Sally, but I am giving you half my shares and leaving the other half between the children.'

'One day we might own all of Harpers?' she suggested.

'Have you fallen out with Jenni?' he asked, raising his eyebrows.

'No – but I think her future lies in the north now, don't you? She is opening that new store – small at first, but then she hopes for larger premises and she may want to sell you her shares.' She hesitated, then, 'You can talk to her when they come down for the wedding.' Jenni still hadn't told them a definite date but it could not be long now.

'I'll buy them if she does want to sell,' Ben promised. 'It will mean borrowing from the bank, but I wouldn't want anyone else to own a part of Harpers.'

'No, of course not,' Sally agreed. 'I hope it will never happen, but she mentioned the possibility to me.'

'Well, we'll face it when we get to it,' Ben shrugged. 'Right now, we have other problems. Where we get a couple of nurses for a start.'

'Perhaps Marco doesn't need a qualified nurse,' Sally suggested. 'Just a nice young woman with some experience of children. There was never a shortage before the war, but who knows what the young women will want to do now.' Life in England had changed a great deal during the war years. Although some attitudes remained the same, for young women it never would or could be the same again. Given so much freedom when they were needed to take the men's places, why would they ever give it up? Rachel had remarked on it more than once, telling Sally that she saw confident young ladies everywhere these days.

'Some of them might want to be managing directors or take over the Government,' Ben said in reply to Sally's musing and she saw that he was only half joking. Sally nodded and laughed. She couldn't see a lot of women simply going back quietly to the lives they'd had before the war, content to be just a wife that knew her place or a dutiful daughter who stayed home with her parents – they were going to want more.

* * *

'But will you be happy just living in the Hampshire countryside with William and Lizzie?' Sally asked when Rachel came to tea with her later that day. Rachel had told her that she'd decided she must do whatever William wanted and Sally looked at her doubtfully. 'You've enjoyed working at Harpers, haven't you?' Rachel had always seemed to thrive in her job.

'Yes, very much, and I shall miss it,' Rachel told her. 'I've told you that I want to be sure you have the right person to take over my job – but then I shall go with him. Otherwise, it would mean living apart for much of the time and I don't want to do that, Sally.'

'No, of course not – if you are sure it's what you want, then go and be happy.'

'He has been very ill,' Rachel said, 'and I thought I might lose him – so I shall go with him. I was a bit worried about Hazel, but he says there is a cottage she can have that he owns in the village and she is ready to move with us. I think it is for Lizzie's sake.'

'Yes, she loves that child – and William didn't try to prevent you adopting her properly?'

'He made it easy for me. His lawyer did it and so...' Rachel hesitated, then, 'I owe it to him, Sally, and I love him. You would go wherever Ben wanted, wouldn't you?'

'Yes, I would.' Sally sighed. Despite the vote for older women, it seemed there were still ties that bound women, but they were of love and who could wish to break them? 'I'm just going to miss you, Rachel – and I'm afraid you will find it a bit dull in the country, quiet...'

'Yes, I expect I shall for a while,' Rachel agreed. 'I shall find something to keep me busy, Sally. Get involved with the local women's groups – or sit on the board of a charity. William suggested that. He says that as his wife I'll be asked to do all sorts of things – teas for the local children and their mothers, hospital visiting, all kinds of stuff.'

'Yes, there is always that,' Sally said, because she sometimes still visited the hospital that her friend, Marlene, had told her about, though only occasionally these days, because her children took up all the time she had to spare from Harpers. She got up and bent down to kiss Rachel's cheek, 'I shall miss you a lot.'

'I imagine I'll miss you and Harpers more,' she replied. 'I really don't have a choice, Sally – or not one that I would wish to make.'

'And when do you leave?' Sally asked, frowning.

'William says there is a lot to do to the house, before we can move in,' Rachel replied. 'It may be a couple of months – so until then I shall continue to work for Harpers.'

'Good.' Sally sighed. She knew she was being selfish, wishing that Rachel wouldn't go, but it sometimes seemed that she was losing all her friends and that made her feel sad. Her life was full; she had Ben and her children and she was lucky – but a part of her believed that Rachel would hate the life she was planning and so it wasn't all for her sake that she'd questioned it. Yet, in her heart, she knew her friend was right. Rachel really didn't have much choice if she wanted her marriage to be close and loving – living apart wasn't an option.

* * *

'It is a shame that she's retiring to the country,' Ben said after Rachel had left them to return home that afternoon. 'She was good at her job and you'll miss her friendship.'

'Yes, I shall, quite a bit,' Sally admitted. 'I missed Maggie when she went off to be a nurse and then married Colin – but she is happy and I see her now and then.'

'Not the same, though, is it?' he said. 'It brought it home to me how few real friends we have when I visited Marco in the hospital and saw how ill he still is.' Ben sighed. 'This war has a lot to answer for. I felt so awful telling him that Sadie had died of a fever.' Ben shook his head, looking sad as he thought about colleagues and friends they would never see again.

Sally put her arms around him. He was thinner and she noticed a few strands of grey at his temples. 'I know you can't tell me – but I'm guessing that whatever went on out there had something to do with his work in France during the first part of the war. I know that whatever Marco was doing then was important.'

'Yes, that much I can admit,' Ben said, sounding weary. 'At least we have him back. I fear that some of Harpers' people won't be coming home ever.' He sighed as they thought about young men lost to the war. 'Lord, I hope Jack Burrows gets back all right. Beth told you his ship was overdue again, didn't she?'

'Yes,' Sally frowned. 'I've hardly seen her for three weeks. She used to come as often as she could, but I think she's worried about Jack and finding things hard to manage at the moment.'

'I don't want to lose more friends,' Ben said. 'Jack and I had plans for after the war. I know that sounds selfish, but I just feel we've lost too many of our people already.'

Sally agreed. That morning, they'd had a letter from the parents of one of the young men who had worked in the clothing department before the war. Alfie Smith had been killed in action, receiving a posthumous medal for bravery under fire, and his family had wanted to share the news with them. He was just one of thousands who had died for his country – but he'd been one of Harpers' people and his loss was another cause for sorrow; it just seemed too much at times.

'I haven't heard from Mick for ages either,' she told him. Mick O'Sullivan, the Irish friend she'd known since before she worked at Harpers, had returned to his unit after Maggie's wedding had taken place and Sally had not heard anything from him since. He'd fallen in love with Maggie, seeing her bravery after her fiancé was killed in the war, but he'd been injured himself and then she'd met Colin. 'I think I might visit Marlene tomorrow, Ben. She may know how he is.'

Marlene half-owned a pub-come-restaurant with Mick and she managed it for them. Mick also owned several other restaurants that he'd set up and were run by his various managers. Sally had often visited them with him before the war, advising and giving her opinion of the food and décor. She still ate at one of them with friends sometimes, though a couple seemed to be not as busy or as well run as they had been when Mick was there to keep an eye on them. The one Sally frequented the most was still as busy and efficient as ever and she'd complimented the manager on it more than once.

'Yes, do that,' he said and looked thoughtful. 'I think I might take a trip up north and see how Jenni is, Sally. I'd like to be certain she is happy and sure of what she's doing up there.'

'Yes, that would be a nice thing to do, Ben,' Sally said and hugged him. 'I'm so glad you're home safely. I had a few moments when I feared the worst – you were so long away this last time.' Her eyes searched his face. 'I know that what you did was for Marco – but you won't be doing anything like that again?'

'I certainly hope not,' he told her frankly. 'If I had a slight hankering to be more involved in the war what I saw over there cured me, Sally. I never want to leave you again if I can help it – and I would love you to come on this trip to visit Jenni with me, if you can manage it?'

'Yes, why not?' she said and smiled up at him lovingly as she saw anxiety for her in his face. 'Don't worry, darling. I am all right. I was just concerned for Rachel earlier. I'm not sure she will be happy in the country and I know you must feel the same about your sister being up north. I shall come with you, Ben.'

23

'So, if you don't need the loan I made Harpers some years back, I'd like the money to invest in my business here,' Jenni said when they all sat talking over a cup of tea on the second evening of their visit to Newcastle. 'Of course if you do need it, I'll leave it with you.'

'Have we used any of Jenni's money?' Ben asked and Sally shook her head.

'We've managed without it so far...' She hesitated, because their reserve funds were slender and she'd been thinking that she might have to use a small amount of Jenni's emergency fund soon, but she didn't like to say so. It was like admitting failure in her eyes. 'No – if Jenni needs her money, she should have it.'

'Good,' Jenni said. 'There are two premises I have been offered – one much larger than the other and I've decided I'll go for more space and increase the range of my stock.' She frowned, clearly a little annoyed with the Government for bringing in restrictive measures. 'With the change in the clothing regulations, I can't do what I intended and sell beautiful clothes – so I'll go for a small department store instead. Like yours, Ben, but not as big – and not as well stocked either, at least until we can get shipments from

New York again. Besides, I'll be busy with other things for a while.' She placed a hand on her swelling midriff and smiled. 'If I get everything set up, we'll delay the opening until after my baby is born.'

'Make sure you do,' Ben told his sister. 'Sally was forever looking through stock lists and catalogues or talking to a supplier on the phone...'

Sally shook her head at him. 'Ben, that's not quite true,' she said and laughed and then looked at Jenni curiously. 'You spoke of shipments from America – are you intending your stock to be mainly American?'

'When I can, I shall buy mostly from home,' she said and looked thoughtful. 'I think we're ready for modern ideas and fresh stock – and women will be eager for something new once things get better. I'd like to do things a little differently to you, Ben.'

'Sounds interesting,' he said. 'We shall buy more from overseas again when we can do so without damaging the war effort. The country still needs the basics, Jenni. Sally has done wonderfully well to keep us more than half-fully stocked from local and regional sources throughout the conflict. I'm not sure how she's done it.'

'With a lot of hard work,' Jenni said, smiling at them both. 'I'm not going to use the name Harpers, Ben – that wouldn't be fair and it would be confusing.'

'I'd like to buy your share of Harpers one day,' he said, and then, as Sally drew in her breath, he looked at her. 'Not yet, darling. I know we can't afford it.'

'If Jenni needed her money, I suppose we might raise a loan from the bank?'

'I only want the loan returned for now anyway,' Jenni told them and Sally nodded.

'We've never paid a penny interest...'

'Well, you didn't use it and the bank paid interest so that was all right.' Jenni looked at her. 'You don't mind that I want it for my business, Sally?'

'No, of course not,' Sally said. 'I admire you for being brave enough to set up business now – it isn't going to be easy to find enough stock.' To say nothing of the coming birth. Sally knew how hard it was to juggle home and work life with a young child. She'd managed because she had good people around her and a dogged determination.

'I've been making contacts for months,' Jenni replied with a confident air. 'And I think that by the time I'm ready to open, things will be getting better again. As soon as it is safe, I'm going back to America to source the stock I want over there.'

'What does your husband-to-be say to that?' Ben asked, frowning. 'You are happy with what you've done, Jenni, moving in with him?'

Her smile lit her face. 'Andrew says I should do what I want and doesn't care what I do – as long as I come back.'

'Well, I guess that's all right then,' Ben said and gave his sister a quick hug. 'I was a bit worried about you – but it seems you've got it all under control.'

'When have I ever not?' Jenni said and, as she met Ben's gaze, 'Well, yes, I know I messed up with Henry – but that's over now. We're divorced and by next week I'll be married. Yes, we've managed to get a date to fit in with Andrew's workload. We're coming down to London and we'll have the wedding, a couple of nights in a nice hotel and then come home.' Her smile lit up her face. 'I'm fine, Ben. You don't need to worry about me.'

* * *

'Jenni seems fine,' Ben remarked to Sally as they settled in the train taking them home the next morning. 'I had no need to worry about her at all.'

'Jenni is very capable when it comes to business,' Sally said. 'She was vulnerable for a while when she was breaking up with Henry – but she's turned her life around and I think she seems happy...'

Ben looked at her, his brows raised. 'What is it then, Sally? I know there is something on your mind – something to do with Jenni or Harpers?'

'We don't have much in our reserves, Ben. If Jenni takes her money – and I agree that she should – we shall have to keep our fingers crossed and hope that things soon start to improve.'

'I know there isn't a lot in the bank,' Ben said, his expression serious. 'I haven't been around much to help you, Sally, but I've kept my eye on things as much as I could. We don't need Jenni's money – that loan was her idea. I never asked for it and if she needs it...' He shrugged. 'We'll manage, and I can raise another loan from the bank if I have to.'

He'd taken a small loan when they expanded just before the war started and Sally had been making the regular repayments from the cash flow, which was one of the reasons there wasn't as much to spare as she'd like. Their sales were patchy, sometimes excellent when new and good stock was fresh in and then tailing off, for the simple reason that there wasn't enough stock arriving to keep a constant turnover.

'As Jenni says, once things settle down again, we'll be able to buy more stock and trade will pick up again. We have no shortage of customers wanting to buy, Ben – it's just that I can't get enough stock to satisfy that demand, and it's going to be worse in the clothing department now the restrictions have come in. I don't think Jenni will find it as simple to bring goods into the country as she thinks – at least for a while, even after the war is over, and we don't know for sure that it's ending yet.'

'A few months at most,' Ben assured her. 'Even the Germans can't fight with empty stomachs and no fuel in their tanks. It has been a war of attrition, Sally. Whoever manages to last the longest is probably the winner – though how anyone can claim victory when so much has been lost and so many have died, I don't know...'

Sally's cheeks were wet with tears as she looked at him. 'I know – and it makes me so sad. I've been lucky, Ben. I found my mother and I see her as often as we can manage these days – but so many others have lost their loved ones.' She wiped her cheek. 'I can find a replacement for Sadie in the department, but Marco has lost his wife and Pierre his mother – and so many others have lost fathers and sons, brothers, cousins and friends.'

Ben nodded. 'We've been lucky. A financial problem at Harpers doesn't seem much compared with that, does it?'

Sally shook her head. 'I just can't stop thinking of Marco, how he must be feeling – and what is going to happen to his little boy. I know he thinks the world of Pierre...'

* * *

Marco struggled to concentrate on what the doctor was saying. The fever had gone at last and his wounds were healing, but he felt so weak – and so lost and useless lying here in this hospital. When Ben told him that Sadie had become ill and died of a fever, he'd been devastated. It was so unfair that a young, blameless woman had died just like that – whereas he had survived against the odds.

He knew that it was unlikely he would be asked to serve his country again. Ben Harper had seen to that and told him that he would be getting an honourable discharge from the Army. He would

– when he was fit enough – be able to return to his work at Harpers, though at the moment the thought didn't fill him with joy. Yes, it was what he wanted when he felt able – but right now he was emotionally drained. It was as though Sadie's death had taken all purpose from his life. Marco had realised that he'd come to love her – as much as he could ever love a woman. Not in the way he'd loved Julien, but quietly and with a deep warmth that had made him feel safe and secure. He'd wanted to spend the rest of his life looking after her and Pierre.

What about Pierre? The question hung like a dark shadow, hovering at the back of his mind. He'd been Sadie's husband and the child had been his in all but blood. Marco had intended to adopt him legally after the war. He realised now that he should not have waited. Had the boy been his legally, Marco could have claimed him, but he'd waited, not wanting to push Sadie into anything – and now it was too late.

Lying back against a pillow that smelled of starch and disinfectant, Marco longed to be home, to have his own things around him. Perhaps there he could think about what was right for him – but, above all, it must be right for the boy he thought of as his son. He might be able to persuade Sadie's parents to give him up – but was it the best thing for the boy? He would be at work most of the day once he was on his feet again and have no choice but to leave him with a nurse. It wasn't ideal and he might be better off with his grandparents. Sighing, Marco realised that he would have to discuss what to do with Sadie's family. If they would look after him while he worked and allow Marco general custody, he could fetch him home for the evenings and the weekends.

A faint smile touched his mouth. Perhaps an agreement could be reached. It depended on whether or not they knew how unusual their daughter's marriage had been in that it had not been consummated for some months after the wedding – and that Marco's preference had always been for men until he met Sadie and gradually began to love her.

They were upright folk with high morals and if they knew the truth might think he would corrupt Pierre – which was something Marco would never do. He had often felt himself cursed to be different and wished for a home and family – children of his own. He loved Pierre as if he were his own and had thought it possible that Sadie and he would have more children. Marco knew that Pierre was his only chance of having a son now and he just prayed that he would be allowed to keep him.

24

Beth read her letter three times and tears of relief trickled down her cheeks. Jack wasn't often able to write but he did so whenever they were in port if they were not due to return immediately. He'd told her his reasoning long ago: *'it's often not worth writing, because I'd be home as soon or even before you received it,'* so she'd got used to the idea, but it was months since she heard anything of him and so when the letter came informing her that Jack was in an English hospital, wounded in the leg this time, but recovering, the relief was overwhelming.

Rushing down the stairs as she heard her father-in-law come in that evening, Beth called to him joyfully. 'Jack is back in England, Dad. He is in hospital and hasn't been able to write himself just yet, but he asked a nurse to write to me – and she says he is making good progress. I can visit him in Portsmouth if I like...'

Fred's face lit up like a torch that had just been switched on and she knew that he'd been worrying as much as she had. 'We'll both go and take the children. I'm due some holiday and I'll take a week off to make the trip worthwhile.'

'Thank you.' She felt the warmth of gratitude and love as she saw the new lines at the corner of his eyes and the grey hairs that had now spread out from his temples so that most of the colour had been stripped from what was still a remarkably thick head of hair. The grey hairs had begun to appear when his son, Tim, had died and got steadily more prevalent with worry over Jack's long absences. 'I should like that.'

'You've been a good daughter to me, Beth,' he said and smiled at her. 'I couldn't have wished for a better wife for Jack – or a kinder and more loving companion. I'm not sure what I would have done without you these past years.'

Beth hesitated, then, 'Perhaps you might have married, Dad. I am sure Vera would say yes if you asked her.'

'Yes, she probably would,' he agreed and sighed. 'It was never meant to go that far, Beth. I like her. She's a generous and helpful lady – but I'm a bit long in the tooth for marrying.'

'Not if it was what you wanted,' Beth told him. 'Vera doesn't expect hearts and flowers, Fred. She just wants company as she gets older – and so do you... I mean, we'll always be around, but we might not always be here with you.'

Fred nodded. 'You should have your own home and would have done before now if it were not for the war, love. I don't mind living alone.'

He said the words stoutly, but she saw a flicker of doubt in his eyes and hoped she'd set him thinking. Vera was a good decent woman and would make sure he had clean clothes and ate properly if she and Jack and the boys were not with him every day. Naturally, they would visit, most days if they weren't too far away, but it might be that the only time they could come would be weekends when Fred was at home – and that meant long hours spent alone in the evenings after work. Beth wouldn't badger him, he must make up his own mind, but she felt he needed to think about it for his own sake.

'When are you going to visit Jack in the hospital?' Fred asked her, obviously deciding on a change of subject.

'I'd like to go soon– but it might be a bit difficult with the children; it's a long train journey for them.'

'We'll manage them between us,' he said. 'Or we might ask Vera if she'd like to come with us... have a bit of a holiday, at my expense, naturally.'

'I'll mention it to her when she comes round, see what she says.'

They talked some more, because Fred would need to let Mr Stockbridge know that he wanted to take his holiday, and decided to go down that weekend so that it would actually be more like nine days they could have away.

'We'll telephone a few hotels this evening and see where we can get in,' Fred suggested, but Beth smiled.

'I can do that myself, Dad. Sally will be back from her visit to Jenni now, so I'll pop round and tell her that we're going down to see Jack and she'll suggest that I use her phone. She may know which is the best hotel for us. She always knows things like that...'

Fred smiled and nodded his agreement. 'Yes, Mrs Harper keeps her fingers on the pulse. She talks to a lot of travelling salespeople and they tell her things like that... I always find her interesting to talk to when she visits me in the basement.' He smiled at Beth. 'I've only taken a day off at a time since I started working for Harpers – knew they couldn't manage the stockroom without me, see – but I've got a couple of good lads now.' Fred nodded to himself. 'When our boys come back from overseas, I might think of retiring, let the youngsters take over.'

'What would you do all day?' Beth asked, shocked by the suggestion. 'How would you manage?'

'I've got a few ideas,' Fred told her. 'Haven't decided yet, Beth – but things change, life moves on, and if you leave it too late you don't get a chance to do things you might have liked to do.'

Beth would have liked to press him further on his plans for a life after retirement. Of course, he did have a small pension from his former work as the headmaster of a school, but she wasn't sure it was enough to keep him in comfort – besides, he would be alone all day then... She hesitated to ask and Fred picked up his newspaper, settling down to read the latest news from the war.

'Postage has gone up to a penny-halfpenny,' he muttered. 'That's been the same for as long as I can recall – just a penny it was to post a letter.' Fred shook his head over it. 'And that standard clothing won't please Sally Harper one bit. You can't expect Harpers' customers to buy that kind of stuff – no, they'll make do with what they've already got and have it remodelled.'

'I expect a lot of women have been doing that for a while now,' Beth said. 'Sally was concerned the women's clothing department wasn't doing as well as some others. Even when she could buy what stock she chose and not what the Government allows, it was in short supply. They had a rush whenever something nice came in and then, when the new stock was gone, it was slow.'

'It's been a bad year all round,' Fred cleared his throat. 'Mrs Harper set up that department for children and employed a nurse – wonderful thing to do – and then Mr Marco's wife dies of a chill... at least that's what they say. Sounded worse than a chill to me. Must have been pneumonia that killed her.'

'Yes, probably,' Beth said and frowned. 'Sally was going to interview some more nurses this week – Pearl, who looks after Jenny for her, has told her about two young women who are looking to make a change. They've both been nursing overseas and they've been released and told they've done enough and should return to their old lives.'

'Yes, that will be happening a lot once things quieten down and the men return,' Fred agreed. 'Of course some never will... like young Alfie...'

'Harpers has been lucky though,' Beth mused. 'We've only heard of three or four deaths.'

'There will be injuries we haven't heard of and it isn't quite over yet,' Fred reminded her. 'It looks more hopeful of late, but there may be some nasty surprises yet awhile.'

Beth was silent. It was too sobering to think of all the lives lost and ruined and all the damage done to the country. Harpers had struggled through due to Sally's hard work and that of her staff and sister-in-law, all of whom had contributed to its survival. Many shops and businesses had not been so lucky, but even Harpers couldn't have made much of a profit during these past years. It would be awful if, like some others, it was forced to close.

Beth shook her head over it but then she remembered her own news and smiled. Jack was in hospital in Portsmouth and very soon she would be able to see him. She just had to book the hotel and then they could all go down on the train.

25

'Jack! Oh, Jack, it's wonderful to see you,' Beth cried in surprise and rushed to greet her husband as he entered the kitchen two days later and then stopped short of hugging him as she saw his drained look. He was so grey in the face and he was standing badly, leaning on a stick, his eyes drained of their usual vitality. He'd got here somehow, but he was looking so pale and weak. 'We were all coming down to visit. You're ill, my darling...' Tears started to her eyes. 'How on earth did you manage it?'

'I'm better than I was,' Jack said, but he was obviously weary as he limped to the nearest chair and sat down. 'They let me come home to you, Beth, because I never gave them any peace, but I have to report to the doctor and ask for a home visit. I'm better, but I need to take it easy for a while.' He closed his eyes for a moment and then opened them and looked at her. 'I'm lucky to be alive. I thought for a while I wasn't going to make it back.'

Beth knelt by his side and took his hands, noticing the scars that were still red. His injuries had been more extensive than she'd known. She kissed his fingers gently, understanding that he still hurt in several places and holding back her tears to see him looking so frail and unlike himself. 'I love you,' she said, eyes misting over. 'I'm so glad you're back, my love. So very glad.'

'I am too,' Jack replied and smiled wearily. 'All I could think of when I lay in the hospital was of you and the boys and Dad. I couldn't wait to get back to you. When you come close to death, Beth, you know what is important.'

'Home and family,' Beth agreed, still holding his hand carefully. 'You didn't let us know you were coming home...'

'I came the instant they said I could,' Jack told her. 'I didn't have time to write and telegrams are frightening to receive – so I just begged a lift in the ambulance that was bringing another patient to London for treatment – and here I am.'

'Thank goodness for that,' Beth breathed deeply as she looked into the face of the man she loved. 'Your father will be so happy to see you. He'd actually decided to take his annual holiday to visit you. We were all coming.'

Jack glanced around the familiar room with its old Welsh dresser set with blue and white porcelain and the curtains that had been washed so many times that the colour had faded from bright blue to pale. Yet it was comfortable and welcoming and home.

'Dad must have been worried if he was going to take his holiday,' he said and the tiredness vanished from his face for a moment. 'I've saved you all the trouble – but where are the boys?'

'Upstairs having a nap before tea,' Beth said with a fond smile. 'Dad likes to see them when he gets in, so I give them a nap in the afternoons and then let them stay up to play with Grandad when he gets home.'

Jack nodded, a faint echo of sadness in his eyes. 'Dad loves them – they know him better than their father...'

'Jackie doesn't forget you, I see to that,' Beth told him, a glimmer of tears in her eyes. 'But Tim may be a little uncertain at first – he wasn't very old the last time you were home, Jack. It has been months since you got leave...'

'At least two in the hospital, abroad first and then here once I could travel...' At her gasp of dismay, he smiled. 'I didn't want you to know how ill I was at first, Beth, so I wouldn't let them tell you until I knew I was on the mend.' His fingers gripped hers, his strength returning for a moment. 'At least I shan't be going back to sea again, my love. They've officially discharged me. I've done my share and they say I'm not up to long voyages any more.' He sighed and then shook his head. 'We can begin to look to the future now, Beth. The money we got from the sale of the hotel lease and at least part of our savings... I'm going to ask Ben Harper if I can invest it with him.'

Beth nodded. 'You were thinking of opening a restaurant together before the war...'

'Yes, and I'm still thinking of it now.' Jack nodded. 'It will suit me very well to manage a small restaurant – and, hopefully, Ben will still be of the same mind.'

'If he can afford it,' Beth frowned. 'I know Sally is a bit worried about the financial side of Harpers. They still trade as much as possible, but the war has been hard for them – as it has for others.' Some businesses had prospered and made money, but others had suffered. Wages had to be paid even when times were difficult. Harpers had been through a vulnerable period, but the store was hardly established when the war began, unlike some others that had a firmer grounding. The problems had begun when Ben Harper's uncle had died suddenly, leaving him to take over but with less financial backing than was necessary. He'd pulled it all together and was just beginning to expand when the war began and it was marvellous that they'd come through as well as they had.

'Yes, I dare say,' Jack agreed. 'I think they have a lot of space on their top floor. We could just expand the staff canteen and make it into a restaurant the public can use for the time being – build up slowly. After all, now isn't the time for anything too fancy. Plenty of time for that after the victory bells have rung.'

Beth inclined her head in agreement. 'As far as I'm concerned, it is a victory to get *you* back,' she told him. 'If you want to invest in Harpers that is fine with me, Jack. When will you visit Ben – or would you like me to invite them here for Sunday lunch so that you can talk?'

'That would be ideal,' Jack told her. 'I should go myself if I felt able – but it would be easier if they came here.' He looked at her as they heard a wail from upstairs. 'Is that Jackie or Tim?'

'At a guess, I'd say Tim,' Beth said. 'I'll just pop the kettle on and then fetch them down. I'm sure we could all do with a cup of tea – unless you need something stronger? I think there is whisky and half a bottle of brandy left.'

'Just a cup of tea,' Jack said and nodded as she got up.

Beth glanced at him after she'd moved the kettle onto the hob to boil. He looked so tired, but his spirit wasn't broken, just subdued. The news that he wasn't going back to war filled her with a quiet joy. Jack wasn't well. He might have difficult times ahead until he completely recovered from his multiple injuries – far worse than he'd ever let her know. She felt the flow of love between them as he looked up and knew that together they would meet whatever life threw at them and win. She was smiling as she went upstairs to fetch her children down and warn them Daddy wasn't quite well just yet but loved them and was home for good.

* * *

Fred's face when he saw his son sitting in the chair by the fire was a picture. For a moment, Beth thought he would burst into tears, but then he grinned at Jack and took his customary seat by the fire opposite him.

'Well, this is a nice surprise,' he said. 'I suppose Beth told you we were coming to visit at the weekend. I'd taken my holiday. I suppose I could cancel that now—'

'You take it, Dad,' Jack said. 'We haven't spent much time together in years. It will be an opportunity for us to talk, catch up on all that has happened over the years.'

'That sounds as if you're not planning to go back on the ships, son?'

'My days at sea are finished,' Jack told him with a grimace. 'It was sheer determination that kept me going. I wanted to come home to my family and they've told me my body has taken enough punishment. It is a quiet life for me in future.'

'You need some good home cooking and a lot of rest and then you'll be as right as rain.'

Jack nodded but didn't say anything and Fred frowned.

'Unless there is something you're not telling us?'

'The doctors patched me up as best they could – but I have a weakness in here.' Jack touched his chest. 'I haven't told Beth. They've given me a fifty-fifty chance of making it to my forties...'

Fred shook his head. 'Take no notice of them, Jack. I've got little faith in doctors since your mother died long before her time. You rest up while you can and let us look after you. I've lost one son and I've no intention of losing another.'

'Glad to hear it,' Jack smiled and then gave his father a warning look as Beth entered the kitchen. 'Boys settled again now, love?'

'Yes, they're fine,' Beth said and glanced at Fred. 'I let them see Jack for a while, but they got a bit upset, so I put them back to bed.

I'll bring them down later for a few minutes.' She smiled at them both. 'Isn't it wonderful to have him back, Dad?'

'Yes, it is – and he's told me he's not rushing off again this time, so you can feed him up a bit and have some time together.'

'Yes. It is such a relief,' Beth said. 'I'll get supper now – it's just chops, mash and veg this evening. I didn't have time to make a pie. I'll do that tomorrow.'

'I shan't want much,' Jack warned. 'I haven't got my appetite back yet – some soup would probably be enough for me.'

'Nonsense!' his father said. 'You'll eat proper food in this house, Jack. I remember you being difficult to feed when you were just a little lad, but your mother made you sit at the table until you ate your dinner.'

'Jack can have just a small meal if he wants,' Beth said. 'You usually like lamb chops, Jack?'

'I still like them but not too much yet,' he said with a smile. 'I'll eat what I can, love.'

Fred retired behind his newspaper, but not before Beth noticed the anxiety in his eyes. She didn't comment and got on with dishing up their meal, giving her husband less than she would eat herself and he ate about half of it. Fred made no comment, but after Jack went up to bed, Beth asked him what was going on.

'What has Jack told you that I don't know?' she said. 'Don't try to lie, Fred. I know you – and I know you're upset...'

'He is so tired and exhausted,' Fred replied. 'That's all it is, love. He needs a lot of love and care and I know that's what he'll get from you – but we have to make him eat and try to get well. His mother was ill, but she thought she was getting better – until the doctor told her she probably wouldn't live much longer and then she went downhill rapidly, wouldn't try to eat or bother about anything. I lost her because she gave up. I won't let it happen to my son.'

'What did the doctors tell Jack?'

'That he may not live to be as old as I am,' Fred replied with a sombre look. 'He didn't tell you, but I think you have the right to know – because we can't let him sink into himself and slip away as his mother did.'

Beth nodded, smothering the cry that rose to her lips. She'd seen Jack's weariness for herself and known he was hiding something. 'I don't know why your wife died,' she said softly. 'It was very sad and I can see it has haunted you over the years – but Jack isn't his mother. He already has plans for the future. Besides, we'll make him well – you, the boys and me. We'll make him happy, Fred, and we'll make sure he does whatever is right for him.' She would seek the advice of other doctors and talk to Sally, who always knew how to get things done.

'I know you'll look after him.' Fred looked uncomfortable. 'You won't tell him I said anything?'

'Of course not. If he wants to tell me, he will,' she said. 'But I know Jack and he won't give up now. He didn't give up when the Titanic sank and he won't now. He'll fight and together we'll make sure he wins. After all he has been through, he is bound to get down in the dumps at times, but we'll bring his smile back and we'll give him something to live for.' She hesitated, then, 'I know I wasn't there, but perhaps your wife didn't just give up, perhaps the doctor was right and she just couldn't hang on any longer.'

Fred shook his head sadly. 'Her decline was sudden and swift. I've always blamed that doctor and it has made me wary of marrying again – it hurts to lose those you care for, Beth.'

'Yes, it does,' Beth agreed and then hugged him. 'But sometimes you have to trust in the future, Fred. You have to believe that you can change things for the better – that it is worth striving for. Otherwise, we'd all give up.' She drew back and smiled at him. 'You'll see, Dad. We'll make Jack better. I promise...'

Inside, Beth's heart might ache and maybe she wasn't quite as brave or confident as she sounded, but she knew Fred needed her to be strong. Jack and the boys needed that too and so she would be. Whatever life threw at her, she would take it and carry on smiling for their sakes.

26

Kathy finished making the treacle tarts. Hilda had asked her to make individual tarts rather than the large one she would make for her family at home.

'We make them a bit fancy like,' she said. 'It's worth the extra trouble when I've got a nice big tin of golden syrup, Kathy. Just make your filling in the normal way with the breadcrumbs and simply measure equal amounts on to each pastry case. It isn't often we can get walnuts these days, but when we can, I'd pop one on top – the men like that, I find.'

'I like cooking with you,' Kathy replied. 'You make things sound easy.'

'Well, they are if you use your head,' her mentor said. 'You won't need the more complicated knowledge here, but if you study those books I lent you, it will help you move up the ladder in future.'

'You mean – cook for a posh hotel?' Kathy asked, frowning a little. 'Some of those recipes use expensive foods. I'd never be able to afford the ingredients to practice.'

'I was thinking you could get a job as a cook in service one day if you wanted – and a good household will expect something a bit fancy now and then.'

'I don't think I'd want to do that,' Kathy replied. She thought it was a good job working for Harpers – but it would be even better if she could be promoted to the fancy restaurant she'd heard Marion mention. It wasn't certain but Mrs Bailey had told Marion that she thought Mr Harper might open a restaurant after the war. Kathy was learning lots of little tricks from Hilda and she thought in a year or two she might be ready to move on if the chance came.

* * *

'How did you get on today, Kathy?' Sarah asked when she got home that evening. It was a pleasant summer evening. 'Are you enjoying the work?'

'Yes, I am,' Kathy replied, smiling as she bent down to lift Sarah's little boy up for a kiss. 'I am learning a lot. Hilda was nice to let me have those recipe books of hers – but I can't practice at home, because everything is so expensive.'

'Some of the dishes would be,' Sarah agreed, 'but I don't see why we shouldn't have some of them now and then. If I buy the ingredients, you can cook them for us on a Sunday.'

'You're so generous,' Kathy exclaimed and, putting the child down, she kissed her sister-in-law. 'But are you certain you can afford it?'

'I'm getting more and more commissions for my sewing,' Sarah told her. 'Besides, I had a surprise this morning. My father sent a registered envelope with twenty pounds inside!'

'How exciting,' Kathy exclaimed. 'Has he said how sorry he is for throwing you out?'

'Well, he didn't exactly throw me out,' Sarah corrected, 'but he refused to accept my marriage or the fact that I was with child and when Marion went to ask if there was a letter for me, he was awful to her. In answer to your question, he didn't enclose a note, just the money. I only know it came from him, because he had to write his name and address on the back.'

'I've never seen a registered letter...' Kathy examined the thick envelope and nodded. Sarah's father had put his name on the back. 'Will you go and see him now?'

'No, I don't think so. Not yet. I am grateful for the money, of course, but he doesn't want to see me or he would have written.'

'Then why did he send the money?'

'Because it was owed to me, I suppose. I have a small income from my mother. My father prevented me from having it for a while – and I think this is what was withheld.'

'Yes, but the fact that he sent it must mean something?'

'Perhaps,' Sarah agreed. 'However, unless he writes and says he accepts my marriage to Dan, I shan't visit him. Would you wish to visit your father if—' She stopped and looked upset. 'You suffered at your father's hands I know. Mine only shouted at me.'

'Father was a bully, Kathy said, feeling the coldness at her nape she always felt when thinking of the man she'd learned to fear. 'He killed my mother and I'm glad he is dead – but if he hadn't hurt Ma, I think I would have visited him, even in prison. It upset me the way he died there – and yet I'll never forgive him for what happened...' she glanced round. 'Where is Marion?

'She went next door to speak to her mother-in-law. Now if my father was more like Mr Jackson, I'd visit him tomorrow.'

Marion came in then and their conversation ceased. Kathy helped serve the simple dish of macaroni cheese with cabbage they had for their supper. It was filling and tasty and something that they'd never had until Sarah came to live with them.

'Did any letters come today?' Marion asked as they all sat down at the table to eat.

'No, none,' Sarah sighed. 'I had several from Dan last month but none at all since then.'

'And I haven't heard from Reggie either,' Marion said. She looked at Kathy. 'You're growing up now – any boyfriends yet?'

'Not for me,' Kathy replied. 'I don't think I'll ever want to marry – unless I meet a famous chef who wants to share his life and his restaurant with me.' She giggled as she saw Marion's face. 'Well, why not? If I do decide to marry, I want to get something out of it – a good income and a better life.'

'What about love?' Marion asked and Sarah nodded. 'Don't you think that important?'

'I'm not sure I believe in it.'

'Well, we do,' Sarah told her firmly. 'I know you had a bad example in your parents' marriage, Kathy, but look at Dan and me – don't you think we're happy?'

'Yes, I do,' Kathy agreed. 'But Dan is special and there aren't many like him... besides, so many men have been killed out there I probably shan't get the chance. I think a lot of this generation will either be war widows or spinsters...'

It was a sobering thought and everyone lapsed into silence as they reflected on the truth of Kathy's words.

27

'I shall miss you once you've moved,' Beth told Rachel and gave her a hug when she visited to say her goodbyes. It had taken longer to get the house right than she'd expected but now it was ready for her and she was going down that weekend. 'We've been friends for a long time now.'

'Yes, we have,' Rachel agreed, smiling as she hugged her back. 'William says I must keep my apartment and then I can visit sometimes. I think it is an extravagance, but he insists on paying the expenses. If I find the solitude of the countryside too much, I can escape to London for a week or two.' She smothered a sigh. 'I am going to miss my friends and working at Harpers, though it means I'll have more time for Lizzie and I'm looking forward to making a new life for us all.'

'They will miss you in the department,' Beth looked thoughtful. 'Have they found anyone to take your place yet?'

'Yes, a very pleasant young woman named Deborah Carter,' Rachel replied. 'She has been working with me for a week now, just to learn our ways – but she has had quite a bit of experience and worked at another store in the West End for five years.'

'Why did she change her job?' Beth asked and frowned. It seemed strange that the young woman should move from the West End to Oxford Street.

'Her mother is unwell and Debbie – as she likes to be called by friends – wanted to be closer. Her mother only lives a short distance from Harpers and she has moved in with her so that she can look after her.'

'I see.' Beth's frown cleared. 'I'll pop in and take a look at her one day.'

'I am sure you will like her,' Rachel said. 'She is more your age than mine and Sally is delighted with her. She thinks she is lucky to get her.'

'How is Sally?' Beth asked. 'I haven't seen her for a week or two – not since Jack got home. I invited her to come to lunch with Ben, but she wasn't too well so they put it off for another time – though Ben came round to talk to Jack and they're full of plans for the future.'

'I believe Sally caught a nasty chill when they were up north visiting Jenni the other week,' Rachel said. 'She had to spend a few days in bed on their return – and you know how much Sally likes that... She got herself up for Jenni Harper's wedding, but then had to go to bed straight after. Mrs Alexander was a bit upset over that... she brought some cake in for the staff and asked me to let her know if Sally needed anything.'

'She never stays in bed unless she feels really ill,' Beth said, looking anxious. 'Is she all right now?'

'Mr Stockbridge said that she was on the mend but working at home for a while,' Rachel replied. 'I dare say Ben insisted. After all, it isn't long since Sadie died of what they thought was a chill.'

'Yes.' Beth's forehead creased. 'That is why I am worried. Marco's wife seemed a perfectly healthy woman to me and she died so quickly. I was reading something in the paper the other day –

they think there's some nasty illness going round various countries that they're calling Spanish flu now.'

'Yes. I believe it has killed a lot of people there and other places too; it has caused some problems with the armed forces too. Do you think it was what Sadie died of?'

'I don't know – but it could well have been and it worries me that Sally might have caught it.' Beth was anxious.

'Well, she is certainly on the mend because her secretary told me that she phoned her and asked her to take her some accounts and other paperwork to the house.'

Beth smiled her relief. 'That sounds like our Sally.'

'Yes, she never gives in.' Rachel paused, then, 'I've written to Maggie to tell her of my decision to leave Harpers, but I haven't heard anything back, which is unusual. She normally writes most weeks, but I haven't heard for a while now – you don't think she is ill?'

'I do hope not,' Beth said, anxious again. 'That is the trouble when people move away... you will keep in touch, Rachel? I don't want our friendship to end just because you live in the country.'

'No, of course it won't,' Rachel said. 'I'll write often and I'll visit when I feel able to leave William.' She glanced at the little watch pinned to her smart dress. 'And now I must go. Hazel and I are taking Lizzie to the toy shop and then for tea. It isn't her birthday but it may be the last chance we get for a while.'

28

'So you've still heard nothing from Mick either?' Sally asked when she visited her friend, Marlene. 'This summer seems to have flown. I know I've been busy but time just rushes by for me.' She frowned. 'I am really worried about Mick now. It isn't like him not to keep in touch. I do hope he is all right.'

'I think I would have been contacted if he'd been killed or was wounded,' Marlene said but looked concerned. 'I expect he's just too busy or too damned tired to write letters.'

'Yes, you are probably right,' Sally agreed thoughtfully. 'The men must all be very tired.'

The two women were silent for a moment, thinking of the hardship and suffering the men had been through these past years and then Marlene smiled at her. 'And how are your children?' she asked, clearly wanting to change to a less painful subject.

'Gorgeous,' Sally said. 'Jenny had a birthday not too long ago and she was given lots of presents – from friends and family, and some of the salesmen who've seen her at Harpers – but all she wants is a dog.'

Marlene laughed. 'Children are funny that way, but will you let her have one when you move? You are going to move into that lovely house you told me about, aren't you?'

'Yes, I think so,' Sally said. 'It is what Ben wants and it will be better for the children.' She smiled. 'Now tell me about you, Marlene – are you managing?'

'Yes, thank you, Sally. I miss Mick, because he was always around and making me laugh – but otherwise, I'm fine.'

'Yes,' Sally nodded. 'Mick was a good friend to both of us. We must hope that he comes home and soon.'

Sally was thoughtful as she took a taxi home later that morning. It was a lovely day, warm and sunny. She had left Marlene feeling a little sad, but the warmth of the sun made her feel better. Something told her that Mick was alive; he was just too busy to write – and that reminded her that she wanted to write a nice long letter to her mother. Sally didn't see her mother as often as she'd like, but the fact that she was alive and well was enough to bring a smile to her face. She would try to get down to visit her soon and take the children.

* * *

Sitting on the sofa at home a few days later, Sally read the latest letter from her mother with a frown. Her husband was ill with what she feared might be this terrible flu. She told Sally she must not come until he recovered. Sally's mother had been up to London twice since last Christmas and Sally had promised she would go down for a day or two soon and she'd planned a visit before the end of the month, but that would need to be postponed for a while.

'Why the sigh?' Ben asked, looking up from his newspaper. 'Something bothering you? The letter from your mother – nothing wrong is there?'

'I was just thinking I ought to try to source some fresh suppliers,' Sally said. 'We could do with something new and exciting to brighten the shelves in the hats and accessories department.'

'I dare say the stock could do with a boost in a lot of departments, Sally,' her husband said. 'Don't let it worry you. You've done wonderfully to keep us going all this time – some stores have not been as lucky, or as well run, and have closed their doors for the duration.'

'Yes, I know.' Sally was subdued, uncertain, worried over her mother's news but not wanting to tell him. 'I dare say we'll manage. Is there anything interesting in the papers?'

'There's an article about why the police went on strike and what effect it has had on their union – many thousands more police are joining it apparently, despite the huge debate going on about whether they should be allowed to strike.'

The strike, which had happened at the end of August, hadn't lasted long, because their march to Whitehall to demand better wages and the reinstatement of one of their men, whom they believed unfairly dismissed, had paid off. The Government had caved in, giving way to the angry police officers. Although most people agreed that the police were underpaid and had been for a long time, the issue of whether they should strike or not caused heated discussion.

'Of course they should if they've been unfairly treated,' Sally said, though she knew Ben didn't altogether agree. He thought the police force should put duty first and negotiate while continuing to work. 'But I meant – anything important happening with the war or the Spanish flu?'

'Seventy-nine men died when *HMS Glatton* caught fire and was scuttled in Dover Harbour,' Ben said and folded his paper. 'It was a terrible disaster, Sally. That ship had never gone into action and they had to sink it to prevent an explosion... but too many were killed.' He looked at his wife. 'What is on your mind, darling? It isn't just Harpers? Or the war? You must not worry. I can raise a bank loan if I have to...'

'Yes, I know.' She smiled at him, realising that she had to confess her true problem. 'I do think about Harpers and I want to do my best for the store – but it isn't business. Mum's husband isn't too well again and that means she can't leave him to come up to town and I can't visit.'

'Oh, I see,' Ben frowned. 'He's not well enough to travel, I suppose—' He hesitated. 'Why don't you go down for a couple of days? I can look after the children... with Mrs Hills' help.'

'Yes, I know, but Mum said not to,' Sally shook her head. 'I was wondering what she would do if...'

'If he gets worse?' Ben nodded. 'That would be very sad, Sally. They haven't had long together. His accident was terrible, but I thought the hospital said he was getting better?' Ben's gaze narrowed. 'You're not thinking it might be Spanish flu?' The pandemic had now been officially named after causing terrible havoc amongst the troops and spreading to many countries, leaving many dead in its wake.

'There have been more cases of it again. I thought it was almost over,' Sally said and her forehead creased with worry. 'It has killed a lot of people, Ben... and Mum thinks it may be that.'

'That is serious, Sally.'

'If he dies it will devastate her.'

'There have been more deaths in other countries than here,' Ben replied with a frown. 'I think it has been bad amongst the American troops and it is a killer... If you think your step father's illness may be Spanish flu, you can't go, Sally.'

Sally nodded. 'Yes, I know, Ben. I hate to think of her coping alone – that is just what I was thinking. I feel guilty if she needs help – but I do have the children to think of as well as us and Harpers.'

'I know it must hurt you,' Ben told her. He got up to place a hand on her shoulder and then bent to kiss her. 'For so many years you never knew your mother and to lose her or see her suffer loss would be terrible – but in this case I am going to insist. You and our children come first.'

'Yes, I know – and they have a good hospital there,' Sally said and sighed. 'I can hear Jenny calling. I'd better go and see what she needs.'

'And I have a meeting this morning,' Ben said and touched her hand as she got up to see to her daughter. 'Try not to worry, Sally, you couldn't do much if you went to your mother. Your stepfather will recover or he won't – exposing yourself to this wicked sickness won't help him or your mother. I doubt if she'd want you to...'

'No, she wouldn't,' Sally forced a smile. 'She told me not to go down until he is over this – whatever it is.'

Sally went through to the bedroom. She could hear Ben getting ready for his meeting and fought to bring her thoughts back to her children, who needed attention and were ready for a game before getting dressed. The Spanish flu pandemic had been a terrible thing, spreading amongst the troops and in other countries and causing serious illness and many deaths. So far, Sally, her family, friends and staff had not been severely affected – apart from Sadie's sudden and sad death. They hadn't been sure at the beginning of the year but now she and Ben thought it must have been the flu and although Marco had accepted it as an act of nature, she knew he was still suffering from the tragedy of it.

Supposing her stepfather died of it? What would Sally's mother do then? It made her eyes sting with tears, but she blinked them away as she picked Jenny up. Ben was right, there was nothing she could do...

* * *

Mrs Hills answered the door when the bell rang. Sally's youngest was sleeping after a feed and Jenny was playing with her doll's house as a man was shown into the room. She had been checking a stock list and looked up in surprise as Marco entered.

'I had hoped to see Ben,' he said and hesitated. 'I just wanted to tell you that I shall be returning to work next week, Mrs Harper. I've been given the all clear as far as my physical health is concerned and I've formally been discharged from the Army so there's nothing to stop me.'

'That is good news for us,' she told him. 'The windows need your special touch, Marco, but are you sure you feel up to it?'

'Yes – I think it is the only way,' he replied and gave her a smile that was a faint echo of his former bright smile. 'Life goes on – and I need to for Pierre's sake. I have come to an arrangement with my son's grandmother. She is to care for him during the day while I work and I shall collect him in the evening.'

'Oh, I am so pleased,' Sally said. 'I believe you were worried about what to do for the best?'

'You know that he isn't mine?' Marco's eyes met hers and she nodded. 'I thought Sadie had told you. She liked you and felt able to tell you things – and she mentioned how kind you were to her.'

'I did very little, Marco. I wish I could have done more. I never even knew she was ill.'

'It was too sudden and swift,' he said regretfully. 'But Ben told me about the department you set up. Sadie would have loved that – and you did it for her sake.'

'Sadie was a part of it,' Sally replied, 'but there were other reasons – quite a few of Harpers' girls will benefit.'

'Yes.' Marco's smile was a little brighter. 'I am sure they will – and it is a credit to you, Sally Harper. I'm sorry I haven't felt able to come back until now.'

'We just want you back, whenever you can manage it,' Sally told him. 'We're your friends, Marco, not just your employers.'

'I know – and I'll never be able to repay what you've both done for me.'

'You don't need to,' she said and looked at him. 'We care about our friends. Now, will you have coffee with me?' She indicated her pile of books and papers. 'I think I deserve a break.'

'Perhaps soon Harpers will be back to its old glory,' Marco said. 'I think you deserve your coffee and more – but I shall not stay. I have a few things to set in order. I need to make a new will that takes care of Pierre and I have an appointment with my solicitor. With this Spanish flu, we all need to set our affairs in order.'

'Yes, we do,' Sally agreed. 'No one is safe until it is over.'

She went to the door with him. Marco's parting remarks had brought back the anxiety over her mother. If her stepfather had this horrid sickness he could pass it on to his nurse and... Sally shook her head. There was no point in torturing herself over it. She had no choice but to do as Ben asked. Sally had to think of her children first, even though she would be devastated if anything happened to her mother. All the years of not knowing if she was alive and then the happiness of discovery – it would be awful if she lost her now and couldn't even go to see her...

29

Rachel looked round her new home and drew in her breath. She hadn't known what to expect and had been a little anxious in case the house was overpowering or too stately to feel like home, but it was beautiful – especially the small parlour that William had had done just for her. It was decorated in shades of rose and cream with touches of dark crimson, and so very much what she liked that tears came to her eyes as she glanced at him.

'It is so beautiful, William,' she said to her husband. 'How did you know what I feel comfortable with – these colours and the lovely furniture. The whole house is nice – but this is special...'

'I guessed what colours you like – you so often choose them,' he said and smiled at her, visibly relaxing as he saw her pleasure. 'I want you to be happy here, Rachel. I do appreciate what you're giving up for my sake, my dear. I know you may not like this style of living – so I tried to make it comfortable for you.'

'I think I shall be happy here with my sewing and my books – and we shall spend more time together in future, William. We've had so little time for ourselves since we married. You had to go away to fight and then you were ill.'

'And you were busy at Harpers. I think you will miss that very much, Rachel.' His gaze was grave, questioning.

'Yes, perhaps, at first,' she agreed, 'but I used to be content at home. I had to work to support myself, William – now I don't. I have a home, a kind and loving husband and Lizzie – and Hazel, of course. She will undoubtedly visit us here most days.'

'Of course she must,' he agreed. 'She is your friend, Rachel, and I want you to make friends and have a good life. While my mother lived, you would not have enjoyed being here, but now you are mistress of your own home and may do as you please.'

'As *we* please, William,' she said and looked at him earnestly. 'You do not dislike Lizzie being with us I hope?'

'She is a delightful little thing,' he told her and smiled. 'Had I been there when you found her I should no doubt have done exactly as you did, my love. I should have liked children, but I doubt it will happen now – neither of us is very young and my health is not marvellous, so we shall thank God for the gift of our daughter and make the most of what life has to offer. She will go to the village school and make friends – and the house will ring with their laughter. Isn't that what you hope?'

'Yes,' Rachel agreed and her doubts began to fade. She'd been so anxious about the move to the country, wondering what she would do with herself, but now she understood that she would simply live. There was a beautiful garden to tend, a house to run and meals to supervise, as well as Lizzie and the friends she and William would make and entertain. 'I think we shall both enjoy her growing up, William. As for Harpers, well, it was my job and I enjoyed it – but friends are the most important and I shall keep in touch with them all.'

'You must visit them sometimes, I insist,' he told her with the warm smile that had won her at the start of their friendship – and, above all else, they were friends. Rachel realised how much she'd missed him. They'd spent so much time apart that she'd almost forgotten how much she enjoyed his company, but now she remembered and happiness flooded through her. She was lucky. For her the worst of the war was over. She could only pray that it would end soon so that everyone could be happy. The sooner victory bells rang all over the country, the better!

It wouldn't be just yet. Many men were still fighting and dying. There were still shortages and hardships to be born, but in this quiet part of the Sussex countryside, Rachel knew a kind of victory. Life had been hard for many years. She'd lost her first husband and grieved for him, finding some solace in her work at Harpers and her friends. Then she'd remarried again and since then life had been like a storm that blew her this way and that, giving her no rest or peace, but here in this lovely house she would find both. More, she would find happiness with her husband and child and her friends.

'Why don't you ring for tea?' William asked her. 'Then you might like to go up and rest for a while before dinner?'

Rachel nodded. It felt strange to just ring for tea when she was used to preparing it herself, but she would become accustomed to it in time. 'Yes, I should like a cup of tea,' she agreed. 'Afterwards, I think I shall write some letters and perhaps take a walk in the gardens before I change.'

'Perhaps I'll take a walk with you,' he said. 'There are some particularly fine roses I should like to show you.'

'Minnie and Mr Stockbridge love roses,' Rachel said. 'Would you mind if I asked them to come and stay for a few days? Minnie was a little upset that I was moving and I'd like her to see the house and garden – they could come for a long weekend.'

'They can visit for as long as you wish and as often,' he assured her. 'It is your home, my love, and you must run it as you please – and your friends are always welcome.'

Rachel nodded and rang the bell for tea. Minnie would love it here. She and her husband often spoke of retiring to a cottage in the country one day so he could grow more roses, though it would not be for a few years yet when he retired from Harpers. Perhaps when they did, they might choose to live nearby... the thought made her smile. She would write to her friends in Harpers as soon as she had time and she might ask William if she could have some photographs of the house and garden to send to them. If they saw the wonderful tranquil gardens and this room, they would be easier in their minds – and she would ask Minnie and Mr Stockbridge to stay for a few days when he could be spared from his work at Harpers, Maggie, too, if she could spare the time from her busy life.

Maggie was seated at a table in the window of the cottage she'd rented for Becky's sake. Now that the child was born and Becky was much stronger, it was time to think of the future. Decisions had to be made, because Colin had asked Maggie when she was coming home and she knew his patience was wearing thin. It was time for her to think of her own life – but Becky was still visiting David Morgan in the hospital every day and had said nothing of the future. What was she hoping to do now? She hadn't told her father, but she would have to soon if she was determined to keep her child.

Pushing Becky's problems aside for the moment, Maggie looked down at the letter she was writing. She had neglected her other friends of late, because even though Colin had brought her all her letters, it was difficult to reply without revealing where she was – and inadvertently Becky's secret. However, she could delay it no longer and was writing to Rachel now. She looked down at what she had written so far:

My dearest Rachel…

Maggie sat with pen in hand, wondering how best to explain why she'd been so long in answering her letters. Bending her head to her task, she went on:

I am so sorry I have not written for a while, but I have been staying with a friend and did not receive your letters immediately. Your news is exciting and I am sure you will be happy in the country with William. It is so wonderful that he is better again. I know you must have feared you would lose him when he was so ill and it is surely a huge relief to have him safely home with you – and you have your darling little Lizzie too. It is nice that Hazel has chosen to move down there to be close to you and will live in a cottage that belongs to your husband. It means you can look after her, too, and she can continue to be Lizzie's granny.

I loved Lizzie when we met while I was staying in London earlier this summer. Colin and I intend to adopt a child fairly soon now and we may take in more as time goes on. Colin's father was doubtful about the idea but has come round to it now and we shall be returning to his home shortly for a visit. I look forward to it and consider myself lucky to have Colin and such a wonderful home. Sometimes, I have to pinch myself to make certain it isn't a dream – and the stress and pain of those years in France has all but melted away. I wish you good fortune in your new home and pray that you will be happy there, and I think you must be. I should love to visit you one day, when you've settled and if you would like me to come...

I must close now. I will write again when we are at home.

Love from Maggie xxx

It was shorter than her normal letters, but they were usually filled with what she had been doing and she could not reveal Becky's secret, even to Rachel. That was for Becky herself to decide and she would do it in her own way and in her own time. Once or twice, Maggie had tried to raise the subject, but Becky simply dismissed it with a little shake of her head, because she did not wish to face it – but it had to be faced. The man she believed to be her lover had shown no sign of recovering his memory. It was an awkward situation and Maggie had no idea how to solve it.

She'd spoken to Colin about it when he'd visited and brought Maggie's letters to her. There had been one for Becky, too, which she'd accepted with a pale face and scared eyes.

'It is from my father. He thinks we're staying at your house,' she'd whispered after reading a few lines. 'He wants me to go home...'

Maggie shook her head. The time was fast approaching when Becky must decide what to do.

Maggie looked up from her letters as Becky entered the small parlour. 'May I talk to you?' she asked in a small voice. 'If you're too busy—'

'I am only writing a letter to my friend. What do you want to talk about, Becky?'

'I think I should speak to David tomorrow and ask him what he feels about things... remind him that it is his child but we aren't married – and I need to know if he will marry me. Do you agree?'

'I think you have to,' Maggie agreed. 'If you don't, this could go on for a long time. Besides, he promised you marriage – and he should honour it...'

'Yes,' Becky blinked hard. 'I was afraid to tell him, Maggie – but they are saying he will be allowed to leave hospital soon now, and I must tell him or tell my father the truth about my child.'

'It is what you truly want – to marry David?' Maggie questioned and Becky nodded. 'And what if he feels unable to because he can't remember who he is?'

'Then I have to tell my father and Minnie—' Becky gulped back her tears. 'They will be ashamed of me – my father may cast me off, but I should give him the chance to know his grandchild.'

'Yes, you should,' Maggie hesitated, then, 'I have spoken to Colin about this and he said if all else fails and you have nowhere to go, we can find you a home on the estate. Colin says you can help to keep the accounts for the estate, which would give you a living.'

Becky's eyes filled with tears. 'You are both so kind, but I couldn't be a burden to you for the rest of my life.'

'You wouldn't be – and I know you're good with office work. In time, you may fall in love again,' Maggie told her and saw the tears well over. 'Don't cry, Becky – perhaps it will be all right. If David accepts his responsibility and asks you to marry him.' She looked at the younger girl uncertainly. 'You are certain this is what you want?'

Becky didn't hesitate. 'I love him, Maggie – talking to him in the hospital, just being with him, makes me feel calm and happy. Sometimes he says things that make me laugh... just like he did before. I am certain it is David and I love him... I love the man with the scarred face. And the redness is fading one side...'

Maggie smiled at her. 'Then make sure to tell him that you love him as he is,' she said. 'Let him see that he is loved and wanted despite the scars – and then he will know what a lovely girl you really are.'

'Yes, I shall,' Becky said and her tears had gone. 'I have to take my chances and I shall this afternoon.'

31

Becky's stomach was churning as she entered the ward that afternoon. She was pleased that it was a sunny day after several days' rain and the other patients had been wheeled outside to enjoy what might be almost the last warm day of a lovely autumn approached fast, leaving them privacy for what must be said. A smile lit David's eyes as he saw her.

'Becky,' he said eagerly and held out his hands to her. 'I hoped you might come this afternoon. Did you bring our daughter?'

'Maggie is in the garden with her—' Becky faltered. 'I wanted to talk to you about something...'

'And I you,' he replied. 'You go first.' She noticed that he was wary, anxious.

'You know that we're not married, even though the nurses think we are, but they wouldn't have let me see you if they'd known the truth,' she said the words hurriedly. 'The child is yours, David. You were the only one ever. You were going away and we went to your home in London—'

'Where I took advantage of your innocence?' he said softly. 'I did – didn't I, Becky? It was so wrong of me because you were so young and I had not even spoken to your father, had I?'

She stared at him in shock as his words made her realise what he wanted to tell her. 'You've recovered your memory, haven't you?'

'Yes, a little...' His hands held hers tightly. 'And that is because of you – because of all your visits. The doctors may think it is their treatment, but it was thinking about you that brought things back. I have thought for a while that I loved you but the idea of you being my wife seemed strange and wrong somehow.'

'You don't wish me to be your wife...' she turned so that he should not see the fear and pain in her eyes. 'You owe me nothing. I was willing...'

'Becky my love...' David held tightly to her hands, refusing to let go as she tugged. 'If you will marry me, I shall be the happiest man alive – but are you sure you can bear it as I am now?'

Becky's gaze moved swiftly to his and she smiled. 'How can you doubt it? I love you so much, my dearest David. I was wretched when I thought you dead. It is a miracle to me that you are here, alive.'

'Then we shall marry,' he said and smiled. 'In two weeks, I shall leave here and then I shall visit your father and tell him everything... Yes, he must be told, Becky. It is the right and proper thing to do and I shall take the force of his anger. He may decide whether he wishes to see us married or not.' His hands held hers even tighter as she trembled. 'In the meantime, you will go down to my cousin's home – and I shall ask their permission to be married from there. I do have my home in London, though I remember nothing of it – but perhaps we shall live in a small house in the country so that you might be near your friend. Maggie has been wonderful to you and I want to thank her, but the rest is your decision.'

Tears of happiness and relief trickled down her cheeks. It was

what she'd prayed for and longed for – and now it seemed that she
had a chance of happiness at last. As for where they would live,
Becky did not mind. She would let David decide once they were
married.

* * *

David watched her leave, leaning back against the pillows and
closing his eyes. He still couldn't remember much, but his distant
cousin had written to him, inviting him to stay, and Colin Morgan
had visited him in the hospital and told him bluntly that it was
his duty to marry Becky Stockbridge. Vague memories had
returned then – something to do with the watch that had apparently been his mother's. Something bothered him about it, but he
didn't know what – and it was comforting to know that he had a
home to go to in the country. Colin had told him there was a job
helping to manage the estate and David thought that sounded
good. Returning to the life he'd known before wasn't truly an
option. His scars were too disfiguring and he simply couldn't find
the courage to face life alone. He would rather hide away here in
the hospital or some home for men like him. Besides, if he'd once
known a lot about being a doctor, he'd forgotten it now. None of
that life had returned – only the watch and what Colin Morgan
had told him about his taking Becky to his home and seducing
her.

Something about that didn't fit. David felt uncomfortable with
the idea – would he truly have done that? What sort of a man was
he? He did not think he was the kind to seduce a young and innocent girl, but if he had, he must have loved her a great deal and
been desperate to make love to her before he was sent to war.

'I can't comment on your private life, but I assume you loved the
girl,' Colin had said, eyes cool and disdainful. 'Therefore, it should

be no hardship to make her your wife. She is a decent girl – and we couldn't offer you a home or a job if you abandoned her to her fate.'

'If it is my child, then of course I'll marry her.' David had accepted it without a struggle. He'd felt something for her from the first and it had grown over the time she'd been visiting. It was just a pity that he had no real memory of their love – though there was something to do with a girl at the back of his mind, if only he could remember.

Colin had spoken again. 'Miss Stockbridge is a decent girl, a friend of my wife, and it's your fault that she has had to lie and hide her condition from her family. Besides, it is the decent thing to do.'

'Yes, I agree.' David did agree. It was what he would have done even if his distant cousin's son hadn't made such a point of it. 'I have been thinking of it and will do so as soon as I am able to leave this hospital...' He'd seen a look of approval and acceptance in Colin's eyes.

'We need someone to care for the estate – and there is a good house that goes with the job,' Colin had told him. 'My father is ill and I don't want to leave all the work to him – but I don't want to be tied there all the time either. I have other things I'd prefer to do and I'd like to live in London for much of the year, though I would visit regularly.' *To check up on you.* The words were implied, if not spoken, and David had been angry inside, his pride touched, though he hadn't let it show.

'I can't give you my answer now,' David had told him, torn between what was an easy option for him and hurt feelings. 'It depends on several factors. I must speak to Becky first – see what she wants from life.'

'Of course. I am not asking for a commitment – it is merely an offer of help if you care to take it... and I would prefer that you told no one of our conversation.'

'As you wish,' David had agreed. He was uncertain, feeling

offended and yet relieved, because he'd lain in this hospital bed so many hours and tried in vain to see a future for himself and now it could all be his for the taking. The only thing he had to do was marry a girl he admired but couldn't truly remember. He certainly remembered something about a country estate and a family quarrel way back in the past, also something about a girl, but he couldn't recall the details.

Now he had spoken to Becky, letting her believe he remembered more than he did – but his feelings for her were not false. He did care for her – and even if the child was not his, he might have offered her marriage.

That thought made David smile. Because it told him that he was not the sort of man Colin Morgan clearly thought him. He could live with his distant relation's disdain as long as he knew the truth for himself. Whoever he was and no matter what he'd done in the past, he was a man of principles.

David would take the new life that had been offered him, but he just wished that he could remember more of how he'd come to make that very pretty young woman pregnant. When Colin had lectured him about his duty, he'd accepted it. Becky might have refused had she known what his relation had said about him marrying her; she might have felt he'd been forced into it and he hadn't, so rather than hurt her feelings, he'd let her believe he'd remembered certain things.

Marriage to a lovely, sweet and gentle young woman like Becky would be no hardship and he was already halfway to being in love with her – and genuinely grateful for her acceptance of him. After all, what else did he have waiting for him? Scarred both physically and mentally, he would have led a lonely and difficult life. Now he had a ready-made family, a lovely wife, a child and a home, to say nothing of a job for as long as he wished.

Becky was already convinced he was David Morgan and so were

his distant cousins, so why should he struggle to prove them wrong when it was so much easier to be who they all wanted him to be? Perhaps he was, but something inside his head made him think there was a deeper mystery.

* * *

'It is like a miracle,' Maggie said. 'For David to remember, just when you'd decided to ask him about the future.'

'He doesn't remember all of it,' Becky said, a slight frown on her face. 'But he remembers that he loved me – and he is going to visit my father, to take all the blame on himself.'

'He is to blame,' Maggie said. 'You were so young and vulnerable, Becky. He should have known better – but these things happen, and if you're happy, I shan't say anything more. Except that if I were you, I should write to Minnie and tell her.'

'Yes, Minnie has always been kind to me,' Becky agreed. 'I will write and ask her to forgive me – I expect she will be very shocked.'

'Oh, I think you will find that Minnie takes it more calmly than you imagine,' Maggie said. 'I know her well and she is the sweetest, kindest person – and, besides, I think she'd half-guessed before I told her I wanted you to stay with me.'

'You don't think she will tell anyone at Harpers, do you? I shouldn't like them to gossip about me.'

'Minnie isn't a gossip,' Maggie said. 'Don't worry, Becky. It is unlikely that you will see any of them again – and those you do need not know anything except that you've married a war hero and had his child.'

Becky nodded and sighed. 'Harpers seems so far away now. I did like being there but then...' She shook her head. 'No, I shan't think of it. I have a new life now.' For a moment, tears filled her eyes, but she blinked them away. 'Sally Harper was always kind to me, so perhaps I wouldn't mind her knowing...'

'Sally is always kind to her friends and those who work for her,' Maggie said and smiled. 'If your father tells her in confidence, she won't repeat it to anyone.'

32

'I wanted to talk to you,' Marlene said when she was invited into Sally's sitting room that morning in late September. 'I've been so worried about Mick... and no, I still haven't heard from him, have you?'

'I just had that one letter before he left England on his third posting. Naturally, he didn't say where he expected to be sent,' Sally sighed. 'I knew he was upset, because of...' She stopped it was not her place to tell anyone Mick's private business.

'Because of the girl he'd fallen in love with out there in France?' Marlene nodded. 'He told me there was someone – she was a nurse, I think?'

'Yes, she was,' Sally said and relaxed, since Marlene obviously knew about her friend's feelings for Maggie. 'He met her through me. I was worried about her and he delivered a message to her in France – and he kept visiting every so often and believed she felt something for him, but then she married someone else.'

'Heartless...' Marlene shook her head over it, clearly thinking Mick had been let down.

'It wasn't quite like that,' Sally corrected. 'She'd been through a lot and I think she met her husband at a time when she was vulnerable and they just fell in love. I know it upset Mick, but it wasn't done deliberately to give him pain.'

'Well, it did,' Marlene looked angry. 'We've known each other for more than ten years and worked together a lot of that time – and I've never seen him look the way he did when he returned from seeing her. I don't mind telling you I was frightened. I thought he might take his own life he was so wretched.'

Sally looked at her anxiously. 'He wouldn't do anything stupid?'

'If he didn't kill himself that night, I doubt he would,' Marlene said, 'but his job as a tunneller is dangerous and any carelessness, any lack of concern for his own safety...' She left the suggestion unfinished and Sally nodded. During a war and in the field of conflict, men needed to be alert and eager to live to stand a chance of survival.

'I wish I knew where he was – if he is all right...' Sally sighed because Mick was a good friend and they'd been close for a while.

'If I get a letter or even a postcard, I'll let you know.' Marlene frowned, hesitated, then, 'It was something Mick said before he left that last time—' she shook her head. 'He told me that if he didn't come back, I'd be all right and... No, that's not for me to say. I keep worrying over it, Mrs Harper. I think he may not have intended to come back and I know he'd made his will, because he told me his lawyer's name.'

Sally looked at her, feeling cold at the nape of her neck suddenly. 'Don't – please don't,' she begged. Sally had known that her friend had been badly hurt by Maggie's decision to marry Colin Morgan, when he'd believed she might care for him – but so desperate that he didn't want to live? It was a chilling thought and stayed with her long after Marlene had departed.

This terrible war had caused so much death and destruction, so much heartache and pain. Harpers had lost young men and she'd lost friends – please God don't let it be that Mick had died because of a broken heart. Sally believed that Maggie had cared for him, but he hadn't been around when she most needed him – and someone else had…

The thought of Mick's pain haunted Sally, staying with her as she tried to work for the rest of the day. She decided that the following morning she would visit Mick's restaurants and ask if any of the managers had heard from him.

* * *

Two of the managers said that they hadn't heard anything from their owner in more than six months, but the one Sally usually frequented was more forthcoming.

'Yes, Mrs Harper, I have heard something,' he told her when she asked. 'Mr O'Sullivan sent word through his solicitor. I'm to take over the management of all three of his restaurants. He isn't pleased with the returns from the other two so I've been asked to sort them out.'

'That is good, Mr Stephan.' Sally looked at the man and nodded her approval. 'I think they need a good shake-up. I noticed tables uncleared, food dropped on the floor and not cleaned – and the glasses weren't sparkling clean the way Mick likes them.'

He beamed at her. 'I can see you have an eye for things, Mrs Harper. I shall sort them out, don't you worry.'

Mr Stephan was a man of some forty years. He walked with a slight limp, a disability that he'd been born with, which had kept him out of the war. Sally knew that he did firewatching some nights as his contribution to national safety, but as a restaurant manager he was a treasure and Mick was lucky to have him.

'I am so glad Mick has you to take care of things,' she told him.

'I would have done what I could – but you need to be a full-time manager to keep things right.'

'You certainly do,' he agreed with a warm smile. 'Those lazy managers at Mr O'Sullivan's other restaurants will find themselves out of a job if they don't pull their socks up. I know of one or two likely candidates to take their place – and you might like to know that one of them is a woman.'

'Ah, that sounds interesting,' Sally said. 'You must let me meet her. I shall book for lunch next week and you can tell me more of your plans.'

'We shall be delighted to see you as always, Mrs Harper.'

Sally shook hands with him and left, feeling very much better. If Mick had written to his lawyers and given Mr Stephan the power to hire and fire his other managers, then he was still alive and still thinking of his business.

Feeling better about her friend, Sally's thoughts turned to her own life. Everything seemed much brighter and better now that Ben was at home more often. She'd spent many hours alone while he was away on war duties and it was so good to hear his voice when he walked in at night. She had so much to be grateful for.

* * *

'I managed to get a loan from the bank,' Ben told Sally when he came home that evening. 'So I've arranged for the release of Jenni's money – and we shall go ahead with the new restaurant.'

'I'm not quite sure where you intend to fit it in,' Sally said, frowning. 'There are no vacant adjoining properties – unless you intend to use another site altogether?'

'I need to discuss that with Jack,' Ben said, looking thoughtful. 'I know it interferes with what you did, Sally – but I think we may have to move your crèche to the basement and use the whole top floor that side as a restaurant.'

Sally nodded. She could see the logic in that and it was possible the basement could accommodate the department she'd envisioned for taking care of the children and employees who became ill at work. 'Yes, that is one idea,' she agreed. 'But where will you fit the toys then?'

'On the ground floor – and we'll move the lingerie into your old department, Sally, and put the flowers and sweet shop on the middle floor of the end section of Harpers.'

'I think the sweets and chocolate would be better with the restaurant,' she said, giving his ideas more thought. 'I know I said they were better on the ground floor, but they would fit with the restaurant – and I've sometimes thought they don't have a big enough turnover these days to have the whole of the ground floor of that section. I believe the toys and perhaps a book section there – children's books with a place where they can sit and read, or someone can read to them now and then. We might have a reader on Saturdays and perhaps one weekday for very small children, who aren't at school. Their parents can bring them in to listen to stories and perhaps buy books and sweets for them.'

'Books?' Ben looked doubtful. 'I know nothing about books. It isn't something I've ever dealt with – but I suppose we could try it. It will make more work for you, sourcing material – unless you already have?'

'I've thought about it,' Sally said and smiled. 'It's just that these days we need something extra to bring people in, Ben. A lot of families have learned to make do with what they have – and we've had so few toys for them to buy, except the handmade wooden toys I sourced a couple of years back. They sell well, as do jigsaw puzzles – but there aren't a lot of dolls or mechanical toys around just now. I think we might be luckier with books. I can investigate anyway.' He still looked doubtful. 'If you would rather I didn't...?'

'No, of course I agree,' he said and smiled. 'You always have lovely fresh ideas to keep the customers interested, Sally – but it is more work for you, my love.'

'I don't mind.' She laughed. 'You know how much I like to be busy. I was a working girl from the East End when you met me, Ben, and I still am.'

33

'How will you feel about your relation living and working on the estate?' Maggie asked when Colin told her that David had accepted the offer and was preparing to move into the manager's house with Becky once they were married.

'He can't make more mess of it than the last manager we had – and it means we can live in London for much of the time,' Colin said with a smile. 'You've been wonderful living here and taking an interest in the estate – and you can still do that when we come down as we shall every few months, but you'll be able to see your friends in London.'

'Yes.' Maggie looked him in the eyes. 'What if your father decides to leave him the estate? Will it upset you?'

'That's his choice,' Colin replied with a shrug. 'It isn't entailed, so Father can do as he pleases.'

'But it made you so angry when he first spoke of it?'

'He was trying to blackmail me and that did make me very angry,' Colin agreed. 'Yes, it is my home and I do love it. I should be sad if we could no longer visit – but I've realised there are more important things. I found a wonderful house for us in Hampstead.

It has a huge garden and a studio where I can paint. Plenty of bedrooms and a big nursery.' He smiled at her. 'You would be able to shop in Harpers and even help out sometimes if you chose – perhaps for a while at Christmas – and it isn't too far from where Sally and Ben Harper will be living soon.'

She laughed. 'You don't have to convince me, Colin. I'll be happy wherever we live.'

'Yes, you are happy, aren't you?' he said and his look was warm as he studied her. 'You don't regret marrying me – or that you didn't marry the other one? That Irishman?'

'No, I don't regret anything,' she told him. 'I feel sorry that Mick was hurt when I married you – but I love *you*.'

'Good.' He reached out to touch her cheek. 'I may have a surprise for you soon, Maggie my love – but I'll keep that until after Becky's wedding, when we're back in London and thinking of settling in our new home. I haven't bought it yet – I want you to see it and be sure you like it, but I have reserved it, because I am certain you will.'

'It sounds wonderful,' Maggie said and felt a little thrill of excitement. She would never have confessed how much she missed Harpers and working there – but now she would be able to visit as often as she wished.

Perhaps now that Becky's problem was solved, they could think about their own lives again.

* * *

Becky's father may have had some harsh words for David, but when he came down to see her and attend her wedding at the end of September, he just kissed her cheek and told her that he hoped she would be happy.

'Of what has happened, I shall say nothing,' he said in a quiet voice that made her hang her head. 'Your husband-to-be has explained that it was all his fault and – since he has been so heroic in the service of his country and so clearly loves you and wants to put it right – I can have no objection.'

'Thank you, Father,' Becky said meekly. 'May I visit you and Minnie sometimes?'

'Yes, if you wish,' he replied. 'Minnie is longing to see the child, though I know she was hurt that you did not confide in her...' He looked anxious for a moment. 'She has a nasty chill at the moment or she would have come with me. You will not mind if she comes down to see you another time?'

'Of course not, Father,' Becky replied feeling relieved that he had not been angrier with her. 'I am sorry I deceived you and Minnie, but I was so ashamed. Please give her my love and tell her that I hope she is soon better.'

'She has sent you a letter and a present,' Becky's father said and allowed himself a small smile. 'I have given you a string of pearls and a pair of matching earrings that were your mother's – but Minnie has made you something personal.'

Becky thanked him and accepted the gifts gratefully. She had not been sure he would come and her heart lifted as she saw the beautiful silk underwear Minnie had made and embroidered for her. She really did excel as a seamstress and her work always sold well at Harpers. It must have taken many hours for her to make and embroider the nightdresses and petticoats she had made for Becky and it brought tears to her eyes. The material was so soft against her skin and would look wonderful on her once her figure was back to normal.

Maggie had managed to find some beautiful bridal clothes in the chests stored in the linen at her father-in-law's house. It had belonged to a long-ago bride of the family and with her father-in-law's permission, Maggie had had it washed and altered to fit Becky. The dress

was of heavy white silk overlaid with silver embroidery and sewn
with pearls, and after one of the villagers – who had a talent for such
things – had remodelled it to fit Becky, it looked wonderful on her.
Her friend had also given her a blue garter to wear on her stockings
for luck. She had the precious jewels David had given her before he
went to France, but she felt that they were too valuable and had asked
Colin if he could place them in the bank for safekeeping. For her
wedding, she wore a simple gold locket and chain that David had
asked Colin to buy for him to give her as a wedding gift.

'So you have something borrowed and something blue and this
is new,' Maggie presented her with a lovely lace handkerchief on
her wedding morning. 'I think that's all you need, dearest Becky.
David clearly thinks the world of you and his daughter so you
should be happy.'

'Yes, I shall be...' Becky blinked away a few foolish tears. 'I am so
lucky, Maggie. All this is due to you – to your kindness. I can't begin
to thank you.'

'You don't need to thank me,' Maggie replied, smiling at her.
'David is going to be helping to run the estate. Colin and I will
remain here for a few weeks until you're both settled and he's sure
everything is running well – and then we shall go to the house he
has bought in Hampstead. We shall visit several times a year and
keep in touch by letter – and you must visit us in London now and
then. We have several bedrooms so there will always be a place for
you – even when we get our children.'

'Have you heard anything about the adoption?' Becky asked a
little awkwardly. 'You do understand why I couldn't let you have my
little Julie?'

'Of course,' Maggie assured her. 'Don't worry, Becky. I love your
little darling, but I shall not break my heart over her. Colin is
already in touch with the authorities and it looks as if we may have

two children quite soon – a boy and a girl. Their father was killed overseas earlier this year and their mother recently died of the Spanish flu. The boy caught it, too, but is recovering in hospital and his sister is being cared for by her grandmother, but it can only be a temporary arrangement, as she is too old to care for two young children. Jane is six and Billy is almost five.'

'They will be a handful,' Becky said and looked surprised. 'I thought you wanted a baby?'

Maggie smiled dreamily. 'Oh, a baby would have been nice, but these children need a home and we thought we would foster them and see what happens. If they are happy with us, we shall adopt them.' She smiled at Becky as she placed the little crystal coronet on her head and arranged her veil. 'You look beautiful, Becky. No more talk now – it is time we left for the church.'

* * *

Becky looked at her husband and smiled. He looked smart in his grey wedding suit and white shirt with a silk cravat at the neck. She was accustomed to the scars on his face now and hardly saw them, gazing into his eyes that looked more grey than blue.

'I am glad it is over,' David said. 'I feel a little tired, Becky. All those people from the estate that came to wish us well. I hadn't expected it – I thought it was to be a quiet wedding.'

It had been quiet by many standards, with only a handful of guests invited to the wedding breakfast, but the church had been filled with people, all curious about the man who was to be in charge of the estate. They had treated him as a war hero and brought lots of small gifts for the bridal couple and Colin had set up a table in the barn with food and drinks for them so that they felt a part of it.

'It's a family tradition that the bride and groom pop in for a while after we've eaten – if you feel up to it?'

David had agreed to carry on the tradition, but it had exhausted him to smile and thank everyone who wanted to shake his hand. His scars were thought honourable, gained in the service of his country, and as a distant relation of the family he'd been warmly welcomed, as had Becky, but now she could see that he was tired.

'Why don't you go to bed?' she suggested. 'If you fancy it, I could make you a cup of cocoa – or hot milk and brandy if you prefer?'

'Could I have the hot milk *and* brandy?' he said and smiled wryly. 'It might help us both to relax and get a good night's sleep. I'm still not as strong as I hope to be...'

Becky nodded and went to the kitchen. She'd spent some hours here since they'd come down to prepare for the wedding, learning how to manage things while Colin had been teaching David about the estate, and she found it simple enough to heat their milk on the range. She added a little sugar and brandy and took it upstairs to their room, feeling nerves in the pit of her stomach. While it was true that she'd given birth to this man's child, she did not know him well and felt a little strange at going to bed with him. She went in and closed the door softly, carrying the tray to the bed and then she saw that David had already climbed into bed and was sound asleep.

She placed the hot milk on the little table beside the bed and sat in a chair to drink hers, waiting to see if he would wake, but when he didn't, she went behind the dressing screen and took off her clothes, slipping into a sensible cotton nightgown. The silk under-wear that Minnie had so lovingly made her could wait for another time.

34

'I wanted you to know the truth, Mrs Harper,' Mr Stockbridge said on his return to work. They were alone in Sally's office at Harpers with the door firmly shut. 'However, my daughter is now respectably married and I would not like it generally known that she gave birth to a child out of wedlock.'

'I should not dream of gossiping about Becky,' Sally assured him. His words had confirmed what she'd suspected but hadn't allowed herself to think about Becky's moods. It was just like Maggie to take her away and help her sort things out. 'I shall not speak of it to anyone – but it is not so very surprising that it happens when we have been at war for so long. You would have preferred it did not, of course, but your new son-in-law clearly intended to marry her – so perhaps we can forgive their indiscretion?'

He smiled and nodded. 'I think she has a good chance of being happy. Captain David Morgan is a gentleman and the family is good.'

Sally looked thoughtful. 'It is a strange coincidence, is it not –

that they should have two Army captains within the same family, both bearing the same surname?'

'Indeed, I thought so too,' he agreed. 'Apparently, they are distant cousins and Captain Colin Morgan did not know of his relation until a few months ago.'

'It was good of the family to take him in,' Sally observed. 'If he has been so badly wounded, he might find it difficult to return to his old life perhaps.'

'Yes, I dare say. He was a doctor but says he has forgotten everything he knew about medicine.'

'How odd,' Sally said. 'I would have expected him to recall some things, if not all – since a part of his memory has returned...'

Mr Stockbridge nodded. 'Yes – but if you saw the extent of his injuries, you would not wonder, Mrs Harper. The poor brave man has been through so much.'

'Yes, of course. I have seen the kinds of injuries you describe and I do understand that it would cause terrible trauma. We must just hope that he remembers a little more as time goes on... and be glad that Becky is happy again.'

'Oh yes, she seemed quite content when I left there the day after the wedding,' he replied, nodding his satisfaction. 'The family gave her a lovely reception and she had some beautiful gifts.'

'Good, I shall send her something – but how is Minnie now? Has she recovered from the chill that prevented her attending with you?'

'Yes, thank goodness!' He smiled at her. 'I could not have left her had you and Mrs Burrows both not promised to look in and see her while I was away for two days – and we have a good neighbour who went in and made her hot drinks and food. Minnie insisted that I go to the wedding and promised she would be fine, but I worried that it might be that terrible flu.'

'We must all be happy that it wasn't,' Sally said and smiled. 'We are all very fond of Minnie and that awful illness has already claimed too many.' Her own problems at Harpers always seemed so insignificant when compared to all the death and destruction caused by the war and now the disease that had spread all over the world. 'But let us not speak of these things. I am delighted that Becky is happy at last and I shall be sure to send her a wedding gift. What do you think she would like?'

'I am sure she will be pleased with anything you send, Mrs Harper. I gave her some trinkets and money, of course, but they have very little, although the house was furnished. However, they need linens, glass and porcelain, which are all scarce at the moment.'

'I have recently discovered a pleasant second-hand shop, where they have beautiful porcelain tea and dinner services and some cut-glass items. I bought a few things for my own use in our new house and I will return and see what I can find as a gift for Becky.'

His brows lifted. 'I am surprised such things remain unsold. I would have imagined they would all have been purchased, due to the shortage brought on by the war.'

'I was surprised, too, but when I asked, the owner told me he had recently cleared a large country mansion and everything came from there. He had boxes he had not even unpacked. I told him I would return in a few days to see what else I liked.'

'You should have bought all he had,' Mr Stockbridge advised. 'On our shelves they would sell easily.'

'You think we could sell second-hand porcelain and glassware?'

'If it is good, I am sure we can – providing it isn't chipped or damaged.'

'I shall return immediately and see what I can find.' Sally sighed. 'I do hope this war is finally over. The papers seem to be hopeful that we're close to the end.'

'We must all pray it is so,' he replied and stood up. 'I shall pass on your good wishes to my wife, Mrs Harper.'

'Thank you – and tell her that I should like you both to come for tea on Sunday, if she is well enough.'

'Thank you.' He beamed at her. 'I know that will please her. She speaks fondly of you and Mrs Burrows and Mrs Bailey. You were all so kind to her, giving her a home when her sister died.'

'I did not live with her long, but I should have been happy to do so,' Sally said. 'We are all very fond of your wife, Mr Stockbridge.'

He looked pleased and left her to make his rounds of the store. Sally decided that she would visit the second-hand shop straight away. Some of the porcelain she'd glimpsed still packed into boxes had looked wonderful. Since her manager seemed to think they could sell it, she would go back to the shop and see if she could do an advantageous deal for Harpers.

* * *

The shop was set down a side street not far from the hostel where she'd lived for a while when she first started working for Harpers. Mick O'Sullivan had worked in a pub just across the street and that was how they had met. Inside the shop, it was gloomy and dusty and many of the boxes were still just as they had been on Sally's last visit. The owner greeted her with a weary smile.

'I am sorry, Mrs Harper. My wife has been unwell and I haven't had time to unpack.'

'Those boxes there with the porcelain and glassware – how much do you need if I take them all?'

'But you may not like what is inside,' He frowned. 'I gave fifty pounds for everything in the house. Would twenty pounds be all right?'

'I am happy if you are,' Sally agreed and they shook hands. 'I'll send someone to pick them up later this afternoon. Is that all right?'

'I'll be glad to get them out of the way,' he told her with a sigh. 'To be honest, I probably shouldn't have cleared that house, but it was such a bargain that I couldn't resist. The solicitor just wanted it done and accepted my first offer. However, my wife wants me to sell the shop premises and retire. We've been here for forty-odd years and she says we'd do better to spend our last days in a nice little cottage by the sea...'

'And do you agree?' Sally asked, counting out his money. 'Twenty pounds.'

'Thank you,' he put the cash into his trouser pockets. 'I suppose it is time, but I shan't know what to do with myself.'

Sally looked at him thoughtfully. 'You could still buy nice things when you get the chance – but you could buy them for me, Mr Samuels. I think that Harpers might be able to continue to sell good porcelain that we class as antique or good second-hand, even when the war is over. I am always looking for interesting things for our shelves.'

He stared at her in astonishment. 'Would you entrust such a job to me? You hardly know me, Mrs Harper.'

'I know an honest man when I meet one,' she replied with a little laugh. 'Besides, you have a good eye for furniture and other things, Mr Samuels. If you decide to retire let me know – I think I might buy a couple of your lovely cabinets for my own home when we move and perhaps other things too.'

'You're the best customer I've had in a long while. I mostly sell a few silver spoons or a tea set now and then as a wedding gift,' he confessed. 'I haven't sold a piece of furniture for ages – oh, that's a lie, I sold an armchair just this week. A customer I hadn't seen since before the war.' He smiled and nodded. 'Mr O'Sullivan... he used to buy things for his restaurants quite often, but I hadn't seen him in years.'

'Mick O' Sullivan?' Sally looked at him in surprise and pleasure as he nodded. 'You've seen him this week?'

'Yes, Mrs Harper. Looked proper poorly he did, but told me he's getting better. He's been in hospital somewhere overseas for a long time, but he's recovering at last.'

'Thank you.' Sally flashed him a brilliant smile. 'His friends have been worried about him. I'll send someone this afternoon to pick up my boxes and I'll be in touch again soon.'

Sally left the shop but didn't return to Harpers immediately. Instead, she hailed a taxi and gave them the address of the pub that Marlene managed for Mick near the river. If Mr Samuels was right, Mick was home and recovering from whatever had afflicted him... so *why* hadn't he been to see her?

* * *

Marlene greeted her with a beaming smile when she entered the restaurant. 'Sally, I've just been trying to get you on the phone. Have you heard? Mick is back in London.'

'Yes, I've just been told he bought an armchair...'

'Yes, he has been looking for some items of furniture for a small house he's rented and is planning to live in for a while.'

'I thought he lived over one of the restaurants?'

'Yes, he did – but he is selling two of them,' Marlene replied. 'He says he has other plans.'

'Oh...' Sally was surprised because Mick had spoken of owning a chain of restaurants more than once. 'Did he say what they were?'

'No, not to me, but he'll probably tell you.'

'Did he say why he hadn't written for so long?'

Marlene hesitated, then, 'He just said that he'd been in a bad place in his life but now knew just what he wanted to do with the future.'

'Oh, well, as long as he is alive and well, the rest is up to him. I was just surprised that he would sell up when he was so set on opening a chain of restaurants at one time.'

Marlene shrugged. 'I suppose it is the war, Mrs Harper. War does change men. I've heard some dreadful stories – changes in behaviour and things. Men who have been sent home, maimed in body or mind.'

Sally nodded. 'Yes, I've heard a couple of stories myself. It alters some men's personality. Is that what has happened to Mick?'

'Oh no, he seems the same as always – a bit pale and not breathing as easily as he did, but still the same old Mick.'

Sally nodded and smiled. 'Perhaps he will come and see me then.'

* * *

Sally went home for lunch, which Mrs Hills had prepared. After lunch, she took her two children for a walk in the park with Pearl, their nurse, and then left them to have their tea at home while she returned to Harpers and sought Fred in the basement. He had already unpacked the six boxes and set out the contents for her to see.

'You've bought some lovely things here, Mrs Harper,' he told her, looking impressed. 'There are three good dinner services – antiques I reckon. Flight Barr and Barr, Worcester, Derby – and tea services to match the Worcester and Derby sets. You also have a Sevres coffee set complete with the pot and a tray. There's thirty-six good crystal wine glasses and a dozen crystal sherry glasses, also three good crystal fruit bowls, a Derby dessert service, a set of port glasses – and then there is a collection of glasses with air twist stems. Twenty-four of those but one is chipped. However, that doesn't matter, because you can sell those singly rather than as a set; they're all different...'

'Good gracious!' Sally was astounded. 'All that came out of those six boxes?'

'Mr Samuels had found another two and he said you might as well have them as he was going to sell the lease of his shop and move to the sea.'

Sally was examining the porcelain and glasses. It was such fine, delicate porcelain that she marvelled it had survived all this time without damage, but everything seemed perfect apart from the one glass that was chipped.

'I shall visit him again and see what else I can buy,' Sally said and smiled. She saw a pile of linen tablecloths and picked one up. It smelled faintly of lavender and had little yellow marks at the edges.

'They will wash out,' Fred told her. 'Shall I drop them off at the laundry for you on my way home?'

'Would you mind?' Sally asked. If they came back in as pristine a condition as she hoped, she could give some to Becky as part of her wedding gift. 'She picked up a Spode dinner plate. 'Is this a full service too?'

'No, that's just six of everything,' Fred told her. 'Just a half service – but all perfect, Mrs Harper.'

'You can pack that as a wedding gift,' Sally said. 'Becky Stock-bridge has just got married and I will send her that set as a gift.'

'Well, I never,' he replied. 'Her sweetheart came home then – lucky girl.'

'Yes. Yes, Becky has been lucky,' Sally agreed. Fred would probably never see Becky again, so there was no need to tell him about her husband's scars. 'Well, that all seems rather good, Fred. I think we need to wash the porcelain and glasses before we put them out –

and we'll be displaying them in the corner by the lift. I shall want a sign advertising them as second-hand.'

'Oh no, Mrs Harper,' Fred told her firmly. 'These are antiques and must be sold as that.' He smiled at her. 'When I was headmaster at the boys' college, we had a wonderful collection in our cabinets. We used them for special occasions. I learned quite a bit about antique porcelain and I know these are valuable items.'

'Do you know what they're worth?' Sally asked. 'I was thinking about ten or fifteen pounds a set for the dinner service.'

He was shaking his head and smiling. 'I think they are worth double that,' he said. 'If you'll take my advice, Mrs Harper, you will charge at least thirty pounds for the Worcester service and the same for the Derby one – and the Flight Barr and Barr is rare. I'd put forty pounds on that and see what happens. The glasses are similar to what we normally charge for a set – but the air twists are worth more, of course. At least ten pounds each glass, don't you think?'

Sally nodded. 'I suppose the antiques are almost irreplaceable, though the modern sets are very expensive, too. We'll price them fairly and see what sells.'

Sally was smiling as she left Fred to finish up for the day. He would see to it all and she could go home to her husband and her children, secure in the knowledge that she'd left the new stock in safe hands. She didn't know what they would do without Fred Burrows. He'd been with them from the beginning and she hoped he wasn't thinking of retiring just yet.

35

'Sally did well again then,' Beth said, nodding as she listened to Fred recounting the day's work. She had made him a fresh pot of tea and served him a plate of beef and ale pie with buttered carrots and cabbage and mashed potatoes for his supper. 'I'd like to have seen her face when you told her what that porcelain was worth...'

'She deserved a nice surprise, taking a chance like she did,' Fred said. 'Not many would have had the courage to pay twenty pounds without even looking at what was inside.'

'I certainly wouldn't,' Beth agreed.

'She has a good business head on her,' Fred nodded. 'She didn't know what she'd got, though, until I told her.' He smiled in a satisfied way. 'Worth a lot more than she'd thought, I can tell you.'

Beth nodded and smiled. 'I'll bet she was surprised you knew so much about it?'

'Perhaps. She didn't show it, just accepted my word that it was worth a lot of money and said she would price it fairly and see what happened. I reckon it will run out of the shop. Folk can't buy new very often at the moment and some of that porcelain is irreplaceable. They stopped making it a while ago... the modern stuff doesn't truly compare in my opinion. It would probably sell for more than I told her, but I didn't want to go over the top.'

'I should be afraid to use it,' Beth said. 'It sounds as if it should be in a museum cabinet rather than on the dining table?'

'Well, yes, some of it would be safer that way – but it is too beautiful not to be used. We used our collection at the boys' college just for special occasions – when we entertained important guests. It was still possible to replace items then, but I'm not sure it is now.'

Beth nodded. She turned as Jack entered the room. He looked tired but pleased as he sat down and Beth made another fresh pot of tea.

'Did your meeting with Ben Harper go well?' she asked.

'Yes, we're going ahead with the restaurant at Harpers, but he is already talking about others for the future.'

'So he has sorted out his financial worries then?' Beth asked. 'I know it was a bit uncertain...'

'Oh, he got a loan for our restaurant some weeks ago,' Jack told her. 'Now he is thinking further ahead – but he had some news today...' He shook his head as Beth looked at him. 'No, not my business to say. That pie looks good – any left for me?'

'It is good,' Fred said and cleared his plate as Beth fetched the dish she'd put aside for Jack.

'Would you like some jam roly-poly?' she asked her father-in-law.

'No thanks, Beth,' Fred said with a smile. 'I'm going down the road to see Vera this evening and she is sure to have made a cake.' He stood up and went to put his thick jacket on. 'I'll do the washing-up later if you leave it.'

'We'll do that, Dad,' Jack told him. 'You have a good time.' He looked at Beth after the door had closed behind his father. 'Do you think they will marry?'

'I'm not sure. I hope so. Vera is a nice woman and she is fond of him – he could do a lot worse.'

'He's had chances in the past,' Jack said, surprising her. 'He always said he couldn't replace my mother – but it would be better than him living alone if we move one day.'

'I'm in no hurry to move – unless he does get married,' Beth said. 'I know you would like to, Jack.'

'We need a bigger garden for the boys. Dad's vegetable garden takes up most of the space and as they grow and start to play games... yes, I'd like to move. If I can find the right place to rent. We can't buy our own for a while, Beth...'

'I still have quite a bit left over from the sale of those shares.' After her mother's death, some old shares had come to light and because of a new discovery of a valuable mineral, she had inherited several thousand pounds.

'Keep it for you and the boys. I don't anticipate anything going awry now, but if it should...' Jack frowned. 'For us the war is over. We have the future to look forward to, but life can be cruel at times. If we're lucky and things go well, we can buy our own house in a few years. Meanwhile, we'll look for a decent place to rent – close to the one Ben Harper bought.'

'I wonder how he managed that as well as the restaurant,' Beth mused. 'I thought money would be tight the way things have been at Harpers these past years. I know sales have not been what they were, because Sally was worried.'

'Ben knows what he is doing,' Jack told her. 'So do I, Beth, and neither of us will take more risk than we think right.'

* * *

'I was delighted to get the porcelain and the glasses,' Sally said to her husband that evening. 'They are so beautiful, Ben. I know they are probably not quite the same as we could buy these days – if some of the factories are even still going – but I'd like to stock new when it is possible. I think they may be very expensive to buy new. I shall have to make inquiries.'

'You do that, love,' Ben agreed. 'I'm all for taking Harpers upmarket – and so is my new partner.' He saw the surprise in her face and laughed. 'I'm not just talking about Jack's investment in the restaurant. I have a new partner in Harpers. Jenni has offered to sell her shares to him and he is prepared to put money in for us too.'

'Who is – your cousin from America?' Sally felt shocked. It was the first she'd heard of it and she didn't like the idea that Ben hadn't told her what was going on after the way she'd kept the place viable all through the war. 'Why didn't you tell me?'

'It was to be a surprise, Sally. I knew you were worried about Jenni pulling out, so when the chance to make us solid again came up, I agreed,' Ben said. 'No, Jenni didn't sell her shares to my cousin – someone much closer to home... you know him well and you will be pleased...'

'Not Mr Selfridge?' she said, puzzled and wary. 'He would want to take us over, Ben.' Why hadn't he consulted her?

'No, not Mr Selfridge – Mick O'Sullivan...' Ben grinned at her expression of disbelief. 'He has sold some of his restaurants and he owned the properties. They were in an area that is earmarked for better-class housing and he got a good price – so he is investing his money in Harpers. You knew we were thinking of going into business with him, because we discussed it years ago – and now we have...'

'Mick is your new partner?' Sally questioned, feeling bewildered, though her anger had evaporated as Ben explained. 'I trust Mick – but why did you keep it from me?'

'Because Mick didn't want to disappoint you if the sales on his property didn't go ahead. He asked me not to mention it until he was sure he could do it and at one time he wasn't certain he would get his price.'

'But you said you hadn't heard from him...' Sally stared at him, hardly knowing whether to be happy or cross over the deception. 'Didn't either of you realise that I was very worried about him?'

'Sorry,' Ben apologised, as he realised his neglect had upset her. 'I should have told you, but I hadn't heard from him until a few days ago and I would have told you then, of course I would, but Mick made me promise not to say a word. He knew that if he saw you, he couldn't keep the secret.' Ben grinned. 'It's wonderful, Sally, don't you see? Jenni wanted out, because setting up the store is costing her more than she'd expected. She asked if I wanted her shares and I couldn't afford to buy them just yet, so when Mick came up with the suggestion, it seemed a good idea. She wouldn't have sold to anyone I didn't approve of. Mick has invested another ten thousand pounds besides, to match the money I borrowed from the bank. It means we have no financial worries and I still own 60 per cent of Harpers...' He looked slightly deflated. 'It is all set up but not signed – so if you're against it...'

'I'm not and I understand why the pair of you thought it would be a lovely surprise. It is, but I would have liked to be asked.' Sally smiled as she realised that it was an answer to her concerns. 'It is wonderful news, Ben. Mick has a good head for business and he's a friend – but we don't know whether business will pick up again once the war is over...'

'Of course it will,' Ben said. 'You've done marvels, Sally, but with a partner like Mick and you putting your heads together, things are bound to take off. Once we can start shipping goods from abroad again, it will all be fine.'

'I do hope so.' Sally smiled. She felt some of her anxiety of the past months slip from her shoulders. With Ben always so busy with his Government work, which looked set to continue even when the war was done, because there were so many loose ends to tie up, the task of running Harpers had fallen to her. He'd juggled his finances so many times and she didn't really know how he'd managed to get the loan from the bank. She had very good staff and Mr Stockbridge was an excellent manager, but he'd spoken once or twice of retiring in a couple of years, and finding another she could trust as implicitly was going to be difficult. However, Mick was an excellent judge of character and a good businessman. She was glad he would be there to help out if and when she needed him.

'Mick is sailing for America before Christmas,' Ben went on. 'He is going to source some suppliers for us and visit some relatives there at the same time – but I've invited him to dinner next week so he can tell you all about it himself.'

Sally looked at him thoughtfully. 'How much do you owe the bank, Ben? I know you managed to borrow another ten thousand pounds to use as standby money in case it is needed for stock... but the new house – are you sure we can afford it?'

'I shall sell this flat to cover part of the house price – as for the rest...' He shrugged his shoulders. 'My aunt made me a personal loan. She felt that my uncle should have left more of the shares in Harpers to me at the beginning and wanted to give me the money, but I shall pay her back when I can.'

'I see... I know it isn't my business, Ben, but I feel responsible for Harpers and I would hate us to lose it because we were over-stretched at the bank...'

'I'm sorry, Sally.' Ben gave her an apologetic look. 'I don't always tell you these things because I know you worry over Harpers and you have enough to think of with the buying and the children.'

'Yes, there is plenty to do,' she agreed. 'We are fortunate that Harpers is owned by family – at least it was. Mick has a percentage now...' Sally hesitated. 'I don't think he will – but supposing he sold them to someone else?'

'I have the first offer legally,' Ben said. 'It was a part of the deal.'

Sally was aware of unease, though she couldn't have said why. Mick was a good friend and she was sure he would work in the best interests of Harpers – but supposing his shares did pass to someone else? She shook her head. It was foolish to worry about things over which she had no control. Sally must just have faith that everything would turn out well.

* * *

'It's sorry I am that you worried over me, Sally Harper,' Mick said with the smile and Irish charm that won him so many friends. 'I wrote to you weeks ago and told you that I was fine – but it seems you didn't get my letter?'

'No. I hadn't heard from you since the time...'

Mick nodded as she hesitated. 'You thought I was still breaking my heart over that lovely Maggie?'

'Yes. I thought...' Sally drew a deep breath and shook her head.

'I knew Ben would tell you about the deal we were doing if you got wind of us meeting so I asked him to keep my secret – but I'm sorry you were anxious, Sally. He wanted to tell you. I told him not to, because had I not been able to sell my properties for the right price, I couldn't have invested with Harpers.'

Sally nodded, but her gaze fixed on him accusingly. 'You didn't even write to Marlene?'

'No – well, I didn't want to be persuaded out of selling up. I sold my interest in the pub as well as two of my restaurants.'

'But the pub was doing so well.'

'That's the truth of it,' he agreed, 'and Marlene is not best pleased with me for not consulting her until the last minute.'

'What will she do now?' Sally asked him.

'Marlene made a lot of money out of it,' Mick said. 'At first she was against it, but then she realised it was for the best. She is going to work in the one restaurant I have left until she decides what she wants to do next.'

Sally shook her head, feeling puzzled. 'I thought you really cared about having your own chain of restaurants? Why did you decide to make the change?'

Mick shrugged his shoulders. 'Two of my managers let me down – I've kept the one that did well.'

'But the manager there was going to turn them around for you.' Sally felt uncertain as she looked at him. 'What is really going on, Mick?'

He hesitated and then inclined his head. 'Since you're the only person I truly care for, Sally Harper, I'll tell you the truth. I'm thinking I may stay in America,' he said. 'I know I can trust you and Ben to look after my investments in Harpers and with Marlene at the restaurant my investments here would be secure...' He shrugged his shoulders. 'I haven't decided yet.'

'Does Ben know that's what you plan?' Sally looked at him uncertainly.

'No, he doesn't,' Mick admitted. 'Because I'm not sure – besides, you don't need my help, Sally Harper. You managed all through the war and I'm certain you can manage now – but I shall act as a buyer for you over there. I'll source things for you and buy them if you authorise it, so I'm not abandoning you and mebbe I'll come back in a year or two. Sooner if I miss you all too much.' He gave her a rueful smile. 'Don't you be worrying your head over me. 'Tis restless I am and don't ask me why for I couldn't tell you.'

Sally met his gaze and saw the underlying pain. He'd told her he was over Maggie and perhaps this restless urge was because of what he'd suffered in the war – who knew what men like him had gone through and what they might suffer, because of it?

'I do understand, Mick,' she said. 'Thank you for telling me and thank you for investing with us. It will ease some of the strain this war has caused – but I would have enjoyed working with you.'

'Would you?' His grin was much as it always had been. 'Then perhaps I will come back in a while...'

36

Marion looked up as Mrs Harper approached. This was her first week back at Harpers. She'd been working on one of the windows alone, because Mr Marco had told her she should finish it off as she had come up with the idea. Mr Marco was busy stripping the next window, which was to have a victory theme, with bunting and flags, because it looked as if the war was winding to a weary close. It could not truly be called a victory for anyone, in Marion's opinion, although an armistice with Austria-Hungary had recently been signed.

'It is the beginning of the end. Germany can't hold out much longer – they don't have the money or the manpower and their allies have had enough,' Mr Marco had told her cheerfully before he went off to start on the next window. 'Harpers will reflect a moment of hope for peace for the world, Mrs Jackson. Let's give our windows a joyful look, shall we?'

They weren't quite ready to do the Christmas windows for another few weeks, but they were doing their best with bright colours and happy messages. Marion's window was centred on women making the home look warm and comfortable and depicted a woman and children at play in front of a fire. The models were dressed in warm winter clothing, all of which was available for sale at Harpers, and the room was furnished with porcelain and linens that were also to be found on the shelves. The little marble-topped tables were antiques that Mrs Harper had found, as was the rocking chair by the fireplace and the dresser in the corner that displayed some beautiful porcelain and glass. Marion had never seen anything so fine. Not that she could afford to buy anything like that, because it was far too expensive for her. However, it gave an air of luxury to the setting and might remind people of life before the war and all the shortages that had made things so hard these past months and years. It was a promise of better things to come and made you feel warm inside.

Mrs Harper had wanted to advertise the new venture into antiques. She had found a good source of antique and second-hand furniture, glassware, porcelain and ornaments and she had made room for it on the ground floor, putting some of the other departments together to make space. The stationery and pens were now relegated to one counter with some extra shelves on the walls behind, which Marion thought much better and the new department took centre stage.

Mrs Harper was always moving things round these days, trying to make the stock look more plentiful than it was. Before the war, every shelf had been fully stocked, as well as all the glass counters, but some had spaces on them these days. The new department had filled a sizeable area and three glass counters had been cleared to the basement for the time being.

'The window looks wonderful, Marion,' Mrs Harper said as she reached her. 'It reflects the hope of a homecoming for the men who may soon be returning. I am hoping it will bring back some of the customers we haven't seen for a while.'

'I'm glad you like it,' Marion said. 'Mr Marco let me do most of it

– and the window he is working on will be linked to it, though he hasn't told me exactly what he intends to do.'

Mrs Harper nodded. 'I think he wants to give the impression of victory – and the armistice is certainly that... even if the war isn't quite finished.'

'Surely, they will give in now?' Marion said and frowned. 'They must know they can't win?'

'You would think so – but a battleship – *HMS Britannia* – has just been sunk off Trafalgar... It was in this morning's paper...'

'Oh no, not another!' Marion groaned. 'Why must they keep on doing it when they know they're beaten?'

'I suppose it is hard for them to accept defeat,' Mrs Harper said. 'The paper says it was an act of defiance – and probably the last action of the war.'

Marion's eyes watered with tears. She wiped them away with her handkerchief. 'So all the men that died on that ship lost their lives for nothing.' A shudder went through her. 'My brother Robbie was lost at sea... they were on their way home when they were attacked. He was younger than me.'

'I know. Rachel told me. I was so very sorry.'

'He was doing what he wanted – but it all seems such a waste to me, Mrs Harper.'

'Yes, I suppose you could say that,' Sally Harper agreed. 'They think around fifty men were lost in this last disaster, which was definitely a waste – but perhaps you could say the same of every action. I mean, what was it all about really? I know we had to fight once it started – but it should never have got to that.'

'I just hope it is all over now...' Everyone was saying it all they time. As a nation the British were hopeful but still anxious.

'Yes.' Mrs Harper looked thoughtful. 'Are you expecting your husband home soon? I know he has been in hospital for a very long time. You must miss him terribly?'

'I do,' Marion nodded. 'I wanted to visit him in hospital – but he didn't want me to. He said it was best if I waited until he was on his feet again. I know he was a lot worse that he pretended but... he'll be home soon. He was coming home some weeks ago but there was a setback – his wound flared up again and he had to have another operation.'

'I am so sorry. You must be so anxious – and he hasn't even seen his baby yet...'

'I miss him a lot.' Marion bit her lip. 'I can't help wondering why he won't let me visit...'

'You should go down anyway,' Sally Harper told her. 'I would if I were you.'

'Reggie might not like it...' Marion looked thoughtful. 'My sister-in-law, Sarah, told me to go, but I'm not sure...'

'Well, it's up to you – but if I can help at all with anything, don't hesitate to ask.' Mrs Harper smiled, then, 'If you ever need anything – someone to talk to or to sort out a problem for you – I am always available, Marion. Just come to my office – or ask Ruth to telephone me and I'll come in... and you know you are welcome to use our crèche.'

'Yes, thank you. You're so kind – giving me this job. I couldn't have worked behind the counters with a family to care for, but these few hours are precious...' Marion wiped her tears as she saw Mr Marco wave to her. 'I think I am wanted now, Mrs Harper. The window is ready to be dressed and I have to help.'

'Yes, you go,' Mrs Harper said. 'I can't wait for the windows to be revealed.'

Marion nodded and went to join the window dresser. Mr Marco showed her his drawing for the new window and she nodded. In anticipation of the war ending, he'd designed a window to depict men returning home and greeting their wives and children smiling in front of a warm fire with all the comforts of family around him.

'It's lovely,' she said and smiled. 'Mrs Harper and I were talking, saying as there wasn't much to celebrate in the war ending – but this turns it into victory.'

'I'm glad you see it, Marion,' he said and smiled at her. 'The victory is in the men coming home, you see. It doesn't matter that some of them are badly wounded and will never be the same. They did their duty and can stand tall and proud and life will be all the sweeter for what they suffered.'

'Yes, I do see that,' Marion agreed. 'We can be bitter and angry and wonder what it was all for – or we can just celebrate the home-coming and enjoy that we did what we had to, that we stood up to be counted.'

Mr Marco smiled at her. 'You are a clever girl, Marion. We all have to make the best of what is left – and build on it. Most of us have lost something because of this war...' For a moment, his voice cracked and she thought he was remembering his wife. 'But death is always with us in life and we can't allow personal grief to stop us. We have to build the future in whatever way we can. If our windows make people smile and give comfort, then we've done our part. First the homecoming and then we'll start planning the Christmas cele-brations, which is what most people will do if they can.'

Marion nodded. 'Reggie will be home soon. I hope I'll still be able to come in, but I'm not sure... it depends how he is...'

'Well, let's wait and see,' Mr Marco said. 'Let us know if it is necessary to stay home for a time and I'll find someone else to help – though not many have your talent.'

'I'm not as good as you,' she replied, blushing.

'I've had years of practice,' he told her with a smile. 'Now, we have several hours work ahead, so we'd best get on with it...'

* * *

It was dark before Marion got home that evening. When she opened the kitchen door, Sarah was at the stove. 'I'm sorry I was late,' she said, apologising, 'but the windows took longer than I expected—'

'I don't mind but...' She broke off as Marion closed the door behind her and then a heavy tread was heard on the stair. 'Reggie is here – he isn't very pleased that you weren't—'

'Reggie? He didn't let us know...' Marion felt a thrill of pleasure and yet she was nervous. It had been so long since she'd seen him and she felt apprehensive.

Marion's eyes went towards the door to the hall. It opened and her husband entered. Her breath expelled in relief as she saw that although he was walking with a limp, he hadn't lost any limbs, but then as he walked into the light, she saw the vivid scar across his right cheek; it reached from above his eye to his chin and his right eye was covered with a patch.

'Reggie...' She moved towards him eagerly, but he put out a hand to ward her off as she would've hugged him. 'I'm so glad you're home!'

'Is that why you stayed out all day?'

'I was working at Harpers. I didn't know you were coming home today...'

'I expected better of you,' he muttered. 'You have a young baby, Marion. Why are you still working? You don't need to. You should be able to manage on what I send you; most women do...'

Marion stood stock-still and looked at him, feeling as if he'd slapped her face. This wasn't like her husband – but he looked so tired and pale. 'I am sorry I wasn't here to greet you – but the money I earn buys extras,' she said defensively. 'I like working at Harpers, Reggie – and it is usually only for a few hours, but today we had two windows to dress.'

'I should have thought your child would come first,' he said.

'How is Sarah supposed to look after two very young children at the same time.'

'I don't mind,' Sarah said quickly. 'Really, I don't – it was just they were both crying at the same time when you arrived.'

'I know you did your best to keep them quiet while I had a sleep,' Reggie's voice was softer, but Marion could see he was still angry with her. 'It would not have happened had my wife been at home, where she should be.'

Marion's chest felt tight with disappointment and the tears were close. She'd longed for him to be home and now he was so angry. She'd known Reggie wouldn't want her to work full-time when he got back from the Army, but she hadn't expected this. She loved her work and didn't want to give it up completely. The routine they'd worked out for themselves was fine for both of them and Sarah worked extra hours on her sewing when Marion was home and she looked after both children so Sarah could do her embroidery.

Deciding not to force the issue, Marion took off her coat and started to prepare the evening meal. Sarah had put a slow casserole in the oven earlier, but the vegetables needed washing and cooking and Marion normally did that when she got in, though sometimes Sarah had everything ready. Marion could see that her sister-in-law was tired and apologised to her in a low voice when they met in the scullery a bit later to wash up after they'd all eaten.

'I shouldn't have stopped late,' she said. 'I'm sorry the children were a handful, Sarah.'

'It's fine, Marion, it really is. You know we all have off days – I reckon Reggie is having one today. Surely he can't mean that he wants you to give up your job? It isn't as if you were working long hours every day.'

'I suppose it may happen occasionally,' Marion replied. 'That's if he will let me continue. I know he has never been keen on the idea of my working once we were settled with a child – and probably more young ones soon enough, now he is home.'

'I'll be sorry if you have to stop,' Sarah told her. 'You normally come home glowing and full of interesting things to tell us. I know how much you love it, Marion.'

'Yes, I do,' Marion agreed. 'But I love Reggie, too, and our child – if it upsets him because I'm working, I shall have to stop, though I'll need to give notice. I can't just walk away and leave them in the lurch, no matter what Reggie says...'

'Of course you can't – but when he thinks about it, he will see that it is good for all of us that you work a few hours once a week.'

Marion nodded. 'It will probably be two mornings next week or another long day. I have to be flexible, Sarah...' She sighed. 'Reggie is probably tired after his long journey. Perhaps he will be in a better mood in the morning.'

'Yes...' Sarah looked thoughtful. 'Dan asks my opinion and what I want rather than dictating, Marion. I think he probably knows that I wouldn't accept anything else. The way Reggie spoke to you – well, I wouldn't put up with it. Some men can become bullies if you let them and it's best to let them see you won't just take it at the start... but I can't tell you what to do.'

Marion met her sympathetic gaze and felt like crying. 'It isn't like him, Sarah. I expect it is because he has been ill and he's tired...'

'You stand up to him,' Sarah replied and left it there.

Marion thought about what she'd said and felt a tight knot in her chest. She'd been so happy to think that Reggie was coming home but she'd suffered enough verbal and sometimes physical abuse from her father, especially when he was drunk. She didn't think she was prepared to take it from her husband for the rest of her life. As yet, she was willing to give him a little time and see how things went – but if she had to, she would ask him to leave. This was her home and she had a right to decide what she did with her life, at least to a certain degree. She would do what she could to make her husband happy, but she wasn't a doormat and she wouldn't be treated like one.

* * *

Later that evening, when they were alone in their bedroom, Reggie put his arms around her and apologised.

'I'm sorry I was nasty to you when you got home,' he told her. 'When I arrived, both the children were screaming their heads off and my head ached. I just wanted a little peace and to be with you.'

'Does your head ache much, Reggie?' Marion asked in a soft voice full of understanding. 'Is it because of your injuries?'

'Yes...' She saw his grimace. 'It was pretty rough where I was, before I was injured this last time. The hospital patched up my leg and some other injuries, but my eye has gone and the damage to nerves in the area is what causes the headaches and the mood swings.'

'I'm sorry I wasn't home sooner. We wanted to get the windows finished so they could be revealed tomorrow morning. The customers love it when a special display is unveiled and it is a spectacular window this time – Mr Marco excelled himself.'

'Yes, I dare say, but I want you here with us, Marion, not stuck at work for hours.'

'Don't let's quarrel about it,' Marion replied carefully. 'It usually works very well.'

'I don't want to quarrel with you, Marion,' he said softly. 'I've been dreaming and longing to come home. Come here and let me kiss you...'

Marion went to him, slipping her arms around him. He felt thin and she could see he was weary. When they went to bed together,

Reggie held her tightly but didn't make love to her. It was the first time since their marriage that he hadn't loved her after a parting and she snuggled up to him, wanting her old Reggie back, but he stiffened and then turned away with a muffled goodnight.

Soon, he was fast asleep and after a while Marion slept too. She had an odd little ache inside her because she knew something wasn't right. They'd always enjoyed the intimate side of marriage and it had made them complete, together. Now as she settled into his warmth, she was glad he was there but uncertain of the future. Would he ever be the same? Or had the war changed him for ever? She'd heard that war did change men's personalities and Reggie had been through a lot, been injured both in the trenches and during a bombing raid from the air. Had that affected him so badly that he would never be the same?

37

Sally snuggled into Ben's body as he lay deep in slumber. She had slept too for a while after they'd made love and she'd drifted off in his arms. It was light outside and a new day was almost here. For a moment, she wondered what had woken her and then heard a cry from the children's room. Her son had woken and his cries had disturbed Jenny. She wailed and Sally smothered a sigh. It was warm and comfortable beside Ben and she didn't want to get up, but she had no choice.

The carpet was cold beneath her feet and she could feel a very definite change in the weather. It was winter now and she shivered at the thought of it.

She padded softly into the kitchen, not wanting to disturb Ben, and put the kettle on. No doubt her youngest child needed a feed and Jenny would also want some warm milk. While the kettle was boiling, she went into the bedroom and bent to kiss Jenny, soothing her and lifting her out of her cot and then she picked up little Peter and discovered he was soaking wet.

'Oh dear,' she said softly. 'We'd better get that changed quickly, darling. Jenny – can you fetch Mummy's basket please. I'll get you some nice milk with a little honey as soon as I've changed Peter's nappy.'

Jenny had stopped crying as soon as she was out of the cot. She ran to fetch the little basket that had Peter's bits and pieces in it and then stood watching as her mother changed the wet nappy, sucking her thumb.

'Don't suck your thumb, darling, you'll make it sore,' Sally told her.

Jenny took her thumb out of her mouth. 'When can I have a doggie?' she asked, which was often the first thing she said in the mornings and the last at night. 'Daddy said I could have a doggie.'

'Yes, he has promised to buy you one when we get to the new house.'

'When will that be?'

'I think we're moving in the next week or two,' Sally said. 'The house needed decorating and new carpets – but it won't be long.'

'Before Christmas?' Jenny asked, looking at her earnestly.

'Yes, before Christmas,' Sally said as she tickled her son's tummy and saw him laugh up at her. 'Let's go in the kitchen now and have our drinks. Peter needs a feed and I'll make you some hot milk.'

'Can I have a biscuit too – one with chocolate?'

'Yes, if there are any left. You and Daddy both like them and they don't last long!' Sally smiled as she cuddled her now dry and sweet-smelling son, taking him through to the kitchen with Jenny following.

She had just given Jenny her milk and biscuit and was making up Peter's bottle when Ben came into the kitchen wearing a dark blue dressing robe, his feet bare and his hair tousled. He looked totally gorgeous and her stomach clenched. She was lucky that their marriage was so good in every way and she still felt the pull of physical attraction whenever she saw him.

He saw what she was doing and smiled lovingly. 'Carry on with the main job,' he told her. 'I'll make coffee and some breakfast for us both – do we have bacon?'

'Yes – but it is only streaky. That's all the butcher had,' Sally said apologetically. 'However, I did manage to get some sausages and there are mushrooms and tomatoes. We could have a real treat today if you felt like it, the way we used to before the war. To celebrate today and the end of the war.' Ben had told his staff to close for the day so that they could all go out and celebrate in the streets, because they would be lined with people waving flags and cheering. He and Sally had wanted everyone to enjoy the day.

'Wonderful,' Ben said appreciatively, his eyes moving over her as her silk robe fell open, revealing that she wasn't wearing anything underneath. 'You look good enough to eat, Sally...'

She laughed up at him as her son sucked eagerly at his bottle. 'You had a good go at that last night.'

He grinned and looked pleased with himself as he filled the percolator and soon the kitchen was redolent with the delicious smells of fresh coffee and frying bacon.

When Peter had finished his bottle and been burped, Sally took him back to the bedroom, where he lay looking up at her for a few moments and then curled his fist against his face and went back to sleep. He was such a good boy, far less demanding than Jenny had been.

Returning to the kitchen, Sally found breakfast waiting. Jenny was sitting on her father's lap being fed crispy bacon, tomato and toast. She didn't like mushrooms and refused them, spitting them out when she'd first tried them. Her toast had thick marmalade on it and had transferred itself to her hands and face. Sally's throat caught with love as she watched father and daughter.

'We're so lucky, Ben,' she said and he looked up and smiled.

'Yes, we are,' he agreed. 'But this is such a momentous day, Sally.

They sign the Armistice with the Germans today. It's 11 November 1918 and that wretched war is finally over.'

'It's wonderful that it's finally ended, but I meant us – our family,' Sally said and sat down, nibbling a piece of bacon that crackled as she ate and was delicious.

'Yes, we've done well as a family despite it all,' Ben said with a sober look. 'But this is a good day for everyone, Sally. It means the war is finally over. They will ring the bells today for victory and the country will celebrate. Everyone will go mad with joy and there will be celebrations in the streets. What shall we do? It is a day to have fun and do something special – something we shall never forget.'

'We'll take the children somewhere,' Sally said, catching his mood. 'Buy them something nice – whatever we can find – and take them for ice cream and cakes.'

'We might go to the zoo,' Ben said. 'I know it's cold, but we can all wrap up warm and some of the animals are inside.'

'Oh, I don't like caged animals much,' Sally said. 'Why don't we show them the new house – and we could perhaps look at some puppies too? Jenny asked me again this morning.'

'Doggie, Daddy,' Jenny said, picking up on the conversation. 'Jenny wants a nice doggie.'

'What sort do you want?' Ben asked and Jenny's face lit up.

'Like this...' She wriggled down off his lap and ran out of the room; within minutes she was back with a picture book. She thrust it at him and pointed to a little brown dog with curly fur, a pretty face and long ears.

'That is a nice doggie,' Ben agreed. 'But I'm not sure we can find one just like it...'

'It looks a bit like a spaniel, but I'm not sure exactly,' Sally said. She wrinkled her brow. 'It has long ears like a spaniel and fluffy... it may be a bit of a mongrel or a crossbreed.'

'Quite possibly,' Ben agreed. 'I'll make some phone calls while you and the children are getting ready, shall I?'

'Yes, do that,' Sally agreed. 'If we find one that we all like, we can buy it and ask them to keep it until we move.'

'All right,' Ben agreed. 'I'll wash first while you finish your breakfast and then I'll see what I can find...'

* * *

It was nearly two hours before they were all ready and Mrs Hills had arrived to do the washing-up and tidy things a little. She smiled to see the children, eyes shining, wide with wonder, and ready for their special day out. Even Peter was awake and not crying, as if he'd got the holiday feeling too.

'It is a special day, Mrs Harper,' she said. 'You all get off and enjoy yourselves. I'm going to tea with my friends this afternoon and we're going to the palace to wave at the King when he comes out to the balcony – so we'll have something to remember too.'

'There will be crowds of people in the Mall, celebrating. We should all remember this day,' Sally said. 'It is such an exciting day. I can hardly believe the war is over at last. There were times I thought it would never end and I wondered if we might lose it – until the Americans came in and helped.'

'We've had help from all our allies and friendly countries, but it has been a long and terrible time,' Mrs Hills said, shaking her head. 'And what was it all for – that's what I want to know...'

Sally, Ben and the children left her grumbling to herself. Nothing could spoil their mood of release and happiness that morning as they took Ben's car out to Hampstead and the house Ben had bought. Jenny had brought her favourite doll and a book with her but sat looking out of the window most of the time, talking to her brother even though he just looked at her with his big blue eyes and didn't answer.

The house looked lovely despite the frosty day and inside the decorator was putting the finishing touches to the downstairs hall, which had been painted in a pretty duck egg blue with white skirting, cornice and doors. It all looked fresh and clean and smelled nice. Jenny scampered from room to room, giggling with excitement and thoroughly enjoying herself.

At the back was a long light room with big windows, a French door that opened on to the garden and a big lawn with shrub-filled borders and an old apple tree. It was cold out, but they all went to explore and look at what would be a pretty rose arbour in the summer. Jenny ran everywhere, screaming in delight, with Ben chasing her and laughing.

Sally watched them and smiled. She hadn't wanted to move at first, but now she was completely won over and already planning where things would go. This would be the room they lived in, where the children could play and go in and out when it wasn't too cold or raining. There was a room at the front for dining and a cosy sitting room for when she and Ben were sitting alone by the fire in the evenings. Upstairs were five bedrooms and two bathrooms. There was a big kitchen with a housekeeper's sitting room beyond the dining room on the ground floor.

Mrs Hills had told them she wanted to come with them when they moved. 'I'm on my own most of the time these days,' she'd said. 'My husband has been gone some years, as you know – and my children have married. If you've a place for me, Mrs Harper, I could live in.'

'Of course there is room for you – a bedroom upstairs next to the nursery and your own sitting room downstairs,' Ben had said, pleased by her decision. 'We needed a live-in housekeeper if Sally is to continue her work, Mrs Hills, and you are like part of our family. Jenny loves you and she doesn't take to everyone.'

Sally had yet to find someone to help with the housework, but she had inquired at an employment agency for a woman who could come in the mornings to help. Pearl would come in most days for a few hours with the children and, of course, Sally could do much of her own work from home. But she would need to go in to Harpers at least twice a week to keep her finger on the pulse of things, watch and feel how business was going. It was still her habit to walk the floor at least twice a week to make certain the departments were looking their best and check on stock.

In the early days, Harpers had employed a floor walker, but after a while that had been stopped. Mr Stockbridge, their manager, and Sally normally did the job between them, relying on the department heads to tell them if anything was seriously wrong. It was a part of her job that Sally particularly liked, because she always made a point of speaking to staff, from the errand boy who worked in Fred Burrow's department right the way up. Just a few words here and there to make sure everyone was happy.

'Are you pleased with the house, Sally?' Ben asked when he finally brought Jenny inside. 'It is almost finished now. The carpets come tomorrow and the decorator is finished this evening.'

'It looks wonderful,' she agreed. 'This long room will be just right for us all to sit in and the children can play.'

Ben showed his agreement in his expression of satisfaction. 'I knew it was right for us the moment I first viewed it. You were not sure you wanted to move – but it will be so much better for us, Sally.'

'Yes, it will. I'm not sure if it will be best to take a taxi in when I go to Harpers or travel on the underground...'

'I don't like to think of you travelling in with the crowds, darling,' Ben said. 'I'd rather you had a car to take you. I can either employ a driver – or arrange with a taxi firm to fetch you and bring you back in the evenings and you can learn to drive.'

Sally nodded. If they were living in the country, she would have her own car and drive herself, but in the city, it was probably more sensible to use a taxi in town, because the drivers knew all the best routes and where the bottlenecks were if an accident had happened, as it often did in the busy streets. Carts overturned, horses got frightened by the noise of motor vehicles and sometimes even fights would break out between rival firms and they would deliberately block a road as they argued.

'Sometimes we can go in together,' she suggested and he smiled.

'Once I can get rid of my other work, I'll be going in several times a week,' he agreed. His face lit with enthusiasm. 'I'll be around to help more now. Things should get better soon, Sally. One day I want to expand Harpers even further – and I've told the local agents I want first offer on any adjoining properties.'

'Oh Ben,' Sally laughed. 'Give us a chance to catch a breath – we've only just come through the war by the skin of our teeth.'

'I know and that was due to you,' he agreed. 'With Mick's investment and Jack as a partner in the restaurant, I think we're secure now, Sally. So in a year or two I want to make us bigger.'

Sally looked at his eager expression and smiled. 'What departments do you want to add?'

'Well, you gave me the idea with your antiques,' Ben said. 'We could have a bigger antiques department – and a modern furniture department if we had the space. The other successful departments could be made larger with more stock once it is readily available too.' His grin was infectious and Sally found herself agreeing.

'I think that would be wonderful, Ben – we might have a food hall too, attached to the restaurant, when we can buy anything we want. I thought it might be nice to stock specialities from Scotland and good Cheddar cheese, as well as foreign varieties of cheese, and various gourmet foods. We could invite the producers to show us their wares – or set up little stalls of their own in the store. We would receive a proportion of the sales turnover, but they would be responsible for their own produce.'

Ben stared at her in surprise. 'What a fantastic idea, Sally. We could have luxuries from all over the world – stuff that keeps in tins and—'

'Daddy!' An impatient little hand grabbed his trouser leg. 'When are we going to see my doggie?'

Ben looked down and laughed. 'I hadn't forgotten you, Jenny darling.' His eyes met Sally's in amusement. 'We've been brought down to Earth – we'd better go and investigate what I found.'

'What kind of a dog did you find?' Sally asked. 'Will they be anything like her picture?'

'Well, perhaps not quite the same – but I have found some puppies that have a bit of spaniel and a bit of poodle in them. The owner said they were family pets who bred by accident and have produced some pretty puppies – so we'll just see what they are like.'

* * *

Both Jenny and Sally fell in love with the little balls of fur that were just big enough to sit in the palms of Ben's hands when he picked them up. The puppies were chocolate brown in colour with sweet little faces and big greenish eyes and curly fur.

One of them came prancing towards Jenny and she sat down on the floor with it and immediately began to play. Sally watched. The puppy clearly had a lovely nature as it allowed her to pull it about and merely licked her hands and her cheek.

'I want this one,' Jenny announced as she put her arms around its neck and it responded with enthusiasm, licking her and jumping into her arms.

'Is that a boy or a girl?' Ben asked the woman who had bred the pups.

'It's a girl,' the woman told him. 'A lot of people want a male...'

'I know we need to be more careful with a girl,' Ben agreed. 'This one has a sweet nature though – and I think my little girl has made up her mind. When are the puppies ready to leave their mother?'

'You could take her now,' the owner suggested. 'She is eight weeks old. I'm just trying to find good homes for them all. I show my spaniels and they have won prizes, but I didn't intend for my spaniel to breed with my daughter's poodle. However, the puppies are pretty little things if you're not looking for a pure breed?'

'No, my daughter just wants a little dog.' Ben hesitated for a moment. 'We're in a flat until next week. Could we leave her with you until then? I'll pay for her now.'

'I'll keep her for you,' the woman agreed with a smile. 'I'm keeping the other bitch myself and the male dogs will sell easier. I don't want much for them as they are not a recognised breed – would a pound be satisfactory?'

Ben took out his wallet and paid her. She gave him a receipt and tied a little pink ribbon to the collar with a tag on it.

'That shows she's sold,' she explained. 'I'll have her ready for you when you come – and I hope you'll be pleased with her.'

'Oh, we shall. She's a lovely puppy,' Ben replied. 'Come on, Jenny. We have to go and eat ice cream now...'

'Lulu come too,' Jenny said, pointing to the puppy.

'Not yet – next week when we move,' Ben told her. For a moment, her face screwed up and Sally thought she would throw a tantrum, but instead, she kissed the puppy on its nose and told it she would see it next week. Then she put her hand in her father's and looked up at him.

'Strawberry ice cream?'

'Yes, if we can find some,' Ben agreed. 'Then we'll find something nice in the shop – some gifts for Lulu perhaps. She is going to need all sorts of things.'

Jenny's face lit up and she skipped happily by her father's side.

Sally stopped to speak with the owner. 'Can you give me a list of what Lulu will and should eat?' she asked. 'I've never had a dog before and I want to look after it properly.'

'Yes, of course. I'll write it all down for you,' the woman said. 'You have a lovely family, Mrs Harper. I am particular where my dogs go, even those I didn't intend to breed – but I can see that Lulu will have a good home with you.'

Sally laughed. 'Lulu – where did she get the name from? I would never have thought of calling her that and yet it fits somehow. She's such a pretty little thing...'

'She was the last born and the smallest, but I've hand-fed her to make sure she survived and she's quite healthy now. I am sure your daughter will love her.'

'I think we all shall,' Sally agreed. 'She will probably be thoroughly spoiled.'

* * *

The remainder of the day went just as well, and they passed crowds of happy cheering people on their way home after tea at a nice café. Men in uniform with their arms round their wives and girlfriends, some in groups and a little merry, though whether from drink or sheer relief it would be hard to say. When in the evening they sat reading the paper and looking at pictures of the various men who would have been at the meeting to sign the treaty between the Allies and Germany, both Sally and Ben were feeling content.

'It has been a good day,' Sally said as Ben poured her a sherry and a small brandy for himself. 'Jenny is so happy – and all those bits and pieces you bought for the dog; I never knew a puppy needed so much stuff...'

'Well, a dog like that is going to need brushing to keep its coat right and a collar and lead, also its own feeding and drinking bowls, a bed and blankets and a few toys. If we don't give Lulu her own toys, she may take Jenny and Peter's and then there will be tantrums.'

'She probably will anyway,' Sally said. 'She seemed very lively. I think she may turn out to be quite a handful.'

'Oh, we'll soon have her trained,' he replied. 'So, my darling, let us drink to the future – of Harpers and the family.' He smiled and looked at her. 'To peace and happiness for the world – and us.'

Sally raised her glass to his. It had been a glorious day and for them as a family the future looked bright. She hoped – believed – that things would steadily improve at the store now and for her friends, for everyone. Yet she knew in her heart that despite the victory bells being sounded all over London, there were some people for whom the peace was too late...

38

Becky picked up her baby and inhaled the clean freshness of soap, powder and fresh linen. Babies were so lovely when they'd been bathed and changed. She smiled down at her little girl, her eyes moist as she remembered how close she'd come to giving her child away to Maggie. If she'd done that, she would have regretted it all her life and yet she'd felt she had no choice – until she discovered that David was in hospital, still alive, despite the feeling inside that had told her he was dead...

Becky looked down at her child's fairness. Her eyes were open now and so like David's... like the man she would learn to call father. A little tingle went down Becky's spine as she thought about it. She had remembered David Morgan's eyes – and they were not the eyes that looked at her across the breakfast table or when she woke next to her husband in the mornings. His eyes had been darker. The man she'd married had blue-grey eyes – and so, strangely, had her daughter.

Her husband wasn't David Morgan. Becky had convinced herself that the man in the hospital was the man she'd loved. Of course she hadn't known him long enough to be sure – but she did remember certain things and, gradually, as she lived with the man she'd married, a niggling doubt entered her thoughts. A terrible wound to his face had changed his appearance forever, but it wouldn't change the way he sat, walked or held his head – would it? Although he was the same height and build and the back of his head had the same shape. At first, she'd ignored any differences, but now things had come back to her. Silly little facts that David had told her. He didn't take sugar in tea. Her husband liked two spoons. David Morgan didn't like dogs. She remembered he'd been annoyed when a dear little dog followed them in the park. Her husband loved them and had suggested they get one. Becky liked them too.

Could his injuries have changed him so much? Yet her instinct was telling her it was a different man. He didn't make love in the same way. Her lover had been demanding, sweeping her off her feet – her husband was gentle, slow and sweet with his kisses. Becky's body didn't respond in the same way... she'd known the first time they made love that it wasn't the man she'd fallen in love with before he went to war. Or had she changed?

Why would David say he'd got his memory back if he hadn't? Becky wasn't certain of anything. She felt inside that he wasn't the same man – but was that just because of what he'd suffered? It might be. Becky was reluctant to question. She couldn't bear to hurt his feelings because he'd become very dear to her. It didn't feel the same as it had when they were courting. Then he'd had a confident, even bold manner that had appealed to a young girl and she'd been swept along on a tide of excitement and passion – what she felt now was softer, quieter but... nice. Yes, it was nice. Becky liked her life with her husband. She liked the home they shared and she felt happy.

She was afraid to question him in case everything went wrong. Becky didn't know what she would do if he became angry and accused her of trying to wreck their marriage by doubting him. She didn't want to go back to the uncertainty and fear that had haunted her before she saw him in the hospital. With her husband, she felt safe and cared for. What did the truth matter? Becky tried not to let it. She had nothing she wanted to return to. Her old life meant little to her and her father would be hurt and upset by the lies.

No, it was best just to leave things as they were...

* * *

David looked in the mirror as he was shaving and knew that he'd done a terrible thing. He'd married Becky under false colours and he was living a lie. Their marriage had remained unconsummated on the wedding night because tiredness had overcome him and he'd fallen asleep. The following day had been spent together, walking, relaxing and laughing as they got to know their new home and the beautiful estate he'd been given the opportunity to manage. Later that evening, they'd made love in a gentle, sweet way and since then it had happened several times – and now, he knew that he'd done the woman he loved a great harm. She'd married him believing he was David Morgan, an Army captain, who had been wounded fighting the enemy – and it was all a lie.

David's hand shook as he tried to shave and blood spurted as he cut his skin. He swore beneath his breath. How could he ever explain to Becky and, worse, how could he put right what he'd done? It could not be put right; he knew that and as a man of honour he felt it keenly.

Why had the memories eluded him for so long come sweeping back that morning? He knew suddenly and quite clearly who he was – and what had happened.

His name was David Norris with a courtesy title of Captain and he was an ordained vicar serving with the Army in France. Captain

David Morgan had been brought into the field hospital he was attending, conscious but mortally wounded. David had sat with him, praying and trying to give him comfort throughout two agonising days and nights when he lay dying, in terrible pain. They had talked for a long time about the war, about God and about what was uppermost in Captain Morgan's mind.

The dying man had told him about the young woman he loved and was afraid he had deeply wronged. 'I always intended to marry her,' he'd said, gripping David's hand tightly with a strength that was surprising given his wounds and loss of blood. 'Please, find her and tell her what happened to me. Tell her I loved her to the end and give her this watch – it belonged to my mother. I have little else of value other than my furniture. The house isn't mine – merely rented. I had debts to pay... family debts. One day I hoped I might inherit wealth. My mother always said I was entitled to some of it... but there was a quarrel in my great-grandfather's day and my family was cheated of their share of a fortune... that was how Mother saw it, though I am not sure she really knew.'

'Don't talk,' David had hushed him as his breath came in gasps. 'Money doesn't matter now. Make your peace with God, my friend.'

'You will find Becky Stockbridge, tell her everything and say I loved her to the end – please?'

'Yes, I give you my word. I will help her if she needs it,' David had promised.

Captain David Morgan had died that night – the night of the attack on the field hospital. Death had rained down on them from the air and David had been leaving the hospital tents to return to his own accommodation when he was caught in the blast of a bomb dropped from Gothas bombers overhead. He'd been thinking of the man who had just died and of the letter he would write to Miss Becky Stockbridge, when he was rendered senseless by the blast.

No wonder Becky's story had rung a bell with him! It was the last thing in his mind when he was injured. In the confusion of that night, a lot of bodies had been buried together and mistakes had been made... David remembered that he'd placed his coat over Captain Morgan as he lay dying, because he'd been cold – perhaps it had misled those who had buried what remained of bodies, already mangled and dying, who had been burned where they lay. Incendiary bombs robbed a corpse of everything, even identity.

David had been found badly injured and taken to another hospital, the first of several as he was nursed back to physical health, while unable to recall a single thing from his past. When Becky claimed to be his wife, he'd begun to remember things... first of all the sound of guns and explosions and then the smell of sickness and the cries of men in terrible pain. He knew that he'd tried to help those men – and he'd been told that a watch in his possession proved he was Doctor Captain David Morgan. The name David seemed right. He had the watch in his possession when he was taken to hospital – and there was a vague thought about a young woman who needed something from him.

Becky's story had rung true when she told him what had happened between her and Captain Morgan. He'd believed her and he'd wanted to believe that he was the man she loved – he'd wanted to believe it because he'd begun to love her from the first time that he saw her. Perhaps even before he met her – when he'd heard how young, innocent and lovely she was from the lips of a dying man. He'd wanted to help her even then, because he was an honourable man, a good man. David knew that if he'd been in Captain Morgan's shoes, he would never have done what he did – he would never have exposed her to the risk of giving birth to a child outside wedlock.

He met his eyes in the mirror. Yes, he had wronged Becky by letting her believe he was Captain Morgan – and he'd deceived the good people who had given him a job. He would have to tell them the truth, but first he must tell Becky. David closed his eyes, because all the peace and happiness of the past few weeks could disappear with a few words, but it had to be done. He could not live a lie... and yet Becky was happy. He'd seen it in her eyes. If he told her the truth, it might destroy her life.

David sat down on the edge of the bath. He wasn't sure he had the courage to face what had to be done, but, somehow, he must.

* * *

The letter from Maggie came that morning when David was out with his employer on the estate overseeing some building work. Maggie had written to say that they had been given the chance to foster two small children.

> *A girl and boy. The girl is just three and her brother is four. Their father was killed fighting for us and their mother died of the Spanish flu. They wanted to stay together and the authorities did not want to put them in an orphanage as there is a chance their father's family may claim them. We have them for six months. At the end of that time – if their uncle and aunt don't come forward – we can apply to adopt them. I am beyond excited, Becky. Jane is the sweetest little thing and Billy is a naughty little monkey but very lovable...*

Becky smiled as she read on about the things Maggie had bought for her foster children from Harpers. She was also going to help Mr Marco with the windows for a while.

> *Marion Jackson has unexpectedly resigned. She wrote to say she could not come in for the foreseeable future but would see if things improved – whatever that means. She says her husband is*

ill, though he has just come out of hospital. Sally asked if I would like to help for a while and, of course, I said yes. I love Harpers and although, I don't have time to work behind the counter all day any more, a few hours helping dress the windows is an opportunity I couldn't resist. Colin doesn't mind at all. I can even take the children with me if I like, because Sally's new department for the childcare is running again. Although Colin says he can manage them for a short time – and his driver is so obliging. He does all the things Colin can't; they are becoming firm friends – and of course I have a housekeeper. Fancy me having a housekeeper! I couldn't imagine why I'd need one, but it is rather nice to have tea served in the front room and not have to boil the kettle or make sandwiches. I find plenty to do with the children, Colin and a little charity work I've taken on – but dressing the windows with Mr Marco is my playtime. I am nowhere near as good as Marion was and I shall go to see her and ask why she gave it up. I know she loved it but I think her husband may have forbidden her to work.

Becky folded her letter away as her husband entered the sitting room. He looked pleased and smiled at her when she asked if he would like a pot of tea and some sandwiches. He didn't eat a proper lunch when he was working as he could never spare the time.

'Did your morning go well?' she asked.

'I believe Sir Edmund was pleased with the way things had gone with the new cottages. He took my advice and had those old ones that were so damp and unhealthy torn down and the new ones will make wonderful homes for the workers – and men who have fought for this country deserve good homes, don't you think?'

'Yes, I do,' Becky agreed. 'I am glad you like it here, David.' She looked at him, a question in her eyes. 'You have no desire to return to your old life?'

'I believe I can bring comfort here,' he told her and then seemed to catch himself up. 'My job is worthwhile, Becky. Are you happy here?'

'Yes, I am,' she said and smiled at him.

'You do not regret our marriage?'

'Not at all. Why should I?'

'No reason,' he replied, but his eyes did not meet hers.

'Do you want to talk about something?' Becky asked and he hesitated.

'Not at the moment,' he said. 'Perhaps we shall talk later...'

He finished eating his meal, got up, kissed her cheek and went back to work. Becky washed the cups and plates and then went to get her baby up and change her. She had decided to walk to the village. The vicar's wife was very friendly and had asked Becky if she would like to help with the Christmas bazaar and she'd decided that she would.

39

Maggie looked at Marion Jackson as she sat sewing a baby's dress. Her eyes looked a bit red and she seemed tired, almost listless – not a bit like the bright pretty girl she'd been only a few months ago when Maggie had last seen her on a visit to Harpers.

'Mrs Harper is wondering what has changed,' she told her as Marion's sister-in-law offered tea and cake. 'Has someone upset you at Harpers? Everyone misses you and we all thought you were happy to come back for a few hours a week.'

'I can't manage it,' Marion mumbled. 'I'm sorry, but it's just too much.'

'Why don't you tell her the truth?' Sarah said and Maggie looked at her. 'She loves it and she wanted to keep coming – but her husband refused to allow it and when she argued with him, he hit her.'

'Sarah, please don't,' Marion said, but the misery in her eyes showed quite clearly that Sarah was telling the truth.

Maggie was shocked. She hated that kind of brutality. Her own father had been a kind and gentle man and although Colin had a bad temper when provoked, he would never dream of raising his hand to her. 'That is so awful for you, Marion. I didn't think Reggie was like that?'

Marion looked up at her, a curious mixture of defence and defiance in her eyes. 'He isn't – he wasn't before the war. My father was like that when he got drunk and Reggie used to condemn him for it. He would never have done it before – but he has changed.' She wiped a tear that escaped from the corner of her eye. 'I don't think he knew what he was doing at the time. He just got angry, started shouting, hit me around the head twice, and then went storming off. When he came back, he seemed to have forgotten what he'd done.'

'He didn't remember hitting you?'

Sarah snorted her disbelief. 'You should let me tell Dan,' she said. 'He would sort him out...'

Marion shook her head. 'Reggie is ill, Sarah. He's not like my father was, a bully. Reggie wouldn't do that... he is so moody now.'

'Well, if he hits you again, I'm telling Dan,' Sarah retorted. 'I shan't just stand by and let him do it – and I'm not moving out until he's more like he used to be.'

'He might never be,' Marion said and looked so desperately unhappy that Maggie wanted to hug her and make her feel better – but it wouldn't help. A violent husband was the worst nightmare for a woman. A bad temper and quarrels were one thing – but a husband who hit his wife was quite another.

'Perhaps you should seek help from a doctor,' she suggested. She hesitated, then, 'Do you want me to see if I can find one who deals with that sort of thing...'

'What do you mean?' Marion demanded. 'Reggie isn't mad.'

'No – but he has suffered some sort of trauma to do with the war,' Maggie suggested. 'I don't know if anyone understands it – but I could try to find out. I do know some doctors and nurses who might have an idea...'

Marion hesitated and then inclined her head. 'I should be glad of some help. I don't know what to do. He's been quiet since it happened – sort of brooding and I'm... afraid of what might happen if he loses his temper like that again.'

'I'll do what I can,' Maggie said, 'and I'll tell Sally you can't come in for a while, because your husband isn't well – but I won't tell anyone what is wrong, except the right doctor.'

'Thank you.' Marion blinked back her tears. 'I do love him, Maggie – it's just... I'm afraid of what he might do.' She choked back a sob. 'The other day he was looking at our baby oddly and... he asked me if he was the father...'

'You didn't tell me that!' Sarah exclaimed. 'He's losing his mind, Marion. How could he accuse you of something like that...?'

'I don't know...' Marion bent her head and covered her face with her hands as the tears came. 'When he picked her up later, I was terrified he would hurt her.'

'I'm so sorry,' Maggie said. She decided on a hug and Marion returned it before pulling away. 'I promise I'll try to find some help for him as quickly as I can.'

Marion nodded. 'Thank you. I can bear having to give up my job. I can even put up with him hitting me sometimes – but I won't let him hurt my baby.'

'No, you mustn't,' Maggie and Sarah said at the same moment.

'It isn't his fault... it's the war...'

'Even so, he mustn't be allowed to continue,' Maggie said firmly. 'If we don't do something, he could hurt you or the child... or both.'

'I know.' Marion was very still, her face pale. 'I saw my mother live in fear of a violent husband for years. I can't – I won't – live like that.' She raised her head. But I don't know what to do or where to go...'

'Reggie needs help,' Maggie replied. 'Keep your chin up, Marion. I'll see who I can find to help you – and in the meantime, you must keep an eye on her.' She looked at Sarah. 'If you think he is getting worse, ask your husband to talk to him. Perhaps he truly doesn't understand what he's doing...'

* * *

Maggie told Colin about it later that evening. She wouldn't tell anyone else, but Colin's advice was always good and he might have seen erratic behaviour from men he knew, either in the trenches or at the hospital. He looked grim when she'd finished and was silent for a few moments, then nodded.

'Yes, I've seen similar behaviour in the trenches. It was the waiting and what you heard and saw Maggie. I'm sure you saw cases of it at the hospital... some of the men had what we called the shakes...'

'Yes, I've seen that,' she admitted. 'Mainly, I was dealing with men who were too ill to think or do anything – but there was one case. He was normally very quiet, but one night he went berserk and attacked two nurses. It took two soldiers to calm him and we had to sedate him. He was shaking at first and then angry, striking out with his fists. It sounds to me as if Reggie Jackson is suffering the same way.'

'Yes, that's about right,' Colin agreed. 'Some of the fellows couldn't take the mental strain. Was he in hospital for a long time?'

'Yes, he was wounded several times, I understand. He wouldn't let Marion visit last time – his face has been scarred. Perhaps he feared that she wouldn't want him like that...'

'I'm sure it went through his mind,' Colin said. 'Serious injury does things to a man. I didn't think anyone could love me as I am.' He smiled at her. 'You changed all that, darling Maggie. Perhaps Reggie will come to accept that his wife still loves him and settle down.'

'If he uses violence, how long can their relationship continue? Maggie is nervous, afraid he might hit their child. He questioned the paternity...'

'That shows his insecurity. He knows in his heart it is his child but fears the worst – that's the way we lived out there, Maggie. On the edge, always waiting for the next attack and the bullet that had your name on it – and then, after you've been wounded, you wake up and realise you can never be the same and for a while you just want to die.'

'Oh, Colin, is that how you felt?' Maggie put her arms around him and they held each other. Then she drew back and looked at him searchingly. 'How did you come through it, my love? You have, haven't you?'

Colin smiled and touched her cheek. 'It was meeting you,' he said simply. 'The bitterness was eating at me when we met – but our clashes woke me up and I had something to look forward to. After our marriage, I discovered what love was all about and you gave me a reason to live – you quite simply made me whole and happy. I'm lucky – but some poor devils don't have all the advantages I have.'

'I love you,' she said and kissed him. 'You've made me happy.'

'And you love the children?'

'They are wonderful,' Maggie said. 'After what they've been through, I wondered if they might not settle, but they have. They both call me Mummy and Mrs James says they are no trouble when I'm out, as long as she tells them that Mummy is coming back. She said Billy was a bit naughty when he thought he'd been abandoned, but she told him I would give him some sweeties when I got back.'

Colin nodded. 'I had Jane on my lap and read to her while you were out the other day and Billy played with his bricks, but he was listening. I started their portraits and they were fascinated.'

Maggie nodded and smiled. 'You are very talented, Colin. Are you enjoying the freedom to paint?'

'I enjoy everything about my life now,' he told her and hesitated. 'I haven't told you, Maggie, because I'm not certain the treatment will work – but my specialist thinks I may be able to walk a little one day soon.' He saw her eyes light up and shook his head. 'I'll never be able to go for long walks or play football, but I should be able to manage things like getting in and out of bed and walking to the bathroom.'

'That is a miracle in itself, Colin. Didn't they tell you at the military hospital that you would never walk again?'

'Yes, they warned me that it was likely I wouldn't,' he told her. 'I have had some feeling return to my legs recently and I can manage a few steps, but I'm not sure how much improvement I can make...'

'Whatever it is, we'll accept and be glad of it,' Maggie said and smiled at him. 'You and I both know we're happy, so anything else is a bonus.'

'Yes, that is what helped me,' he told her. 'I knew that I had plenty of time to get myself right so I haven't pushed it too far too fast. I was warned that if I overdid things, it might set me back – but I don't have to worry, do I, Maggie? If I get stronger and it happens that is good – but we're happy as we are.'

'Yes, we are,' she agreed and looked at him thoughtfully. 'I think Becky is happy now she is married – and I know Sally is very content with her life. I think Rachel will be, too, and Beth seems all right. It's just Marion Jackson that I'm anxious about.'

'I know a few doctors at the hospital who were good with patients suffering from that kind of trauma – and that's what it is,' Colin told her. 'He isn't mad, Maggie. He's probably just scared – too frightened to live and love. They must find a way to help men like him, because there will be thousands who are suffering just the same terrors. It comes out in different ways and Marion's husband just needs the right help.'

40

'I shall write and tell Marion that her job will be here for her when her husband is better,' Sally told Maggie when she went to visit her at home the next day. 'It is so sad, Maggie. So many men are suffering from their injuries, physical or mental, and I feel sorry for their wives. Coping with illness can be very difficult at the best of times and I doubt the doctors truly understand how deep the effects of the war have gone in some men.' She hesitated, then, 'Mick was here a few weeks ago. He was wounded but seems better – but the war unsettled him. He sold most of his restaurants and invested money in Harpers. Then he went off to America... it wasn't like the old Mick. He would have shrugged any setback off and got on with it.'

'I am sorry he was wounded again,' Maggie said thoughtfully. 'I've always felt a bit guilty about Mick, Sally. I never intended to hurt him – and there wasn't anything between us, really. He was a good friend to me after Tim died and I thought for a while I might come to love him – but when they sent him away, he didn't write and I didn't see him for a long time. He wasn't there when I was so ill and then Colin came into my life... but I am sorry if Mick suffered because of me.'

'I know,' Sally smiled at her. 'I don't think he still has a broken heart, Maggie love. He is suffering from the effects of the war mentally and perhaps physically. He told me he might stay in America...'

'He is restless and unsure,' Maggie agreed. 'Colin says the war affected most of the men in the hospital that way. They lived under such pressure and with the fear of death for a long time – and then they suffered terrible physical pain. What their mental anguish must have been like – well, no one who didn't go through it could hope to understand it really.'

Sally agreed. 'Ben says some elements of the Government are very worried about the effect it will have on stability in the workplace – but some of them believe it is all tommyrot. They don't believe there is such a thing as shell shock.'

Maggie looked at her thoughtfully. 'Shell shock is a good name for it. In France, I saw men hide under the bed every time there was a loud noise anywhere near them. The poor things were shaking and terrified and it was ages before we could coax them out.'

Sally looked at her sadly. 'How do they get over things like that, Maggie? Especially if the doctors don't believe in the condition?'

'There are some that do sort of understand it,' Maggie said but didn't elaborate. She'd promised not to tell Sally or anyone at Harpers the true nature of Reggie Jackson's illness. 'I think it may be just patience and understanding – and helping them to stay safe, but sometimes whatever you do, you can't help them. We had one patient that recovered from his physical wounds, but rather than be sent back to the front line, he shot himself in the head...'

'Oh no!' Sally stared at her in horror. 'The poor man. What must his mental state have been like?'

'A lot of them were frightened to return to the fighting, but if they were needed and deemed fit, they had no choice. If they tried to run away or refused, they could be shot as a coward – so it must have seemed there was no way out.'

Sally shivered. 'I knew it must have been bad, but I never knew that could happen, Maggie. We've all been overjoyed to hear the churches ringing their bells for victory and peace – but it makes me wonder how many of those men returning from war will ever know true peace and happiness.'

'Some will manage it,' Maggie said. 'Colin has – but I think a great many more will find it difficult to return to normal life. You set up a place of rest for your staff, Sally. I imagine you were thinking mostly of female staff, but I dare say some of the men will have need of a safe place at times.'

Sally nodded and looked at Maggie sombrely. 'I shall tell all my managers that they must treat our returning heroes with respect and sensitivity. Men who have been through hell must be given a chance to ease back into normal life. We shall not be penalising them for late arrival at work or for taking time off if they are unwell. At Harpers we shall give them the care they deserve – but I'm not certain they will get the same treatment everywhere.'

'I think it makes some of them short-tempered, which might make it more likely that they would fight if pushed. They've had to fight for fear of their lives. We cannot expect that to just go away without a ripple – and if it does, trouble may be building underneath.'

'Your nursing experience has made you very wise,' Sally said and smiled at her. 'If you ever want to return to Harpers, we could do with you in the restroom as well as the window-dressing department...'

'I only go in for a little fun,' Maggie told her. 'I like to see my friends – and I've enjoyed helping Mr Marco, but my home, Colin and the children will take up most of my time in future, Sally.'

'Yes, I know, and I'm glad,' Sally said warmly. 'I think for you the victory bells ring true, Maggie?'

'Yes, they do. I am very happy. I'm almost afraid to say it, because things have a habit of going wrong – but I have everything I could ever want.'

'Yes, I feel the same way,' Sally agreed. 'I think Rachel and Beth feel the same – but there are others for whom it must seem a hollow victory. I want to help as many as I can. I think perhaps we should form a committee to set up something to help our brave men...'

'You mean like a community room where they could go for help?' Maggie said sitting forward, her senses tingling. 'That's a wonderful idea! We'd need to raise money, Sally, and we'll have to find somewhere suitable... Would it just be somewhere they can go for warmth and food, or would we provide a bed for the night?'

'I think we need to do all of that,' Sally replied. 'We need good women who can be there and help them to find homes, locate their families if they've lost touch, and provide the information they need to get medical and monetary assistance.' Sally smiled. 'I think we shall have many volunteers for the work, because quite a few women will lose their jobs as the men who can reclaim them. So our ladies will have time on their hands and will be happy to help.'

'A bit like the Sally Army but without the banging cymbals and the hymns,' Maggie said with a hint of mischief was in her eyes. 'Do you recall when we attended the Women's Movement meetings, Sally? We could find some of those women to join in and help – because there are a lot of men who may need us out there, and not just in London.'

'That is a brilliant suggestion,' Sally said. 'I shall ask Marco to dress a window that illustrates what we need and I'll get in touch with the Movement. If we can enlist enough of them, we can have our first hall of welcome up and running in no time.'

'I love that name – Harpers Hall of Welcome.' Maggie laughed. 'Oh, Sally, it is good to be back with you. I can see you will have lots of ideas to keep us all busy. It is a pity that Rachel isn't here to help. She would have known lots of people...'

'I'll write to her,' Sally said. 'I believe she is happy with William in the country – but she will know the addresses of a lot of the women we need. I'll be asking women to volunteer and apply to us here at Harpers. Perhaps if we can collect enough donations, we could even pay them a small wage.'

'A lot of women would be grateful for just a few shillings. After they lose their jobs, they will find it hard to manage without them – especially if they do not have a husband coming home...' Or were drunk and abusive, she thought.

'So it is another way to help the widows as well as the injured men,' Sally agreed. 'Thank you, dear Maggie, for giving me the idea – and for wanting to help.'

'I'm not sure I did anything,' Maggie said and laughed. 'I think the ideas came from you – but of course I'm glad to help. Colin has his painting and he can get lost in it for hours at a time. I need to spend time with him and the children – but being involved with Harpers is going to be a big part of my life in the future, one way and another.'

'You were one of the original Harpers' girls,' Sally said. 'Beth will want to be involved too. It will mean we all get to spend lots of time together – because there is going to be a lot of fundraising to do.'

'We could have a flag day,' Maggie said. 'We could have women on every street in the country collecting money for our charity.'

'Yes, it will have to be a proper charity – I'll probably have to register it,' Sally said. 'I'm going to ask all my friends to help – and that includes Minnie and Marlene.' She laughed. 'I have a lot of friends with the letter M as the start of their name. I shall ask

Pearl to inquire amongst her friends too. A lot of them are nurses...'

'And all the VADs will be home and suddenly have nothing to do.' Maggie laughed. 'We can start a revolution, Sally – but a good one. Not like they've had in Russia, where after they stopped fighting the Germans, they started fighting themselves...'

'It was so awful what happened to the Russian royal family...' Sally shivered. 'Thank goodness nothing like that could ever happen here. Everyone loves our King and Queen.'

The shooting of the Czar and all his family had been such a violent and unnecessary tragedy and shocked everyone and the conflict over there was still ongoing.

Maggie nodded. 'Yes, that was terrible – but I'm more interested in helping our men when they come home.' She stood up and pulled on her gloves. 'Well, I must go, Sally. I need to get back to make sure everyone has lunch and the children have their afternoon nap – and I have lots of letters to write.'

'As do I,' Sally said. 'I know you're busy, so I won't ask you to lunch – but come for tea at the weekend. Bring Colin and the children and I'll ask Beth and her family too.' She laughed as she saw Maggie's face. 'We shall have moved into our new house by the weekend and be your neighbours – or within walking distance anyway. It will be wonderful to be so near one another. It's actually tomorrow that we move.'

'Goodness! I've taken up so much of your time and you must have such a lot to do...'

'Not really,' Sally assured her. 'We've bought a lot of extra furniture for the house and most of this will go in the van when it comes. Ben will see to that and I simply have to take the children by taxi to their new home... and Lulu of course.' She saw Maggie's mystified look. 'We have a new addition to the family and you can meet her when you come to tea...'

* * *

'You have been busy between you,' Colin said when Maggie told him all about her talk with Sally. 'I think it's wonderful what you intend to do. A lot of men will have no homes and no family to go to, I'm afraid. Some of them may have died or been forced to move on – and there are many marriages broken by war. Those are the men you can help, Maggie. The others – the ones like Marion's husband – they need medical help...'

'We shall give out advice about all kinds of things,' Maggie told him. 'We can't treat them and we can't force them to seek medical advice – but sometimes a place of safety and kindness is all that is needed.'

'It is certainly necessary,' he agreed. 'Some of the men I knew will never leave hospital because they can't face the world alone. When the doctors have done all they can, they will be transferred to a convalescent home, but they'll never leave it until they die. I don't think you can help them, darling Maggie.'

'Not immediately,' she agreed. 'But if we can form a legion of willing helpers all over the country, we can arrange for those men to have visitors. Perhaps it won't help them all – some of those poor men can never be helped – but if we can reach a few, it must be worthwhile, mustn't it?'

'Yes, I am certain it is,' he agreed. 'And I shall help all I can, darling. I'll write to my father and involve him. He can help locally. David and Becky can try to get a small refuge going locally. I am certain that some of the estate workers will be willing to help – especially the women. I know some of the wives worked when their husbands were away. They will almost certainly be glad of something to get them out of the house, even for a few hours a week.'

'That is exactly what we thought,' Maggie said and embraced

him. 'I am so lucky to have you, Colin. You never try to put me down or laugh at my ideas.'

'How could I when you have such good ones?' he said with a smile. 'I would argue with you about who is the lucky one in this marriage, but I shan't – I'm just glad you have something more to keep you busy when I'm not around.'

'I have loads to do,' Maggie said, laughing. She did a little twirl and swept Jane up as she looked at her with wide inquiring eyes. 'We are all lucky in this family, Colin – and now I'm going to write some more letters.'

41

Reggie Jackson woke to find himself lying under a hedge. He was cold and wet and, as he realised where he was, the fear overtook him and he started to shiver and shake. What had he done? He sat up warily and looked around him, trying to piece together the events of the last couple of days.

He'd had a quarrel with his wife over something... Oh, God, no! He'd hit Marion. Hit the woman he loved more than life itself! How could he have done such a terrible thing? Reggie sat on the icy cold grass of the park and wept, his hands over his face. He would never forgive himself for what he'd done. It was over something trivial... she wanted to work for a few hours a week at Harpers helping to dress the windows. It was a step up from a counter assistant and she'd loved it – Reggie had forbidden her and when she'd argued, he'd hit her – and he'd questioned the paternity of his child. How could he have said something so hurtful? The anger had just soared up inside him so that he couldn't control it. His anger came from fear and his fear came from worrying about dying and leaving his family to fend for themselves – from a terror of losing all that he loved.

If he hit Marion again, he would lose her. Reggie knew that deep down inside. She'd lived with a brutal father and would not take it from him; he wouldn't want her to. Rather than put her through all that misery, he would top himself.

Shuddering, Reggie climbed to his feet. He had to go home and apologise to his wife and family – and then he had to find somewhere, a place of refuge where he could live until he could trust himself to be near his family again. The hospital hadn't wanted to release him because they said he wasn't ready. Reggie had argued, saying he would discharge himself and so they'd let him come home – but he couldn't settle. The terror he'd lived through was still there in his mind and he needed to get it out. Was there someone who could help him?

He stared bleakly ahead as he trudged on icy pavements to the nearest bus stop that would get him home. Reggie knew he needed help because he would rather be dead than live this way...

* * *

Marion looked apprehensively at her husband as he entered the kitchen. He looked terrible, as he ought after staying out two nights and frightening them all.

'Reggie,' she said and started towards him. 'Where have you been? You look cold and hungry. Sit by the fire while I make you something to eat and a nice cup of tea.'

The tears started to roll down Reggie's face as he looked at her. 'I hit you,' he mumbled. 'How can you forgive me?'

'I forgive you because I love you – and because you went through terrible things. You're lucky to be alive, Reggie, and we're lucky to have you back.'

'I can't control it...' Reggie choked. 'The things I say and do... I can't stop myself. It might happen again. I shall have to go away to get help...'

'Where would you go?' she asked in a small voice. 'Back to the hospital you were in?'

'I'll try to get a place nearer home.' He sat down, bowing his head. 'I'm sorry for what I did – so sorry. You know I love you?'

Marion stroked his hair. 'I know. It isn't you – it's what they did to you, Reggie. You've been through too much, my love.' He looked up at her and she bent and kissed him. 'Will you let me help you – find somewhere you can be helped properly? Somewhere they will stop the nightmares in your head?'

'How did you know about them?' he asked.

'I heard you talking in your sleep,' Marion said. 'It wasn't you that hit me, Reggie – not the man I love. It was the horrors you've seen and what you've endured. No one could put up with it and you aren't the only one to suffer. I've read about it in the paper – and I'll find someone to help you, if you'll let me...'

'Thank you...' Reggie caught her hand and kissed it. 'I should go away. I don't trust myself not to hurt you.'

'You can stay next door with your mum if you want,' she said, knowing that his mother was a strong woman who could cope with his moods. 'But don't go to some horrid little hostel and make yourself sick with neglect and worry. Let us look after you. We all love you – and I will find someone to help you, I promise.'

Reggie looked at her humbly. 'I know I'm lucky to have you – and you can work at Harpers, Marion. I know you love it and if Sarah can look after the baby... Besides, you may need it if anything happens to me.'

'Nothing bad is going to happen,' Maggie told him and held his hands, which were shaking a little. They stilled as she held him and she smiled. 'We'll find help, Reggie, and you will get better – and we'll forget these awful times and be happy again, my love. The war is over. You have a lot to look forward to in the future – and so do I...'

Reggie looked up at her, hope in his eyes. 'I love you, Marion.,' he said. 'If you can believe in me, perhaps I can too... Perhaps with the right help I can make all these bad things up here go away...' He touched the side of his head. 'I feel so sick sometimes and they haunt me... but perhaps I can learn to forget...'

Marion nodded.

Sarah had watched from the doorway and now she made the tea and then brought a hot sweet cup of fragrant liquid for Reggie. 'Stay with him, love,' she said quietly. 'I'll make him a bacon sandwich and see if some hot food will bring him round.'

* * *

Later that evening, when Reggie was in bed asleep, Marion wrote to her friend and told her it was urgent that somewhere was found for Reggie close to home.

He needs help desperately, but I think he might despair if he was sent a long way off. I need to be able to visit regularly so that he has something to hope for, Maggie. I realise you haven't had much time, but I am asking if you can do something quickly. It is too much to ask I know – but he is so desperate that I fear he might do something awful unless we get help.

Marion took her letter and posted it. She would write to Mrs Harper another day and ask if she could resume her job, but she had to make sure that Reggie was safe first. Tears stung her eyes as she walked back from the post box. Reggie had been so humble and so ashamed of what he'd done and she was glad that she hadn't taken her baby and left him. He wasn't to blame for his actions.

Reggie wasn't like her father – a hopeless drunk and bully – he was just a man who had been made ill by the most terrible war.

* * *

'Tell me what is happening with Marion Jackson,' Sally said after Maggie admitted her to her sitting room. The two children she and Colin had fostered were sitting by the large French window and playing with their toys. 'I had a letter from her asking if she could come back – very apologetic and a little odd. I know her husband is ill – is it mental or physical?'

'I promised I wouldn't tell anyone at Harpers...' Maggie looked at her reluctantly. 'He has been badly affected by the war... in the way we spoke of the other day.'

Sally nodded her understanding. 'Yes, I thought as much – and I shan't be sharing what you've said with anyone – but I have this name and address. If she needs to find a doctor that will listen...' She produced a piece of paper from her handbag. 'Jenni's husband – you may recall that he is brilliant at putting badly injured men back together? He gave me that address when I was trying to help some of the men at the hospital. For some men, it is less their physical wounds and more what's going on inside – emotional trauma he called it. If Marion contacts Doctor Pearson, who has his own clinic in London, he may be able to help.'

'He holds a clinic for new patients once a week at a small private hospital,' Maggie said, reading what was on the sheet of paper. 'And men who need it can stay at the clinic for treatment.' She smiled at Sally. 'I'll give this to Marion, but I'll telephone first and make sure they will see him.'

'Yes, that's always best,' Sally said. 'Well, that's a start, Maggie – and I've got some good news. I've made contact with some of our old friends from the Women's Movement and they've agreed to help us spread the word. I am looking into organising a flag day for raising money for our project and I am going to write to some of the other large store owners in London and see if they will contribute.'

'Oh, good,' Maggie replied. 'I wrote to quite a few nursing friends and asked them to contact us if they were interested in helping to set up a chain of restrooms for soldiers that feel abandoned when they leave the Army.'

'Abandoned? Yes, I suppose they may feel something like that,' Sally said. 'Their lives have been strictly controlled; they've been ordered what to do, told when to eat and when to fight and they must be bewildered to find themselves back home, many with no money and no job. The lucky ones have homes to return to but some do not and they will feel the worst – but others may not be able to settle in their homes and feel uncomfortable at work. We need to help them, too, if we can.'

Maggie nodded. 'You know I'll help all I can and Colin is happy for me to be involved – and will help in any way he can, though he is busy with various things himself. He has to visit his father to sort out a little problem...' Maggie sighed. 'His cousin has something important to tell them apparently and he wants Colin there. I shall not go this time as we've just got the children – though I expect to take them down at Christmas.'

'I thought that was all settled?' Sally said. 'I hope nothing is seriously wrong.'

'Colin hopes so too. To be honest, I think he is worried that his cousin has changed his mind about the job – and that would mean Colin spending a lot more time there again.'

'That wouldn't please him,' Sally agreed. 'I know it is his home, but he wanted the chance to lead his own life, didn't he?'

'Yes, he has always wanted to paint and he can become immersed in his work for hours on end. If he hadn't been for the war, I suppose he would have taken over the estate and probably never had the chance to indulge his artistic side. He can only do it now, because his father likes his cousin... and Colin says he can't trust a stranger after what happened when he was away fighting.'

The manager they'd employed had been a cheat and a thief and Colin's father had been too ill to see it. It had taken Colin nearly a year to sort out the mess, but things had been running smoothly when he'd handed it over to his cousin. Perhaps if Colin and his father got on better, he might have been able to live there and paint in his spare time – though running the estate left little time for what Sir Edmund thought of as an indulgence. If Colin was obliged to return, he would not be as happy as he was here in London.

'How will you feel if Colin decides he needs to go back there?'

'I don't really mind much,' Maggie said. 'I should come to London for a few days now and then and see my friends. Colin is determined to keep our house, so I can only wait and see...' She frowned. 'It is puzzling and a bit of a worry, too. I just hope Becky is all right with whatever is going on down there.'

42

Becky looked at her husband as he prepared to meet his employer and Captain Morgan that morning. It was a typical foggy late November morning, damp and cold and she had insisted that he wear a scarf tucked inside his coat.

'You're very nervous, aren't you?' she said and reached up to kiss his cheek. 'Please don't worry, David. If he dismisses you, you can go back to the church or... or something.'

'I'm not sure that I could, Becky. I told you the truth, everything, so you know what my life was – and I have thought about it long and hard. I'm not sure I could just go back to that life. I had not long been ordained and was awaiting a parish of my own when I joined up. I had been assigned as a deacon in the East End of London for a large church and we did a great deal of work amongst the poor; it was not a life I would wish to take you to – this is so pleasant here...'

'Yes, it is pleasant and we are happy – but I would go anywhere with you, David. You must know that?' Becky knew that she loved this man with her whole heart. She'd loved him when she thought he was David Morgan, the man whose child she'd carried, but his kindness and gentleness had won her heart and the confirmation of her suspicions made no difference to her feelings.

'I was afraid I might lose you once you knew the truth?'

'No. I had guessed before you told me, but I said nothing because I didn't wish to lose what we have.' He hadn't lied to her. His mind had been confused and being told the watch was his had made him believe it.

'I am blessed indeed.' He looked at her for a moment in silence and then inclined his head. 'I still can't believe how lucky I am to have you, dearest Becky. But I have so little to give you – and this place here is more than I could have hoped for.'

'I know and I'm happy here too – but you have to tell them the truth. We cannot live a lie forever. Someone who knew you might recognise you and if it came out that way it would be terrible...'

David pulled a wry expression. 'With this face? I doubt many would know me – but the honourable thing is to own up and so I must.'

'Would you like me to come with you?' she asked, but he shook his head.

'I have to do this alone, Becky, but they may want to speak to you later – to see how you feel about things... or they may simply ask me to leave.'

'If they do, we'll look for somewhere else in the country,' Becky said and reached for his hand. 'We'll find something – you'll see. You're good at what you're doing, David. I don't know how you managed to pick it up so quickly.'

'Colin explained my duties very well – and I simply listen to the workers, Becky. Men who have had years of experience on the land know when the time is right to sow and to plough and to harvest. All I have to do is listen, look after them and tell them to get on with it. I've always been good at listening and observing and I'm good with figures and book work. So it came easily.'

'Well, let's hope Sir Edmund is happy to keep you on despite the fact that you are not his cousin.'

'I pray that it will be so,' David said and kissed her. 'I must go. I do not want to be late.'

* * *

'You lied to us? You deliberately took the identity of another man?' Sir Edmund said, a high colour rushing up his neck. 'That is not the act of a gentleman, nor an honest one…'

'It sounds worse than it is, Father,' Colin said, frowning. 'You weren't sure who you were when you married? What does your wife think now she knows the truth – you have told her?'

'I am very fortunate that she has forgiven me and still loves me. She admitted that she had already begun to suspect something when my memory returned and I told her.'

'How very convenient that your memory returned after you had married and taken up a position of trust,' Sir Edmund said drily. 'Of course you cannot continue—'

'Father, please think about it,' Colin said carefully. 'David didn't have to tell us. Your cousin was killed over there – he was dead before the attack that wounded David and caused him to forget who he was. The mistake was made by other people. Because of the watch our relation had given David for Becky, everyone assumed that he was Captain David Morgan, when in reality, he was Captain David Norris – an ordained cleric. It was a case of mistaken identity at the hospital – and if Becky is happy knowing the truth, why should we make a fuss?'

'Because he is a liar and a cheat!'

'Has he stolen anything from us?' Colin asked reasonably. 'I may be in London, but I have looked at the books and I've spoken to our people, Father. Everyone likes David. I for one do not believe he will cheat us.'

'Thank you for your good opinion,' David said. 'I know it all sounds suspicious and I must appear to be a cheat – but the story Captain David Morgan told me was fresh in my mind when I was hurt – and it all seemed to be right when Becky visited the hospital. He'd told me about this estate... and of the old family quarrel...'

'A family quarrel?' Colin's gaze centred on his father's face. 'You didn't tell me about that, Father?'

'It happened too long ago.' Sir Edmund cleared his throat. 'I inherited as the son of a second son... My father's eldest brother was a black sheep. He quarrelled with his father and went off in a temper, declaring he would never return. He died abroad and his family never heard of him again – but then some years later a woman turned up and said she was his daughter and she had a son. She said her mother had told her she had a claim on the estate. My father sent her away without a penny, refused to believe her. Later, she sent copies of her birth certificate, her marriage certificate and her son's birth certificate. She tried to make a claim for her son, David, through a lawyer, but the court said that as a female she couldn't inherit and there was no proof David was blood-related as some doubt was cast on his paternity...'

'That is a sorry tale, Father. If she was your cousin's daughter, she deserved something surely?'

Sir Edmund glared at him and then inclined his head. 'I thought so myself as a young man, but my father was a mean old devil and wouldn't give her a penny. I did try to trace them once when I inherited, but I wasn't able to – until just before the war when I had a letter...'

'I believe that was written by Captain David Morgan's mother,' David said. 'We talked for a long time as he lay dying. She wrote to you from the hospital in which she died.'

Sir Edmund stared at him, frowning. 'So, you are telling me that your wife's child was his?'

'Yes, the child is a distant relation to you, sir. I am not... but I would have helped Becky had I not been wounded...'

'Father, you can't turn them out – Maggie would never forgive us,' Colin said firmly. 'Becky is entitled to our care and consideration. Our cousin should not have placed her in such a position – I believe that Captain Norris has behaved as a gentleman ought and I am willing to trust him.'

'You just don't want to come back and look after the estate yourself,' his father grumbled. 'But I suppose the girl has a right – and I will admit the estate seems to prosper.' His gaze narrowed. 'If we trust you to continue – will you give me your word as a gentleman that you will not let us down or try to take advantage?'

'Certainly, Sir Edmund,' David agreed instantly. 'I am sorry that you've been placed in this position, and, if you would prefer that we left, we shall of course do so.'

'No, no, my son is right,' Sir Edmund said. 'Becky's daughter belongs here – and I like your wife. She is a nice little thing. Behave yourself and we'll forget this... unfortunate business.'

'Thank you.' David looked at Colin. 'Thank you, Captain Morgan. I am very grateful.'

'Everyone believes you to be our cousin, so I think you should change your name to Morgan by deed poll, to make it legal,' Colin said. 'If anything should happen to my father and I, it would ensure your future and the future of your family here. No one outside this room needs to know anything about this. My cousin is dead and no one has a claim on him other than Becky. You've taken his place in her life and so all is as good as it can be. I shall walk back with you and speak to her. I have gifts from my wife to yours, sir.'

'They are good friends, I believe...'

'Yes, they worked together before the war and kept in touch.

Maggie is very fond of Becky. I shall not tell her about this, but if Becky wishes to, that is up to her.'

'I will come back with you – and then I have some estate matters to attend to,' David replied. 'I have arranged for some repairs to the old barn down near the ten acres and they are starting this morning.'

'You will excuse me,' Sir Edmund said. 'I have something I need to do.'

'Thank you again, sir,' David said and he and Colin left the room, Colin manoeuvring his chair with practised ease. 'I shall always be grateful – and you may rely on me,' he said as they began the walk to the manager's cottage.

'I know that I can trust you. Otherwise, I would never have given you the job,' Colin told him. 'I didn't offer it to you just because you were related – I knew nothing of the old dispute. I think I know a decent man when I meet one and I was certain of it when Becky told you her story and you married her as soon as we could arrange it. Had you been anything less than honest, you might have pretended not to believe her.' He gave David a frank look. 'I never met my cousin – but I can't condone what he did. Becky was young and innocent and came from a decent family. He should never have put her at risk like that – knowing that he might not be able to marry her if anything happened.'

'He said he never meant for it to happen,' David said. 'It seems he was overwhelmed by his feelings for her and the knowledge that he might never return, might never see her again...'

'Yes, I understand the feeling of desperation,' Colin replied. His eyes met David's. 'But I do not think that either you or I would have done the same...'

'No, perhaps not – but we should not judge. Perhaps neither of us has been in his position?'

'There was someone in my life – but she was not young and

innocent,' Colin said, 'but you are right. Perhaps I have no right to judge.'

'You must forgive me. Sometimes I forget I am no longer a member of the clergy.'

'You were the deacon at your church – a position of trust,' Colin said. 'I am pleased to meet you, sir, and I wish you a long life and a pleasant one here – though watch out for my father's temper.'

'Sir Edmund is an honourable man, though short-tempered, as my own father was. He was a small landowner – nothing like this, of course...' David gestured to their surroundings. 'However, perhaps that is where my feeling for the land comes from. I have lived in a big city and I do not care for it...'

'For me, it breathes life,' Colin told him. 'I enjoy the variety and the museums, the galleries and theatres. My wife has many friends there and they are about to embark on a great venture. She will be writing to Becky about it and I shall leave her to tell you when she gets the letter...' They had arrived at the cottage. 'And here she is, worried I dare say. Let us put her mind at rest...'

* * *

'How lucky we are,' Becky said after Colin had taken a cup of tea with them and left. 'Captain Morgan is very kind and generous.'

'He is a good man. I do not think he would have been kind if he'd thought I meant to deceive everyone.'

'No, perhaps not.' Becky smiled up at him. 'But you did not – and I think I knew almost from the start, but I wanted to believe you were the man I loved. And now you are – because I do love you and I would not change anything if I could.'

David felt the sting of tears but blinked them away as he embraced his wife. 'I must go,' he told her gruffly. 'I have work to oversee – and if there is one thing Captain Morgan would not forgive, it is neglect of duty...'

* * *

'So is everything all right?' Maggie said when Colin returned home two days later. 'Nothing very terrible has happened?'

'It was just a small problem, easily resolved,' Colin replied and smiled at her. 'My father sends his love, Maggie, and told me to say that he is looking forward to our visit at Christmas – and to hear childish laughter in the house again. The staff all wanted to know about the children and are looking forward to providing lots of treats for them.'

'That's Millie,' she laughed. 'I'll bet she was excited when you told her we were coming down until after the New Year.'

'Beyond excited,' Colin confirmed. 'She was in tears, some of it because the war is over and I told her what you were planning for the men who would be coming home. She said that if she can help in any way, you have only to ask...'

'How wonderful,' Maggie exclaimed. 'She and Becky can get something organised down there – but we are having a lovely response from most of the ladies we've contacted. It seems everyone wants to help. They all want to thank our men for the sacrifices they've made for us.'

Colin nodded. 'I think you will find that a lot of women feel as you do, Maggie – but you may get opposition from some quarters, especially as time goes on. If you need help, my darling, don't be afraid to ask for it. I may not be able to do much, but I might know people who can.'

'I shan't forget,' Maggie said and laughed. 'To be honest, all I do is hang on to Sally Harper's coat-tails and let her take me along...'

He laughed. 'I know Sally Harper and there aren't many who

can resist her – but you are every bit as remarkable in your own way, my love. Don't forget to put on your medal when you meet influential people. You earned it and it will make sceptic men listen if you tell them about the hell we all had to endure out there.'

'It was the men who fought that had the worst of it,' Maggie asserted.

'And you nurses patched us up and kept us going when we were close to despair,' he said. 'I don't think you realise what a heroine you were, Maggie, or how much I admire you for what you did – you and the other girls who came out to help.'

'Yes, it wasn't easy.' Maggie sighed and looked sad. She put her hands to her breast. 'It hurts in here when I think of what happened to Sadie. She went through the same things I did out there, and more in a way – having Pierre's child and losing him – and then, just as she was feeling happy again, she died.'

'Yes, that was tragic,' Colin said. 'Do you think her husband and the boy are coping all right? Is there anything we can do to help?'

'I'm not sure,' Maggie admitted. 'I've been helping with the windows while Marion wasn't able to go in, but they won't need me now. However, I shall pop in on Monday and see if Mr Marco needs anything.'

'Yes, you do that,' Colin said, 'and now I have something to ask. Would you consider putting on your nursing uniform for a portrait please? I'd like to do several of you, Maggie, but to capture all your different virtues, I want to paint you as a nurse against a background of war – and then with the children to show what a difference peace makes.'

'Yes, if you wish,' she agreed. 'Although the uniforms are very ugly.'

'But you will look beautiful,' he countered, 'because you always do.'

* * *

'You know that Sadie and I were good friends,' Maggie said to Mr Marco on Monday morning when they were having a cup of tea at Harpers. 'You must miss her terribly – you and Pierre. I wondered if you needed any help. If you need someone to look after your little boy...'

He smiled at her. 'You are very kind, Mrs Morgan. Sadie was so fond of you and there may be times when Pierre's grandmother can't look after him. Mrs Harper has told me I can bring him here until he is ready for school – but I do thank you for the offer.'

'Well, you know that I will always help if you need me.'

'Thank you, Maggie,' he said and his eyes were warm. 'You were a good friend to Sadie and you know that our marriage wasn't for love in the first place – but we did come to love each other and I do miss her a great deal. I like to think we would have been happy had she not been taken so cruelly.'

'It was so sudden – such a sad thing to die after all she did...'

'Thousands have died of the Spanish flu,' Marco said. 'The pain their loved ones feel is mine, too, so I am not alone in my sorrow. I have good friends and life goes on and we must make the best of what we have.' For a moment, the grief and agony of loss was in his eyes, and then it was gone. 'I am lucky I did not die on some foreign shore. I have Pierre, Sadie's family, and my job at Harpers – as well as my friends. I have so much more than many. I shall survive, but I do thank you for your kindness.'

'I wish there was more I could do.' She smiled suddenly as she thought of something. 'You must bring Pierre to tea with my two on Sunday. Let them become friends, Mr Marco. And you must come for Christmas too.'

'I shall be pleased to come on Sunday – but I have already been invited to Sadie's parents' home for Christmas, as well as the Harpers', and Fred Burrows invited me, too.'

Maggie laughed, pleased with his answer. 'I can see I need not worry too much about you, Mr Marco.'

'No. I have many friends,' he told her. 'They cannot replace Pierre's mother of course, but we shall manage.' He smiled. 'I am already hiding things all over the house, so I think we shall have a lovely time together this Christmas.'

43

'I think we should have our Christmas grotto this year again,' Ben told Sally that evening. 'I understand you couldn't manage much last year, but we'll do our best this time.'

'I'm not sure where we shall buy small gifts, Ben,' Sally told him. 'Things like colouring books and toys are in short supply. I've been looking for presents for Jenny and Peter – but there isn't much about. We have a few things at Harpers for their main presents. I've got a little wooden horse you pull on a string for Peter and a doll's pram for Jenny – but it is the little things that are hard to find. I'm afraid I'm giving a few sweets and money to the children of all our friends, unless I can find something suitable in the meantime.'

'I've found some pretty painted wooden beads, necklaces and bracelets,' Ben told her. 'I went to see an old soldier who makes them – he can't do enough to make them viable as a sales project for Harpers, but I've bought enough for the Christmas gifts at the store. For the boys, I have wooden puzzles and penknives.'

'Are you certain penknives are a good thing?' Sally asked.

Ben thought about it and then nodded. 'I always had one and

we'll only give them to boys aged nine or over. I had my first when I was eight.'

'Well, if you think so, but ask the mothers if it is all right first,' she suggested and he agreed. Sally smiled. 'We've still got all the decorations I bought before the war, so we can make the most of it for the children. You were hardly here last year, Ben, but this time we'll be together as a family all through Christmas.'

'Yes, we shall,' he agreed and hesitated. 'Next year, they may want me to go to America – talk to a few people about various things. I was thinking, if we went by a luxury passenger liner now that it's safe again, we could all go, Sally. I'd like you to meet my relations. I don't have many, but they would make you welcome – and they would love to see the children. You might like to visit the store in New York...' He looked at her speculatively. 'How do you feel about that? We could ask Pearl if she'd like to come along, too, and then you wouldn't be tied to the children the whole time.'

'Really?' Sally gave a little shout of joy and hugged him. 'I should love it, Ben. It would be a wonderful chance to see all the big stores and to source a supply of goods for Harpers.'

'You're not going just for work,' he said, laughing. 'We can visit friends, go to the big shows on Broadway and walk in Central Park – oh, and I do have a cousin on my mother's side who owns a ranch. If we had time, we might visit him.'

'It sounds very exciting,' Sally said and laughed. 'Oh, I am so glad the war is over at last. Now we can really start to live again. Life has been hard these past years, Ben, but we're both still young enough to have fun now that we can.'

'We've got the rest of our lives, darling,' he said and hugged her. 'Harpers has chugged along nicely during the past years. It was a little miracle that you brought us through the war and we didn't lose everything – but now that it's over we have the chance to expand and grow and we shall. Not just at Harpers but in our own lives. We can plan on taking the children to the seaside and perhaps for a holiday abroad when they're older – and we can go out more ourselves now that Mrs Hills lives in.' Ben smiled. 'What would you like to do most, Sally – go to a dinner dance or the theatre?'

'Either, both,' she said, laughing with excitement.

For so long all she'd seemed to do was worry about shortages at Harpers, feel grief at the untimely passing of friends and worry about those whose suffering went on, but now Ben was reminding her that as a family they had so much to look forward to. Harpers had survived the war and now the future could only get brighter, opening up in so many ways. Sally had lost friends, but many of them had come through. Everything seemed to be changing for the better. Very soon now, women would be able to stand for parliament for the first time and there would be a general election.

She looked at Ben, feeling truly happy for the first time in ages. 'Mum says things are getting better for her and Trevor too. He has turned a corner and is improving steadily. She says they will be able to come and stay with us at Christmas after all.' It would have been nice to have Jenni and Andrew, too, but Jenni's baby was imminent and she couldn't travel so they would visit her in the New Year.

'That's wonderful, darling.' Ben took her in his arms and kissed her long and hard. 'We're so lucky to have our family, Jenni, her husband and quite soon her baby, too, and a few really good friends – and Harpers. We're going to soar, Sally. You wait and see – and when we do, we'll take our friends with us. We won't forget them. When Harpers prospers, we'll make sure our staff does, too, and we'll take care of our friends as the years go by.' He smiled down at her. 'It is going to be a wonderful life from now on.'

Sally touched his cheek with her fingers. 'Beth told me how excited Jack is about the future – and she is investing her own funds in a house not too far from us, even though Jack told her they would rent.' A giggle burst from her. 'And do you know what – Fred

Burrows is getting married next spring! He finally popped the question and of course Vera said yes. They will be living in Fred's house and Beth and I will be neighbours.'

'You've never had that before,' he said, smiling as he saw how happy she was. 'Maggie and Colin aren't too far off either.' He looked thoughtful for a moment. 'I was wondering if we might rent some extra space as an art department, Sally. We could have shows for new artists like Colin Morgan – and we can sell paints, crayons, pastels and canvases, whatever, as well...'

She looked at him in astonishment. 'I've been thinking something like that, too... Did you see that premises just two doors away from Harpers is up for rent now?'

'Yes, of course. I've already inquired about the lease,' Ben said and grinned. 'If our next-door neighbours decide to move, we'll be able to link it all up one day and then...' He expanded his arms. 'The sky is the limit...'

Sally laughed out loud. 'Oh, Ben,' she said. 'I do love you so much!'

'And I love you,' he replied, looking at her. 'I always have and I always will.'

MORE FROM ROSIE CLARKE

We hope you enjoyed reading *Victory Bells For The Harpers Girls*. If you did, please leave a review.

If you'd like to gift a copy, this book is also available as an ebook, digital audio download and audiobook CD.

Sign up to Rosie Clarke's mailing list for news, competitions and updates on future books.

http://bit.ly/RosieClarkeNewsletter

Why not explore the rest of the *Welcome to Harpers Emporium* series from Rosie Clarke!

ABOUT THE AUTHOR

Rosie Clarke is a #1 bestselling saga writer whose most recent books include *The Shop Girls of Harpers* and *The Mulberry Lane* series. She has written over 100 novels under different pseudonyms and is a RNA Award winner. She lives in Cambridgeshire.

Visit Rosie Clarke's website: http://www.rosieclarke.co.uk

Follow Rosie on social media:

 twitter.com/AnneHerries

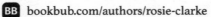 bookbub.com/authors/rosie-clarke

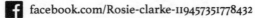 facebook.com/Rosie-clarke-119457351778432

Sixpence Stories

Introducing Sixpence Stories!

Discover page-turning historical novels from your favourite authors, meet new friends and be transported back in time.

Join our book club
Facebook group

https://bit.ly/SixpenceGroup

Sign up to our
newsletter

https://bit.ly/SixpenceNews

Boldw**oo**d

Boldwood Books is an award-winning fiction publishing company seeking out the best stories from around the world.

Find out more at www.boldwoodbooks.com

Join our reader community for brilliant books, competitions and offers!

Follow us
@BoldwoodBooks
@BookandTonic

Sign up to our weekly deals newsletter

https://bit.ly/BoldwoodBNewsletter